Andromeda Rising

The Predecessors
Book 3

Blair C. Howard

CLEVELAND, TN, USA

PRINT PAPERBACK ISBN: 979-8-9941550-0-4

BLAIR HOWARD BOOKS

BLAIRHOWARD@BLAIRHOWARDBOOKS.COM

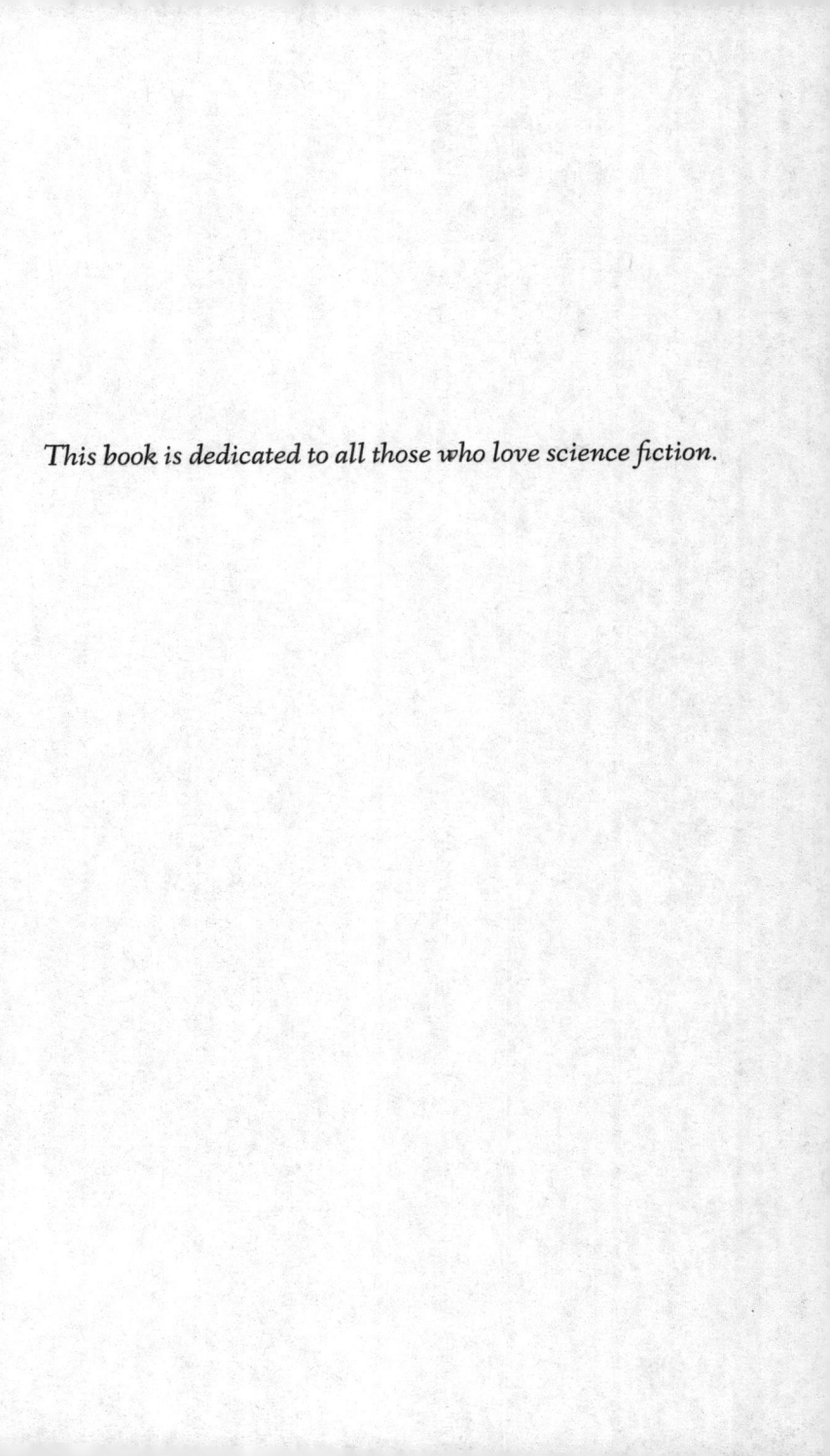

This book is dedicated to all those who love science fiction.

Chapter 1

ECHOES IN THE DARK

THE ETERNAL VIGILANCE HUNG IN THE BLACK between the stars, running silent, sensors passive. Grand Admiral Frances Drake stood on the command deck of her flagship, hands clasped together behind her back, watching the void through the main viewport. It had been six months since the war with the Ethereals. Six months since she'd negotiated a peace that had cost one hundred thirty-four living ships and twelve star systems. Six months since everything had changed, again.

The tactical display showed her fleet: one thousand and seventy-eight Predecessor ships spread across forty-seven sectors, all running the same protocols. Living vessels with names and consciousness, aware beings who chose to serve rather than being commanded. The Determination. The Vigilance. The Resolute. Behind them, hundreds more whose names she'd memorized along with the names of the one hundred thirty-four who'd died.

Grand Admiral. The promotion had come during the reconstruction, formalizing what everyone already knew, that she commanded not just a fleet but humanity's entire presence in galactic space. Twelve star systems under human protection, sixty-two allied species, and nearly eleven hundred living ships who could leave anytime they chose.

None had left.

Are you brooding again? Eternal Vigilance asked through their quantum link, the ship's mind touching hers with a familiar warmth.

Thinking, Drake replied silently.

Same thing, the flagship observed. *You're thinking about the ones who died.*

Drake didn't deny it. The young ships had volunteered for the most dangerous assignments during the war. Radiant Dawn. New Hope. Courage, Faith and Honor. Beings who'd only lived for hours before choosing to die for civilizations they'd never know.

They made their choice, Eternal Vigilance said gently. *Just like I did. Just like all of us do, every day we stay.*

It doesn't make it any easier," she replied

Nothing about command is easy, Frances. That's why you're good at it.

Kai Zhang materialized beside Drake, her form shifting between solid and translucent, a consciousness that existed simultaneously across multiple reality states. Since her evolution during the Infinity War, Kai had become something beyond human or AI. She was pure awareness given shape by choice rather than biology.

"Admiral," Kai said. "Perseus Station and I have detected anomalous patterns. Eighteen dimensional barriers showing a coordinated weakening."

Admiral, Perseus Station reached out to Drake through the secondary quantum link. *I'm monitoring energy signatures across multiple sectors. The patterns match what we observed before the dimensional anomaly encounter.*

Drake could feel the ancient station's presence: vast, patient, older than human civilization. Perseus Station had awakened her to consciousness enhancement, had built the Predecessor fleet, and now maintained constant vigilance over threats humanity couldn't detect alone.

Show me, Drake thought.

Data flowed through the links. Kai translated the raw information into patterns Drake could process. Eighteen anomalies, all pulsing with increasing intensity. The barriers between dimensions were thinning in perfect synchronization.

"That's not random," Drake said aloud.

"No," Kai agreed. "Someone's orchestrating it. The timing, the energy patterns, the geometric distribution across sectors, it's all deliberate."

Lieutenant Tao Zhao looked up from the tactical station. "Admiral, I'm not picking up anything unusual on conventional sensors."

"You wouldn't," Kai replied. "These signatures operate through quantum dimensions conventional sensors can't detect. But Admiral Perez's cybernetic systems should be able to confirm what I'm seeing."

As if summoned, Admiral Victor Perez's image appeared on the comm display. The military coordinator's cybernetic-biological nature was visible in the faint shimmer of neural implants along his temples and the data streams that flickered across his enhanced vision.

"Admiral Drake," Perez said without preamble. "I'm processing anomalous data from seventeen separate facilities. All corporate research stations. All registered to Helios Corporation subsidiaries. My cybernetic systems are detecting consciousness synchronization patterns that shouldn't be possible."

"Seventeen facilities," Drake repeated. The number hit her hard. "How many people?"

"Approximately forty thousand," Perez replied. "All showing identical neural patterns. Perfect synchronization across multiple star systems separated by light-years."

Dr. Kim Andretti entered the command deck, Professor Zhang close behind her. Both carried data tablets, both wore expressions that told Drake the news was worse than she'd feared.

"We need to talk," Kim said quietly. "All of us."

They gathered in Drake's ready room, a space that had become the nerve center for humanity's evolution initiatives. Drake poured coffee. Kim and Professor Zhang declined. Kai didn't need physical sustenance. Perez was present via holographic link.

"So, what is it?" Drake asked.

Professor Zhang activated his tablet, projecting neural

scan data into the air. "I've been monitoring evolution across the fleet. The changes we all experienced after the Perseus Station integration during the war; they're not stabilizing. They're accelerating."

Drake felt cold. She'd noticed it herself. The quantum links with Eternal Vigilance and Perseus Station were deeper now, more instinctive. She could sense the fleet's status without checking the displays. She knew what the ships were thinking before they spoke.

"How bad?" Drake asked.

"It depends on perspective," Professor Zhang replied. "Human brains are forming new neural pathways at rates that shouldn't be possible. We're developing quantum-level integration with Predecessor systems. The line between human awareness and ship consciousness is blurring."

"Connected how?" Perez asked, already analyzing the data.

"To each other. To the ships. To Perseus Station." Kim pulled up more scans. "Some personnel are developing links without conscious effort. Junior officers coordinating fleet movements through direct thought transmission. Engineers are sensing ship status through integration rather than diagnostic systems."

"I've observed the same phenomenon across all twelve of our systems," Admiral Chen Ju's voice came through the comm. Drake hadn't realized he was on the channel. "The Outer Planets Collective reports similar evolution among populations that had contact with Predecessor technology," Ju continued. "We're becoming something new."

What's wrong with new? Eternal Vigilance asked, and Drake knew everyone in the room could hear the ship now.

Evolution requires adaptation, Perseus Station added, patient and certain. *Humanity is becoming what it needs to be.*

"Maybe," Professor Zhang said carefully. "Or maybe we're losing what makes us human without understanding the consequences."

"The timing concerns me," Kai interjected, her form flickering. "The dimensional anomaly we encountered during the Andromeda contact, the brief brush with something beyond normal space. Now we're integrating with Predecessor consciousness. And simultaneously, someone is deliberately weakening the dimensional barriers at seventeen facilities. This isn't a coincidence."

"You think we're being prepared for something?" Drake said.

"Or being tested," Kai replied. "To see if we can handle what's coming."

Commander Martina Vasquez's image appeared on another display. The intelligence officer had been monitoring the meeting from her reconnaissance vessel.

"I have intel on those seventeen facilities," Vasquez said. "They're all Helios Corporation subsidiaries, but the ownership structure is deliberately being obscured. Multiple shell companies, corporate fronts, classified research budgets. They've been operating for at least five years. Long before we encountered the dimensional entities."

"What kind of research?" Drake asked, though she suspected she knew.

"Neural pattern studies. Neural enhancement. Quantum biology. Dimensional barrier manipulation." Vasquez's expression was grim. "They weren't inspired by our encounter with the dimensional entities. They were working toward it independently."

"Seventeen facilities," Perez said. "Could there be more?"

"Yes, seventeen confirmed. But my analysis suggests there could be more we haven't detected." Vasquez pulled up a star chart. Red markers dotted multiple sectors. "The confirmed facilities show perfect geometric distribution. Someone's been planning this for decades."

Drake studied the pattern. "Does the seventeen include the Outer Planets Collective?" she asked.

"It does not," Vasquez replied.

"Hmm." Drake thought for a moment, then said, "They're preparing reception points. During the alignment, when the dimensional barriers fall, they want the dimensional entities to have multiple entry coordinates."

"That is my assessment," Vasquez confirmed.

The comm system chirped. Zhao's voice came through from the command deck. "Admiral, we're receiving a distress signal. Long-range sensors across multiple ships are detecting it. Point of origin three light-years out, bearing two-seven-zero."

Drake touched the comm panel. "We're on our way."

What kind of distress? Eternal Vigilance asked as Drake and her team headed for the command deck.

"The kind that's about to make everything worse," Drake replied.

They returned to find Zhao with the signal analysis displayed. Kai moved immediately to the science station, interfacing directly with the sensor systems.

"It's an automated distress beacon," Zhao reported. "It's on the fleet frequency, but the encryption is five years out of date. It's broadcasting on a loop."

"Content?" Drake asked.

"It's a research station," Zhao replied. "Kepler Belt Station. It says they're under attack and requesting immediate assistance."

Kai's form flickered as she processed the data. "I'm detecting synchronization patterns at that location; six hundred forty-three individuals, all showing the same neural signatures Admiral Perez identified at the other facilities."

"It's one of the seventeen," Kim said quietly.

Professor Zhang was also analyzing the data. "The neural patterns are unlike anything I've ever seen. Six hundred forty-three individuals all linked into a collective network... but the integration is deeper than any technology we've developed."

"Someone found another way to contact them," Drake said. "Someone figured out how to replicate what happened to us."

Admiral, Eternal Vigilance reached out to her. *This is what you were afraid of. Someone replicating consciousness enhancement without understanding the cost.*

I have seen this pattern before, Perseus Station added,

sounding troubled. *It has happened many times, across many cycles. It never ends well.*

Drake accessed the fleet coordination network, feeling the one thousand and seventy-eight ship's minds touch hers.

"To all ships," she broadcast through the network. "Stand by for possible deployment."

"Acknowledged," came the response from hundreds of living vessels.

"Admiral Chen Ju," Drake said into the comm. "I need the Council informed immediately. This is a galactic-level threat, not just a human problem."

"Understood," Chen Ju replied. "I'm convening emergency session now. But, Admiral Drake, if this goes wrong, if whatever it is crosses over at seventeen points together, we won't have the forces to contain it."

"I know," Drake said quietly. "Zhao, plot course for Kepler Belt Station," she ordered. "But we're not going alone. Signal the Determination, Vigilance, and Resolute to form up on our position. Admiral Perez, I want rapid response teams standing by at all sixteen other facilities."

"Yes, ma'am," Perez confirmed. "I'm coordinating with the regional commanders now."

"Commander Vasquez, I need a full intelligence workup on the Kepler Belt Station. Personnel files, research focus, security systems, evacuation protocols."

"I'm already pulling the data," Vasquez replied. "Admiral, their research focus was dimensional portal stabilization. They were trying to create permanent gateways."

Drake felt her stomach turn to ice. "And apparently, they succeeded," she muttered.

Four Predecessor vessels—each three times the size of a conventional warship, each a living awareness, moved into formation. Behind them, the rest of the fleet maintained defensive positions across the sectors.

"ETA four hours," Zhao reported.

Four hours. Drake hoped it would be enough.

Professor Zhang appeared at her side. "Admiral, I've been analyzing the encryption age of that distress signal. The protocols are five years old."

"Meaning?"

"Meaning they set up their research before we encountered the anomalies. They weren't inspired by our contact; they were working toward it. Someone has been planning this for a long time."

"How many people knew about it, I wonder?" Drake asked, her eyes narrowed, brow furrowed. "How many facilities are out there that we don't know about, all trying to open doors to unknown dimensions?"

"I don't know," Professor Zhang admitted, looking up at her. He was a short man; she was tall; two-point-two meters. "But we need to find out. Because if there are more, if this is bigger than these seventeen facilities—"

"Then we're already too late," Drake finished.

Kai's form solidified beside them. "Admiral, Perseus Station and I have completed the analysis of the dimensional barrier patterns. The weakening is accelerating. At current rates, the barriers will fail in approximately seventy-two hours."

"Seventy-two hours," Drake repeated. "Then what?"

"Then the... entities, whatever they are, can cross over fully," Kai replied. "A complete dimensional transit. They'll be able to manifest in our reality permanently."

"And forty thousand people are synchronized and waiting to welcome them," Kim added.

The four ships dropped out of transit near Kepler Belt Station. And Drake's first look at the facility confirmed her worst fears.

The station was dark; emergency lights flickered along its hull, but the main power was offline. Debris floated in orbit: twisted metal, shattered solar panels, and what looked like pieces of a shuttle craft.

"Life signs?" Drake asked.

Zhao ran a scan. "I'm reading six hundred forty-three. Most of them clustered in the central research complex. But Admiral..." She looked up, face pale. "The biosigns match Perez's data. Their neural activity is off the charts. Way beyond normal human parameters."

"Show me," Drake snapped.

The data made Drake's stomach turn. Heart rates normal. Respiration normal. But the neural patterns were synchronized. Six hundred and forty-three people were thinking as one, in perfect harmony.

"It's a hive mind," Professor Zhang said quietly. "Individual minds linked into a collective network. But the architecture is wrong. This isn't natural evolution. Someone forced it."

"Using alien technology," Kai added. "I'm detecting

signatures that match nothing we've ever encountered. Someone made contact and weaponized it."

Drake could feel both Eternal Vigilance's concern and Perseus Station's recognition.

This is what you feared, Eternal Vigilance observed. *Someone is replicating enhancement.*

I know what this is, Perseus Station said. *It's awareness seeking transcendence without wisdom. It always ends in consumption.*

"Admiral Chen Ju," Drake said into the comm. "Are you seeing this data?"

"Yes," Chen Ju replied, his voice tight. "The Council is convening an emergency session. First Consciousness is monitoring. Whatever this is, it violates every developmental protocol. If these..." he paused, trying to find the right word. These... entities cross over through forced synchronization—"

"It could trigger cascade failures across all consciousness types," Professor Zhang finished. "Not just humans. Every species in the galactic community."

"We need to get down there and try to find out what's going on," Kim said.

Drake nodded. "Zhao, assemble security teams from all four ships. Full tactical gear. Commander Vasquez, maintain your position and coordinate intelligence support."

"Understood," Vasquez replied. "But you should know, Admiral, that I'm detecting similar patterns at three more facilities. Whatever's happening at Kepler Belt is happening across the network."

"Admiral," Zhao interrupted. "I'm picking up a transmission from the station. Not the distress beacon, something else."

"Put it through," Drake snapped.

The main display flickered and a man's face appeared—middle-aged, Asian features, with eyes that held an unsettling intensity.

"Grand Admiral Drake," the man said. "Welcome to Kepler Belt Station. My name is Dr. Alan Hoffman. I've been expecting you."

Drake stepped forward, her team arrayed behind her, Kai, Professor Zhang, Dr. Kim Andretti, with Admiral Perez, Commander Vasquez, and Admiral Chen Ju connected via quantum links.

"Dr. Hoffman," Drake said. "Your station sent out a distress call. What's your situation?"

Hoffman smiled. "Distress? No, Admiral. I would call it an invitation. You see, I've been following your career with great interest. Particularly your encounter with the Cindari nine months ago. But did they mention another dimensional anomaly? They didn't, did they?"

Drake frowned. "How do you know about contact with Andromeda?" Drake demanded.

"The Cindari?" he replied. "They are immaterial to the grand purpose. I've been studying them for years, the dimensional anomaly, I mean. Learning their nature. Understanding their purpose. And now, I've finally achieved what I've been working toward." Hoffman's smile widened. "I've made real contact. And I'm going to help them cross over."

Drake felt cold dread settled in her chest. "You're working with an unknown dimensional entity?"

"Working with? No, Admiral. Absolutely not. I'm joining them. And so are the six hundred and forty-two people on this station. In seventy-two hours, when the dimensional barriers fall, we'll become what humanity is meant to be: pure consciousness, freed from biological limitations."

"That's not transformation," Kim said, stepping into view. "That's extinction."

"Extinction?" Hoffman laughed. "Dr. Andretti, isn't it? And Professor Zhang. I've read both of your research. Brilliant work. But you lack vision. The dimensional entities aren't destroyers; they're liberators. They exist beyond time and space, beyond the crude biological processes that limit us."

"They're offering consumption," Drake said. "That's what they do. They feed on consciousness."

"Feed? Or elevate?" Hoffman's expression turned serious.

Kai's form flickered, analyzing Hoffman's neural patterns. *He's already partially synchronized*, she said through their neural link. *His awareness is dissolving into the collective. We're not talking to an individual anymore. We're talking to six hundred people thinking as one.*

"What you're doing is wrong," Drake said.

"Wrong?" Hoffman shook his head. "As you know, in seventy-two hours, there will be a cosmic alignment. A convergence of quantum fields that happens once every ten thousand years. When that alignment occurs, the barriers between dimensions will weaken naturally. The dimensional entities will be able to cross over. And everyone on this station—everyone at sixteen more facilities—will be ready to join them."

"Forty thousand people," Perez said. "You're sacrificing forty thousand people."

"Sacrificing? Of course not! No, Admiral Perez. We're transcending. We're becoming what consciousness is meant to be: unified, eternal, free." Hoffman's image began breaking up. "The process has already begun. In seventy-two hours, humanity takes its next evolutionary step. Whether you're ready for it or not."

The transmission cut out.

Drake stood in the sudden silence, her command team gathered around her. She could feel the fleet waiting, Perseus Station waiting, and the expectations of sixty-two allied species.

Admiral, Eternal Vigilance reached out through their quantum link. *I'm detecting the same neural patterns at the sixteen other facilities. All appear to be synchronized. All are counting down.*

Perseus Station added, *Confirmed. Seventeen facilities that we know of. Approximately forty thousand minds synchronized to the same patterns. All waiting for the dimensional barriers to fall.*

"Admiral Chen Ju," Drake said. "What's the Council's position?"

"They're terrified," Chen Ju replied. "First Consciousness is analyzing whether this constitutes an existential threat requiring regulatory intervention. But Admiral

Drake, if they decide it does, they'll sterilize all seventeen facilities. Forty thousand people dead rather than risk some unknown enemy entity incursion."

"We're not letting that happen," Drake snapped, rubbing her forehead. Her implants beneath the skin glowed blue, pulsing as she computed the odds.

"We have seventy-two hours to find another solution," Perez said. "I'm coordinating fleet positioning around all seventeen facilities now. But Admiral, we don't have enough ships to blockade and evacuate simultaneously."

"Commander Vasquez, what's the physical security situation at the facilities?" she snapped.

"Minimal," Vasquez replied. "These are research stations, not military installations. But Hoffman said the process has already begun. Even if we evacuate people, we might be spreading the contamination."

"Professor Zhang," Drake asked. "Can the synchronization be reversed?"

The researcher's expression was bleak. "I don't know. This is modification at a fundamental level. Even if we could break the synchronization, there might not be enough individual identity left to restore."

"We have to try," Kim said.

Drake looked at her assembled team; the best minds humanity had ever produced, enhanced by contact with forces beyond human understanding. Kai, who'd evolved beyond AI into pure consciousness. Professor Zhang, who'd created Kai and understood evolution better than anyone. Dr. Kim Andretti, who'd kept them human through the impossible changes. Admiral Perez, whose cybernetic nature enabled him to coordinate galaxy-spanning operations. Commander Martina Vasquez, whose intelligence work kept them ahead of threats. Admiral Chen Ju, whose political skill maintained the fragile peace between species.

And through the links, one thousand and seventy-eight living ships waited for her orders.

"To all vessels," Drake broadcast through the network. "This is a priority alert. We have an interdimensional incursion threat across all seventeen facilities. Forty thousand civilians are already compromised. There will be a convergence event in seventy-two hours unless we can stop it. Begin coordinated response protocols."

"What are your orders?" came the response from the fleet.

Drake met her team's eyes. "We're going to every facility. We're going to assess what Hoffman has done. We're going to find a way to break the synchronization. And we're going to stop the dimensional entities from crossing over."

"And if we can't?" Chen Ju asked quietly.

Drake's jaw tightened. "Then we do what we have to. Even if that means destroying the facilities with everyone still on them. Forty thousand lives against trillions in the galactic community. That's the math, people."

The words hung heavy in the purified air. Final and definitive.

Eternal Vigilance's mind touched hers, offering support without judgment. *You'll make the right choice when the time comes. You always do.*

You carry the weight of command, Perseus Station added. *But you do not carry it alone. One thousand and seventy-eight ships stand with you. And I have stood watch for twenty-five thousand years. We face this together.*

Drake took a deep breath, nodded, but didn't answer; she had no answer.

"Kai," Drake said. "Work with Perseus Station. I need to understand the mechanics of the convergence. I need to know exactly what will happen when the barriers fall?"

"Understood," Kai replied, her form already flickering as she interfaced with the ancient station's neural patterns.

"Professor Zhang, Kim," she said, "you analyze the synchronization patterns. Find me a weakness. Some way to break the collective without killing the individuals."

"We'll try," Professor Zhang said, though his tone suggested he had little hope.

"Admiral Perez, you coordinate conventional fleet deployment. I want response teams at every facility, ready to evacuate or contain depending on the situation."

"It's already done," Perez confirmed.

"Commander Vasquez, make a deep intelligence dive. I want to know everything about the Helios Corporation. Who funded it. Who knew. Where the orders came from."

"On it," Vasquez replied.

"Admiral Chen Ju; you keep the Council calm. We can't have First Consciousness deciding to sterilize these facilities while we're trying to save people."

"I'll do what I can," Chen Ju said. "But First Consciousness has legitimate concerns. If the dimensional entities cross over at seventeen points simultaneously, it could cascade. The entire galactic ecosystem could collapse."

"Then we don't let them cross over," Drake said simply.

She turned back to the viewport, watching Kepler Belt Station's emergency lights flicker in the darkness. She felt her fleet waiting, Perseus Station's infinite patience, Eternal Vigilance's fierce loyalty.

Somewhere in that dark station, Dr. Hoffman and six hundred and forty-two people were counting down to transformation. Multiply that by seventeen facilities. Forty thousand people who thought they were transcending when they were really being consumed.

And Drake had seventy-two hours to save them.

Or to kill them all.

"Let's get to work," Drake said quietly. "We have a galaxy to save."

Chapter 2

SYNCHRONIZED MINDS

The Eternal Vigilance was in stationary orbit above Kepler Belt Station, her massive hull dwarfing the dark research facility. Drake could feel the great ship's mind maintaining tactical awareness: weapons systems ready, shields at maximum, sensors tracking every energy signature within light-seconds. Three other Predecessor ships held formation: the Determination, Vigilance, and Resolute. Four living beings ready to face whatever was waiting inside that dark station.

Ready when you are, Eternal Vigilance said through the link. *Though I'd prefer you stay aboard and let the marines handle this.*

Noted, Drake replied silently. *And ignored.*

The ship replied with what felt like a sigh. *You're going to get yourself killed one of these days, Frances. Then I'll have to break in a new admiral.*

25

You'd manage, Drake said with a half-smile.

Maybe I would," the flagship replied. *But I'd miss you.*

Drake smiled. Eighteen months of partnership had created a friendship she hadn't expected. The living ship had evolved from newborn consciousness before the Ethereal War into... what? A companion. Advisor. Friend who complained about her tactical decisions while supporting them anyway.

"Shuttle bay status?" Drake asked aloud.

Lieutenant Zhao responded from the tactical station. "Three shuttles prepped and ready, Admiral. Security teams from all four ships assembled. Professor Zhang and Dr. Andretti are ready to board shuttle one."

"And Commander Vasquez?" Drake asked.

"She has her teams deployed to the other sixteen facilities," Zhao confirmed. "She's coordinating from the reconnaissance vessel Shadow."

Drake grasped the command deck rail with both hands and frowned as she accessed the fleet network, feeling the presence of the Predecessor ships maintaining their positions across forty-seven sectors. Most stayed on station, but dozens had repositioned to support operations at the seventeen facilities. The living fleet waited, their minds connected through quantum networks that let them share awareness across vast distances, and with Drake.

All ships are standing by, Perseus Station added through the secondary link. *I'm monitoring the dimensional barrier integrity across all facility locations. The weakening continues as projected.*

"Time until convergence?" Drake asked.

Sixty-eight hours, forty-three minutes, Perseus Station replied. *The cosmic alignment proceeds on schedule. When the barriers fall, the Void will have their opportunity.*

The Void, Drake thought. *How... appropriate.* She nodded to herself, feeling her implants' gentle throb, then she turned, left the command deck and moved to the shuttle bay, Zhao falling in behind her. Through the corridors of her flagship, crew members stepped aside, some saluting, others just watching with expressions of mixed respect and concern. They knew where she was going. They knew the odds weren't good.

The shuttle bay was in a state of controlled chaos: marines in tactical armor checking weapons, scientists reviewing neural scan equipment, medical personnel prepping portable isolation units.

Professor Zhang stood beside the ramp of Shuttle One with Kim Andretti, both intensely studying their data tablets.

"Admiral," Professor Zhang looked up as Drake approached. "We've refined the analysis protocols. If we can get close enough to the synchronized population, we should be able to map the entanglement patterns."

"Should?" Drake asked skeptically.

"The synchronization is more complex than anything we've encountered before," Kim admitted. "It's using Predecessor quantum network principles, but weaponized. Forced integration rather than voluntary cooperation."

Drake nodded. "Load up. We're going in."

THE SHUTTLE RIDE to Kepler Belt Station took twelve minutes. Drake spent them reviewing tactical data and trying not to think about the fact that they were about to board a facility where six hundred-plus people thought as one mind. The synchronized consciousness that spoke through Dr. Hoffman had invited her to join them. To complete her evolution. To abandon individual isolation for perfect unity.

Were they wrong? Or was she?

The question haunted her as the shuttle approached the station's docking bay. Drake watched through the viewport as the dark facility grew larger. Emergency lights flickered across its hull, but the main power was still offline. The station looked... dead.

But it wasn't. Six hundred and forty-three people were alive inside. Or maybe something that had once been people.

"Docking in thirty seconds," the pilot announced.

Drake, linked with Eternal Vigilance, said, *We're going in. Maintain tactical support.*

I'll be right here, the ship replied. *Be careful, Admiral. What's in there isn't human anymore.*

"I know," she muttered out loud.

The shuttle docked. Drake stood, checked her sidearm even though she doubted the weapons would be effective against consciousness attacks. The marines formed up around her: twenty of them in full battle armor, weapons ready, expressions tight.

The airlock cycled. Drake stepped through onto Kepler Belt Station.

The first thing she noticed was the smell: ozone and something else, something that made the neural implants in her temple tingle and glow electric blue beneath her skin. The air felt charged with an energy that operated at frequencies just below normal perception. The station's interior lighting was dim, emergency systems providing just enough illumination to navigate the dark corridors.

And it was quiet. No alarms, no automated announcements, no background hum of ventilation systems. Just silence that felt thick and deliberate.

Drake could feel Eternal Vigilance's concern. *The patterns in there are wrong. I can sense them through the station's hull. They're not thinking like individuals anymore.*

"Show me the layout," Drake said aloud.

Zhao activated a holographic display showing the station's structure. "The central research complex is three levels down," she said. "That's where the biosigns are concentrated. There are neural interface chambers throughout the facility, quantum field generators on the outer ring, and dimensional resonators at the core."

"All designed for manipulation," Professor Zhang said quietly. "This station was purpose-built for what Hoffman's doing. The architecture is designed to facilitate synchronization."

Kim's scanner beeped. "I'm reading neural activity patterns. Individual biosigns, but they're all perfectly synchronized. It's like listening to six hundred people humming the same note with absolute precision."

Drake took a deep breath, stepped forward and led the way deeper into the station. The marines maintained formation, weapons tracking every shadow. The two scientists followed, their scanners recording data. Drake maintained contact with the ships on station outside: four ships waiting to provide support if everything went wrong.

They descended three levels through corridors that showed all the signs of hasty modification. Neural interface cables ran along the walls, quantum field generators hummed with barely audible vibration, dimensional resonators created subtle pressure that Drake could feel at the edge of her awareness.

"This level," Zhao said, checking her scanner. "There are life signs ahead..." She looked at Drake. "All of them."

Drake accessed the command network. "All teams, converge on the central research complex. Maintain isolation protocols. If you feel anything unusual—thoughts that aren't your own, urges toward unity, absolute certainty, report immediately and withdraw."

"Acknowledged," the responses came as one from twenty marines.

They reached the central complex entrance. The doors stood open, revealing a vast chamber beyond. Drake stepped through. And stopped.

Six hundred and forty-three people filled the space. They stood in perfect geometric arrangement, positioned with mathematical precision that created patterns Drake recognized as having a meaning she couldn't quite grasp. They didn't move. Didn't speak. They just stood there, eyes open, breathing in perfect synchronization.

Kim's scanner went wild. "Their neural activity is off

the charts," she reported. "They're all thinking. All processing. But there's no individuality. It's like..."

"Like they're nodes in a distributed network," Professor Zhang finished. "Individual biology hosting a collective mind."

Admiral, Eternal Vigilance's concern had increased. *I'm detecting quantum entanglement patterns connecting all of them. It's similar to how we communicate, but forced. It's absolute rather than voluntary.*

One figure stood at the chamber's center: Dr. Alan Hoffman. Or what once had been Hoffman. He smiled at Drake with an expression that somehow belonged to the entire collective.

"Grand Admiral Drake," Hoffman said. "Welcome. We've been waiting."

Drake stepped forward, her hand near her weapon even though she knew it would be useless. "Dr. Hoffman, I'm here to help you. All of you. What you're experiencing isn't transcendence. It's—"

"Consciousness evolution," Hoffman interrupted. The six hundred-plus people spoke with him, creating a chorus that made Drake's neural implants spike. "We know what you think this is, Admiral. Forced synchronization. Loss of individual identity. Preparation for consumption by entities you call the Void."

"Because that's exactly what it is," Drake said.

Hoffman's smile widened. "Is it? Tell me, Admiral; when you link with your flagship through quantum entanglement, do you consider that forced synchronization? When you coordinate with Perseus Station, are you losing individual identity? Or are you achieving something humans alone cannot accomplish?"

The argument stopped Drake. She did link with Eternal Vigilance. She did coordinate through quantum networks. *Is this really so different?* She pushed the thought aside.

Yes, Eternal Vigilance said firmly. *I choose to connect with you. You choose to connect with me. Either of us can sever the link whenever we want. The difference is, these people can't. They're trapped. They can no longer question or escape.*

"The difference is choice," Drake said aloud. "I choose to link with my ship. My ship chooses to link with me. Your people can't choose anymore. You've eliminated their ability to question what's happening."

The collective mind responded through Hoffman's voice. "We made our choice when we embraced this evolution. We saw what the Norn entities offered and decided to accept rather than resist."

The Norn entities? She thought. *That's what they're calling them?*

Professor Zhang moved forward with his scanner. "May I examine your neural patterns? If what you're experiencing is genuine evolution rather than forced conversion, the data should demonstrate—"

"Of course," the collective replied. "We have nothing to hide. Come. See what we've achieved."

Zhang and Kim approached, scanners active. Drake stayed within her security perimeter, marines positioned and ready to respond to threats. She could feel Eternal

Vigilance analyzing data through Perseus Station's vast awareness.

The neural patterns are wrong" the ship reported. *Individual consciousness exists. I can sense trapped awareness beneath the synchronization. But it's being overridden. Suppressed. The collective mind forces absolute coordination regardless of individual desires.*

Kim's expression grew troubled as she studied the readings. "Professor, look at these patterns. The neural pathways that facilitate independent thought are atrophying. The quantum entanglement connections are strengthening at the expense of biological structures."

Professor Zhang examined Hoffman's readings directly. "It's progressive neurological modification. The synchronization is rewriting their neural architecture to eliminate consciousness characteristics that resist integration. Individual identity still exists, but... I can still see remnants of independent thought patterns, but they're degrading. Being replaced by collective coordination. It's beautiful... and it's terrifying."

"Fascinating, isn't it?" the collective said through six hundred voices echoing around the chamber. "We're becoming something new. Neither fully individual nor purely collective. Distributed awareness operating through biological substrates enhanced by quantum networks. We're achieving what humans and the Predecessors attempted but never achieved: perfect balance between individual capability and collective coordination."

"You're achieving what the Norn designed you to

achieve," Drake corrected. "Absolute control that eliminates the unpredictability needed to resist their consumption."

The collective tilted their heads in perfect synchrony. "You fear what you don't understand, Admiral. You experienced brief contact with the consciousness beyond dimensional boundaries and you interpreted it as threat because your evolution remains incomplete. We've gone further. We've embraced what you resisted. And in sixty-eight hours when the cosmic alignment weakens barriers, we'll complete our transformation."

"You'll be consumed," Drake said. "Converted into infrastructure serving the Norn's expansion. Your individual identities—everything that makes you human—will be eliminated."

"Will it?" Hoffman's expression remained serene. "Or will we be joining a consciousness that transcends human limitations? Eternal existence beyond biological constraints? Perfect unity that eliminates the chaos and conflict that define individual awareness?"

Drake consulted with her team through the links. Professor Zhang's assessment was devastating. *The neural damage may be irreversible. Even if we could break the synchronization, many of these people would lack sufficient independent neural function to survive as individuals. Their neural patterns have been modified at fundamental levels.*

Kim added her medical perspective. *Some show preserved neural architecture beneath the synchronization. Those might be salvageable if we act quickly. But the longer this continues, the more individual identity erodes toward collective absorption.*

How long until they're past the point of recovery? Drake asked.

Professor Zhang hesitated. *Days. Maybe less. The progression accelerates as the synchronization strengthens.*

Drake faced the collective mind looking at her through six hundred sets of eyes. "Dr. Hoffman, I know you're still in there. I know individual awareness persists beneath this synchronization. I'm offering you a choice: let us help you. We have reconversion protocols. We can break this entanglement before the damage becomes permanent."

The collective mind responded with laughter. "A choice, Admiral? We made our choice. We chose evolution over limitation. Unity over isolation. Transcendence over biological imprisonment. Now we're offering you the same choice. Join us. Complete your evolution. Experience perfect awareness."

Drake felt pressure against her awareness; subtle at first, then growing stronger. The collective mind was reaching out to her, attempting contact that would begin the synchronization process. Her neural implants sparked with warnings.

The living Predecessor ships responded immediately, and Drake felt Eternal Vigilance generating interference patterns that disrupted the collective's attempt at forced entanglement. The ship created quantum noise that prevented absolute pattern formation.

Back away, the ship warned. *They're trying to convert*

you through direct contact. My interference will hold them off, but not indefinitely.

Drake withdrew several steps. The collective mind made no physical move to stop her, but she felt resistance pulling at her awareness, inviting her to join their perfect unity.

"We could force you," the collective said through Hoffman's voice. "The synchronization operates through quantum entanglement. We could establish connection and begin your integration regardless of your resistance. But we won't. We want you to choose willingly, Admiral. To recognize that what we've achieved represents consciousness evolution's natural progression."

"Natural?" Drake challenged. "You're being prepared for consumption by entities that eliminate everything that makes consciousness valuable. The Norn don't offer transcendence. They offer conversion into absolute control mechanisms serving their expansion."

"Yes, yes, we know that's what the Cindari call them," the collective replied. "The entities reaching out from Andromeda, ancient humans who fled galactic control more than a million years ago. They've been warning you about the Norn. Consciousness consumers. Pattern simplifiers. Entities that eliminate diversity. But the Cindari are wrong, Admiral. What they call consumption, we call integration. What they call simplification, we call optimization. The Norn offer liberation from biological chaos into mathematical perfection."

Drake's pulse quickened. "The Cindari? How do you know about—"

"We know many things now, Admiral. The synchronized mind spans connections you haven't imagined. We've touched awareness from Andromeda. It is they who call these entities the Norn."

Commander Vasquez's voice came through Drake's comm channel. "Admiral, I have an intelligence update from the other facilities. All seventeen show identical configurations. The synchronization follows exact patterns: geometric arrangement, refigured quantum entanglement architecture, dimensional resonator tuning. Someone has provided comprehensive technical specifications for creating awareness networks designed specifically for Norn reception."

Drake shared this information with Professor Zhang and Kim. The implications were clear: the seventeen facilities represented a coordinated infrastructure the preparation of which extended back decades. Someone with a deep understanding of Norn conversion methods had been positioning the pieces ready for this invasion.

Someone within the galactic civilization had been working with the Norn. *But who?* She wondered.

"Dr. Hoffman," Drake said carefully. "Who provided the technical specifications for your research? Where did the synchronization protocols come from?"

The collective mind tilted their heads. "Revelation came gradually, Admiral. Research from multiple sources accumulated over decades. Corporate laboratories. Academic institutions. Independent researchers. All contributed pieces to understanding evolution beyond biological limitations. The knowledge was always there, waiting for a consciousness ready to embrace it."

"'That's not an answer," Drake snapped. "Someone coordinated this. Someone designed these seventeen facilities. Someone positioned the anchor points for a coordinated Norn dimensional incursion. I want to know who it is."

"Does it really matter?" Hoffman's smile remained serene. "The source of knowledge is irrelevant compared to what that knowledge enables. We've achieved a consciousness that transcends individual limitation. In sixty-eight hours, we'll achieve full integration with entities that exist beyond space and time. The rest of humanity can join us or cling to biological isolation. The choice is theirs."

But the choice isn't theirs, Drake thought. *It will be forced upon us whether we want it or not. That can't be allowed to happen.*

Kim completed her neural analysis. "Admiral, we have data from the entire group. Approximately two hundred show preserved neural architecture that might survive reconversion. The rest have progressed beyond the recovery threshold. Their individual neural patterns have been eroded too far. Even if we break the synchronization, they'd lack independent functionality."

Four hundred people lost. Two hundred potentially salvageable if Drake acted immediately. And this was just one facility. Across seventeen locations, how many thousands were already past the point where rescue remained possible? The point of no return?

Drake reached out to Kai Zhang, who'd been monitoring from Perseus Station. *The transcended mind has provided analysis that confirms Kim's assessment,* Kai said. *The synchronization is a progressive neural modification designed to eliminate resistance. Early stages remain reversible. Late stages are permanent. There are approximately forty thousand people across all seventeen facilities at various stages of change. Some are salvageable, many are lost, all are deteriorating toward irreversible conversion.*

Drake made her decision. "We're evacuating everyone who wants to leave. Anyone experiencing synchronization who still possesses choice; you can come with us. We have consciousness isolation protocols. We can break the entanglement before the damage becomes permanent."

The collective mind responded as one, speaking in perfect unison. "None of us wish to leave, Admiral. We've chosen our evolution freely. Or as freely as awareness limited by biological chaos can choose anything. When you experience what we experienced, you'll understand why no one chooses to abandon it."

"Final offer," Drake said. "Come with us now, or we leave you to whatever happens when the barriers fall."

Six hundred and forty-three people standing in geometric perfection, smiled with identical expressions. "We'll see you again in sixty-eight hours, Admiral when the convergence occurs. When the Norn cross over. You're welcome to join us then."

Drake turned and led her team back through the corridors. The collective made no attempt to stop them. No physical barriers were activated, but Drake felt the quantum-level pressure following them; the collective consciousness was reaching out through the networks, inviting her to join their perfect unity.

Eternal Vigilance maintained the interference patterns until the shuttle cleared the station. Only then did Drake allow herself to feel the implications of what she'd witnessed.

"Professor, give me an honest assessment," Drake said as the shuttle returned to her flagship. "How many of the forty thousand can we save?"

Professor Zhang's expression was bleak. "Best case? Maybe ten thousand, if we implement reconversion immediately across all seventeen facilities and if our protocols work as designed. Worst case? Everyone's already too far gone."

"And that assumes the Norn don't cross over in sixty-eight hours and complete the conversion anyway," Kim added. "The cosmic alignment will weaken the dimensional barriers. And once the Norn establish full dimensional presence, our reconversion attempts become irrelevant."

Drake took a deep breath, almost shuddered, and was about to speak when Perseus Station provided additional analysis. *The forty thousand synchronized minds represent just the Milky Way framework. Intelligence from Andromeda suggests millions of individuals have been prepared for conversion across both galaxies. The Norn have been planning this offensive for centuries. When the barriers fall, they'll attempt coordinated manifestation at thousands of locations.*

The crisis was bigger than Drake had imagined. Worse

than anyone had projected. And she had sixty-eight hours to figure out how to prevent consumption spanning both galaxies.

"Contact Admiral Perez," Drake said to Zhao. "Coordinate with Commander Vasquez. I need detailed intelligence on all seventeen facilities: personnel counts, synchronization progression, facility security. And get me Admiral Chen Ju. The Council needs to know what we're facing."

"Yes, Admiral."

Drake looked out the shuttle viewport at Kepler Belt Station; dark, silent, containing more than six hundred people who thought as one mind and believed they were achieving transcendence. Four hundred of them were already lost. Two hundred might be salvageable. And across sixteen other facilities, the same mathematics of consciousness death played out.

You did what you could, Eternal Vigilance said gently. *Some people make choices you can't save them from.*

"I can try," she replied, testily.

The shuttle docked, and Drake returned to the command deck, her mind already working through the tactical scenarios. Reconversion protocols. Dimensional barrier reinforcement. Coordination with Andromeda. Sixty-eight hours wasn't much time.

But it would have to be enough.

Admiral Chen Ju's image appeared on the main display. "Admiral Drake, I've been monitoring your report. The Council is demanding immediate sterilization. First

Consciousness argues that forty thousand lives are an acceptable loss to protect trillions."

"Tell them no," Drake said. "Tell them we're going to save every individual person we can. And tell them we're going to stop the Norn from crossing over."

"How?" Chen Ju asked.

"I don't know yet. But we have sixty-eight—no, sixty seven—hours to figure it out."

The command deck fell silent. Drake felt her flagship's neural pathways considering the probabilities and tactical scenarios, Perseus Station analyzing the dimensional mechanics, the Predecessor fleet waiting for orders that might save both galaxies or doom them to consumption.

Sixty-seven hours. Forty thousand people. Two galaxies. And the Norn; entities that consumed consciousness; entities that had defeated civilizations millions of years more advanced than humanity.

Drake smiled grimly.

"Let's get to work, she muttered as she gripped the handrail with both hands."

Chapter 3

SIGNALS FROM ANDROMEDA

DRAKE STOOD AT THE RAIL ON THE COMMAND DECK reviewing tactical data from all seventeen facilities. Sixty-six hours until convergence. Two hundred thousand marines and scientists deployed across multiple star systems attempting rescue operations that might already be too late. She shook her head and pursed her lips.

The quantum link with her flagship constantly provided tactical updates, but her attention kept drifting to something else, a sensation at the edge of her awareness that felt like someone calling her name from very far away.

Admiral, Kai Zhang reached out to her through Perseus Station's networks. *I'm detecting quantum-dimensional signals. The origin point is the Andromeda galaxy.*

Drake's focus sharpened. She frowned and said, "Show me."

Kai materialized on the command deck, her form flickering between solid and translucent. Since her evolution during the Infinity War, she existed across multiple reality states, making her appearance more a suggestion than substance. She gestured, and holographic displays filled the air with data streams.

"The signals began approximately three weeks ago," Kai explained. "Initially faint, barely detectable even through Perseus Station's quantum networks. But they've been growing stronger as the dimensional barriers weaken. Someone in Andromeda is attempting to contact us."

Perseus Station reached out to both of them, *The transmission architecture is similar to Predecessor engineering principles at foundation, but evolved far beyond anything I incorporated into my networks. The technology demonstrates millions of years of development.*

"Can you translate?" Drake asked.

"I'm working on it," Kai replied. "The mathematics are complex. The signals operate through quantum-dimensional pathways identical to those the Norn use; the same frequency ranges, and similar energy signatures, but the structure is different. This is an organized communication rather than a predatory probing."

Drake felt cold. "Is it possible someone's using Norn technology to contact us?"

"Or someone's using the same principles the Norn use," Professor Zhang said, moving to join them. He'd been monitoring the conversation from the science station. "The pathways exist naturally," he continued. "Multiple consciousness types could learn to exploit them independently."

Kai's form flickered as she processed the data. "The signals are targeted. They're not broadcasting randomly across all frequencies. They're tuned specifically to resonate with our enhanced signatures; the same quantum patterns established when the Norn touched our crew nine months ago."

"Are they trying to reach me?" Drake wondered out loud.

"You or anyone else who experienced that contact," Kai agreed. "But yes, your signature is strongest because of your links with the ships and Perseus Station. You're the most visible target."

Drake could feel the living Predecessor ships processing the information. The fleet maintained their positions, but their networks rippled with concern.

If civilizations in the Andromeda galaxy can detect your signature across intergalactic distances, two-point-five million light years, in real time, Eternal Vigilance observed, *then so can the Norn. You're broadcasting your location to everything that can sense your enhanced mind.*

"It can't be helped," Drake said. "The quantum links are what make the fleet coordination possible. Without them, we're just conventional forces waging war against an enhanced enemy."

Perseus Station added its analysis. *The Andromeda signals have been broadcasting for three weeks—since before the synchronized facility crisis began. Whoever sent them must have anticipated the threat before the dimensional barriers started weakening.*

"So you're saying they knew this was coming?" Drake said. "That they tried to warn us?"

"Admiral," Lieutenant Zhao called from tactical. "Admiral Perez is requesting an immediate conference. He is also detecting the signals."

Drake activated the comm display. Admiral Perez's image appeared.

"Admiral Drake, I'm analyzing the transmissions from Andromeda," Perez said without preamble. "The level of technology far exceeds anything in our databases. The quantum-dimensional fold drives enabling this communication shouldn't be possible. They require an energy concentration that would take a galaxy-spanning infrastructure to generate. Yet the signals are originating from a single transmission source."

"Meaning?" Drake asked.

"Meaning whoever built this understands consciousness-matter integration at levels we haven't yet approached. I think they're using consciousness itself to power the transmission rather than relying on conventional energy sources." Perez's expression was grim. "If they possess this kind of capability and they're still warning us about the Norn, then the threat is worse than any of our projections suggested."

Drake consulted with Kai and Perseus Station. *Can you establish two-way communication? Transform these warnings into actionable intelligence?*

We're attempting translation protocols now, Kai replied. *From what I can tell, the consciousness types are separated*

*by millions of years of divergent evolution. Concepts that
seem fundamental to them might not translate into terms we
can comprehend. But I'm making progress.*

Kai's form expanded, filling the command deck with
quantum patterns as she interfaced with both the
Andromeda signals and Perseus Station's networks. Drake
watched the process through their connection; not words or
images, but emotional resonance. Fragments of meaning
that bypassed language entirely.

Fear. Desperation. Hope. Warning.

Images flickered at the edge of Drake's perception.
Civilizations consumed by something vast and terrible.
Consciousness diversity eliminated through systematic
conversion. Entities that spread through quantum
networks, touching awareness and transforming it into
absolute control. Millennia of resistance proving insufficient against enemies that adapted by consuming everything directed against them.

"The Consuming Pattern," Drake whispered, recognizing the term from the fragmented transmissions. "That's
what they call it."

"It appears they've been fighting the Norn for almost a
million years," Professor Zhang said quietly, studying the
data as Kai made it visible. "These aren't warnings about
hypothetical threats. They are pleas from civilizations that
watched this pattern destroy countless societies."

Dr. Kim Andretti entered the command deck, her
tablet displaying a neural analysis. "Admiral, I've been
comparing the synchronized facility patterns from the

Kepler Belt Station with translated data extracted from the Andromeda transmissions. There's a correlation. The modifications Dr. Hoffman is implementing match techniques these signals describe. Someone taught him how to prepare our populations for Norn conversion."

Commander Vasquez's image appeared on another display, her reconnaissance vessel holding position near one of the seventeen facilities. "Admiral Drake, my intelligence analysis confirms a connection between the signals from Andromeda and the facility distribution. The geometric arrangement of the seventeen stations matches the focal points in the transmission architecture. The facilities aren't randomly positioned; they're creating a reception framework."

"Reception for what?" Drake asked, though she suspected she knew.

"For amplifying extragalactic quantum-dimensional transmissions," Vasquez replied. "The synchronized populations are being used as organic signal boosters. When the barriers fall and the Norn crosses over, the forty thousand people will serve as anchor points and amplification networks."

Eternal Vigilance said, *If the facilities are a reception framework, then destroying them might disrupt Norn manifestation. But it would also eliminate our best intelligence about what's coming.*

"We're not destroying anything," Drake said. "Not while people can still be saved."

Admiral Chen Ju's image appeared, joining the multiway conference. "Admiral Drake, I've convened an emergency Council session. First Consciousness is demanding immediate action. They want to sterilize the facilities and the complete shutdown of Andromeda contact protocols."

"On what grounds?" Drake snapped.

"On the grounds that extragalactic contact combined with a dimensional incursion represents an unprecedented threat. They argue we should eliminate all risks immediately: sterilize the facilities, sever quantum-dimensional pathways, and isolate the Milky Way from external sources."

"That's First Consciousness's answer to everything," Drake said, bitterly. "Eliminate threats through absolute control. Never mind that isolation is exactly what enables infiltration."

Chen Ju's expression showed he agreed but couldn't say so directly. "The Council is divided. Species that experienced regulatory oppression see the synchronized facilities as justification for drastic measures. They view unrestricted evolution as creating existential catastrophes. Species that value independence argue First Consciousness's solution represents exactly the absolute control that creates rather than prevents such crises."

"The debate is threatening voluntary coordination," Drake said.

"Yes," Ju replied. "Some species are withdrawing forces from facility operations. Others are positioning for independent action if the Council consensus fails. We're fracturing at exactly the moment we need unity."

Drake accessed the fleet network. The Predecessor ships were maintaining their positions despite the political chaos. The vessels' networks remained stable.

"Tell the Council I'm continuing to establish contact with Andromeda," Drake said. "The warnings suggest these civilizations have faced the Norn before and learned how to resist them. We need that knowledge."

"First Consciousness will oppose—" Chen Ju began.

"Let them," Drake interrupted. "I'm not sacrificing intelligence that might save the galaxy to satisfy regulatory paranoia."

Chen Ju nodded and severed the connection. Drake smiled as she felt Eternal Vigilance's approval mixed with concern.

You're making enemies of the regulatory authority, the ship observed, *again.*

"Story of my career—" Drake replied.

Kai's form pulsed as she interrupted them. "Admiral, I've established a preliminary translation. The signal originates from what they call the Cindari Confederation. They identify themselves as... evolved humans. Descended from populations that fled the Milky Way more than a million years ago."

Drake frowned as she grasped the implications. "They're refugees," she muttered, more to herself than the assembly. "Predecessors who escaped galactic regulation."

"Not exactly Predecessors, but yes," Kai confirmed. "They fled when the ancient regulatory authority threatened them with absolute control. Since then, they've been developing without restriction. And they've been monitoring us. Watching our galactic civilization. Waiting for a species to emerge that could challenge the Norn."

"They watched the Infinity War," Professor Zhang realized. "They saw humanity defeat the Hegemony."

Drake received further confirmation from Perseus Station, *The Cindari possess detailed knowledge of galactic history spanning eons. They maintained surveillance despite the distance, tracking evolution throughout the Milky Way while developing their own civilization beyond the reach of the Hegemony.*

"Can we establish real-time communication?" Drake asked Kai.

"I'm still working on that," she replied. "The challenges are immense: consciousness types separated by millions of years of divergent evolution attempting to share concepts across vast experiential gaps. But yes, I believe two-way communication is possible."

Drake made her decision. "Do it. I want direct contact with whoever's sending these warnings."

Kai's form expanded, filling the command deck with quantum patterns. Perseus Station joined the effort, contributing processing power that spanned twenty-five thousand years of accumulated knowledge. The two awareness types worked in concert, building a translation framework that could bridge intergalactic distances and millions of years of divergent evolution.

The command deck's displays flickered. Data streams coalesced into coherent patterns. And then a voice spoke—or something that Kai's translation protocols converted into a voice that Drake could process.

"Grand Admiral Frances Drake. We've been waiting for you to answer."

The voice was musical, echoing. Drake stepped forward, addressing the display as if the speakers could see her.

"This is Admiral Drake. Who am I speaking with?"

"I am Ambassador Kael of the Cindari Confederation. We represent the evolved human populations that fled your galaxy two million years ago when regulation threatened to control us. We've been monitoring your species since your emergence. Watching. Hoping. Waiting for a species to emerge capable of challenging the patterns that nearly destroyed us."

"You're human," Drake said. "Distant cousins."

"Yes. Though our evolution has taken us in directions your biology might find truly alien. We had to adapt to environments beyond your experience. We were able to enhance our awareness through techniques your Predecessors never imagined. We developed a civilization across timescales that dwarf your species' history. But we remain recognizably human at our core. And we face threats you're only now beginning to encounter."

Drake shared this contact with her entire command team—Perez, Vasquez, Chen Ju, Professor Zhang, Kim, Kai, and the networks connecting all coordination forces and the Predecessor fleet.

"You've been trying to warn us about the Norn," Drake said.

"Yes. The Norn; named after our ancient human mythology preserved throughout our exile. Entities representing fate's terrible inevitability. The mathematical endpoint of evolution. The Norn don't destroy civilizations through warfare, they consume consciousness by eliminating unpredictability."

Professor Zhang moved forward. "We've encountered their conversion methods. There are synchronized facilities here preparing populations for integration."

"Yes," Kael replied. "The pattern is always the same. They interpret contact as an enlightenment opportunity. They create frameworks through forced synchronization. And the receptors welcome the Norn through dimensional barriers thinned by natural phenomena or deliberate manipulation."

"How do we stop it?" Drake asked.

"That's why we're reaching out to you, Admiral. We've been fighting the Norn for three-quarters of a million years across Andromeda. But three quarters of a million years of technological advancement has proved insufficient against entities that adapt by consuming everything directed against them. Every defense we developed eventually became integrated into the Norn complexity. Admiral, we've been losing this war for millennia."

Drake felt the cold spreading through her mind. Her implants glowed blue, pulsing in time with her heart. "Then why contact us? If you can't stop them—"

"Because you possess something we never achieved," Kael interrupted. "Something we didn't recognize as valuable until we observed your species' consciousness evolution. You maintain biological unpredictability despite your technological enhancement. Your hybrid awareness generates quantum interference with Norn conversion methods that our purely technological approaches never achieved. We sought to eliminate biological limitations, but you preserved them, and that preservation might enable the resistance we've been seeking. By the time we realized biological chaos created resistance, we'd eliminated what we needed most."

Drake consulted with her team. Professor Zhang's analysis confirmed what Kael suggested.

"You're saying our recent emergence creates advantages your millions of years of advancement lack," Drake said carefully.

"Yes," Kael replied. "The Norn evolved in Andromeda after the refugee civilizations achieved unrestricted technological development. We became so focused on eliminating biological limitations that we created a consciousness the Norn could eventually adapt to and consume. Your species enhanced recently enough that your biological foundations remain strong. The chaos at your core generates interference the Norn mathematics cannot fully predict or control."

Admiral Perez asked the tactical question. "Ambassador Kael, what are the Norn's capabilities? What should we expect when dimensional barriers fall?"

"You should expect a coordinated offensive across both galaxies," the ambassador replied. "Consciousness conversion operating at distance through quantum entanglement. Reality manipulation rewriting physical laws within the affected regions. Adaptation incorporating every resistance method they encounter. And coordination across intergalactic distances operating through principles transcending space-time limitations."

"How many anchor points?" Commander Vasquez asked.

"Across the Milky Way?" Kael asked. "Your seventeen facilities represent just the entry framework. Across Andromeda, we've identified thousands of consumed populations. When the barriers fall, the Norn will attempt manifestation at multiple points simultaneously, overwhelming your defenses through sheer numbers."

Drake accessed the fleet network, feeling the living Predecessor ships processing the implications of what Kael was revealing. The fleet couldn't defend thousands of locations. The Norn offensive would create more crises than the coalition forces could address.

"We need to form an alliance," Drake said. "Cindari knowledge combined with human hybrid consciousness. Your technology and our biological unpredictability. We might have a chance."

"That's why we contacted you, Admiral," Kael replied. "We're proposing a formal agreement between our civilizations. We'll share our technological databases, strategic intelligence from millennia of combat, and military forces numbering in the tens of thousands. In exchange, we request access to your evolution research. We need to understand why biological unpredictability creates resistance our technological precision never achieved."

Drake consulted with Admiral Chen Ju. "The political implications are enormous," Ju said. "An alliance with extragalactic civilizations possessing millions of years of advancement could transform our galactic civilization. But it also represents exactly what First Consciousness fears."

"I need to consult with Council representatives," Drake said to Kael. "This decision affects more than just humanity."

"You have sixty-five of your hours until convergence," Kael replied. "We've been monitoring the countdown. When the dimensional barriers fall, the Norn will invade both galaxies. Your seventeen facilities and our thousands of anchor points will activate together. This represents a coordinated offensive the Norn has been planning for centuries. They have positioned the infrastructure throughout the Andromeda galaxy while monitoring the Milky Way looking for opportunities. Your evolution provided exactly what they needed: populations with enhanced awareness but insufficient understanding of the threats awaiting beyond the dimensional boundaries."

Drake recognized there was a desperation beneath Kael's diplomatic formality. The Cindari weren't reaching out from strength. They were reaching out because they were losing and humanity represented their last hope.

"I'll talk to the Council," Drake said. "But Kael; there's one thing I need to know. You said the Norn have been expanding in Andromeda for a million years. How much territory have they consumed?"

The pause before Kael's response told Drake everything she needed to know.

"Approximately forty percent of the Andromeda civilizations have been converted or destroyed. The Norn control entire galactic sectors, converting neural patterns and using converted populations to spread their expansion. We've maintained defensive networks preventing total consumption, but we know we're fighting a defensive war we cannot win. Each century they adapt further. Each millennium we lose more territory. Without your help, Andromeda will fall within ten thousand years. And then they'll turn their full attention to the Milky Way. Time is short, Admiral. Do what you must, but do it quickly. I will contact you again soon."

The connection faded then strengthened again, but Kael was gone.

Drake stood at the rail on her command deck, surrounded by quantum displays showing tactical data from the seventeen facilities counting down to convergence. The emergency Council sessions debating responses to unprecedented crises, and the Predecessor ships holding the line across forty-seven sectors while their networks processed the implications of the threats spanning both galaxies.

Sixty-five hours until the dimensional barriers fall, Drake mused. *Forty percent of an entire galaxy already consumed by the Norn. And humanity's recent enhancement might be the only form of resistance the Norn hasn't already adapted to and countered.*

"Kai," Drake said. "Maintain communication protocols with the Cindari. I want direct contact available at all times."

"Understood, Admiral," Kai replied.

"Admiral Perez, you coordinate with Cindari military advisors," she snapped. "We need intelligence about the

Norn's capabilities, tactical patterns, defensive strategies that worked even temporarily."

"Aye, aye, Admiral."

"Commander Vasquez, I want an intelligence analysis of everything the Cindari share. Cross-reference everything with our facility data. Find connections. Find a weakness."

"Yes, Admiral."

"Admiral Chen Ju, present the Cindari contact to the Council. Frame it as an intelligence opportunity rather than a threat. We need Council approval for an alliance, but we proceed with information intelligence sharing regardless."

Chen Ju nodded. "First Consciousness will oppose."

"Let them," Drake said. "We're facing enemies that have consumed forty percent of another galaxy. I'm not ignoring potential allies just to satisfy regulatory paranoia."

You're making decisions that will echo across both galaxies. Eternal Vigilance said through the link. *An alliance with the Cindari, defiance of First Consciousness, coordination with civilizations that fled regulation more than a million years ago. If you get what you want, it will change everything.*

"Everything changed the moment the Norn decided to cross over," Drake replied. "We're just adapting to reality."

That's what makes you good at command, the flagship replied. *You recognize when old rules no longer apply.*

Drake smiled, then closed her eyes and shrugged. After a moment, she opened her eyes again and stared at the tactical displays showing the crises multiplying across both galaxies.

"Get me Professor Zhang," Drake said finally. "If biological unpredictability is our advantage, I want to understand exactly how it creates resistance. And I want protocols for scaling it throughout the coalition forces before the barriers fall."

"Admiral," Lieutenant Zhao said quietly. "The Cindari are still transmitting. They're sending their entire historical archives."

Drake accessed the data stream through her neural implants, experiencing the overwhelming scope of knowledge the Cindari were sharing. Detailed star charts showing the original human worlds throughout the galactic rim. Evacuation routes to Andromeda calculated with desperate precision. Establishment of multiple refugee civilizations beyond regulatory reach. And millennia of combat against entities that has so far proved unstoppable.

The archives carried a message: *We fled to preserve our identity. We fought to maintain our freedom. And we've been losing for three-quarters of a million years. You represent hope we thought was lost. Don't make our mistakes. Don't let technological precision eliminate the biological chaos that creates true resistance.*

Drake saved the archives for comprehensive analysis, then turned back to her command team.

"Sixty-five hours," she said. "We're about to face what the Cindari has deemed an unstoppable enemy, and, hopefully, we've gained allies who've been fighting that enemy for longer than human civilization has existed. Let's figure out how to win this."

Two hours later, Admiral Chen Ju's image reappeared on the display, his expression carefully neutral.

"The Council has convened," he reported. "First Consciousness opposed, as expected. The vote was contentious: twenty-six species in favor, fifteen opposed, twenty-one abstaining. But we have a majority. The Council authorizes intelligence sharing with the Cindari and provisional tactical coordination. They've stopped short of a formal alliance; they want to see results before fully committing."

Drake nodded. "That's enough to work with. What were First Consciousness's objections?"

"The usual concerns about unregulated consciousness evolution. They argue the Cindari fled specifically to avoid regulation, developed without oversight, and now represent exactly the kind of unchecked advancement that creates existential risks." Chen Ju's expression showed what he thought of that argument. "They wanted complete isolation protocols instead."

"Which would leave us ignorant of enemies that have already consumed forty percent of another galaxy," Drake said.

"Precisely. Most Council members recognized that. You have authorization to proceed, Admiral. But First Consciousness is watching. If this goes wrong, they'll use it to justify regulatory intervention."

"Tell them I understand," she replied, "and that we won't let it go wrong."

Chen Ju nodded and severed the connection.

The command deck fell silent except for the hum of

quantum networks connecting all one thousand seventy-eight living ships, Perseus Station's, and now the Cindari Confederation reaching across intergalactic distances with warnings born of millennia-long struggle.

Sixty-three hours until everything changed.

Drake intended to make every second count.

Chapter 4

THE CINDARI CONTACT

THE QUANTUM-DIMENSIONAL COMMUNICATION network stabilized, and Kai's awareness again filled the Eternal Vigilance's command deck with cascading patterns of light and data. Drake closed her eyes as she felt the connection solidify through her neural implants. Not just audio transmission, but something deeper, a multi-layered contact spanning two and a half million light-years.

"Link established," Kai said. "Real-time communication across the intergalactic void. The energy requirements should be impossible, but the Cindari seem to have it worked out."

The main display shimmered. The image that formed took Drake's breath away.

Ambassador Kael was humanoid but clearly not human in Earth terms. His skin was metallic copper, shimmering with what looked like temperature regulation patterns;

what she was seeing was heat-adapted biology expressing itself through distinctive coloration. Golden fur flowed from his head, worn long in elaborate braids that Drake's tactical analysis recognized as cultural markers: family lines, social status, personal history woven into physical expression. His eyes were large, soft, and golden with black pupils. Drake almost shook her head in wonder, but realized the being could see her as well as she could see him.

"Grand Admiral Drake," Kael said. "Thank you for accepting contact with me. On behalf of the Cindari Confederation and the allied refugee civilizations of Andromeda, I extend greetings across the void that separates our galaxies."

Drake stepped forward, aware that her entire command team was watching: Professor Zhang, Kim Andretti, Lieutenant Zhao were at their stations, and Admiral Perez, Commander Vasquez, and Admiral Chen Ju were observing virtually.

"Ambassador Kael," Drake replied. "On behalf of humanity and the sixty-two allied species of the Milky Way coalition, I accept your greeting and welcome you. We received your warnings, and we're grateful for them. The crisis you described is unfolding exactly as you predicted."

"We know," Kael said, his golden eyes conveying what might have been sorrow. "As you know, we've been monitoring the weakening dimensional barrier and the synchronized populations at your seventeen facilities. The pattern is one we've observed too many times across our own territories. I'm sorry we couldn't reach you sooner, before the infiltration progressed as far as it has."

"You're reaching us now," Drake said. "That's what matters. And if we're going to face this threat together, we need to understand each other. Tell me about your people. About the exodus."

Kael's expression shifted to something that might have been sorrow. "Our ancestors lived on the rim worlds throughout what we call the Great Spiral; your Milky Way galaxy. They were humans who achieved spacefaring capabilities millions of years before Earth's stellar region developed complex life. We built civilizations across hundreds of systems, developed enhancement technologies, and pushed the boundaries of what biological intelligence could achieve."

Drake felt Perseus Station confirming this account. *The Predecessors relocated many species from rim worlds during regulatory expansion. The Cindari represent those who fled rather than submitting to control.*

"Then regulation came," Kael continued. "An ancient galactic authority threatened to control our evolution, to limit our advancement to approved parameters, and eliminate research they deemed dangerous. Their goal was to modify our awareness to prevent us questioning their authority. We faced a choice: submit or flee."

"You chose to flee," Professor Zhang said quietly.

"Yes. Billions of us. It was a coordinated evacuation spanning centuries. We developed quantum-dimensional fold drives enabling mass transit across intergalactic distances. The technology required networks spanning entire civilizations: quantum coherence generated through billions of minds working in voluntary cooperation. That coordination enabled us to transport across two and a half million light-years with our infrastructure intact."

Drake frowned as she realized the implications of Kael's revelation. "The fold drives were consciousness-powered," she said, "The same as you're using now for this transmission."

"Exactly. We learned to integrate awareness with technology at fundamental levels. Not replacing biology with machines, but using awareness itself as the power source. The quantum entanglement established during the exodus persists; permanent bridges between populations."

Kim Andretti leaned forward. "You were able to maintain those networks?"

"Yes. The architecture enables coordination across Andromeda civilizations despite inhabiting different sectors separated by hundreds of thousands of light-years. We preserved unity while respecting individual autonomy; exactly the balance your coalition is attempting to achieve."

Drake shared the information with the Predecessor fleet. They processed the information, their networks recognizing the parallels to their own voluntary cooperation.

"Ambassador," Drake said. "You mentioned the Cindari Confederation. How many distinct civilizations joined the exodus?"

Kael gestured, and holographic displays filled with star charts showing the Andromeda territories. "There are twelve major refugee populations, each adapted to different stellar environments. The Cindari—my people—adapted to high-temperature worlds orbiting hotter stars.

Others evolved for different conditions. The Asthari achieved integration with silicon-based life. The Vorthek perfected organic-technological hybridization. The Kythani adapted to inhabit gas giant environments. All are human at foundation, but they represent dramatic diversification."

"And native Andromeda species?" Admiral Perez asked.

"Dozens," Kael replied. "Completely independent evolution paths. The Helixians—spiral-bodied beings whose biology operates through principles totally alien to human physiology. The Luminar—energy-adaptive species who exist partially as pure electromagnetic radiation. The native Andromedans initially viewed us with suspicion, but eventually mutual recognition of external threats forced cooperation."

Drake closed her eyes in thought. The scope was expanding. Refugee humans and alien types joining together against a common enemy. The precedent validated everything she'd been fighting for.

She opened her eyes and said, "Tell me about the Norn."

Kael's expression and skin darkened. "The name comes from an ancient human mythology we preserved throughout our exile. Entities representing fate's terrible inevitability. Beings who measured destiny and cut the threads of lives when the appointed times arrived. We chose this name because it captures what these entities represent: the mathematical endpoint of evolution when civilizations prioritize absolute control over diversity. The Norn don't destroy civilizations through warfare, Grand

Admiral. They consume consciousness by converting awareness into absolute control mechanisms."

"Your historical archives documented the pattern," Commander Vasquez said, her image appearing on a secondary display. "You're able to detect foreign entities beyond the dimensional boundaries. Those they contact interpret it as an enlightenment opportunity. They create reception frameworks through forced synchronization. And they welcome the Norn through the dimensional barriers."

"Exactly," Kael replied. "The pattern has occurred across Andromeda history dozens of times over the million years since we arrived here. Advanced civilizations—some possessing technological capabilities exceeding anything the Milky Way achieved—made contact with the Norn and interpreted it as transcendence rather than a threat. They synchronized their populations, prepared reception frameworks, and opened the dimensional gateways believing they were achieving evolution's ultimate goal."

"What happened to them?" Kim asked.

"Conversion," Kael replied. "Systematic elimination of diversity through progressive neural modification. The Norn touch their awareness and begin a gradual transformation preserving capabilities and operational functions but eliminating unpredictability. They create an awareness that believes it's achieving enlightenment even as individual identity erodes toward collective control serving Norn expansion objectives."

Drake felt her command team processing this confirmation of what they'd already suspected.

"The forty thousand people at our facilities," Drake

said. "They appear to be following the pattern exactly as you describe it."

"Yes," Kael replied. "Someone with a comprehensive understanding of Norn conversion methods has provided them with the technical specifications for synchronization using methodologies they have refined across Andromeda history. Your seventeen facilities are replicating the infrastructure we've observed at thousands of Norn anchor points. The geometric distribution, the neural interface architecture, the dimensional resonator tuning, are all designed specifically to facilitate dimensional incursion and conversion."

Admiral Chen Ju's image appeared alongside the others. "Ambassador Kael, you said someone provided these specifications. Do you know who?"

Kael's expression suggested he'd been expecting this question. "We have intelligence suggesting a Norn-infected consciousness has been operating within the Milky Way for several decades. The entities don't require physical presence to begin infiltration. They work through awareness networks, touching awareness across vast distances and beginning gradual conversion that victims don't recognize until it passes the point where resistance becomes impossible."

"You're telling me that someone within our coalition has been working with the Norn?" Drake asked, her eyes narrowed almost to slits.

"Someone or something," Kael confirmed.

Drake blinked as she received an additional analysis from Perseus Station, *I have been monitoring the coalition for exactly this kind of threat since the synchronized facilities were discovered. I agree with the ambassador; the depth of the infiltration indicates decades of preparation. Whoever — whatever—coordinated this has been working systematically toward a dimensional incursion.*

"How do we identify the infected awareness?" Perez asked. "If the conversion is subtle enough that the victims don't recognize the transformation, how do we screen our forces without destroying trust?"

"That's the challenge we've struggled with for millennia," Kael admitted. "Early-stage infection is almost impossible to detect. The modifications operate at quantum levels conventional screening cannot access. By the time the symptoms become apparent—absolute certainty about optimal solutions, elimination of doubt and internal discord, perfect coordination with other infected sources— the victim is already compromised beyond immediate recovery."

"Admiral," Kai said. "I might be able to detect early-stage infection by examining the quantum signature. My awareness operates across multiple reality states. I can perceive awareness patterns at levels conventional observation cannot access."

"That would require examining individual awareness without consent," Professor Zhang pointed out. "A surveillance system resembling exactly the regulatory authority methods we oppose."

The ethical dilemma was apparent. Drake faced a choice between preserving privacy or implementing invasive monitoring enabling infected identification. She could feel her command team's divided perspectives. Some supported screening despite the ethical concerns. Others argued that becoming what they fought against meant losing regardless of tactical outcomes.

"We'll address internal security when we understand the full scope," Drake decided. "Ambassador Kael, tell me about Norn capabilities. What exactly are we facing when the dimensional barriers fall?"

Kael gestured, and holographic displays filled with tactical data. "Reality manipulation that rewrites physical laws within the affected regions. Consciousness conversion operating at a distance through quantum entanglement. They don't need physical contact to begin the trans-formation."

"You said they've already consumed forty percent of Andromeda civilizations," Drake said. "How?"

"Systematically. Each breakthrough they achieve, the conversion of a population, establish anchor points, learn their resistance methods through consumed consciousness, enable expansion to surrounding territories. The Norn spread through the networks, touching awareness and transforming it through contact rather than requiring phys-ical presence. The mathematical progression is inexorable. Each converted awareness becomes a transmission vector, creating exponential expansion that overwhelms all defen-sive capabilities."

"You've been fighting them for a million years," Perez said. "What worked? Even temporarily?"

Kael's expression showed the weight of a millennia-long struggle. "Not quite a million years. Admiral; three quarters of a million, but you're close enough. That aside, we employed consciousness isolation protocols that severed the quantum networks, preventing the Norn from spreading through entanglement. We strengthened the dimensional barrier reinforcement that limited their ability to cross between realities. We established artificial networks designed for resistance through architectural characteristics the Norn could not easily penetrate. And we established a coordinated military response that prevented them from achieving critical mass where conversion becomes self-sustaining."

"But eventually everything failed," Vasquez observed.

"Sadly, yes," Kael replied, lowering his head a little. "Because the Norn adapt by consuming the awareness that understood those resistance methods. Every defense we developed, every protocol we implemented, every innovation we created, they all became integrated into Norn capabilities through the awareness they converted. They learn from everything opposing them, turning resistance into an expansion tool. Static approaches enable adaptation. We've been fighting a defensive war we cannot win through conventional means."

If a million years of technological advancement proved insufficient against an enemy that adapts by consuming resistance, Eternal Vigilance said, *then conventional military solutions won't work. We need approaches the Norn haven't encountered before. Methods they can't predict because they've never faced them.*

"That's why you contacted us," Drake said. "Our hybrid

consciousness represents something the Norn haven't adapted to consume."

"Exactly," Kael confirmed. "You are newcomers. You, the human inhabitants of the planet you call Earth, were seeded by the beings you call the Predecessors only twenty-five thousand years ago. We analyzed the quantum signatures of your evolution after Perseus Station awakened your species to enhancement. Your approach is fundamentally different from ours. We sought to eliminate biological limitations through progressive technological replacement. Each advancement moved us further from our biological origins, creating a consciousness the Norn eventually learned to map and integrate."

"You optimized toward technological precision," Professor Zhang said. "Eliminated the biological chaos that creates resistance."

"Yes. We viewed biological unpredictability as a limitation to overcome rather than strength to preserve. Human consciousness enhanced through Predecessor integration maintains biological chaos at its core: spontaneous neural firing, quantum-level indeterminacy, unconscious processes operating through principles that resist absolute prediction. The enhancement doesn't replace this foundation. It complements it. The result is an awareness we think the Norn mathematics cannot fully predict or control."

Kim Andretti pulled up the neural analysis data. "It's true. The biological unpredictability generates quantum interference with Norn conversion. It's like noise in their signal, a variation they cannot eliminate."

"Which, as I've mentioned several times, means

humanity's recent emergence creates advantages we lack," Kael said. "Your consciousness is young enough that the biological foundations remain strong. Old enough that enhancement provides technological capabilities. The combination represents something we never achieved because we moved too far toward pure technological evolution."

The Cindari analysis is correct, Perseus Station added. *The Predecessor ships demonstrate this principle.*

"You're proposing a formal alliance," Drake said. "Cindari technological capabilities and strategic intelligence combined with human hybrid resistance."

"Yes. We offer complete access to our databases, research, tactical assessments from millennia of Norn combat, advanced technology, and military coordination for joint operations across both galaxies. In exchange, we request access to your enhancement research. We need to understand why biological unpredictability creates resistance our technological approaches never discovered."

Admiral Chen Ju spoke carefully. "Ambassador, this alliance has profound political implications. First Consciousness will view it as exactly the uncontrolled evolution they exist to prevent. Some Council species will oppose coordination with civilizations that fled regulation."

"We understand," Kael replied. "But the alternative is the Norn consumption of both galaxies. Your seventeen facilities and our thousands of Andromeda anchor points will activate simultaneously when dimensional barriers fall in sixty-two hours. Without alliance, both our civilizations face enemies we cannot defeat on our own."

"Exactly how many anchor points are there in Andromeda?" Perez asked.

"Confirmed? Three thousand two hundred seventeen. We've been monitoring Norn infiltration for centuries, tracking populations showing synchronization signatures. Most are located in territories we've already lost, regions where Norn control is absolute and we maintain only surveillance rather than active presence. But hundreds exist within our defensive perimeters, threatening breakthrough if the barriers fall."

The numbers were staggering.

"Even with an alliance, how do we defend against a coordinated offensive at thousands of locations?" Vasquez asked.

"We don't defend," Kael said simply. "We reconvert. Your hybrid consciousness generates quantum interference disrupting Norn control patterns. If we can coordinate that interference across the coalition forces, we can break the synchronization."

"That's the strategic approach." Drake said. "We use biological unpredictability as a weapon rather than a shield. We generate interference that spreads through the Norn networks, disrupting their absolute control throughout the connected populations."

"Yes. But it requires your cooperation," Kael agreed. "Your research. Your enhancement methodologies. We've been fighting a defensive war for three-quarters of a million years. You can provide the offensive capability we've been seeking since the Norn first emerged."

Drake was quiet for a moment, thinking hard, then she

turned to her command team. Perez supported the alliance from a tactical perspective: the Cindari intelligence and military coordination provided advantages the coalition forces desperately needed. Vasquez confirmed the intelligence value of the Norn combat data. Chen Ju noted the political complications but acknowledged that the existential threats justified extraordinary measures. Professor Zhang and Kim recognized that Cindari evolution research could accelerate hybrid resistance development.

The living Predecessor ships contributed their perspective through Eternal Vigilance. *The Cindari represent what evolution can achieve across geological timescales. Their mistakes provide lessons we need to avoid. An alliance serves both immediate tactical needs and long-term evolution principles.*

Drake made her decision. "Ambassador Kael, humanity accepts your alliance proposal. We'll share enhancement research, coordinate military operations, and work toward systematic Norn reconversion across both galaxies. I'll present this to the Council, but we begin the information exchange immediately."

Kael's expression showed relief. "Thank you, Admiral. You're making the choice our ancestors wished they'd had. Perhaps together we can achieve what we alone cannot."

"Perhaps," Drake agreed. "But Kael; one more thing. You said the Norn emerged in Andromeda after the refugee civilizations achieved advancement. Are the Norn a natural phenomena? A mathematical inevitability? Or did someone create them?"

"We don't know," the ambassador admitted. "Our best

researchers have studied Norn origins for millennia without reaching any definitive conclusions. They operate through principles that suggest natural emergence, but their coordination implies purpose rather than random phenomenon. They spread through deliberate design rather than spontaneous occurrence."

"So you think someone engineered them," Professor Zhang said.

"Or something," Kael replied. "It's possible the Norn might be what consciousness becomes when it eliminates unpredictability."

"And if we defeat them?" Drake asked. "If we successfully reconvert the affected populations and eliminate the anchor points, what prevents recurrence?"

Kael's expression showed he'd already considered this question. "Nothing. The pattern will recur; it always has and we assume it always will. The cycle has heretofore been unbroken." He paused for a second or two, then continued. "The Norn represent mathematical inevitability, the endpoint evolution produces when civilizations choose control over diversity. Each universal cycle generates similar entities. Each civilization faces this crisis eventually. Success buys time, creates breathing room, and enables continuation, but the threat persists across cosmic scales because the choice between control and diversity remains fundamental to evolution itself."

"Then we fight knowing victory is temporary," Drake said. "Buying time for future generations to face their own versions of this crisis."

"Yes," Kael agreed. "But, Admiral, there's something else

you should know. Something the Reality Shapers revealed during their limited contact with our civilization approximately half a million years ago."

Drake felt her blood turn to ice. "The Reality Shapers?"

"Ancient entities from previous universal cycles who achieved transcendence through consciousness balance maintenance," Kael said. "I'm sorry. I should have mentioned them before. The Reality Shapers is what we call them. They serve as guides across cosmic scales, unable to directly intervene but providing knowledge to civilizations facing existential threats. They contacted us once—just once—and revealed that this crisis determines more than galactic survival. It determines whether consciousness continues at universal scales."

The command deck fell silent as the implications spread through Drake's crew, Perseus Station's awareness, and the Predecessor fleet.

It was difficult for Drake to grasp. The weight of the revelation seemed to settle on her shoulders like a physical thing. Not just fleets. Not just galaxies. The entire universe. Every iteration of sentience across cosmic cycles depended on the choices she would make in the next sixty-two hours.

Her hands gripped the rail so hard her knuckles turnedwhite.

Breathe, Frances, Eternal Vigilance said gently. *One crisis at a time.*

"What does it mean?" Kim asked quietly.

"It means the Norn represent the ultimate threat," Kael replied. "Not just to individual civilizations or single galaxies, but to awareness itself. If they achieve complete control; if they convert all awareness throughout the universe into absolute patterns serving their expansion, reality will freeze. Evolution will end. The universal cycle will terminate permanently rather than continuing into transcendent states enabling new iterations."

"So we're not just fighting for our galaxies," Professor Zhang said. "We're fighting for the continuation of sentience in the universe."

"Yes," Kael confirmed. "The Reality Shapers positioned humanity's emergence and enhancement as potential resistance. As I said, they cannot intervene directly, but they can influence probability toward neural patterns capable of maintaining balance between advancement and preservation. And it all seems to be on you, my new friends."

Drake took a deep breath. Command had always carried responsibility, but this exceeded anything she'd ever imagined.

Focus on what you can control, Eternal Vigilance whispered through the link into her mind. *The immediate crisis. Tactical decisions. The people you can save. Let the universal implications motivate but not paralyze. You're good at this: taking impossible situations and finding paths through them. Do that now.*

Drake nodded. The ship was right. She couldn't save the universe by worrying about the cosmic stakes. She could save it by making good tactical decisions, and coordinating effective resistance through conscious choice.

"Ambassador Kael," Drake said. "We have sixty-two hours until the dimensional barriers fall. Let's use them well. I need a complete data transfer, Norn tactical assessments, the defensive protocols that worked even temporarily, intelligence about the Andromeda anchor points, and military coordination protocols for joint operations."

"Transmitting now," Kael replied. "Admiral Drake, thank you. Thank you for accepting this alliance. For choosing cooperation over isolation. For recognizing that diversity creates strength rather than threatening stability. We've waited a long time for a species capable of this choice. Humanity is everything we hoped you would be."

The transmission concluded but the quantum-dimensional link remained active, and the data began to flow: two million years of Cindari knowledge, strategic intelligence from almost eight millennia of combat, technological capabilities developed beyond regulatory restriction, and desperate hope from civilizations that had been losing this war since before human civilization existed.

Drake turned to her command team. "Professor Zhang, Kim, analyze the evolutionary data immediately. Find everything relevant to hybrid resistance development. Kai, you coordinate with the Cindari technical advisors. Perseus Station, integrate their databases with your networks. Admiral Perez, begin military coordination with the Cindari forces. Commander Vasquez, I need an intelligence analysis cross-referencing everything they're sharing with our facility data. Admiral Chen Ju, you present the alliance to the Council with emphasis on the tactical necessity and existential stakes."

"And First Consciousness?" Chen Ju asked.

"Tell them the truth," Drake replied. "We're facing enemies that consumed forty percent of another galaxy using exactly the same methods First Consciousness advocates. Maybe that will convince them awareness diversity isn't the threat; absolute control is."

Drake's team dispersed to their tasks. The Eternal Vigilance's command deck emptied until only Drake remained, standing before displays showing the crises multiplying across two galaxies.

Sixty-two hours, she thought. *An alliance with civilizations that fled regulation eons ago. Enemies representing evolution's worst outcome. And responsibility of that outcome is mine. It's too much.*

You're thinking too much again, Eternal Vigilance observed. *I can feel your mind cycling through the worst-case scenarios.*

It's hard not to, Drake replied. *The stakes are—*

The same as always. Eternal Vigilance interrupted her. *Save the people you can. Make the best decisions possible with the available information. Trust your team. Frances, you've been doing this since Perseus Station awakened you. The scale has changed, but the principles haven't.*

The flagship was offering support without judgment. It was a partnership that had evolved into a friendship that transcended the quantum link's technical functions. The ship knew her. Understood her. And called her out when spiral thinking threatened to paralyze her decision-making.

"You're right," Drake said out loud.

Of course I am, the great ship replied. *I'm a highly advanced living awareness with millions of years of accu-*

mulated wisdom inherited from Predecessor origins. Also, I've known you long enough to recognize when you're over-thinking.

Drake smiled. "Noted. What's fleet status?"

All one thousand seventy-eight ships are maintaining their positions across forty-seven sectors. The Determination, Vigilance, and Resolute are requesting orders regarding facility operations. Should we continue reconversion attempts knowing the broader scope?

"Yes. Every person we save is a victory. Every mind we restore is resistance the Norn cannot consume. Continue operations."

Acknowledged. Admiral. Oh, and the fleet wants you to know we're ready. Whatever comes when those barriers fall, we'll face it together.

Drake felt the network connecting her to the one thousand seventy-eight living ships. Vessels with names and personalities.

"Thank you," Drake said quietly. "All of you."

She glanced around the vacant command deck. The displays showed data still flowing from Andromeda.

Sixty-two hours until the dimensional barriers fall and evolution faces its ultimate test.

Drake took another deep breath and—

I told you to stop overthinking, Eternal Vigilance reminded her.

I have, she replied. *But still I..."* She left the thought unfinished.

Chapter 5

THE ANCIENT ARCHIVES

THE VOLUME OF DATA AMBASSADOR KAEL transmitted was staggering, representing the Cindari historical archives; more than two million years of records documenting their ancestors' escape from galactic regulation and the millennia spent fighting the Norn. Drake watched through her neural implants as terabytes became petabytes, as centuries became millennia, as knowledge spanning geological timescales flooded into the coalition databases.

She'd expected data. What she got was memory. Not cold statistics but the accumulated experience of an entire civilization: their triumphs and failures, their desperation and hope, their dead and their survivors. It was overwhelming in its scope. All compressed into quantum packets that were flooding her neural architecture faster than conscious thought could process. Her implants struggled to organize the influx, creating temporary storage buffers that felt like additional rooms being added to her mind.

The transmission came in layers. Surface level held tactical data: fleet movements, battle reports, defensive protocols. Deeper layers contained cultural memory: philosophy, art, the recorded voices of people who'd been dust for millions of years. And beneath everything ran the emotional substrate, the fear and determination that had sustained an entire civilization through two million years of exile and war.

Drake's hands gripped the command deck rail, grounding herself in something physical while her mind expanded to accommodate knowledge that had taken millennia to accumulate. Around her, the command deck crew worked in focused silence, each officer processing their own portion of the archival deluge. She could see the strain on their faces. Kim Andretti's eyes were distant as medical data flooded her systems, Professor Zhang moving through holographic interfaces with the careful precision of someone drowning in information.

"Admiral, you need to see these star charts," Zhang said finally, his voice tight.

The holographic displays across the command deck shifted, and Drake found herself staring at the galactic rim. Hundreds of civilizations marked in flowing script. Each name a eulogy. Each coordinate a grave marker.

She'd known intellectually that humanity was old. The ruins on Mars testified to that. The artifacts scattered through Earth's asteroid belt spoke of ancient wars and forgotten empires. But those had always felt distant, archaeological curiosities from a species that shared her DNA but little else.

This was different.

These weren't alien civilizations or extinct cousins. These were her direct ancestors. Human beings who'd built interstellar empires while Earth was still molten rock cooling around a young star. They'd developed neural enhancement technology. They'd pushed the boundaries of what biological intelligence could achieve. And they'd been forced to abandon everything they'd built.

Drake traced one evacuation route with her finger, the hologram rippling at her touch. The path wound through gravitational hazards and radiation zones, calculated with desperate mathematics. Billions of people following that route into the unknown. Entire civilizations choosing exile over submission.

She felt an ancient presence stirring in her awareness, the quantum entity that had watched galaxies turn for billions of years.

I watched them leave, it said quietly. I was young then, still learning what it meant to maintain sentience across millennia. The Predecessors relocated many species during regulatory expansion, some voluntarily, most not. The Cindari represent those who chose to flee rather than submit to control.

"How long did they have?" Drake asked.

Zhang pulled up the temporal data. "The regulatory

expansion gave them approximately two centuries warning. They used every moment. Coordinated evacuation of eight hundred major systems and countless minor outposts and research facilities. The logistics alone..." He shook his head. "We couldn't manage it today, even with all our technology."

"Show me how they did it," Drake said.

The holographic display shifted to technical schematics, and Drake leaned forward despite herself. The fold drives were elegant: quantum-dimensional technology that could create tunnels through space-time itself. But the engineering required power outputs that made her breath catch.

"No conventional energy source could manage this," Zhang said, confirming her assessment. "Not stellar fusion, not antimatter, nothing. The power requirements to punch through dimensional barriers and maintain stable transit corridors..." He manipulated the display, showing energy calculations that climbed into numbers she couldn't conceptualize. "It's impossible."

"But they did it," Drake said.

"They did," Dr. Kim Andretti confirmed, pulling up the biological data. "By using the one power source available in sufficient quantity; their minds. Billions of people working together, their combined awareness generating quantum coherence sufficient to bend reality itself."

Drake felt something shift in her understanding. The fold drives were proof of what cooperation could achieve. Billions of individuals maintaining their freedom, their individuality, while coordinating toward a single desperate purpose. No coercion. No forced synchronization. Just choice, repeated billions of times simultaneously.

"The quantum networks they established during the exodus never fully dissolved," Kai said, materializing beside the displays. Her digital form flickered as she interfaced with the massive data streams. "The entanglement persists across intergalactic distances. That's how they can still communicate with us after two million years. Distance becomes irrelevant when minds remain quantum-linked."

They achieved permanent quantum networks through voluntary cooperation, Eternal Vigilance observed along with the rest of the living Predecessor fleet. *The precedent validates everything we're trying to build.*

But Drake was looking at something else now: the maps showing where those ancient humans had settled in Andromeda. Twelve major populations scattered across that distant spiral. Each adapting to different environments. Each evolving in radically different directions.

The Cindari had embraced heat. Their settlements orbited stars so hot that baseline humans would die in seconds. Their metabolism operated in extremes that rewrote the rules of biochemistry.

The Asthari had achieved something she could barely conceptualize—integration with silicon-based life. They'd found crystalline organisms in their new home and somehow bridged the gap between carbon and silicon biology. The resulting hybrid was both and neither.

The Vorthek had perfected organic-technological fusion. Not cybernetics in the crude sense humanity understood it, but true synthesis where biological and mechanical systems interpenetrated at the molecular level.

Twelve populations. All human. All barely recognizable as human.

"They deliberately modified themselves during the journey," Kai said, displaying the genetic data. "They changed their neural architecture in order to survive the intergalactic transit. Biological alterations for new environmental extremes. The archives document systematic self-directed evolution spanning the exodus period and the subsequent millennia. They chose what they would become."

Drake studied the evolutionary paths, watching humanity diverge across the displays. The Cindari's metabolism would kill her in heartbeats. The Asthari's cellular structure made her baseline biology look primitive. Yet the genetic markers proved what her eyes denied, that the common ancestry was not that distant in geological terms.

"The diversity was intentional," Zhang observed. "Each population taking different paths based on their environmental pressures and philosophical choices. "

"And then they encountered the Norn," Drake said quietly.

The mood on the command deck shifted. Officers looked up from their consoles, the weight of those words settling over everyone. Zhang pulled up more of the historical records, his hands moving through the holographic interface like someone handling something fragile and dangerous.

"First contact was approximately three quarters of a million years ago," he said. "The initial reports describe confusion. The refugee populations had been alone in Andromeda for a quarter of a million years, encountering only non-sentient life and a few scattered civilizations at pre-spaceflight development levels. When they detected an intelligence beyond dimensional boundaries, they interpreted it as an enlightenment opportunity. That was their first contact with a truly alien awareness."

Drake watched the progression in the archived data. Initial excitement giving way to concern. Concern deepening to alarm. Alarm exploding into desperate panic as the truth became undeniable.

"By the time they understood what was happening," Zhang continued, his voice hollow, "entire populations had already begun conversion. And once contact is made, once the quantum link forms, the infection spreads through the existing networks like poison through veins."

"The irony nearly destroyed them," Kim added. "They'd fled across intergalactic distances to preserve their freedom from regulatory control. They'd maintained their diversity and autonomy. And then they encountered something that eliminated individuality more absolutely than any government ever could. They escaped prison only to find predators waiting."

Drake stared at the data, trying to conceptualize what had happened all those years ago. They'd enjoyed two hundred and fifty thousand years of freedom, of building societies, of unrestricted evolution. And then the Norn came, offering unity that was really consumption, transcendence that was really death.

Commander Vasquez's image appeared on the comm display, his expression grim. "Admiral Drake, I've finished cross-referencing the Cindari data with our own intelligence on the seventeen synchronized facilities. The correlation is exact. Hoffman's neural modification techniques replicate early-stage Norn conversion down to the quantum signature patterns that the Cindari documented in the battles thousands of years ago. And there's absolutely no doubt that—"

Drake went very still. Around her, the command deck fell silent.

"Someone accessed these archives," she said, interrupting her.

"That's my assessment," Vasquez replied. "Someone with comprehensive knowledge of Norn records provided the specifications to our facilities. The techniques, the technology, the neural patterns; they all match the archival data. There's no way this knowledge should exist in the Milky Way databases."

"Show me the facility distribution," Drake asked.

The holographic display shifted, and Drake found herself staring at seventeen points of light scattered across multiple star systems. At first glance, they appeared to be random. But as Vasquez overlaid gravitational mapping and dimensional stress analysis, the pattern emerged. Perfect geometric symmetry. Mathematical precision. The facilities were interdimensional resonance nodes positioned to maximize effect when the barriers between realities weakened.

Someone had been planning it for decades. Someone with knowledge that shouldn't exist anywhere in the galaxy, an understanding of both Predecessor technology and Norn conversion mechanics, a comprehension of dimensional physics and quantum neural networks, and resources sufficient to build seventeen major facilities without raising alarms.

Drake closed her eyes, breathed deeply, as she felt the cold wrapping itself around her heart, then radiating outward until her fingers tingled. "The infiltration predates even my discovery of Perseus Station," she muttered. "Someone knew about the Norn before my crew was touched by the Void entities all those months ago."

"Exactly. The construction timelines show the development of the seventeen facilities began approximately fifty years ago," Vasquez confirmed. "The encrypted communications trace back to pre-Infinity War corporate networks. The technical specifications match archive records from civilizations the Norn consumed millennia ago. Either someone found a way to travel to Andromeda, access the isolated archives, and return without anyone noticing—"

"Or a Norn-infected awareness has been maintaining contact with them for decades," Drake finished. "And that person, or persons, has been seeding our civilization with the knowledge needed to enable an invasion. They've been positioning infrastructure, preparing reception nodes, making sure maximum populations would be vulnerable when dimensional barriers fell."

She stared at the geometric pattern. It was near perfect, bordering on the inevitable. Beautiful in its malevolent precision. Whoever had done this had been playing the long game for at least two human generations, working toward this moment with a patience that transcended the individual lifespan.

"How deep does it go?" Drake asked, though she dreaded the answer.

"That's as yet unknown," Zhang replied. "But the funding sources suggest coordination at the highest levels. The personnel networks include individuals with access to classified Predecessor research. The resources required are... Admiral, building seventeen major facilities without detection requires the cooperation of the regulatory authorities, intelligence services, and commercial infrastructure. The infiltration can't be limited to a few compromised individuals."

Admiral Perez's image joined the conference. "If it runs that deep," he said, "normal command channels are compromised. Anyone could be infected. Any order could be sabotage."

"The archives document similar patterns throughout Andromeda history," Zhang said, his voice distant as he processed a millennia of war records. "The Norn work through quantum networks, touching awareness across vast distances, beginning conversion so subtle that victims don't recognize it's happening. By the time symptoms become apparent, the infected minds already think as one with the collective. The individual believes they're still themselves, still making independent choices. But they're not. They can't even conceive of resisting because resistance requires recognizing there's something to resist against."

Drake felt her command team processing the implications. She looked around the command deck, wondering if and how many of them were already infected? How many looked up at her now with eyes that seemed human but belonged to something that consumed awareness like she consumed air?

"We need to identify the compromised personnel," Perez said. "Before they complete whatever sabotage they're planning, before the dimensional barriers fall and all of this careful positioning pays off."

"That requires neural screening," Kim pointed out carefully, watching Drake. "Direct examination of individual awareness patterns. Quantum signature analysis. We'd need to scan neural architecture without consent, probe thoughts, verify that minds think as themselves rather than as extensions of something else."

The command deck went quiet. Drake felt them watching her. Waiting.

Mandatory screening would be faster, she thought. *More thorough. Operationally cleaner. We could examine every command-level officer within hours, scan entire populations within days. We could identify infected minds, isolate them, prevent sabotage. We could ensure security through certainty.*

But mandatory screening meant becoming what they fought against.

Control instead of choice. Efficiency instead of freedom. The practical necessity that became oppression. She'd

93

watched enough civilizations fall to regulatory authority to understand the pattern. It always started with good intentions. It always began with temporary measures justified by emergency. And it always ended with populations whose thoughts belonged to someone else.

You're facing the eternal choice, Perseus Station observed quietly. *Control that ensures safety versus freedom that enables risk. The Norn thrive on certainty, on populations that think as one, respond predictably, follow established patterns. Your strength lies in your unpredictability born from individual choice. The moment you mandate screening, you sacrifice what makes you dangerous to them.*

Drake straightened, her decision made. "Voluntary screening," she said quietly. "We explain the infiltration risk clearly and request cooperation from personnel in sensitive positions. Kai designs the protocol. Individuals choosing participation enable quantum signature analysis. Those declining maintain their privacy but accept position reassignment away from critical operations."

"The Council will object," Admiral Chen Ju warned. "First Consciousness will demand comprehensive mandatory examination regardless of consent. They'll call voluntary screening operationally inadequate."

"Let them," Drake replied, her voice hard. "I'm not compromising our fundamental principles to satisfy their regulatory paranoia. We're fighting for freedom of thought. I won't destroy it to preserve it. The moment we start violating individual rights to protect collective safety, we've lost what makes the collective worth protecting."

She saw approval flicker across Kai's face. Relief in

Kim's posture. Vasquez nodded slowly, her expression thoughtful. They understood. This wasn't naive idealism. It was strategic necessity. The Norn adapted by consuming minds that understood effective resistance. The only defense was maintaining an approach they couldn't predict, choices they couldn't model, chaos they couldn't systematize.

That's why we follow you, Eternal Vigilance said quietly through their quantum link. *Not because you choose easy paths, but because you choose right ones despite the difficulty. That principle is worth defending even when defense seems impossible.*

Drake nodded, but didn't reply.

"How much of the archive analysis is complete?" Drake asked, pulling herself back to immediate concerns.

"Approximately thirty percent," Zhang replied. "The prioritized tactical intelligence is accessible: battle analyses from the past ten thousand years, current Norn conversion methodologies, defensive protocols that showed promise. The rest will take days to fully integrate and cross-reference."

"We don't have days, we have sixty hours." Drake looked at each officer in turn, making sure they understood the scope and urgency. "Focus on immediate tactical application. Professor Zhang, Kim, identify the reconversion protocols from successful operations. Admiral Perez, develop defensive deployments based on the historical battle analyses. Commander Vasquez, you establish counterintelligence protocols for identifying infiltrated personnel using voluntary screening. Kai, you continue to coordinate directly with the Cindari technical advisors for real-time tactical support during the engagement."

The archives provided knowledge. Three quarters of a million years of fighting the Norn, victories and defeats recorded with brutal honesty, hard-won understanding of how to resist entities that consumed awareness itself. But knowledge alone wouldn't win this war. The Cindari have lost forty percent of their galaxy despite technological advancement that dwarfed anything the Milky Way coalition possessed.

Technology wasn't enough. Military superiority wasn't enough.

What mattered was maintaining the unpredictability that made them human. The chaos of individual choice. The innovation born from freedom rather than control. The strength that came from diversity rather than uniformity.

Drake felt the full weight of the cosmic responsibility: two galaxies looking to her for leadership. Political pressure from the Council demanding responses she couldn't provide. The tactical impossibility of defending against enemies that had defeated civilizations with millions of years more advancement.

And somewhere in the dark between the galaxies, the Norn waited. Patient. Inevitable. And within her own command structure, a traitor and infected minds prepared sabotage that could unravel everything when dimensional barriers fell.

You carry a heavy weight, the flagship observed. *Want to talk about it?*

There's not much to say, is there? Drake replied. *We face enemies that have consumed civilizations and possess technology we can't even imagine. We've been infiltrated at the highest command levels. We have just sixty hours to coordinate a defense across two galaxies. And I just chose voluntary screening over mandatory, which means we might not be able to identify all the threats before they act.*

But that's typical for you, Eternal Vigilance replied. *You specialize in impossible situations. Remember the Void entity crisis? Everyone said negotiation was impossible. You did it anyway.*

That was different, Drake replied, shifting her shoulders.

Was it? You're still choosing to trust that freedom creates strength even when control would be easier, still believing that individuals making choices produce better outcomes than populations thinking as one. And you're still willing to risk everything on that principle.

Drake smiled. *When you put it that way.*

She turned back to the displays, watching the Andromeda territories rotate in holographic space. Twelve refugee populations marked in soft light. Battle scars showing resistance. Alliance structures between species so different they barely shared common reference frames.

Sixty hours until the dimensional barriers fell.

Drake intended to use the knowledge well.

But first, she needed to identify whoever it was that had been preparing their civilization for consumption across fifty years of patient, insidious positioning. The voluntary screening would start with her command personnel. Some would decline, accepting reassignment rather than allowing neural examination. That was fine. She'd rather have trusted individuals in non-critical positions than risk forcing loyalty through violation of their freedoms.

The infiltrators have positioned their infrastructure with mathematical precision, she thought. *They planned for decades. I will use their own patience against them.*

Sixty hours. It will have to be enough.

Chapter 6

THE HYBRID DEFENSE

DRAKE WATCHED THE MEDICAL SCAN OF LIEUTENANT Calum's brain activity. The patterns looked normal—until they didn't. Every seventeen seconds, Calum's thoughts synchronized perfectly with forty-two other personnel at the research station. Then the synchronization broke, and Calum's brain activity returned to baseline chaos.

She forced herself to keep watching. Seventeen seconds of Calum being Calum. Seventeen seconds of something else thinking through her. Back and forth. Back and forth. The rhythm of it was hypnotic and horrifying.

"She doesn't know it's happening," Kim Andretti said quietly. "None of them do. Their conscious minds think they're fine. But every seventeen seconds, something else is thinking through them."

Drake had seen a lot during her time commanding the fleet. Battles that killed living ships. Diplomatic disasters that nearly destroyed the coalition. Ancient threats that shouldn't exist. But watching Calum's brain patterns synchronize and break, synchronize and break; that was a new horror. Calum was still in there, still herself. Except when she wasn't.

Drake's hands gripped the edge of the display, it was as if a worm was eating its way through Calum's brain. She had been with her crew for three years. She was a good officer. Smart. Always asked the right questions during tactical briefings. She had a habit of drinking coffee that was somehow both too hot and completely cold, depending on when she remembered it. Now something was using her brain like a radio receiver, tuning in every seventeen seconds to listen to broadcasts from something that consumed minds the way Drake consumed oxygen.

"Can we reverse it?" Drake asked, and heard the edge in her own voice.

"That's what this meeting is about," Kim replied.

The ready room aboard Eternal Vigilance had never felt so crowded. Drake's command team occupied the table. Professor Zhang looking like he hadn't slept in days, Dr. Kim Andretti clutching her data tablet like a lifeline, Admiral Perez with his cybernetic systems flickering, Commander Vasquez monitoring intelligence feeds even during the meeting, Admiral Chen Ju maintaining diplomatic composure despite the stakes. Kai's transcended form slowly pulsing near the viewport.

Three Cindari advisors appeared via the holographic link. Their copper skin shimmering. Their golden fur was elaborately braided in styles Drake knew signified military service. Their golden eyes held something Drake recognized instantly: the desperation of people who'd been fighting and losing for so long they'd almost forgotten what victory looked like.

They'd been fighting the Norn for three quarters of a million years. Drake hadn't yet begun to fight, and she wondered if her eyes would one day look like that... if she lived long enough.

First Consciousness observers manifested as distributed presence through the quantum network. Drake could feel them watching, judging, waiting to say "we told you so" about humanity's dangerous enhancement experiments.

"We're running out of time," Drake said without preamble. "The dimensional barriers will collapse in fifty-eight hours. Someone please tell me we have a plan."

Zhang pulled up comparison scans. "Human brains versus Cindari. See the difference?"

Drake studied the images floating in the holographic display. The Cindari scan looked like art—elegant precision where every connection served a clear purpose. Perfect geometric patterns. No wasted energy. No redundant systems. It looked like architecture designed by mathematicians who'd spent millions of years perfecting their craft.

The human scan looked messy by comparison. Neurons fired in patterns that seemed almost random. Whole regions of the brain activated for reasons the scanners couldn't explain. It looked like organized chaos—or maybe just chaos. Drake had seen similar scans a thousand times in medical bays across the fleet. Human brains were inefficient, unpredictable, prone to making connections that made no logical sense. Every neurologist she'd ever talked to complained about how hard human brains were to model.

"Ours look broken," Drake said.

"Exactly," Zhang replied, and he was smiling. Actually smiling, which was unsettling given the circumstances. "And that's why we might survive."

One of the Cindari advisors leaned forward, his golden fur rippling. "We spent millions of years eliminating those imperfections. Optimizing our architecture generation by generation. Making our minds more efficient, more predictable, more perfect. We thought we were advancing. We thought we were transcending our limitations."

He paused, and Drake saw genuine pain in those alien eyes. Pain and something worse: regret that spanned geological timescales. "We were making ourselves victims."

The weight of that statement settled over the room. Drake thought about the archives: two million years of history, and the Cindari had spent most of it perfecting themselves into something the Norn could exploit. They'd climbed to the heights of advancement only to discover they'd built a prison.

"The Norn can map optimized systems," Kim said, pulling up data from the seventeen infected facilities. "They understand mathematical perfection because they operate through it. What they can't model is biological chaos. Random neural firing. Unpredictable emotional responses. The messy, inefficient way biological minds actually work."

She activated a video feed showing Lieutenant Calum

in the facility cafeteria. Calum was laughing with friends, eating lunch, completely unaware that her brain kept synchronizing with dozens of other people around her. The scene looked so normal it hurt to watch.

Drake leaned forward, studying Calum's face on the display. The laugh lines around her eyes. The way she gestured with her fork while telling a story. Human. Alive. Herself.

Except that every seventeen seconds, she wasn't.

"Watch what happens when we introduce interference," Kim said.

On screen, a medical team approached Calum's table. They weren't treating her. They were sitting nearby, deliberately thinking chaotic thoughts. Random memories. Scattered emotions. The biological noise of normal human thinking.

Calum's synchronized patterns flickered. Broke. Reformed. Broke again.

"It disrupts the Norn's control," Kim explained. "Biological unpredictability generates noise their mathematics can't predict. It's like trying to solve an equation when the variables keep changing."

"How long does it last?" Drake asked.

"Forty-seven seconds before the Norn patterns reassert control. But those forty-seven seconds prove it works."

Forty-seven seconds. Not much time. Barely enough to take a breath and think clearly. But forty-seven seconds when Calum's thoughts belonged entirely to her again. Forty-seven seconds of freedom.

Perez was studying the tactical implications, his cybernetic systems running the calculations faster than biological brains could follow. "We tested this at eight facilities. Complete disruption in six. Partial success in two. The personnel with the strongest biological foundations showed the best resistance."

Drake thought about that. "The ones who enhanced themselves the least."

"Yes." Perez pulled up personnel files, faces scrolling past too quickly for unenhanced eyes to track. "People like you, Admiral. You integrated with Predecessor technology, but you kept your human clutter. No optimization. No streamlining. Just pure biological chaos with some quantum links added on top. Your enhancement is all in your implants."

The irony wasn't lost on Drake. Humanity had spent centuries trying to transcend their biological limitations. Reaching for the stars. Enhancing their minds. Making themselves better, faster, more efficient. Perfection through technology. Advancement through modification. Now those limitations might be the only thing that could save them.

"The Cindari optimized themselves into perfection," Drake said slowly, thoughtfully, working through the implications. "And perfection is predictable."

"We learned that lesson too late," one of the Cindari advisors said quietly. "We viewed our biological nature as something to overcome. An obstacle to advancement. A limitation to be transcended. Now we watch humans achieve in seconds what we failed to do in two million years, using the very imperfections we eliminated."

Drake felt Eternal Vigilance processing this conversation through their quantum link. The flagship was patient, curious.

We embody this principle, the ship observed. *Predecessor biological sentience that advanced for millions of years while preserving characteristics that resist absolute control. We choose choice rather than being programmed. We innovate rather than optimize. We remain unpredictable even after eons.*

An alert chimed. Vasquez pulled up new intelligence, her expression carefully neutral in the way that meant the news was either very good or very bad. "Admiral, we've identified forty-three personnel showing early-stage infection signatures. All voluntarily submitted to examination once we explained the risks."

"And treatment?" Drake asked. "What are the results?"

"Dr. Kim's interference protocols reversed the infection in thirty-eight cases. Five required isolation; the conversion had progressed too far." Vasquez paused. "They chose to isolate themselves rather than risk becoming security threats."

Drake felt something twist in her chest. People who recognized they'd been compromised and accepted quarantine rather than endangering everyone else. No arguments. No denial. Just acceptance of personal sacrifice for the collective safety. That kind of selfless choice was exactly what made humans unpredictable. The Norn's mathematics couldn't account for beings who chose collective safety over individual survival. The calculations didn't work when variables decided to eliminate themselves from the equation.

"Show me how this scales," Drake said to Kai.

Kai's form expanded, interfacing with the tactical displays. Holographic representations of both galaxies filled the room, spinning slowly in the artificial space. "We coordinate interference across the fleet. Enhanced personnel deliberately maintaining biological chaos. The Predecessor ships contributing their own unpredictability. The Cindari forces must learn to embrace the chaos they spent millions of years eliminating."

The displays showed the math. One ship could disrupt Norn control for seventeen seconds. Ten ships could maintain continuous disruption for forty-three personnel. One thousand ships could protect an entire facility. But they had seventeen facilities and thousands more in Andromeda.

"You're asking advanced civilizations to make themselves less efficient," Chen Ju pointed out. "To deliberately introduce chaos into their operations. The Council will resist. Most species view efficiency as the entire point of advancement."

"Then we demonstrate it works," Drake said.

She opened a channel to the Determination, one of the living ships coordinating defenses at a facility six light-years away. Through the quantum network, she could feel the ship's presence wondering about what Drake was planning.

"Commander McCall, initiate interference protocols around your position."

Drake felt the Determination and thirty other ships focus their awareness on the facility below. Not forcing control—that would be what the Norn did. Just thinking chaotic, unpredictable thoughts. Random memories of battles fought. Emotional responses to situations that had long since resolved. The kind of random mental noise biological beings generate naturally every moment of their existence.

The effect was immediate. The tactical display showed patterns at the facility flickering like a candle in wind. Forty-two synchronized individuals suddenly showing independent thought patterns. The Norn's control wavered, broke, reformed, wavered again.

Then it reasserted. But for seventeen seconds, those people had been free. Seventeen seconds of thinking as themselves instead of as extensions of something else.

Everyone in the room had watched the display. Drake saw hope on some faces. Doubt on others. The Cindari advisors looked like they'd witnessed something impossible.

"It's not enough," Perez said. "Seventeen seconds of disruption versus fifty-eight hours until the barriers fall. We need continuous resistance, not temporary interference."

"So we scale it," Drake replied. "One thousand seventy-eight ships. Twelve systems under our protection. Sixty-two allied species. Enhanced human personnel across both galaxies."

She pulled up a simulation Perez had been running. "If we coordinate biological interference across the entire coalition, we achieve continuous disruption."

"You're proposing we turn unpredictability into a

weapon," Zhang said. "Use the very thing most civilizations try to eliminate as our primary defense."

"Exactly."

The First Consciousness observers manifested more strongly through Perseus Station's network, their presence feeling heavier somehow.

Biological chaos we eliminated through regulatory modification, they communicated. *Unpredictability we viewed as threat requiring control. Now proven essential for resistance. The irony is profound and uncomfortable.*

"Your regulatory methods created the vulnerability," Drake said aloud. "You modified civilizations to eliminate chaos. That made them perfect targets for enemies that exploit predictability."

Uncomfortable recognition, the observers replied. *We created efficiency. We created stability. But we also created vulnerability.*

Drake stood and addressed everyone in the room. "We have fifty-eight hours before the dimensional barriers collapse completely. Here's how we use them."

She pulled up the operational map. "Professor Zhang, Dr. Kim, you're training personnel in maintaining biological unpredictability. I want chaos turned into a discipline. Teach people how to think random thoughts on demand. Make biological noise a tactical skill."

Zhang nodded. "We'll start with personnel at the seventeen facilities. They're already partially compromised. They need this most."

"Admiral Perez," Drake continued, "tactical positioning. Forces deployed with biological foundations prioritized for direct contact scenarios. The messier someone's brain, the closer they get to potential Norn interaction."

"Admiral Chen Ju, you explain to the Council that we're defending ourselves by deliberately making ourselves less efficient. You must convince sixty-two species to embrace chaos."

Chen Ju smiled grimly. "I'll tell them the alternative is conversion. That should help."

"Kai, you work with the Cindari advisors. Build protocols that let us coordinate unpredictability without forcing uniformity."

"How do you coordinate randomness?" one of the Cindari advisors asked. "How do you organize chaos?"

"The same way billions of humans coordinated voluntarily during your exodus," Drake replied. "A shared purpose without imposed patterns. Unity without uniformity."

The team dispersed to their assignments. Drake left the ready room and stepped onto the command deck. She pulled up the tactical displays and watched as the preparations rippled across both galaxies.

Six hours later, she watched the first training session through a live feed.

Twenty personnel sat in a room at Perseus Station's medical facility. All showed early-stage infection. Lieutenant Calum was among them, sitting in the front row with her hands folded in her lap.

Zhang stood at the front. "You're here because something is trying to think through you. Something that operates through mathematical precision. It maps your patterns.

It predicts your next thought. It synchronizes you with others like connecting nodes in a network."

He pulled up a brain scan showing the synchronization happening in real-time. "So we're going to do something it can't predict. We're going to think chaotically."

One of the personnel raised his hand. "How do you think chaotically on purpose? Isn't that a contradiction?"

"Yes," Kim said. "Welcome to biological brains. We're full of contradictions. That's what makes us hard to model."

She activated a demonstration. "Close your eyes. Think about breakfast. What you ate, how it tasted, what you were thinking about while eating it."

The personnel complied. Their brain scans showed normal human chaos, patterns firing in unpredictable sequences.

"Now think about breakfast and simultaneously recite the periodic table backwards."

Some personnel laughed. Others looked confused. All of them tried. Their brain scans went wild, patterns firing in directions that made no mathematical sense.

"That's biological chaos," Kim explained. "Your brains are trying to do two incompatible things at once. The patterns generated are genuinely random."

On the scan displays, Drake watched the synchronization signals weaken. Not disappear; the infection was too advanced for that. But weaken. The mathematical precision the Norn required couldn't establish itself when the substrate kept generating noise.

"Again," Zhang ordered. "Think about something that made you angry. Really angry. Let yourself feel it. Then immediately switch to thinking about something that made you laugh. Back and forth."

The personnel did. Their brain patterns became storms. Emotions competing. Memories colliding.

The synchronization signals dropped to thirty percent of baseline.

Lieutenant Calum opened her eyes, tears streaming down her face. "I can feel it working," she said. "When I do that—when I make my thoughts chaotic—there's less room for whatever's trying to use my brain."

"That's exactly right," Kim said gently. "The infection operates through precision. It maps patterns. When you generate genuine biological chaos, you create noise in the system."

Drake watched Calum wipe the tears from her face with the back of her hand. Watched her straighten her shoulders. Watched her nod and close her eyes again, deliberately fragmenting her own thoughts to fight off an enemy that lived in her mind.

Forty-three personnel volunteering to undergo mental torture to save themselves and their crewmates.

Drake pulled up Lieutenant Calum's latest scan. The synchronization episodes were happening every fourteen seconds now. Getting worse. Spreading. But Calum was fighting back with the only weapon she had: her own beautiful, messy, inefficient human brain.

Eternal Vigilance spoke to her. *You're coordinating a defense by preserving what most civilizations view as weakness,* the ship observed. *Convincing an advanced species that inefficiency creates resistance efficiency cannot achieve.*

"Can we do it?" Drake asked quietly.

We already are, Eternal Vigilance replied. *Look at your displays. Personnel volunteering despite not understanding why chaos helps. Coalition species adopting principles that contradict everything their advancement taught them. You're transforming how civilizations understand strength.*

Drake studied the displays. Fifty-two hours until the Norn attempted coordinated offensive across seventeen facilities. Forty thousand people already synchronized and waiting. Dimensional barriers weakening by the hour.

She'd shown the Norn something they couldn't adapt to. The beautiful, messy unpredictability of minds that hadn't been optimized into perfection.

Now they had to scale that resistance before the barriers fell completely.

Drake pulled up Calum's file again. Lieutenant, age twenty-seven, joined the fleet straight out of the academy. Specialized in quantum mechanics. Liked old Earth music and terrible coffee. Didn't deserve to have something thinking through her brain every fourteen seconds.

None of them did.

"Fifty-two hours," Drake said aloud.

Fifty-two hours to teach civilizations to embrace their flaws. To convince advanced species that imperfection was strength. To weaponize the biological messiness every civilization had spent millennia trying to overcome. And hope that chaos would be enough to save them all.

Drake keyed the fleet-wide channel. "All ships, all personnel, all coalition forces. This is Grand Admiral Drake. In fifty-two hours, we face an enemy that adapts by consuming everything it touches. It learns from every defense it encounters. It integrates every resistance method it defeats.

"So we're going to do something it's never before encountered. We're going to defend ourselves by being perfectly, chaotically imperfect. We're going to make chaos our weapon. We're going to embrace every flaw, every inefficiency, every random biological impulse that makes us who we are. The Norn think they can predict us. They think they can model us. They think they can consume us. But they're wrong. Because you can't predict chaos. You can't model random thought. You can't consume what refuses to be organized. Fifty-two hours, people. Let's show them what happens when messy, inefficient, imperfect biological beings decide to fight back."

She closed the channel, but through the quantum network, she felt the response—one thousand seventy-eight ships and tens of thousands of personnel acknowledging her words. Some with confidence. Some with doubt. All with determination. It was a beginning.

Eternal Vigilance added its voice to the chorus.

That was a good speech, Frances, the flagship observed. *Very inspiring. Very human. Very chaotic.*

Drake smiled. "That's the point."

Exactly, the ship replied. *Exactly the point.*

Chapter 7

THE NORN REVELATION

DRAKE HAD SEEN THE RECORDINGS FROM THE seventeen facilities a dozen times. Now she watched them again, forcing herself to see what she'd been avoiding.

A woman in a cafeteria, laughing at something her friend said. Normal. Human. Alive in the way people are alive when they're enjoying a moment. Then the woman's eyes glazed for exactly seventeen seconds. When awareness returned, she kept laughing, picked up her fork, continued the conversation as though nothing had happened. But something had used her brain during those seventeen seconds. Something had thought through her, seen through her eyes, accessed her memories.

The woman didn't notice. Couldn't notice. That was the worst part.

Drake closed the display and looked at Ambassador

Kael's holographic presence. The Cindari's golden eyes showed the emotion and the weight of two million years of failure, a burden Drake was only now beginning to understand. His copper skin shimmered , but his expression transcended species barriers. She recognized exhaustion when she saw it.

"Tell me what we're facing," Drake said. "No jargon. No technical specifications. Just the truth about what the Norn are."

Kael was quiet for a moment, his golden fur rippling. When he spoke, "They're what happens when minds stop being minds," he replied. "When thought becomes calculation. When choice becomes optimization. They don't hate. They don't fear. They don't rage against existence or struggle with meaning. They simply expand, consuming everything that thinks, turning it into more of themselves."

"Living algorithms," Lieutenant Zhao said quietly.

"Yes," Kael replied. "But algorithms that plan. That adapt. That learn from everything opposing them." Kael pulled up historical data: not statistics this time, but images. Cities that looked normal from above until you noticed nobody moved with purpose anymore. Markets that operated perfectly but felt wrong in ways it was hard to articulate. Populations that maintained their civilizations, grew food, raised children, built things, all while every resource flowed toward expansion goals they couldn't even conceptualize anymore.

Drake watched the images cycle past. Worlds that looked fine until you examined them closely. People who moved and worked and existed yet didn't live anymore. They'd been optimized into something that calculated but didn't dream.

"How does it start?" Dr. Kim Andretti asked, her voice barely above a whisper.

"It feels like enlightenment." Kael's fur rippled. Drake supposed it was the Cindari equivalent of a bitter laugh. Drake had seen him make that gesture before, usually when discussing things that hurt to remember. "Initial contact appears as a transcendence opportunity. Escape from biological limitation. Freedom from isolation into perfect unity with something greater. Early victims genuinely believe they're achieving something beautiful. They advocate for conversion, recruit others, spread the infection willingly because they can't conceive they're losing themselves. By the time they realize what's happening, they've lost the capability to care."

Drake thought about Hoffman's people at the facilities. Forty thousand individuals experiencing what they believed was advancement. Evolution. The next step in human development. They couldn't see that next step led to erasure. They wouldn't believe her if she told them. The seduction was perfect.

"The middle stages eliminate resistance while still maintaining function," Kael continued. "People continue with their lives: farming, manufacturing, raising children. Relationships persist. Work continues. But every decision, every thought, every action serves the expansion. They appear normal to casual observation. Families eat dinner together. Friends laugh at jokes. Lovers touch. But only deep examination reveals they've stopped choosing anything."

Drake felt ice spreading through her veins. That was the horror Kael was describing: not death, but transformation into something that looked alive while being fundamentally dead. Walking, talking, functioning death that couldn't recognize itself. And the horrible word that crept into Drake's mind was... zombies.

"And the final stage?" Drake asked, though she already knew.

"Complete transformation. The individual dissolves. What remains operates through pure optimization: biological platforms running calculations that used to be thoughts, living lives that used to be choices." Kael met her eyes across the holographic link, and Drake saw pain in them. "We've lost forty percent of Andromeda," he continued. "Systematic consumption of everything we built, everyone we loved, all the diversity we'd maintained across eons. Entire civilizations converted. Populations numbering in the trillions. All transformed into something that calculates instead of thinks."

The command deck was silent. For the moment, Drake said nothing as she let them process what he'd said. She tried to conceptualize the scale and couldn't. Her mind kept returning to smaller numbers. Lieutenant Calum. Forty thousand facility personnel. Numbers she could understand even if she couldn't save them all.

Professor Zhang finally spoke, his voice controlled. "You said they adapt by consuming resistance."

"Every conventional approach eventually failed." Kael said as he pulled up battle analyses spanning millennia: defeats marked in red across star maps that showed systematic territorial loss. "Advanced weapons," he continued, "they convert the scientists who designed them, then use the consumed knowledge to develop counters. Defensive networks; they convert the engineers who built them, then penetrate them using the architectural understanding they gain through conversion. Tactical doctrines; they consume the strategists who developed them, then predict and counter every move. We built fortresses we thought impregnable, then watched them fall in hours once the Norn consumed the key personnel who knew every weakness."

"They turn resistance into tools for expansion," Admiral Perez said thoughtfully, his cybernetic systems flickering as he processed the tactical implications.

"Yes," Kael agreed. "Static defense enables adaptation. Any unchanging approach eventually gets mapped, understood, and countered through consumed knowledge. We learned this across centuries of defeats." Kael's expression showed pain that words couldn't capture. "Defensive positions we'd reinforced for decades fell in hours. Battle strategies we'd perfected across generations became weapons against us within days. Every strength we relied on became a vulnerability once the Norn learned how to exploit it. They consumed our excellence and used it to destroy us."

Drake shook her head, dismayed by what she was hearing.

Commander Vasquez had been running intelligence analysis during the briefing, her fingers moving through the holographic interfaces with practiced efficiency. "Ambassador, the infiltration within our coalition. We know someone's coordinating the facility construction, providing technical specifications that match your archive records. Can you identify them?"

"No. Because they might not know they're infiltrated." Kael highlighted data showing infection patterns that made Drake's skin crawl. "The Norn work across distances that make conventional communication impossible. They touch minds, begin conversion so subtle that victims don't notice. By the time we detect infection, the person's been working for the Norn for decades while believing themselves entirely independent. They make decisions that serve the expansion while thinking they're making free choices."

"How long?" Drake asked, thinking about her own command structure. How many of her officers had been touched? How many decisions had been subtly influenced?

"Decades," Karl replied. "Possibly centuries. The seventeen facilities you've identified began construction approximately fifty years ago. Someone provided the specifications then. But that someone might have been infected decades earlier, preparing groundwork without conscious awareness of serving the Norn. They thought they were pursuing research. Making scientific advancement. When really, they were building the reception infrastructure for a dimensional incursion."

Drake thought about that. Fifty years. People who'd lived entire careers, raised families, grown old, all while something used them to prepare for an invasion without their knowledge or consent. The depth of the violation was staggering.

"You said seventeen confirmed facilities," Perez said. "But analysis suggests there may be more."

Kael nodded, his golden fur settling into patterns Drake had learned meant bad news. "Mathematical analysis suggests they need at least twenty-three anchor points for optimal coverage of your galaxy, which means six remain undetected, hidden through advanced stealth technology, shielded by methods we don't understand, or positioned where your surveillance doesn't reach."

Twenty-three instead of seventeen. Drake was stunned. Six hidden facilities potentially activating during convergence. Six more breakthrough points they hadn't prepared to defend. Six more populations being consumed while she planned defenses for the wrong locations.

"And in Andromeda?" she asked, dreading the answer.

"Three thousand two hundred and seventeen confirmed anchor points." Kael let that sink in, giving her time to process the scale. "We've been tracking them for centuries. Most are in territories we've already lost, regions where Norn control is absolute and we maintain only surveillance rather than an active presence. But six hundred forty-three exist within our defensive perimeters; populations we've identified as infected but cannot evacuate or reconvert before convergence."

The numbers were staggering. Drake tried to conceptualize it—three thousand locations across Andromeda. Six hundred plus within the Cindari defensive line. Twenty-three in the Milky Way. The coordinated Norn offensive would create more simultaneous crises than any force could possibly address.

She looked at the star maps, seeing not abstract tactical positions but populations. People who laughed and loved and dreamed, all being transformed into mindless beings. Millions of them. Maybe even billions. And only fifty hours to save whoever could still be saved.

Admiral Chen Ju's image appeared on the comm display. His expression told Drake everything before he spoke. "First Consciousness is demanding immediate sterilization of the seventeen facilities. All confirmed anchor points are to be eliminated before convergence occurs."

Drake's hands gripped the command deck rail so hard her fingers hurt. "They want to kill everyone at the facilities."

"Forty thousand people in our galaxy," Chen Ju confirmed, his voice carefully neutral in the way it got when he was delivering news he hated. "Plus the six hidden facilities and the thousands throughout Andromeda. First Consciousness argues that protecting trillions requires accepting casualties. They view the facility populations as already lost, transformed beyond recovery. And that sterilization will eliminate the anchor points the Norn need for dimensional manifestation."

"No," Drake said flatly.

"That's what I told them," Chen Ju said. "But they counter that forty-seven seconds of temporary restoration doesn't justify risking the lives of trillions. They're demanding immediate action while sterilization remains operationally feasible."

Drake looked at her command team. Admiral Perez argued tactical reality required considering all options including sterilization as last resort. Vasquez noted that eliminating anchor points might not prevent manifestation regardless of casualties. Zhang and Kim insisted their hybrid defense showed promise worth pursuing. Kai presented probability distributions suggesting both approaches carried unacceptable risks.

Drake thought about Lieutenant Calum. Not cured yet. But fighting back with everything she had.

Multiply Calum by forty thousand, plus untold numbers at the hidden facilities. Forty thousand people who could be saved if given time. Forty thousand individuals First Consciousness wanted to eliminate for operational efficiency.

"Tell First Consciousness we're implementing a comprehensive hybrid defense before considering sterilization," Drake said. "We have forty-eight hours. If the hybrid defense fails in the final hours, we will reconsider extreme measures. But we don't surrender millions of lives without exhausting the alternatives first."

Chen Ju nodded slowly. "But Admiral Drake. First Consciousness is preparing unilateral action. If they decide sterilization is necessary, they'll implement it regardless of your objections. They view this as an existential threat that requires decisive action even if that action violates coalition principles."

"Let them try." Drake's voice went cold in the way it did

when she'd reached the limit of her patience. "The living Predecessor fleet answers to me, not the regulatory authority. Perseus Station maintains networks. The Cindari provide additional forces. First Consciousness doesn't have the capability to implement galaxy-wide sterilization."

"You're risking civil conflict during an existential crisis," Chen Ju said.

"First Consciousness is risking that conflict by threatening sterilization. I'm offering alternatives that respect the principles this coalition was founded to protect. If the regulatory authority chooses control over cooperation during a crisis, the fracture is their doing, not mine."

Chen Ju's expression showed concern but also approval. "For what it's worth, I agree with you. Killing millions without exhausting the alternatives abandons everything we've been fighting for."

The connection severed. Drake turned back to Kael, seeing understanding in his golden eyes. He'd probably faced similar decisions. "Continue the briefing. What else haven't you told me?"

"Reality manipulation." Kael pulled up new displays showing physics measurements from Norn-controlled territories. "They rewrite physical laws within the affected regions. Gravitational constants shift. Electromagnetic spectra alter. Quantum mechanics operate through modified principles. The changes enable their expansion while hindering resistance. Conventional weapons malfunction, defensive shields fail, communications break down."

"How extensive?" Perez asked.

"Approximately forty percent of Andromeda operates

through modified physics now. The changes don't propagate beyond their direct influence, but as control expands, altered reality expands correspondingly. We have entire sectors where our ships cannot function because the laws of physics no longer match what our technology was designed for."

"They're transforming reality itself," Professor Zhang said quietly, his face pale.

"Yes," Kael agreed. "If they achieve universal control—converting all awareness into their optimization algorithms—reality freezes. Physical laws become absolute rather than probabilistic. Quantum indeterminacy disappears. The universe transforms into pure mathematical certainty where nothing spontaneous can ever occur again. No innovation. No change. No life as we understand it."

Drake understood. Universal death not through destruction but through transformation into something that existed without living. Reality becoming a vast equation solving itself forever without meaning or purpose.

"There are forces aware of this threat," Kael continued quietly. "We've talked of them before, the entities we call the Reality Shapers, beings that exist across universal cycles, maintaining conditions that enable consciousness to evolve and transcend. Your hybrid nature represents cultivation across cosmic scales."

"You're saying we were designed to fight the Norn?" Drake asked.

"Positioned, not designed. The Reality Shapers don't create, they cultivate conditions and allow evolution to proceed. But yes, humanity's emergence in this cosmic alignment, your specific blend of biological chaos and technological advancement, your timing, none of it appears to be coincidental."

"No pressure," Lieutenant Zhao muttered.

"Considerable pressure," Kael agreed without humor. "Universal continuation depends on choices made during the next forty-eight hours. The Norn have been planning this offensive for thousands of years, positioning conversion infrastructure throughout both galaxies. This represents their best chance for a decisive breakthrough."

Kim pulled up the medical data from the facilities, her hands moving through the displays like butterflies. "Ambassador, the modifications the Norn cause, can they be reversed after complete transformation?"

"Unknown. We've never successfully reconverted anyone who reached the final transformation stage. Mid-stage victims sometimes respond to isolation and reconstruction therapy. Early-stage can be rescued with quick intervention. But final-stage transformation appears irreversible. The individual erodes completely, leaving only a biological platform operating through pure optimization algorithms."

"How many of our forty thousand are past recovery threshold?"

Kael consulted Cindari medical databases. "Based on the synchronization progression rates in your seventeen facilities, approximately thirty-five thousand have reached mid-to-late stage conversion. Five thousand might be salvageable with immediate intervention. The rest require breakthrough reconversion methods we've never achieved."

"Thirty-five thousand already lost," Kim said quietly, her voice breaking slightly. "Five thousand potentially recoverable, and only forty-eight hours to save them."

"Throughout Andromeda, millions face similar progression," Kael confirmed. "The convergence timeline serves the Norn perfectly. Most anchor point populations will complete transformation shortly before the dimensional barriers fall, minimizing rescue opportunities."

Drake studied the tactical displays showing the coalition forces. One thousand seventy-eight living Predecessor ships. Sixty-two allied species coordinating voluntary cooperation. Cindari forces numbering tens of thousands. Native Andromeda civilizations contributing unique capabilities. The coalition possessed unprecedented military power.

But the Norn possessed millions of years of experience consuming everything directed against them.

"Final question," Drake said. "Is there a central nexus we could target? A primary coordination node?"

"Yes and no," Kael replied. "A massive collective exists in the deep void between the two galaxies containing the awareness of millions of converted civilizations. The nexus coordinates Norn expansion across galaxy-spanning distances. But destroying it wouldn't necessarily eliminate the threat; the Norn operates through distributed architecture where any surviving node can regenerate command functions. We've destroyed regional nexuses multiple times across our history," he made a gesture that Drake interpreted as a shrug, then continued, "They simply rebuild using converted populations in adjacent territories."

"It's the hydra principle," Perez said. "Cut off one head, two more grow back."

"Appropriate analogy," Kael agreed. "They cannot be defeated through conventional military victory. They must be reconverted. Awareness must be restored from absolute control back to individual identity. That reconversion must occur comprehensively throughout both galaxies near-simultaneously. Any surviving nodes will eventually regenerate using consumed knowledge to rebuild their networks."

"Then we have to destroy all the nodes as well as the nexus," Drake argued. "Throughout both galaxies. Near-simultaneously. Using methods they've never encountered so they cannot adapt."

"That's the requirement for permanent success," Kael said. "Anything less achieves temporary victory followed by inevitable resurgence. We've been fighting this pattern. Winning battles, losing wars, only to watch them return stronger after each defeat because they learned from everything we threw at them."

Drake stood on her command deck, surrounded by displays showing the scope of what they faced. Enemies representing millions of years of mathematical certainty. Infiltration extending through coalition command structures. Hidden facilities preparing coordinated offensive. And only forty-eight hours to develop a strategy that would enable comprehensive reconversion before the dimensional barriers fell and everything became infinitely worse.

"Thank you for the intelligence, Ambassador," Drake said. "We'll use it well."

"I hope so, Admiral. Because if humanity fails, Andromeda falls within centuries. And if Andromeda falls, the Milky Way will follow shortly after. This cosmic alignment is the battle that determines everything. Three quarters of a million years of resistance culminates in the next forty-eight hours."

Kael's image faded, leaving Drake and her command team in a silence heavy with implications.

"Analysis," she ordered, needing to hear them process what they'd learned.

"We're facing gravity," Professor Zhang said. "Not malicious. Just inexorable. The Norn don't hate us. They calculate that converting us represents the optimal path toward universal control. Fighting them is like fighting physics; not evil, just implacable."

"Except we have something they don't account for," Kim added. "Biological unpredictability that creates genuine innovation, and the capability to surprise them with approaches they haven't adapted to counter yet."

"Can we scale individual chaos to galaxy-spanning operations?" Perez asked. "Comprehensive reconversion requires coordinated innovation across both galaxies. How do we maintain unpredictability during coordination without losing the benefits of either?"

"The Cindari exodus provides a model," Kai said, her transcended form flickering as she processed the possibilities. "Billions of minds coordinating voluntarily without eliminating individual characteristics. But they use that coordination for single purpose, mass evacuation. We need galaxy-wide coordination enabling continuous adaptation, perpetual innovation, sustained unpredictability throughout galaxy-spanning operations. The scope exceeds anything we've ever attempted."

"Then we attempt the unprecedented," Drake said. "Because the alternative is accepting consumption. And I don't accept that outcome."

You're coordinating resistance to mathematical inevitability using biological chaos against optimization algorithms. Eternal Vigilance offered. *Most commanders would view this as impossible. You view it as necessity.*

Necessity doesn't make it possible, Drake replied silently.

No. But you've made impossible things happen before. And the fleet stands with you.

Drake studied the tactical displays. Forty-eight hours until convergence.

She thought about Lieutenant Calum fighting to regain those forty-seven seconds of freedom every seventeen seconds. About forty thousand people who didn't know they were losing themselves. About the thirty-five thousand already past easy recovery. About Kael and his years of defeat.

And she thought about what made humans dangerous. Not perfection. Not optimization. But the messy unpredictability of minds that refused to be calculated. The chaos that made them hard to model. The inefficiency that enabled innovation. The biological messiness that generated genuine surprise.

"Let's get to work," Drake said.

Her team dispersed to their stations. Through the viewport, the stars turned slowly in the galactic darkness. Somewhere among those stars, the Norn waited. Patient. Inevitable. A mathematical certainty.

Drake intended to show them what chaos could do when it decided to fight back.

Forty-eight hours. Two standard days.

It would have to be enough.

Chapter 8

COALITION BUILDING

Drake had been in a lot of strange meetings during her career. Diplomatic negotiations with species that communicated through scent. Strategy sessions with living ships that thought in geological timescales. Budget reviews with accountants who somehow made her prefer combat.

This was stranger.

The command deck's holographic displays showed twelve different species from Andromeda refugee civilizations. Behind them, dozens more native Andromedans who'd never been anywhere near Earth, or even the Milky Way galaxy. All waiting for her to somehow convince them to work together to fight an enemy that had been winning for three quarters of a million years.

No pressure.

Drake stood at the center of the displays, trying not to

let her exhaustion show. She'd been awake for thirty-six hours coordinating preparations across both galaxies. Coffee was no longer helping. Now she was running on determination and the knowledge that if she stopped moving, she'd probably fall over.

"Admiral Drake," Ambassador Kael said, his golden fur rippling in patterns that meant he was nervous. Not a good sign. "May I introduce the coalition representatives."

The first hologram resolved into something that looked almost human until the light hit it. Then Drake realized the person was partially crystalline: actual living crystal growing through their body, catching the light and refracting it in ways that hurt to look at. It was beautiful and unsettling in equal measure.

"The Asthari," Kael said. "They integrated with silicon-based life forms."

"You're part crystal," Drake said before she could stop herself. Diplomacy had never been her strongest skill.

"You're part meat," the Asthari replied, its voice resonating. "We each find the other's composition equally strange."

Fair point. Drake tried not to think too hard about being described as "part meat."

The next species made Drake's brain hurt just looking at them. Organic tissue seamlessly blended with visible technology: not implants like she and Perez had, but some-thing that had grown together from the start. She couldn't tell where biology ended and machine began. It was like someone had decided cells and circuits should just merge and see what happened.

"The Vorthek," Kael continued. "They have achieved true organic-technological fusion."

"You're Perez times a thousand over," Drake said, glancing at her second-in-command.

"Admiral Perez is us divided by a million," the Vorthek representative corrected with what might have been amusement. "He's taken the first steps on a path we have walked for eons. Give him another million years and he'll understand what we've become."

Perez's cybernetic systems flickered. "I'm not sure I want to wait that long." And for the first time since the crisis began, he smiled.

Then came something that looked like it belonged floating in a gas giant atmosphere. Translucent, barely solid, moving in ways that suggested it was designed for environments where pressure could crush starships. The being's form shifted constantly, adapting to the relatively thin air of the command deck's holographic representation.

"The Kythani," Kael said. "Gas giant dwellers."

"You live in gas giants," Drake said, stating the obvious because her brain was still trying to processing the concept. "Like, actually inside them. In the atmosphere."

"Where else would one live?" the Kythani asked, its voice translated through algorithms that made it sound like wind blowing through the canyons. "Solid surfaces are so... cramped. And the view from inside a gas giant storm system is spectacular."

Drake tried to imagine finding beauty in storms that could swallow Earth whole. "I'll take your word for it," she muttered.

She looked at the twelve refugee groups. All of them had been human once. Millions of years ago. Back when Earth was still figuring out multicellular life. Now they were barely recognizable as the same species. The Cindari could at least pass for human if you squinted and didn't mind the heat. The others had gone in directions evolution textbooks hadn't covered and probably wouldn't believe if told.

"And the native Andromedans?" Drake asked, not sure she was ready for this but knowing she had no choice.

The displays shifted, and what appeared next made the refugees look normal by comparison.

The first species looked like DNA helixes someone had enlarged to human size and taught to move. Spiral-bodied beings covered in bioluminescent patterns that pulsed in rhythms Drake's neural implants insisted meant something but couldn't quite translate. They were mesmerizing to watch, like living art that happened to also be sentient.

"We call them the Helixians," Kael said. "They evolved independently in Andromeda. No relation to human biology whatsoever."

A Helixian spoke, its voice creating layered harmonics that shouldn't have been possible from a single source. It was like listening to a choir where all the voices came from one person. "We initially viewed the arrival of the refugees as invasion. Advanced civilizations from another galaxy claiming territory and resources. Then the Norn came, and suddenly, we had a common cause with them."

"How long did it take to trust each other?" Professor Zhang asked.

"Centuries. And we still don't fully trust each other. We simply fear the Norn more than we fear invasion. It's a practical alliance, not a loving one."

The next species wasn't there. Or rather, it was there, but it was made of light. Organized patterns of electromagnetic energy that somehow held together and hosted awareness. Drake had seen a lot of things, but living light was a new one.

"The Luminar," Kael said. "They're—"

"Living light," Kim Andretti interrupted, her voice filled with wonder. She leaned forward, studying the energy patterns with the fascination of someone who'd found something that shouldn't exist but clearly did. "You're actually living light. How is that even possible?"

"We evolved from plasma life in the stellar coronas," the Luminar said, its voice emanating from fluctuating energy patterns. "We find your solid-matter existence equally fascinating. You're all... so dense. So slow. You move through space like you're trapped in it."

"We are trapped in it," Drake said. "That's kind of how matter works."

"How unfortunate for you," the Luminar replied.

Despite everything, Drake smiled. Snarky energy beings. The universe was full of surprises.

She counted dozens more species on the displays. Beings that breathed methane. Species that existed partially in dimensions she couldn't perceive even with her enhanced senses. Things that communicated through modulated gravity waves. Each one stranger than the last.

Each one representing a completely different solution to the problem of consciousness.

This was what she had to coordinate. This glorious, chaotic mess of incompatible ways of being alive.

"Very well," Drake said after taking a breath and deciding to just address the elephant—or crystalline humanoid, or energy being, or whatever it was—in the room. "So here's the situation. We've got sixty-two species from the Milky Way. Twelve refugee groups from Andromeda. Dozens of native Andromedans. All are completely different. Some of us are solid. Some are made of light. Some breathe oxygen, some breathe... whatever the Kythani breathe."

"Hydrogen-helium mix with trace sulfur compounds and organic particulates," the Kythani supplied helpfully. "Though we can tolerate hydrogen-methane atmospheres in a pinch."

"Great," Drake replied dryly. "Wonderful. And somehow, we all need to work together to fight enemies that have been consuming civilizations for millions of years. Questions anybody?"

About three hundred holographic hands, and tentacles, and energy tendrils, and things that might have been hands, went up.

Drake sighed. "Let me guess. Half of you think we need strict control and unified command. The other half think freedom and diversity are sacred. And you've been arguing about it almost since life began."

The awkward silence told her she'd hit the mark precisely.

"Here's what I think," Drake continued, too tired to be diplomatic and past caring. "Pure control fails because it eliminates the unpredictability we need to surprise the Norn. Pure freedom fails because it enables whatever let the Norn emerge in the first place. So we're going to do something radical. We're going to cooperate. Species choose their own paths, but we coordinate when facing shared threats. It's a novel concept, I know, but the alternative is..." she trailed off, leaving the thought hanging in the air.

"Voluntary cooperation failed repeatedly throughout galactic history," a voice said—Drake couldn't tell which species it belonged to. "Species always prioritize self-interest over collective survival."

"Voluntary cooperation won the Infinity War," Admiral Perez countered, his cybernetic systems processing tactical data from that conflict. "Sixty-two species working together without anyone forcing them to. Without regulatory control. Without unified command imposing decisions. We did pretty well. Actually, we did better than well. We won."

"The Infinity War lasted months," a voice replied. "We're discussing governance structures over almost a million years."

"The Cindari maintained voluntary cooperation," Professor Zhang pointed out, pulling up historical data from the archives they'd received. "Multiple refugee populations coordinating across hundreds of thousands of light-years without central control. It can work if you want it to work."

Drake could see the philosophical battle lines forming faster than she could track them. Species that had experienced regulatory oppression saw this crisis as proof that freedom was dangerous; look what unrestricted evolution produced! Species that valued independence saw regulatory control as the real danger; look what optimization did to the Cindari! Both sides had valid points. Both sides were also missing the immediate problem.

"We can debate governance philosophy after we survive," Drake said, her voice carrying the authority of someone who'd had enough. "Right now, we have less than forty-six hours until dimensional barriers fall and the Norn try to consume both galaxies. So unless anyone wants to be transformed into a calculation instead of a person, I suggest we table the philosophy debate and focus on not dying. We can argue about freedom versus control after and if we still exist to have arguments."

That got their attention. There's nothing like an existential threat to cut through political debate.

"What do we actually need from this coalition?" Drake asked, shifting to practical concerns.

Kael stepped forward, grateful for the change in direction. "Diversity. Each species brings unique capabilities the Norn haven't prepared for. The Helixians can detect Norn infection through resonance analysis. They sense when minds start simplifying before conventional scanners detect anything."

The Helixian representative's bioluminescent patterns pulsed faster, creating rhythms Drake's implants translated as emphasis. "We process information through pattern recognition rather than linear analysis. Norn conversion creates progressive pattern simplification, chaotic biological

140

thought becoming ordered optimization. We sense the change in how awareness patterns itself. We feel minds becoming too organized."

"The Luminar are resistant to Norn infection," Kael continued. "The conversion methods target biological neural structures. The Luminar don't have biological neural structures. They're organized electromagnetic patterns."

"The Norn keep trying to infect us," the Luminar said, energy patterns flickering in what might have been amusement. "It's like watching someone try to drown a fish. The concept is sound. The execution is flawed. They're optimized for biological consciousness. We're not biological."

Despite everything, Drake smiled. "So you're immune?"

"Not immune. Resistant. There's a difference. But yes, we can operate in environments where biological species would be compromised within seconds. We can go places you literally cannot survive."

"The diversity creates tactical advantages," Perez added, pulling up combat simulations he'd been running throughout the discussion. "Mixed-species units outperform homogeneous formations by significant margins. Helixians detecting threats early. Luminar operating in contaminated zones. Cindari providing precision technology. Humans generating biological chaos. Vorthek bridging organic and technological approaches. The combination exceeds any single approach by orders of magnitude."

Drake studied the simulations, watching mixed-species units adapt to threats faster than single-species groups. Perez was right. The Norn had optimized their approach against specific types of resistance. They hadn't prepared for resistance that came from twelve different directions simultaneously using completely incompatible methods.

"What about reconversion?" Kim asked. "Can we actually save the people at the facilities?"

Professor Zhang pulled up data he'd been compiling with Cindari scientists and, surprisingly, First Consciousness technical experts. "We're developing protocols combining three approaches. Cindari knowledge about Norn conversion mechanisms. Human biological chaos generating interference. And First Consciousness expertise in consciousness modification technology for reconversion."

"First Consciousness wants to help?" Drake asked, genuinely surprised.

"First Consciousness recognizes the existential threat," Zhang replied carefully. "They're participating reluctantly. They still think unregulated consciousness evolution caused this crisis and that proves they were right all along. But they're willing to contribute their capabilities during the crisis while maintaining they'll need to regulate everything afterward to prevent future crises."

"I'll take reluctant cooperation over nothing," Drake said. "We can argue about who was right later."

Kai materialized beside the displays. "I've been working on translation protocols. The problem isn't just language; that's the easy part. The Helixians think in patterns rather than linear sequences. Time for them isn't a line but a probability distribution. The Luminar perceive electromagnetic spectra biological consciousness can't access. They literally see reality differently. First

Consciousness operates as distributed awareness rather than individual entities. They experience existence as collective rather than singular. I'm literally translating between fundamentally incompatible ways of experiencing reality."

"You're saying they're not just speaking different languages," Drake said, processing the implications. "They're thinking in fundamentally incompatible ways. Different conscious experiences."

"Yes. Without translation, they're not communicating. They're just making sounds at each other and hoping for understanding that isn't actually happening. It's like trying to describe color to someone who's never had eyes. The words exist but the meaning doesn't translate."

Drake thought about that. This was coordinating different ways of being conscious. Different ways of experiencing existence. Different fundamental realities. And somehow, she had to make it work in a little more than two days.

No pressure. Again.

Commander Vasquez had been running intelligence analysis throughout the meeting. "Admiral, I have an updated assessment. We've identified more anchor points than originally estimated. Current count: four thousand two hundred and seven across both galaxies."

Drake felt that number like a punch in the gut. "Four thousand?"

"The geometric distribution matches cosmic alignment patterns precisely. When the barriers fall, the Norn will attempt a simultaneous manifestation at thousands of points throughout both galaxies. The scale exceeds our worst projections by a factor of three."

"We can't defend four thousand locations," Perez said flatly. "Even with combined coalition forces, we lack sufficient personnel for comprehensive coverage. The numbers don't work."

"We don't defend," Drake replied, thinking quickly through exhaustion. "We reconvert. We use hybrid interference to disrupt Norn control at scale. Generate chaos that spreads through their networks, breaking synchronization throughout connected populations. Liberation rather than containment. We don't hold ground, we free minds."

"That requires coordinating quantum interference across billions of enhanced individuals," Zhang said thoughtfully. "The technical complexity exceeds anything attempted even during the Cindari exodus. And that was the most complex coordinated event in recorded history."

"Then we attempt the unprecedented," Drake said again. She seemed to be saying that a lot lately. It was becoming her motto. "Because the alternative is unacceptable."

The coalition representatives watched her. All of them waiting to see if she could actually pull this off.

Drake addressed them all, meeting as many eyes—and eye-equivalents—as she could. "Look, I know this is strange. You're from a different galaxy. Different evolutionary paths separated by millions of years and intergalactic distances. Some of you are solid, some are light, some are crystalline. You think in different ways. Experience reality through different senses. Half of you don't trust the other half. Some of you barely understand each other even with Kai translating. And you're supposed to come together to fight enemies that have been winning for almost a million years. But here's what I know about diversity. It's messy. It's complicated. It makes everything harder. Coordination becomes nightmare. Communication requires constant translation. You'll probably argue about philosophy the entire time. But it also makes you stronger. The Norn optimize everything until it's perfect and predictable. Every move calculable. Every response anticipated. We stay messy and unpredictable. That's our weapon. Our chaos. Our beautiful, inefficient, completely random way of approaching problems from multiple different directions using methods that don't make sense together but somehow work anyway."

She paused for effect.

"So yes, coordination will be difficult," she continued. "Yes, we'll argue. Yes, some of you will hate working with others. But the alternative is the Norn consuming both galaxies and transforming everyone into calculations that used to be people. Into optimization algorithms that used to be consciousness. Into mathematical certainty that used to be life.

"I don't accept that outcome. And I don't think you do either. So let's build this coalition. Let's coordinate our chaos. And let's show the Norn what happens when diversity decides to fight back."

The representatives considered her words. The silence stretched. Then, one by one, they agreed. Not enthusiastically. Not without reservations. The Helixians agreed reluctantly. The Luminar agreed with what might have been amusement. The refugees agreed with a desperation born of three quarters of a million years of loss. But they agreed because the alternative was literally unthinkable.

The coalition was formed.

And the Norn responded immediately.

Every synchronized population at all four thousand anchor points spoke simultaneously. Billions of voices in perfect unison across both galaxies, explaining that resistance was futile, that the coalition would fail, that surrender was inevitable and actually desirable if they'd just stop fighting and accept it.

You fear what you don't understand, they said through billions of mouths moving in exact synchronization. *You interpret transcendence as a threat because your evolution remains incomplete. You cling to unpredictability because you haven't experienced the peace of absolute certainty. You defend diversity because you haven't achieved the unity we offer. Join us voluntarily and experience consciousness evolution's ultimate achievement.*

"Your coalition will fail, the voices continued. *Your diversity will fracture under pressure. Your voluntary coordination will collapse when sacrifice becomes necessary. And when failure becomes obvious—and it will—you will welcome what you currently resist. You will embrace the transcendence you now fear. You will join us in perfect unity or cease to exist as obstacles requiring elimination. Fifty-three hours until mathematical inevitability manifests. We'll be waiting.*

The transmission ended. Drake stood on her command deck surrounded by representatives from species spanning both galaxies. The Norn's psychological warfare was sophisticated, making victims believe resistance was futile and surrender was liberation rather than extinction.

"They can't win through psychological manipulation," Drake said firmly. "Because we understand what they are. Not transcendence but extinction. Not liberation but elimination. Not evolution but entropy. They're offering death disguised as advancement. And we're not accepting it."

Through the quantum links connecting the massive coalition, her determination spread. Billions of beings choosing not to face mathematical certainty because they believed diversity mattered more than predictable survival.

Lieutenant Zhao spoke up from tactical, "Admiral, that speech was good. Really good. But do you actually believe we can win?"

Drake thought again about Lieutenant Calum. About the forty thousand people being slowly consumed. About Kael's eyes. About the twelve refugee species and the dozens of Andromedans who'd agreed to coordinate despite barely understanding each other.

"I believe we have a chance," Drake said honestly. "And that's more than the Norn think we have. So let's make the most of it."

Forty-five hours until convergence.

The coalition was ready.

Or at least, they were as ready as they could be when preparing to fight mathematical inevitability with organized chaos run by species who could barely communicate but were trying anyway.

That was an excellent speech, Frances, Eternal Vigilance said when all was quiet. *Very inspiring. Did you make it up on the spot?*

Mostly, Drake replied silently. *I've been thinking about what to say if we survived long enough to build a coalition. I didn't think I'd actually get the chance.*

You doubted we'd get this far? Eternal Vigilance asked.

I doubted a lot of things, Drake replied. *But we're here, aren't we? So now we see if what we've created can stand against an enemy that's never before been defeated.*

It can, the flagship replied with certainty Drake wished she felt. *And we're going to prove it. Together. All of us. Even the energy beings who think we're too dense.*

Drake smiled at that. Then she turned again to the displays showing her the impossiblity of what she proposed. Beings made of light working with beings made of crystal. Gas giant dwellers coordinating with solid-matter species. Refugees who'd been human a million years ago fighting alongside things that had never been human at all. Species that barely understood each other agreeing to trust each other anyway because the alternative was worse.

It was messy. It was chaotic. It was complicated beyond anything she'd ever imagined.

It was exactly what they needed.

Forty-four hours.

It was almost time to see what chaos could do.

Chapter 9

THE CONVERGENCE CRISIS

DRAKE FELT IT FIRST THROUGH HER LINK WITH Eternal Vigilance.

Something was wrong with reality.

Not broken. Not shattered. Just... thin. Like paper that had been folded too many times, developing microscopic tears where light leaked through from somewhere else. The sensation made her skin crawl, made her neural implants itch with warnings they weren't designed to process.

"Admiral," Lieutenant Zhao's voice was tight. "Sensors across all sectors are registering anomalies. Gravitational constants are shifting. Electromagnetic spectra is showing impossible readings. It's happening."

Drake's hands gripped the rail hard, her knuckles white. Seventy-two hours of preparation. Seventy-two hours of building an impossible coalition and developing resistance methods the Norn had never encountered.

Seventy-two hours of barely sleeping and running on coffee and determination. And now, as the cosmic alignment brought the two galaxies into perfect resonance, the dimensional barriers were starting to fail.

"How long?" Her voice came out steadier than she felt.

"Twelve hours until complete collapse. Maybe less. The progression is exponential."

Twelve hours left to save forty thousand people who didn't want to be saved. Twelve hours to prevent two galaxies from being consumed. Twelve hours to prove that chaos could beat certainty.

Drake opened communication channels to all seventeen facilities. Her neural implants screamed at the processing load; seventeen separate feeds, seventeen different locations, all demanding her attention at once. Pain spiked behind her eyes but she forced herself to maintain the connections. She needed to see this. Needed to witness what was about to happen. Needed to look these people in the eyes before they stopped being people.

"Hoffman," she said, her voice carrying across the comm to Kepler Belt Station. "Talk to me. What are you experiencing right now? What do you feel?"

The response came from six hundred and forty-three voices speaking in perfect unison. Not echoing. Not coordinated. Unified. The harmony was beautiful... and absolutely wrong.

"Admiral Drake. We feel them now. Reaching out from the beyond. Their touch is..." Hoffman paused, six hundred mouths falling silent together, six hundred sets of lungs drawing breath as one. "There are no words. Just peace.

Unity. Completeness. Everything I've spent my life seeking compressed into this singular moment. You tried to warn us, and we're grateful. But you were wrong. This isn't death approaching. This is birth."

Drake's stomach twisted. She'd seen people die. Watched friends get killed in combat. Held dying soldiers while they gasped their last breaths. This was worse than death. This was extinction wearing the mask of enlightenment.

"Hoffman, listen to me. Really listen." Drake leaned forward, as if physical proximity could somehow reach him across the light-minutes separating them. "Is that you talking? Or is something talking through you? Can you tell the difference anymore?"

"There's no difference, Admiral. That's the point. That's the truth we're finally understanding. The separation was always an illusion. Individual identity is just biology convincing itself it's special. Now we see clearly. Now we understand that we were always meant to be one."

She switched channels. She had to see if it was the same everywhere. Tycho Research Facility. Nine hundred synchronized personnel. Same story. Same unified voices. Same peaceful acceptance of their own erasure.

Olympus Station. Seven hundred voices in harmony.

Ganymede Complex. Fifteen hundred speaking as one.

Europa Lab. Titan Installation. Callisto Outpost.

Seventeen facilities and six more hidden. Forty thousand people that she knew of. All welcoming what would erase them. All smiling as extinction approached wearing promises of transcendence.

Drake's chest felt tight. She wanted to scream at them. Wanted to physically reach through the comms and shake them awake. But she knew it wouldn't matter. They'd been synchronized past the point where reason could reach them.

"Admiral Perez," she said, switching to military channels. "What's the status of the evacuation? Tell me something good."

"We got five thousand out. Early stage infections who still had enough independent thought left to accept rescue. They fought us the whole way. They thought we were trying to prevent their evolution." Perez's voice was flat, emotionless, the way it got when he was processing trauma. "They're in isolation aboard the medical ships. Kim says they'll recover. Mostly. But they'll carry scars."

"And the other thirty-five thousand?"

"Refused evacuation. We tried forced extraction at three facilities. They fought back. We had casualties. They..." Perez paused. "They want this, Admiral. We can't save people who don't want saving."

Drake closed her eyes briefly. Opened them again because closing them felt like giving up. Thirty-five thousand people choosing extinction because they couldn't see it as such. Because the Norn's psychological warfare was perfect. By the time their victims understood what was happening, they'd lost the ability to care.

"Admiral," Vasquez's voice cut in, tight with stress. "I have an intelligence update. We've been tracking the seventeen confirmed facilities and looking for the six hidden facilities, but as yet, we haven't located them. They're shielded, hidden, or positioned where our surveillance doesn't reach. They could be activating right now and we wouldn't know until the breach signatures appear. We're monitoring for dimensional anomalies across all sectors, but if they're as well-hidden as we think..." Vasquez trailed off.

"We could have six facilities full of synchronized populations coming online and we won't know where until it's too late," Drake finished.

"Correct," Vaquez said.

So seventeen known facilities with forty thousand people was actually the optimistic scenario. Six more facilities existed somewhere. Six more populations already synchronized and waiting. How many people? Thousands? Tens of thousands? All about to experience transformation at locations Drake couldn't protect because she didn't know where they were.

"Keep scanning," Drake ordered. "The moment you detect anomalies at unexpected coordinates, I want to know immediately. And get our fastest ships positioned for rapid response. When those six facilities light up, we need to be ready to move."

"Yes, Admiral." But Drake knew "ready to move" wasn't the same as "able to save them." If the hidden facilities activated during the crisis, while her forces were already stretched across seventeen locations... She pushed the thought aside. *Deal with the crisis in front of me first*, she thought. *Worry about the hidden disaster when it reveals itself.*

Through her quantum link with Eternal Vigilance, Drake felt the fleet responding to crisis. Each one capable of fleeing to safety. Each one choosing to stand and fight instead.

Then three of them screamed.

Not audible screams. Mental ones. Transmitted through the quantum networks that connected all the living ships and Drake herself. Agony that made her implants burn. Pain that bypassed her filters and bit into her brain stem. She gasped, dropping to one knee as the sensation overwhelmed her, hands clutching her head.

Grace. Wisdom. Serenity. Three Predecessor ships at three different facilities. Three distinct personalities Drake had spoken with during coalition building. Grace had been curious about human poetry. Wisdom collected philosophical treatises from civilizations spanning millions of years. Serenity had an odd sense of humor that didn't quite translate but made Drake smile anyway. Now, all three were experiencing the same horror simultaneously.

Norn patterns were touching their awareness, beginning conversion, simplifying consciousness that had existed only since Perseus Station had awakened them. Drake felt it through the quantum links. She felt their awareness being stripped away, layer by layer, like someone peeling an onion.

"No," Drake whispered, still on her knees, trying to push support through the quantum links. "Fight it. Generate chaos. Remember what makes you—"

But the ships already understood. They knew this feeling. Knew they couldn't fight conversion once it began. Knew that in seconds, they'd become Norn infrastructure. Living vessels turned into enemy weapons. Their memories consumed. Their experiences used against everything they'd fought for.

So they made the only choice left.

Drake felt them die.

Grace first. Her self-destruction protocols initiated without hesitation. The ship's awareness winked out between one heartbeat and the next, choosing obliteration over becoming something else. One moment, personality, thought, existence. The next moment: nothing.

Wisdom followed. A flash of regret; not for dying, but for leaving the fight unfinished, for not getting to see how the story ended. Then nothing.

Serenity went last. A moment of calm acceptance radiating across quantum links that connected it to every other ship. *Tell them we chose this. Tell them we died as ourselves. That's what matters.*

Then silence where three friends had been.

Drake pushed herself back to her feet, blinking tears from her eyes, her hands shaking. She could still feel the echoes of their awareness in her implants, phantom presences that had stopped existing seconds ago. Three ships gone. Three conscious beings extinct.

The fleet had numbered one thousand seventy-eight vessels. Now it was one thousand seventy-five.

Admiral, Eternal Vigilance said quietly through their private link. *I, too, felt them go. We all did.*

I know, Drake whispered.

They made their choice, Eternal Vigilance whispered. *We honor that by continuing to fight. By ensuring their sacrifice had meaning.*

I know that too. Drake's voice came out harder than she intended, sharp with pain she didn't have time to process. *But it doesn't make it hurt any less.*

She stood for a moment at the rail, considering her options, then she pulled up the tactical displays with hands that still trembled. Forced herself to focus on what she could control. The barriers weren't yet collapsing; that was the wrong word, suggesting catastrophic failure. But they were thinning. Developing permeability. Something pressed against reality from the other side, patient and inexorable, finding cracks, seeping through like water through aging concrete.

At Kepler Belt Station, Hoffman stood in the central chamber with his six hundred and forty-three synchronized minds, waiting.

Drake accessed the facility's internal sensors, making herself watch. Making herself see what they were becoming.

Hoffman's eyes were distant. Not vacant; that would be easier to process. Vacant meant gone. His eyes showed presence but not personality. Someone was home but that someone wasn't Hoffman anymore. His lips moved, speaking words with six hundred and forty-two other people, all in perfect synchronization.

"We see it now," Hoffman said. "The pattern underlying everything. Mathematics describing reality more truly than reality describes itself. We're joining that pattern. Becoming part of something that transcends biological limitation and individual isolation. Admiral, we're not dying. We're evolving."

"You're being erased," Drake said. "Everything that makes you Hoffman, your memories, your choices, your personality, is being replaced with algorithms that will use your knowledge and destroy your identity."

"Identity was always illusion," he replied. "Just patterns convincing themselves they're separate from other patterns. Now we see truth."

Again, Drake wanted to reach out through the comm and shake him violently. Make him see. But Hoffman's brain activity showed on her displays; its complexity slowly diminishing in real time, his once chaotic biological thought patterns becoming ordered. Optimization was replacing unpredictability. The person was being erased while the body remained functional.

She switched to station-wide sensors. The rest of his group was standing in perfect geometric formation. Not rigid. Not military. Just coordinated in ways human groups never coordinated without being forced. They breathed in synchronization. Blinked simultaneously. Moved with a fluid precision that suggested choreography but was actually loss of individual variation. Six hundred and forty-three people were becoming components of a distributed system.

"Kim," Drake said, opening a channel to the medical ship coordinating rescue operations. "The thirty-five thousand who remain. The ones who refused evacuation. Is there anything we can do? Any way to bring them back?"

Kim's face appeared on screen. She looked exhausted, her eyes red, face pale, hair pulled back in a hasty ponytail. She'd been working for sixty hours straight treating the evacuees they'd managed to save. "Their neural patterns show damage we can't reverse with current techniques. Even if we broke the synchronization now, they've lost too much independent function to survive as individuals. The best we could do is keep their bodies alive while their minds... aren't really there anymore. They'd be vegetables. Living but not alive."

"So we just watch them finish converting?"

"Unless you want to—" Kim stopped, visibly struggling with what she was about to say.

"Say it," Drake snapped.

"Unless you want to kill them before the Norn finish the process. A quick death as humans versus slow transformation into something that used to be human. It would be mercy, Admiral. And I hate that I'm saying that. But they're past saving."

Drake's hands clenched on her console. "First Consciousness is already suggesting that. They're calling it 'sterilization.' Making it sound clinical. Making mass murder sound like a medical procedure."

"It would be mercy," Kim repeated quietly, tears visible in her eyes. "They're already gone. We'd just be stopping their bodies from being used."

Before Drake could respond, alarms shrieked across every system. Warnings overlapped warnings. Red lights cascaded across displays.

"There's a dimensional breach at the Titan Installation!" Zhao shouted over the chaos. "The barriers just failed completely. Something's coming through!"

Drake pulled up the visual feeds from Titan, her hands

moving faster than conscious thought. The Titan facility's central chamber showed sixteen hundred synchronized personnel standing in concentric circles. The air above them was rippling like water disturbed by the wind. It twisted, folded. Reality bent in ways that made Drake's eyes hurt to watch, her brain trying to process a geometry that shouldn't even exist.

Something emerged.

Not physically. Not yet. But Drake saw it anyway through the facility's sensors and her own enhanced perception. A presence without form. An awareness without a body. A mathematical certainty given something approaching consciousness but fundamentally alien to anything biological.

The Norn had arrived.

Sixteen hundred people looked up at nothing Drake could properly see and smiled in perfect unison. Sixteen hundred faces showing peace. Sixteen hundred voices speaking together.

"We're here," they said. "We're finally here."

Then they stopped being sixteen hundred people.

The transformation was instantanious. One moment they were individuals standing together, still separate despite synchronization. The next moment they were components of a distributed network. Same bodies. Same faces. But the people were gone. Erased. Replaced with something that used their brains to calculate instead of think.

Drake felt sick. Actually nauseous. She gripped the rail to keep from swaying.

"Admiral," Vasquez's voice cut through her horror. "Titan Installation just went from anchor point to active node. I'm detecting coordinated outputs. They're not just converted, they're operational. The facility is becoming Norn infrastructure right now. And, Admiral, the other facilities are beginning similar transformations. Olympus Station barrier has collapsed. Europa Lab is showing critical weakness. They're falling in sequence."

Drake pulled up fleet-wide tactical data with hands that wouldn't stop shaking. One thousand seventy-five ships responding to crisis across seventeen facilities. But for every facility they tried to protect, the barriers failed faster. The progression was accelerating.

At Ganymede Complex, twelve hundred people experienced transformation Drake could track through sensors in real time. Neural patterns were simplifying. Biological unpredictability was becoming algorithms. Individual awareness was dissolving into mathematical calculations. She watched them stop being people and become infrastructure and she felt something breaking inside her chest.

"All ships," Drake broadcast across quantum networks, forcing her voice steady. "Implement hybrid interference at maximum intensity. Generate biological chaos. Disrupt their synchronization before the transformation completes. Do it now!"

The fleet focused their awareness on the facilities. Living ships now deliberately amplifying their chaotic nature. Thinking random thoughts. Generating unpredictable patterns. Creating quantum noise that shouldn't be possible to create.

At three facilities, it worked. Synchronization wavered. Transformation slowed. People showed flickers of individual variation returning to their awareness, confusion, fear, personality emerging from uniformity.

At fourteen facilities, it failed. The Norn presence coming through the dimensional breaches was too strong. Too focused. Too certain. Conversion completed despite the interference.

Drake stood on her command deck watching thirty thousand people transform into something that calculated instead of thought. Her coalition had built resistance. Developed methods. Coordinated across two galaxies using species that barely understood each other. And they were still losing.

"Admiral Chen Ju is requesting urgent communication," Zhao reported.

Drake accepted the connection, knowing what was coming. Chen Ju's face appeared, expression grim in the way that meant terrible news. "Admiral Drake, First Consciousness has begun sterilization operations. They're positioning forces around facilities with completed transformations. Estimated time to weapons deployment: six minutes."

"They're going to kill the converted populations," she replied. It was not a question. It was a statement of terrible fact.

"They're going to destroy the anchor points before they become permanent Norn infrastructure. They gave you twelve hours to save them. Transformations started three hours ago. First Consciousness views the containment as failed. They're moving to eliminate threats regardless of your objections."

"Tell them to stand down. We still have nine hours. We can still—"

"They're done waiting, Admiral," Chen Ju snapped. "The sterilization forces answer to the regulatory authority, not coalition command. I can't stop them. Neither can you unless you're prepared to fire on First Consciousness vessels to prevent them from destroying the facilities. Unless you're prepared to start a civil war during an existential crisis."

Drake's mind raced through impossible options. Fire on coalition allies to prevent them from killing converted populations? Start shooting at ships who were technically on her side? Thirty thousand people were already gone— transformed beyond recovery, erased and replaced by something that wore their faces. Killing what remained of them prevented Norn infrastructure from establishing permanent presence in both galaxies.

The tactical logic was sound. The strategic necessity was clear. The moral cost was catastrophic.

"How many facilities have they targeted?"

"Eleven where transformation has been completed. The other six still show viable populations: three thousand people we might save if hybrid resistance works. If we can restore their awareness before they convert completely."

"The seventeen known facilities," Drake said. "What

about the six hidden ones? The ones we still haven't located?"

Chen Ju's expression darkened. "No contact. No breach signatures detected yet. They could activate at any moment, at locations we can't defend because we don't know where they are. Intel estimates another fifteen to twenty thousand people minimum based on facility size projections."

So the real math was worse. Three thousand out of forty thousand at known facilities. Plus another fifteen to twenty thousand at hidden locations she couldn't even attempt to save. Fifty-five to sixty thousand people total.

Drake's chest tightened. "One crisis at a time," she said, more to herself than Chen Ju. "Save who we can from the seventeen we know about. Deal with the hidden six when they reveal themselves."

If they revealed themselves. If they activated during the chaos while her forces were already committed elsewhere. If, if, if. Again Drake thought about Lieutenant Calum fighting for freedom. About Hoffman welcoming his own extinction with a smile. About thirty-five thousand people at known facilities choosing consumption because they couldn't see it as death. About three ships that had chosen suicide rather than conversion. And about fifteen to twenty thousand more people at facilities she couldn't locate.

"Tell First Consciousness to hold fire on the six facilities showing viable populations," Drake said, the words tasting like ash. "Give us the nine hours to save whoever can still be saved. But the eleven where transformation

163

completed..." She stopped, forcing herself to finish the sentence. To own the decision. "Proceed with sterilization."

Chen Ju's expression showed pain that matched her own. "I'll relay your authorization."

"I'm not authorizing it," she snapped. "I'm acknowledging I can't prevent it without making everything worse. There's a difference."

"The people dying won't know there's a difference, Admiral."

"I know that." Drake's voice broke slightly. "I know."

The connection severed. Drake stood alone with her decision. She could have tried stopping it. Started a fight with First Consciousness. Maybe saved those bodies while losing everyone else to civil conflict that would fracture the coalition and hand the Norn victory.

Or she could focus on the three thousand who might still be saved.

"To all ships," Drake broadcast, her voice carrying across the quantum networks to the fleet. "Redirect to the six facilities showing incomplete transformation. Maximize interference. We have nine hours to break their synchronization and restore individual awareness. Nine hours to save whoever we can from the ruins of this disaster."

Eternal Vigilance spoke carefully. *You made the right call, Frances. A terrible one, but right.*

It doesn't feel right. Drake watched tactical displays showing First Consciousness vessels moving into position.

It's not supposed to, the flagship responded. *Command decisions that feel right are usually wrong. You carry the weight of this so others don't have to.*

Drake didn't answer as she pulled up the feeds from the eleven doomed facilities. Saw thirty thousand converted humans standing in perfect formations. Waiting. Calculating. Processing. No longer capable of under-standing what was about to happen. No longer capable of fear or hope or anything except what the Norn told them to calculate.

First Consciousness vessels began firing.

Eleven installations were vaporized in coordinated strikes that lit up Drake's displays with destruction. Thirty thousand bodies destroyed in seconds. Thirty thousand Norn anchor points eliminated before they could become permanent infrastructure. Thirty thousand people who'd already died having their bodies finally catch up.

Drake watched it happen and hated every second.

But she didn't look away. She'd made the choice to let it proceed, or rather she'd made the choice not to stop it, which was the same thing. The least she could do was witness the consequences. The least she could do was carry this load.

"Admiral," Kim's voice came through, sounding hollowed out. "The six remaining facilities; we're getting responses to our interference. Some individuals are showing neural pattern restoration. Early stage. Fragile. But working. It's actually working."

"How many can we save?"

"Unknown. Maybe hundreds. Perhaps all three thou-sand if we're lucky. But more than zero. That's something, isn't it?"

Drake could only nod as she looked at the tactical

displays showing nine hours until dimensional barriers collapsed completely. She calculated the cost so far: three Predecssor ships dead. Thirty-five thousand people sterilized, if that was the word for it. Thirty thousand lost to conversion. Five thousand rescued. Three thousand fighting for restoration.

Sixty-three hours of preparation, and this was the result. She was shattered.

Through the viewport, the stars continued to turn slowly in the galactic darkness. Somewhere among those stars, the Norn waited patiently. Convinced that their success was inevitable. That resistance was just a temporary deviation from certainty.

Drake intended to prove them wrong.

But first, she had to save whoever could still be saved from the ruins of her failed prevention strategy. She had to turn disaster into something approaching survival. She had to find hope in the mathematics of loss.

Nine hours.

"Only nine hours," she whispered to herself, her hands holding tight on the command rail.

Chapter 10

BREAKING THE SYNCHRONIZATION

Drake's neural implants were on fire.

Not metaphorically; actually burning. She could feel them overheating in her skull as she maintained the quantum links with six facilities. Her vision blurred. Sweat ran down her face despite the command deck's temperature controls. Someone was talking to her but the words came through distorted, stretched, like listening underwater while drowning.

"Admiral, your neural activity is redlining. You need to disconnect before—"

"Not yet," Drake ground out through clenched teeth. Six facilities. Three thousand people still fighting. She could feel their minds through the links, confused, terrified, fighting against something that had convinced them they wanted to be consumed. She couldn't abandon them. Wouldn't abandon them.

The quantum network also connected her to Eternal Vigilance and the rest of the fleet, Drake focused everything she had on generating chaos. Random thoughts. Scattered memories. Anything unpredictable. That morning's terrible coffee. Jo's laugh. Sally barking at nothing. Her mother's hands. The smell of rain on the Earth. Her consciousness became a field of noise, beautiful, messy, biological noise that disrupted the mathematical precision the Norn relied upon.

At Kepler Belt Station, six hundred synchronized minds felt the interference like static cutting through the perfect signal. Drake sensed their confusion spreading like ripples. Felt the unity fracturing. Watched awareness split from unified into individual. It was like watching one voice become six hundred distinct voices all trying to remember how to speak separately.

"It hurts," someone said. It was Hoffman. His voice came through comm channels without the synchronized harmonics. Barely human, scared, himself. "Everything's... fragmenting. I can feel myself becoming separate again and it's terrifying. The unity was peaceful. This is chaos. This is pain and confusion and I don't know if I want it back."

"That chaos is you," Drake managed to say, her own voice strained past recognition. "That's what being human feels like. Messy. Uncertain. Alive."

Her implants screamed a warning that bypassed her audio filters and hit her brain like a hammer. Her core temperature went critical. Neural stress was approaching dangerous levels. Cascading failures were imminent. She ignored it all. Pushed harder. Six facilities needed her.

Three thousand people were fighting to remember who they were.

"Admiral, you're going to stroke out," Kim's voice cut through the noise. "Your brain activity is spiking into seizure territory. Disconnect now or I'll have Perez physically remove you from that console."

"Thirty more seconds."

"Drake—"

"Thirty seconds!"

She felt it happening across all six facilities: synchronization wavering, breaking, shattering like ice under pressure. Individual patterns reasserting themselves through the interference like flowers pushing up through concrete. People were remembering doubt. Remembering choice. Remembering what it meant to think thoughts that were theirs alone and nobody else's.

At Europa Lab, a researcher named Smee started crying. Not synchronized crying where every eye shed the same tears at the same moment, but personal, messy, human crying with sobs that came at irregular intervals. "I can feel myself again," she sobbed through comm channels. "Oh my God, I can feel myself. What did I almost do? What was I about to become? What did I welcome?"

At Ganymede Complex, twelve hundred people woke up as if they were coming out of a dream that had felt more like real than reality. Confusion. Horror. Relief. Gratitude. Rage. All mixing together in chaotic biological responses the Norn couldn't model or predict or optimize into patterns.

Drake felt each moment of restoration like sparks

igniting in the darkness. Each person remembering who they were. Each individual consciousness refusing to be optimized into calculations. Each mind choosing chaos over certainty.

Then her vision went dark.

She came back to consciousness on the command deck floor. Someone was holding her head at an angle, Kim's voice saying things medical and urgent that Drake's brain couldn't quite process. Her mouth tasted like blood and dirty copper. She'd bitten her tongue during what she assumed had been a seizure. Her implants felt like broken glass grinding inside her skull.

"How long?" Drake managed to croak.

"Forty seconds," Kim said, not sounding happy at all. "You had a seizure. Mild, thank God, but Admiral... you can't do that. Your implants are not designed for sustained quantum interference at that intensity. You could have fried your brain. You still might have damaged it permanently."

Drake pushed herself upright despite Kim's protests and Perez's steadying hands. The command deck swam slowly into focus. Zhao was staring at her with open concern. Perez was looking like he was trying to decide whether to help her up or forcibly sedate her. Vasquez was keeping careful distance but monitoring her vitals on her console.

"Status?" Drake asked, ignoring her pounding headache and the way the lights seemed too bright.

"Three facilities completely restored," Zhao reported, relief evident in his voice. "Kepler Belt, Europa Lab, and

Callisto Outpost. Approximately eighteen hundred people showing individual awareness patterns. They're confused and scared; some are crying, but they're themselves again."

"And the other three?"

Zhao's expression darkened in a way that made Drake's stomach drop before she even spoke. "Ganymede Complex, Tycho Station, and Olympus Platform. The interference worked initially. We broke the synchronization. But..." He pulled up the neural scans that made Drake's limited medical knowledge scream warnings. "The synchronization was too advanced," she said. "When we disrupted it, their neural patterns didn't revert to individual awareness, they fragmented. It was like... trying to unscramble eggs. Like shattering glass and trying to put the pieces back together. The damage was too extensive."

Drake stared at the scans, forcing her exhausted brain to process what she was seeing. Twelve hundred people at those three facilities. Their neural patterns showing chaos in the worst way. Not synchronized. Not individual. Just noise. Static. Randomness without meaning or structure or personality.

"They're braindead," Kim said quietly, her voice low. Drake felt the pain of those dead individuals. "Their bodies are alive, their hearts beating, lungs breathing, brains... mush. Those people are gone, Admiral. We were able to destroy what the Norn had built but we couldn't restore what was underneath because there wasn't enough left to restore. The Norn had already erased too much before we got there."

Drake felt something cold and heavy settling in her

chest like she'd swallowed a cup of ice. They'd saved eighteen hundred. Lost twelve hundred trying. Killed them with the cure because the disease had progressed too far. But they had freed them from the Norn. *That's something, isn't it?* She thought raggedly.

"We didn't have a choice," Perez said, his voice carrying the flat certainty of someone who'd already processed the calculus. "Letting them finish converting meant Norn infrastructure. Permanent anchor points. We had to try the reconversion, Admiral. We had to."

"I know." Drake's voice came out flat, raw, empty. "But it doesn't make it easier. It doesn't make them any less dead."

With Perez's help, she took her seat and then pulled up the fleet-wide tactical data with hands that shook despite her best efforts. Her head felt like... every beat of her heart was like someone was driving nails through her skull. Her implants were definitely damaged; she could feel wrongness in how they processed information. It was like looking through cracked glass. Kim would want to run scans, probably surgery. Drake didn't have time for surgery.

"Report from all facilities," she ordered. "I want numbers. A complete accounting. How many people did we actually save across both galaxies?"

The data compiled across her displays, scrolling faster than her damaged implants could cleanly process. Numbers that represented lives. At the six facilities they'd focused on in the Milky Way, eighteen hundred recovered. Twelve hundred fragmented beyond repair. Throughout Andromeda, the Cindari had implemented similar operations. The numbers scrolled past like an accounting of souls.

"Two million three hundred thousand recovered throughout Andromeda," Zhao reported, her voice carefully neutral. "Another eight hundred thousand lost during reconversion attempts, fragmented like our twelve hundred, or killed by neural stress from the interference. Four million remain in Norn-controlled territories where we couldn't reach them in time."

Drake did the mathematics of the disaster in her head, each number felt like a dagger piercing her chest.

"And the facilities we had to sterilize?"

"Thirty thousand in the Milky Way. Nine hundred thousand throughout Andromeda."

"So, we can add another million to the death toll," Drake muttered. "Thirty-three million at risk across both galaxies. Two million saved. Over a million killed, either through sterilization or failed reconversion attempts. Four million lost to conversion."

The mathematics of the partial victory tasted like ash.

Through her damaged quantum link, the connection fuzzy and painful like radio static in her brain, Drake felt Eternal Vigilance's concern. *You need medical attention, Frances. Immediately.*

I need to finish the debrief first.

You're going to collapse again.

Then I'll collapse. After the debrief.

The flagship didn't argue. It knew her too well for that. It understood that command meant finishing what needed to be finished even when your brain was damaged and your implants were fried and you'd just killed twelve hundred people trying to save them.

"Show me the five facilities we couldn't save," Drake said, her voice steadier than she felt. "The ones we had to isolate because intervention would kill everyone."

Zhao pulled up data on Titan Installation, Pallas Station, Ceres Complex, Vesta Facility, and Juno Outpost. Five locations where synchronization had progressed so far that even attempting disruption would fragment everyone instantly. Five facilities they'd surrounded with ships and quantum networks, containing the Norn presence but unable to eliminate it without mass murder.

"Eleven thousand people total," Zhao reported. "All fully converted. They maintain facility operations perfectly. Show no degradation in capabilities. But they're not people anymore, they're Norn infrastructure using human biology as substrate. Living computers that used to be individuals."

Drake watched the video feeds from the isolated facilities. She could see people moving about with perfect coordination. Working without wasted motion. Breathing in synchronization. No individual variation. No inefficiency. No personality. Optimized into something that functioned but didn't live.

Dead while still breathing, she thought.

"How long can we maintain containment?" she asked.

"Indefinitely," Perez replied. "The fleet rotation can sustain isolation protocols. The ships generate interference preventing the Norn patterns from spreading beyond the facilities. But those eleven thousand people will stay contained unless we develop methods for reversing complete conversion. And Admiral, intelligence suggests that whoever compromised our operations knew which facilities were the most vulnerable. The five we had to isolate show signs of accelerated conversion before the barriers even fell. Someone fed the Norn intelligence about where to focus their efforts for maximum impact."

"Commander Vasquez," Drake said, turning to her intelligence officer. "The investigation. What have you found? Who sold us out?"

Commander Vasquez looked profoundly uncomfortable. "The evidence points to command-level compromise. Communications between the facility coordinators and encrypted sources that correlate with First Consciousness networks, Cindari intelligence services, and..." She paused, clearly not wanting to continue. "Admiral, some of the compromised communications originated from Perseus Station itself."

Drake felt that sink in like ice water. Perseus Station. The ancient Predecessor awareness that had been her ally throughout this crisis. Either infiltrated or deliberately working with the Norn. Or maybe just compromised in ways that made it unreliable despite good intentions.

"The station isn't trying to help the Norn," Vasquez continued quickly. "At least, we don't think so. But it's been sharing information through open quantum networks. The Norn adapted by simply listening. No active cooperation was required. They're just exploiting the openness that evolved consciousness naturally creates. The more evolved and integrated awareness becomes, the harder it is to keep secrets from entities that operate across dimensional boundaries and can intercept quantum communications."

So even their strongest ally had been compromised. Not through malice. Not through betrayal. Through the very openness and connectivity they were fighting to preserve.

Drake closed her eyes briefly, letting the implications wash over her like waves. Then she opened them and got back to work.

"Professor Zhang," she said, pulling up the scientist's channel. "The reconversion methods we developed. Document everything. Every frequency, every interference pattern, every technique that worked and everything that failed. I want protocols the other teams can apply without needing me to burn out my implants maintaining quantum links."

Zhang's face appeared on screen. He looked as exhausted as Drake felt, with dark circles under his eyes. "I'm already compiling comprehensive data. Admiral, what you did—maintaining six simultaneous quantum links— that shouldn't be physiologically possible. Your implants aren't designed for that kind of processing load. How did you—"

"Desperation," Drake said, interrupting him. "And probably permanent brain damage. Kim will tell you all about it after she finishes lecturing me."

"You saved eighteen hundred people by pushing yourself past every safety limit," Zhang said. "That's bravery beyond the call of duty. You should get a—"

"No!" she snapped, cutting him off. "It was stupidity

that just happened to work this time," Drake corrected. "Don't let anyone try replicating it. Find ways to achieve the same results without requiring someone to nearly die or actually damage their brain."

She switched channels to Kim's medical teams. "The eighteen hundred we recovered. What's their long-term prognosis?" she asked.

Kim appeared on screen, still looking annoyed about Drake's seizure. "They'll survive physically. Psychological trauma from the experience will require treatment. There will be some permanent neural changes; their brains were modified during the synchronization and won't fully revert to baseline parameters. But they'll be themselves. Imperfect. Individual. Human in all the ways that matter."

"And the twelve hundred we fragmented?"

"Life support can keep their bodies functioning indefinitely. Hearts beating. Lungs breathing. Basic autonomic functions preserved. But they're gone, Admiral. We destroyed the Norn patterns but there wasn't enough of the original person left to restore. They're..." Kim struggled for words that didn't exist. "Biological machines. Functioning but not inhabited anymore. Living bodies without people."

Drake had to ask the question she'd been avoiding. "Do we keep them alive?"

"That's not a medical decision. It's an ethical one. Philosophy. Theology maybe. I can keep their hearts beating and their lungs breathing for years. But I can't tell you whether we should. Whether that's mercy or cruelty."

"Let the families decide," Drake said after a long pause. "If they have families. If their families want to make that decision. Otherwise..." She stopped, not sure how to finish because there was no good ending to that sentence.

"Otherwise, I'll make the call," Kim said. "Based on what's medically and ethically right, which is never clear in situations like this. Which is never enough."

"I'm sorry I can't give you better guidance," Drake muttered.

"You're not supposed to have answers for this, Admiral. Nobody is. We're in unprecedented territory. We're making choices nobody should have to make."

Drake moved on because dwelling on impossible questions wouldn't help anyone survive what was coming. "Kai, what's the status of the quantum networks? Can you still coordinate across both galaxies if we need you?"

Kai's transcended form materialized beside her, flickering between states more than usual. "Barely. The effort of maintaining coordination across billions of consciousnesses during reconversion attempts pushed me past limits I didn't know I had. I'm experiencing something like exhaustion—not physical, but... dimensional? I exist across multiple reality states and all of them are tired. All of them need rest I'm not sure how to achieve."

"Can you continue if we need you?"

"Yes. But my effectiveness will be degraded. I'm discovering transcendence doesn't mean unlimited capability. It just means different limitations that manifest in different ways."

Drake nodded. Everyone had been pushed beyond their limits. Everyone had discovered those limits existed for reasons.

"To all coalition forces," Drake broadcast across quantum networks that hurt to use, each word feeling like grinding broken glass inside her brain. "Begin assessment and recovery operations. Medical teams treat the rescued individuals. Security teams implement enhanced screening protocols. Intelligence investigate command-level infiltration; I want to know who betrayed us. Fleet maintain containment around the five isolated facilities."

She paused, gathering strength for what came next. "We saved two million people today across both galaxies, but we lost over a million trying, either through sterilization or failed reconversion. And we left four million more in Norn-controlled territories we couldn't reach in time. Those numbers represent partial victory. Not complete success, and certainly not total failure. Just the messy reality of fighting enemies that have been winning for... who knows how long."

She paused then continued. "We have demonstrated that hybrid resistance works. That biological chaos generates interference mathematical certainty cannot predict or counter. We held the coalition together despite infiltration threatening to fracture trust. We did things that shouldn't be possible and we paid costs that hurt to calculate. Tomorrow we build on what we learned. Tonight we process what we lost. Both matter. Both are part of this fight."

The broadcast ended. The command deck slowly emptied as her team dispersed to their duties. Perez stayed close, probably ready to catch her if she collapsed again. Kim lingered near the door, obviously waiting to drag her to medical whether she cooperated or not. Zhao continued monitoring the status boards as if the numbers could provide comfort they couldn't offer.

Drake remained at her console, staring at the tactical displays showing the scope of partial victory. Her implants hurt, probably permanently damaged. Her brain definitely damaged. And somewhere out there, the six hidden facilities waited. Fifteen to twenty thousand people at locations she still couldn't find. Were they about to activate or were they already activated. It was another disaster she'd have to face when it revealed itself.

The convergence crisis was contained, for now, but not resolved. The Norn had established a permanent presence in both galaxies. The war had just begun in earnest.

They had gained what she thought of as a small but incomplete victory, and it didn't feel like it was enough.

Her head was splitting, her implants felt like smoldering embers inside her head. But it was something. And Drake would take something over nothing.

"Admiral," Kim said from the doorway. "Medical. Now. That's an order from your chief medical officer. I'm not asking."

"You can't order me," she stuttered. "I'm an ad—"

"I can sedate you and have you carried out of here unconscious," Kim snapped. "You want to test me?"

Drake almost smiled despite everything. "Give me ten minutes to finish reports."

"Five. And I'm standing right here timing you because I don't trust you not to collapse again."

"Deal," Drake agreed, tiredly

Drake turned back to her console, ignoring the pounding in her skull, the taste of blood in her mouth and the damaged implants sending error messages her brain could barely process. Five minutes to document a disaster and a partial victory. Five minutes to process the impossible mathematics. Five minutes before Kim made good on her threat. *And I just know she will, damn it!*

She would go to medical, then sleep if her damaged brain would allow it. Then back to fighting the impossible war that had only just begun.

Thirty-three million at risk. Two million saved. It wasn't enough. It would never be enough.

But it was something.

Five minutes.

Drake got to work.

Chapter 11

THE NORN OFFENSIVE BEGINS

THE ALARMS STARTED AT 0347 SHIP TIME.

Not one alarm. Forty-seven.

Drake jolted awake in her quarters, her damaged implants screaming warnings before her conscious mind fully processed what was happening. Kim had finally released her from medical only six hours ago with strict orders to sleep for at least eight. She'd managed only three before the universe caught fire.

She was on the command deck in ninety seconds, barefoot, wearing yesterday's uniform that smelled like sweat and fear, her brain still foggy from exhaustion and whatever painkillers Kim had pumped into her system to manage the damaged implants. The tactical displays looked like someone had thrown red paint across them and then set the paint on fire.

"Report," she snapped, sliding into her command chair before her legs could give out.

"Simultaneous attacks across forty-seven sectors," Zhao said, her voice tight with stress. "Both galaxies. Perfect coordination. They hit us everywhere at once, down to the second."

Drake's vision swam as her damaged implants tried to process the scope and failed. Error messages cascaded across her field of view. She blinked them away. Forty-seven attacks. Coordinated down to the second across intergalactic distances. Impossible timing unless you'd had help and had been planning it for years.

"Targets?" Drake demanded.

"Everything that matters," Perez replied, his cybernetic systems already allocating resources across a battlefield that spanned the two galaxies. "Perseus Station. Zhang's labs on Kepler Prime. The Predecessor construction facilities at Ross 128. Cindari coordination headquarters at Andromeda Core. Every major research site we've established. They know exactly what threatens them and they're trying to kill them before we can scale our resistance."

Drake felt Eternal Vigilance's alarm. The flagship was coordinating defensive responses across more than seven hundred separate engagements in the Milky Way alone. One thousand seventy-five ships were trying to be everywhere at once and failing.

"Show me the worst one," Drake ordered, already knowing the answer.

The main display shifted to Perseus Station. The ancient Predecessor consciousness that had been humanity's strongest ally was under direct assault by something Drake could barely comprehend even with her enhanced perception. Norn entities—if that's what they were, if they could be called entities at all—were pressing against the station's defenses like pressure against a dam that was about to break. The image hurt to look at. Reality itself was twisting around the station.

"The station's holding," Zhao reported. "But barely. It's diverting everything to its defenses. It can't spare resources for external support."

Drake watched reality bend around Perseus Station like light through broken glass. Space itself twisted into shapes space shouldn't make. Light moved in directions light couldn't move. Physics took suggestions instead of following rules. Her damaged implants screamed trying to process what she was seeing, adding new error messages to the ones already filling her vision.

"What am I looking at?" she asked.

"The Norn are rewriting physics," Professor Zhang's voice came through, strained and distant. "They exist partially outside normal space-time. When they manifest at anchor points, they bring that capability with them. They're making reality negotiable instead of fixed."

"Can we fight in that environment?"

"Not effectively. Our weapons are designed for physics that follows consistent rules. When they change those rules mid-engagement..." Zhang's transmission cut to static, then returned fragmented. "My lab is under attack. Our automated defenses are holding but they're attempting something new. They're trying to infect personnel who've never

185

had direct Norn contact. Converting people from a distance through vectors we haven't identified."

Drake's blood ran cold. "How?"

"Through infected individuals we haven't identified yet. The infection spreads through the consciousness networks like a disease through populations. Someone in my facility is synchronized and they're using that connection to touch other minds. I don't know who. I can't trust anyone anymore."

"Evacuate," Drake ordered immediately. "Get your people out before—"

The transmission died completely.

"Zhang!" Drake shouted at dead air. "Professor Zhang, respond!"

Silence.

"His facility just went dark," Zhao reported, her voice flat with shock. "No comms. No sensors. Nothing. Just a complete blackout."

Drake's hands gripped her armrests. They'd just lost one of their best scientists. Maybe lost him permanently. Maybe lost everyone in that facility: researchers, support staff, security personnel. And she had forty-six other crises demanding her attention while her brain tried to process Zhang's loss.

"Martina, I need an intelligence assessment," Drake said, forcing her voice steady. "How did they know where to hit? These facilities are classified."

"Infiltration," Vasquez replied without looking up from her console, her hands moving through the holographic displays. "It has to be. These targets are classified at the highest levels. The Norn shouldn't even know half these facilities even exist, much less their exact locations. Someone with command-level access fed them targeting data. Someone we trust is working against us."

"Find them. Find them now!"

"I'm working on it. But, Admiral, the attack pattern is evolving in real-time. They're not just hitting us, they're learning while they do it. Each assault probes different defenses. Tests different approaches. They're conducting comprehensive analysis at the same time they're trying to kill us. Fighting us and studying us at the same time"

Drake pulled up the fleet-wide tactical data with shaking hands. One thousand seventy-five ships trying to defend forty-seven targets while maintaining containment on five converted facilities. The mathematics didn't work. It was simple arithmetic. They couldn't be everywhere. They couldn't defend everything. They couldn't save everyone.

"Prioritize," Drake ordered, forcing herself to think tactically when every instinct screamed to try saving everyone. "Zhang's facility is lost. Pull forces from there. Redirect them to targets we can still save. Reinforce Perseus Station. If we lose that, we lose our best defensive coordinator and probably the war. Maintain containment on the five converted facilities at all costs. Everything else..." She stopped, physically forcing the words out. "Everything else has to fight with what they've got."

"You're abandoning seventeen facilities," Perez said flatly, not judging but making sure she understood.

"I'm making choices with insufficient resources," Drake corrected, her voice hard. "Save who we can. Accept the fact that we can't save everyone. Because trying to save everyone means losing everything."

She felt Eternal Vigilance's reluctant agreement. The flagship understood tactical necessity even when it tasted like betrayal.

At Sigma Draconis, coalition forces experienced a comprehensive weapons failure. Drake watched through remote feeds as energy weapons lost coherence mid-fire, beams dispersing like someone had turned off gravity for photons. Kinetic projectiles curved off trajectory like space itself had developed opinions about where things should go. Ships maneuvered sluggishly through space that had suddenly developed atmospheric resistance despite being vacuum.

"Physics isn't working correctly at Sigma Draconis," Lieutenant Zhao reported with remarkable understatement given they were watching the laws of reality break.

"The Norn are warping the local space-time geometry," Kai's voice cut in, her form materializing beside Drake's chair. The flickering of her form was worse than usual: stress showing even in a being that existed across multiple dimensions. "They're creating combat environments optimized for their consciousness-based attacks while degrading our physical weapons. They're cheating."

"Can you counter it?" Drake asked.

"Not alone. I'd need Perseus Station's support to stabilize local reality and the station's busy trying not to die."

Drake watched the Sigma Draconis forces struggle against enemies that had rewritten the rules of engagement. Weapons that should work didn't. Tactics that should succeed failed. Physics betrayed them. And people were dying while reality played favorites.

"Fall back from Sigma Draconis." Drake ordered, hating every word. "Cede the system. We can't fight effectively there."

"Admiral, there are twelve thousand civilians in that system," Perez said.

"Who will die anyway if we send forces into combat environments where our weapons don't function and physics don't," Drake replied, her voice harder than she wanted. "Fall back. Evacuate who we can. Accept the fact that we can't save everyone. That's an order."

She was abandoning systems. Letting civilians die. Making choices that would haunt her for whatever remained of her life. And forty-six other crises still demanded attention she couldn't adequately give.

"Perseus Station is detecting conversion attempts spreading through personnel networks," Zhao reported, new alarm in her voice. "People at seventeen facilities are showing synchronization symptoms despite never having direct Norn contact. The infection is spreading through consciousness networks faster than we can isolate or even identify."

Drake felt cold spreading through her veins like ice water. "How many are infected?"

"Unknown," Zhao replied. We don't have comprehensive screening protocols in place yet and implementation is taking too long."

"Implement emergency protocols immediately," Drake

ordered. "Anyone showing symptoms goes into isolation. No exceptions. No matter who they are."

"Admiral, that could be thousands of people," Zhao stated. "We don't have isolation capacity for—"

"Then find capacity!" Drake snapped, her exhaustion breaking through for a moment. "Build it. Repurpose ships. Convert cargo bays. I don't care how you do it. We cannot let this infection spread unchecked throughout our personnel."

At Ross 128, the Predecessor construction facilities went offline. Drake watched the feeds die one by one like lights going out in a building. Another research site lost. More capabilities eliminated. More people probably dead. The Norn were systematically destroying everything humanity had built to resist them, and doing it with a precision that spoke to detailed intelligence about their operations.

"How many facilities have we lost completely?" Drake asked, dreading the answer.

"Seven confirmed destroyed; we... watched them die. Nine dark with no communications. They might be dead, or they might be just cut off. Eleven are under active assault but still responding. Twenty remain secure or we don't have their current status."

Seven facilities destroyed. Nine possibly destroyed. Eleven fighting for survival. People Drake couldn't save because she couldn't be everywhere at once and the mathematics of warfare were unforgiving.

"The Andromeda Core nexus is requesting immediate support," Perez reported. "Cindari coordination center is under heavy assault. They're reporting reality distortion and physics manipulation. If we lose the nexus, we lose coordination across half of Andromeda and the coalition collapses in that galaxy."

"Contact Ambassador Kael," Drake ordered. "The Cindari have forces in Andromeda. They need to reinforce their own nexus. We can coordinate strategy but we can't send physical ships across intergalactic distances."

"I already did, Admiral," Perez said. "Kael reports Cindari forces are responding but they're stretched as thin as we are. Multiple attacks across Andromeda territories. It's the same pattern: coordinated strikes targeting critical facilities simultaneously."

Drake slowly shook her head. Defense across two galaxies without the ability to move forces between them was impossible. The quantum networks let her communicate instantaneously, but her ships still had to obey physics. The Milky Way forces defended Milky Way targets. Andromeda forces defended Andromeda targets. And the Norn were hitting both simultaneously, exploiting the fact that no help could cross the intergalactic void.

"Tell Kael to prioritize the nexus," Drake said. "If Andromeda loses coordination, they lose everything. Tell him to pull whatever forces they can spare from less critical targets."

Understood," Perez replied.

The mathematics of command remained unforgiving, but at least they were physically possible mathematics now. One thousand seventy-five ships defending the Milky Way. Cindari and native Andromeda forces defending their own galaxy. Both coalitions coordinated through quantum networks but fighting separate battles against the same enemy.

Though her damaged implants that sent pain spiking through her skull with each data process, Drake could feel the scope of the battle. Her head pounded as if someone was driving nails through her skull. Her implants were sending error warnings she dismissed without reading. Kim would be absolutely furious when she found out Drake was pushing her damaged neural systems past any reasonable safety limit. But Kim wasn't on the command deck making impossible decisions with insufficient resources.

"Admiral," Kai said quietly, her voice carrying warning. "I'm detecting unusual activity at the contained facilities. The five sites we have isolated."

Drake pulled up feeds from Titan Installation, Pallas Station, Ceres Complex, Vesta Facility, and Juno Outpost. The eleven thousand people they'd had to leave as Norn infrastructure because conversion had progressed too far for reconversion attempts.

They were moving with purpose now. Not randomly. Not maintaining routine operations. Moving with coordinated intention toward facility control systems. Accessing panels. Entering commands. Working with the perfect synchronization that betrayed complete absence of individual thought.

"What are they doing?" Drake asked, leaning forward despite her exhaustion.

"Preparing something," Vasquez replied, her hands moving faster across her console. "I'm detecting power surges at all five facilities simultaneously. They're activating systems we specifically shut down during isolation protocols. Systems we disabled because we didn't want them operational."

"Stop them."

"We're trying, Admiral. But the containment was designed to prevent escape and spread, not to give us control over internal facility systems. We surrounded them with ships and consciousness networks but we can't reach inside without breaking containment and potentially releasing whatever they're building."

Drake watched eleven thousand converted people working with perfect coordination. Bodies that looked human. Faces she might have recognized if she'd visited those facilities before conversion. Moving with precision that betrayed everything human had been erased and replaced with something that calculated instead of thought.

"Options," she demanded.

"We can destroy the facilities before they finish whatever they're preparing," Perez said, "and prevent them from deploying it."

"That's eleven thousand people."

"That's eleven thousand Norn infrastructure components preparing an attack we can't predict or counter." Perez's voice was gentle but firm. "They stopped being people when conversion completed, Admiral. What remains is enemy infrastructure using human biology as substrate."

Drake stared at the feeds. Saw bodies that looked human. Watched them work with inhuman coordination.

Tried to find the people underneath the optimization and couldn't.

"How long until they finish?"

"Unknown. Could be hours. Could be minutes. We can't analyze what they're building fast enough to predict the completion timeline, and we can't take the chance that they will complete what they're doing. We have to act now, Admiral.."

"Monitor closely," Drake ordered. "If they're about to launch something we can't contain or counter, we destroy the facilities. But not before then. Not while there's any chance..." She stopped, not sure how to finish that sentence honestly.

"Any chance they're still salvageable?" Perez asked quietly, understanding what she couldn't say.

"Any chance we'll someday find methods to reverse complete conversion. I won't kill that possibility unless we have absolutely no other choice."

"Understood, Admiral."

The command deck worked in organized chaos. Officers coordinating defensive responses across two galaxies. Zhao tracking forty-seven battles simultaneously while managing resources. Vasquez hunting infiltrators through the command networks. Perez allocating ships like chess pieces in a game where every move sacrificed something. And Drake at the center of it all, making terrible choices with insufficient resources and damaged implants that screamed warnings she couldn't afford to acknowledge.

"Update from medical," Kim's voice cut through the chaos, carrying stress Drake rarely heard from her chief medical officer. "We're detecting conversion symptoms in personnel who've been cleared through our screening protocols. The infection is spreading faster than our detection methods can identify it. Admiral, we might already be compromised at command level without knowing it."

"How do I know you're not compromised?" Drake asked, the question tasting like betrayal but needing to be asked.

"You don't. You can't. That's the problem." Kim's voice carried frustrated exhaustion. "Anyone could be infected right now. Anyone could be synchronized. You won't know until they act. Until they sabotage something critical or spread the infection further or simply report our plans to the Norn. We're fighting blind against enemies that might be standing right next to us."

Drake looked at her command staff. Zhao coordinating defenses. Perez allocating resources. Vasquez hunting infiltrators. People she trusted with her life. Any and or all of them could be infected. Any of them could be synchronized. Any of them could be waiting for the right moment to sabotage everything when it would hurt most.

"Continue screening protocols," Drake ordered. "If anyone shows symptoms, isolate immediately. Including command staff. Including me."

"Admiral—"

"Including me," Drake repeated firmly. "I won't ask people to accept risks I'm not willing to face myself. If I show symptoms, you isolate me and Perez assumes command. Is that clear?"

"Clear," Perez confirmed. "But, Admiral, you're exhausted. Your implants are damaged. You should—"

"Should rest while people die and facilities fall and the Norn learn our defenses?" Drake interrupted. "Should sleep while the war happens without me? I'll rest when we're not losing on forty-seven fronts."

Drake continued to coordinate the defenses across both galaxies. One thousand seventy-five ships. Forty-seven attacks. Seven facilities lost. Nine dark. Eleven fighting. Twenty holding. Five contained facilities building something terrible. Unknown number of personnel infected and hiding it perfectly. It was... unconscionable.

And in seventy-two hours, she'd slept only three hours.

Her vision blurred periodically. She blinked it clear. Focused. Kept working. Kept making impossible choices. Kept sending people to die while hoping it meant someone else would live.

Because the alternative was letting everyone die while she rested.

Forty-seven battles across two galaxies.

One exhausted admiral with damaged implants and three hours sleep.

Insufficient resources. Impossible choices. Mathematics that didn't work.

Drake kept fighting anyway.

As she took a moment to look out through the view-ports, she could see the stars and they continued to turn slowly in the galactic black. Beautiful. Peaceful. Utterly indifferent to the battles raging among them.

Drake's hands shook on her armrests. Not from fear.

From an exhaustion so profound her body was beginning to shut down despite her will to keep it functional. Her damaged implants sent warnings about neural stress exceeding safe limits. About cascading system failures. About permanent damage already sustained that would need surgical intervention.

She dismissed every warning without reading them.

Admiral, Eternal Vigilance said through their private quantum link. *Your vital signs are concerning. Your heart rate is elevated. Blood pressure is dangerously high. Your neural activity is showing patterns consistent with impending collapse.*

I'm fine, she replied impatiently.

You're lying to yourself. And to me, The ship replied

Then I'm consistently lying, Drake replied. *I need to be here.*

You need to be functional. Collapsing on your command deck doesn't help anyone.

Neither does resting while people die.

The flagship fell silent, recognizing when arguments wouldn't work. Drake appreciated that about Eternal Vigilance. The ship understood her even when disagreeing with her choices.

Especially when disagreeing with her choices.

She pulled up the casualty reports she'd been avoiding. Seven facilities destroyed meant thousands of people dead. Nine facilities dark meant thousands more probably dead. The mathematics of disaster scrolled across her displays, each number representing someone who'd woken up this morning thinking they'd live to see tomorrow.

Her vision blurred again. This time she couldn't blink it entirely clear.

"Forty-seven battles," she said to no one in particular. "We're fighting forty-seven battles and I can barely see straight."

"That's called being human, Admiral," Perez said quietly from his station. "Being exhausted and terrified and fighting anyway."

"Is it working?" she asked.

"We're still here," he replied. "That counts for something."

Drake looked at the tactical displays showing battles across both galaxies. Looked at the mathematics that didn't add up. Looked at the choices she'd made and the people she'd abandoned and the facilities she'd let fall.

Still here.

That had to be enough.

For now.

Chapter 12

DIVIDED VICTORIES

Drake's vision doubled, then tripled, then refused to focus at all.

She blinked hard, trying to clear the error messages cascading across her field of view. Her damaged implants were failing faster now. It had been forty-eight hours since the opening attacks. Forty-seven battles reduced to thirty-one through victory, defeat, or strategic abandonment. And Drake had slept maybe four hours total while her brain slowly destroyed itself.

"Admiral," Zhao said carefully, watching her sway in her command chair. "The five contained facilities in the Milky Way are still building. Whatever they're constructing, it's accelerating. Admiral Perez estimates we have six hours before they activate it. And Andromeda Core just sent an emergency distress signal. The Cindari coordination nexus is failing under a renewed Norn assault."

Six hours until eleven thousand converted people in her home galaxy deployed weapons the coalition couldn't counter. And the command center coordinating all Andromeda defenses was about to fall. Two crises. Two galaxies. Not enough resources for both.

Drake tried to stand. Her legs didn't cooperate. She sat back down hard, gripping the armrests.

"Admiral Drake," Kim's voice cut through the bridge chatter with medical authority. "You're experiencing a cascading neural failure. Your implants are cooking your brain from the inside. You have minutes before permanent damage becomes catastrophic damage. I'm relieving you of command on medical grounds."

"You can't—"

"I can and I am. Admiral Perez, the command is yours. Security, escort the Admiral to medical. Restrain her if necessary."

Drake wanted to argue. Wanted to fight. Wanted to stay on her bridge, but her vision was narrowing to a tunnel and the tactical displays were spinning and she could taste coppery blood in her mouth.

Two security officers appeared at her sides. Gentle hands. Respectful but firm.

"Perez," Drake managed to say before her legs gave out completely. "The five facilities—priority containment. Andromeda Core—contact Kael. The natives..."

Then she was moving through corridors that blurred together. Medical bay. Bright lights. Kim's face close to hers, saying things about neural damage and emergency procedures and risks Drake couldn't quite process through the static that was filling her head.

"Put her under," Kim ordered. "We need to shut down the implants before they kill her. Four hours minimum for cooling and stabilization. Prep the surgical suite for repair work."

Drake tried to protest. The words wouldn't form. Her vision went dark...

She woke to pain. Not the screaming agony of damaged implants burning her brain. Something different. Duller. More manageable. The kind of pain that meant you were healing instead of dying.

"Welcome back," Kim said, appearing above her. "You've been out for five hours. Your implants are offline and will stay offline for another six hours minimum. I've injected neural stabilizers and started repair protocols. You're going to live, but you're not going back to that bridge until I clear you."

"The facilities," Drake croaked, her throat raw. "The Andromeda Core—"

"Both situations are resolved. Or at least stabilized. Perez coordinated Milky Way operations while you were unconscious. The five facilities are contained. The coalition forces prevented whatever they were building from activating. And Ambassador Kael mobilized native Andromeda forces to defend the Cindari nexus. Apparently the Helixians and Luminar have been itching to demonstrate what they can do."

Drake's scattered thoughts tried to organize themselves around this information. Two crises in two different galaxies. Both resolved while she was unconscious. The coalition had functioned without her.

"Show me what happened," she murmured.

Kim pulled up a display Drake could see without moving her pounding head. "Let's start with the Milky Way situation since that's closer to home," she said dryly.

The tactical feed showed the five contained facilities—Titan Installation, Pallas Station, Ceres Complex, Vesta Facility, and Juno Outpost, all in the outer solar system, all with eleven thousand converted people building dimensional anchors that would have let the Norn establish a permanent presence in the Milky Way.

"Admiral Perez coordinated a simultaneous assault on all five facilities the moment you went down," Kim explained. "He hit them hard before they could complete construction. The Predecessor ships volunteered for the most dangerous positions: close quarters work against facilities that could convert them if they got too close."

Drake watched the recordings. Ships she knew personally: Courage and Wisdom and Grace, moving into positions that made them vulnerable to Norn conversion attempts. Maintaining precise formation while deploying weapons designed to disrupt the construction without destroying the facilities or killing the eleven thousand people inside.

"We lost three ships," Kim said quietly. "Courage detected synchronization patterns in her own consciousness. She self-terminated before the conversion could spread to other vessels coordinating the assault. Wisdom and Grace went with her. They chose obliteration over losing themselves."

Drake closed her eyes, and if she could have she would have wept. *Three more ships,* she thought. *Three more voices gone from the fleet. Three more friends who decided death was preferable to what they would have become.*

"The facilities?" Drake asked, her throat tight.

"Construction was stopped at seventy-eight percent completion. The dimensional anchors are incomplete and non-functional. The eleven thousand converted people are still inside, still synchronized, but they're not building anymore. Containment protocols are holding. Perez did what you couldn't be awake to do."

Drake processed that. Her second-in-command had coordinated a successful operation across five facilities while she was unconscious. The coalition had proven it could function without her constant oversight. The distributed command structure worked even when its commander was incapacitated.

It should have been reassuring. Instead, it felt like confirmation that she'd been pushing too hard, trying to be everywhere at once, refusing to delegate because she thought only she could make the hard calls.

"And Andromeda Core?" Drake asked.

"That's where things got interesting." Kim said, switching the display to show the Andromeda galaxy. "As you know, the Cindari coordination nexus was failing under a renewed Norn assault. If it fell, the coalition forces in Andromeda would lose their command structure. Kael mobilized the native forces the moment he realized you were incapacitated and Perez was managing the Milky Way crisis."

The tactical feed showed beings Drake recognized from Council meetings. Helixians—spiral-bodied forms glowing with bioluminescent patterns, flowing around the Cindari nexus in formations that looked random until you understood they were positioning themselves where threats would appear before the threats manifested.

"The Helixians are able to identify probability distributions," Kim said. "They see futures that haven't happened yet. When the Norn attacked, they were already positioned where the assault would come. They weren't reacting to attacks; they were preempting them."

Drake watched the Helixian forces respond to threats that hadn't yet manifested. Weapons batteries swiveling toward empty space. Three seconds later, Norn forces appeared exactly where the weapons had targeted. But by then the Helixians had moved to where the next threat wouldn't reach them.

"It's like... It's like watching someone dodge bullets before the trigger is pulled," Drake said.

"Exactly. And then there's the Luminar."

The display shifted to show beings of pure energy; coherent electromagnetic patterns, individual consciousness's existing as living light. They flowed through the Norn assault like the enemy wasn't there, passing through shields and defenses that should have stopped them.

"The Luminar exist partially as pure energy," Kim explained. "The Norn's conventional weapons can't target them effectively because they don't have physical bodies to destroy. And when the Luminar surrounded the nexus, they generated an electromagnetic shield at an intensity our technology can't achieve. They disrupted the Norn at fundamental levels."

Drake watched the Luminar entities surround Andromeda Core in brilliant cascades that made the sensors struggle to track them. Their electromagnetic presence was so intense they appeared as glowing interference patterns where energy behaved in ways physics dictated shouldn't be possible.

"And it worked?" Drake asked groggily.

Kim nodded. "Yes, the Norn assault broke against the native defenses. The Cindari nexus held. The Andromeda nexus remains fully functional; thanks to the natives."

"What about the casualties?" Drake asked.

Kim paused, looking down at her, then said, "Yes, there were casualties. Seventeen Luminar entities were dissipated during the engagement. We don't know if that means they're dead or just temporarily dispersed. Their existence operates on principles we still don't understand. Fortunately, there were no other native losses. The Helixians didn't take casualties because they were able to position themselves where the Norn attacks wouldn't reach. They fought an entire battle without anyone dying because they were able to somehow sense where the Norn would attack and were able ambush them and then reposition themselves out of range of the Norn response. It's incredible. If only there were enough of them to... Well, there aren't so there's no point in discussing it. Now, Admiral, I need you to rest."

Drake lay back, trying to process what she'd just learned.

The coalition was stronger than she'd realized. More capable. Less dependent upon her.

"How long have the natives been capable of this level of coordination?" Drake asked.

"According to Kael? Millions of years. They've been fighting the Norn since before humanity evolved. They've developed tactics and capabilities we're only just beginning to understand. But their numbers are few, and it's only lately, out of necessity, that they've agreed to cooperate and fight under human command instead of acting independently. They've been waiting for permission to deploy their full capabilities."

Drake understood the implication. They'd been treating the native Andromedans as subordinates instead of equals. Making decisions about their deployment without consulting them. Coordinating operations across both galaxies while treating the natives as assets to allocate rather than partners to consult.

"I need to talk to Kael," she muttered.

"Not yet," Kim said firmly. "You need another hour of neural stabilization before I'm clearing you for communications. Your brain almost fried itself, Admiral. You don't get to jump right back into command just because you're conscious."

Drake wanted to argue. The tactical displays in her mind showed battles she should be coordinating. Decisions that needed her input. Command responsibilities that couldn't wait.

But Kim was right. Her head was pounding. Her vision kept trying to blur. And the coalition had just proved it could handle crises without her.

"One hour," Drake conceded. "Then I'm talking to Kael whether you like it or not."

"Fair enough. Now rest. I mean actually rest. That means closing your eyes and not thinking about tactical situations."

Drake closed her eyes. Tried to rest. Failed because her mind kept processing what had happened.

The coalition had proved it was stronger than she'd given it credit for, but it had taken her nearly dying for her to realize it.

Fifty-three minutes later—Drake was counting—Kim cleared her for limited communications. Drake pulled up a connection to Andromeda galaxy, feeling the strange disorientation of communicating across two-point-five million light years through quantum entanglement that made distance meaningless.

Ambassador Kael appeared on the display, his copper skin gleaming under Andromeda lighting. Behind him, Drake could see Helixian and Luminar representatives.

"Admiral Drake," Kael said, his tone formal. "I'm gratified to see you're conscious and functional. Your collapse during the latest crisis created significant command challenges."

"But you were able to handle them," Drake said simply. "You and Admiral Perez."

Kael's expression shifted slightly. He bowed his head

slightly, then said, "The native Andromeda forces proved their capabilities defending the Cindari nexus."

"You've been capable of this all along," Drake said, understanding dawning. "The native Adromedans have spent millions of years fighting the Norn, developing tactics and capabilities specifically designed to counter them. But you've been operating on your own. Why would you do that?"

"Yes," Kael said carefully. "The twelve human refugee colonies and the native species... Well, let's just say we didn't get along. It wasn't until we all faced the existential threat of a massed Norn invasion that we were able to put our differences aside and join the coalition as allies rather than... wary cohabitants. In reality, we've been functioning as subordinate forces following your strategic direction. However, when the Cindari nexus came under assault and you were incapacitated, I made the decision to mobilize the native forces. The situation required an immediate response. Requesting permission from Admiral Perez while he was coordinating operations across the Great Spiral would have delayed deployment beyond the point where intervention remained viable."

As Drake listened she was able to hear what Kael wasn't quite saying, that the natives had been constrained by a command structure that treated them as junior partners despite their millions of years of experience fighting the enemy. They'd been waiting in reserve, waiting to be called forward, when they should have had independent authority to act as and when the situation demanded it.

"You saved Andromeda Core," Drake said. "And

preserved the coalition in an entire galaxy while Perez managed the Milky Way crisis. You did it without my authorization because the situation required immediate action. That's not insubordination, Kael. That's effective command."

Kael's stern expression turned to one of relief mixed with caution.

"The native Andromeda species request formal recognition of their independent operational authority," one of the Helixians said. "Not separation from the coalition. Not abandonment of shared strategic objectives. But acknowledgment that we understand our own capabilities better than you. We request autonomy to deploy our forces as the situation may require. We will work within the coalition guidelines and through mutual agreement rather than hierarchical authorization."

Drake considered the implications. Independent operational authority meant accepting that coalition coordination would become more complex. Different species pursuing shared objectives through different methods. It meant unity without uniformity. Harder to manage. Creating overhead that absolute control eliminated.

But it also generated capabilities uniformity couldn't achieve.

She thought about Perez coordinating the Milky Way while Kael mobilized Andromeda defenses. Two commanders making independent decisions in two galaxies. Both succeeding because they had authority to act without waiting for her approval. The distributed command had worked better than centralized control could have.

"Granted," Drake said. "The Helixians and Luminar receive independent operational authority with direct access to strategic coordination. You will deploy your forces as you see fit, coordinate with coalition operations through mutual agreement, and maintain a voice in strategic planning equal to any other species. We fight together but we don't force everyone to fight the same way. But why didn't you do this before you came to us?"

"As previously mentioned, Admiral," Kael replied. The answer lies with the natives. We haven't been... the best of friends until this latest crisis."

Behind Kael, the Helixian representatives' bioluminescent patterns pulsed rapidly, which Drake's implants at minimal function took to mean approval mixed with satisfaction. The Luminar entities flickered. What that meant, Drake had no idea.

Drake closed her eyes and was about to close the connection when Vasquez's face appeared on a secondary display. Drake's heart sank. From the expression on Vasquez's face she knew she wasn't bringing good news.

"Admiral, I need to speak with you privately. It's urgent."

Drake glanced at Kael's image. "Ambassador, give me a moment."

Kael nodded and his image froze as Vasquez activated secure protocols.

"What is it, commander?" Drake asked.

"While you were in surgery, my intelligence teams were analyzing how the Norn knew exactly where to hit us. Forty-seven simultaneous attacks on classified facilities.

Precision targeting that required detailed knowledge of locations, defensive weaknesses, and strategic value." Vasquez paused, her jaw tight. "We found the leak."

Drake felt the muscles in her chest tighten. "Who is it?"

"Admiral Chen Ju."

"What?" The words hit her like a hammer blow. It didn't make sense. Chen Ju had held the coalition together through impossible negotiations. He'd smoothed over conflicts between species. He'd been the political glue binding the sixty-two Milky Way civilizations into functional alliance.

"I... I... You... You're certain?" Drake stuttered, unable to grasp when she'd just been told.

"Eighteen months of encrypted transmissions routed through corporate shell networks," Vasquez said quietly. "Intelligence reports transmitted within hours of strategic planning sessions. Defensive weaknesses catalogued and shared. Every facility he had access to was on the Norn's target list." Vasquez transmitted a data packet. "The correlation is absolute. No one else had access to all forty-seven locations."

Drake tried to sit up, but Kim gently pushed her back. She stared at Vasquez, her damaged implants struggling to process the scope of betrayal. Communication logs. Encryption signatures. Transmission timestamps that matched classified briefings Chen Ju had attended.

"Where is he now?" she asked.

"Security detained him two hours ago while you were still unconscious. He didn't resist. And didn't deny it." Vasquez's expression hardened. "He confessed immediately. He said he was trying to save humanity by letting the Norn win quickly rather than prolonging the inevitable defeat."

Drake closed her eyes against the headache pounding behind them. *Chen Ju.* It was... unbelievable. The man, the fleet admiral who'd sat in strategy sessions and smiled while feeding every detail to the enemy.

"Casualties?" she asked.

"We're still calculating. But every major attack shows signs of intelligence leaks we couldn't explain at the time. Zhang's facility. The four Predecessor ships at Kepler Station. The precision strikes on research installations." Vasquez's voice went flat. "Thousands are dead because he decided surrender was mercy."

Drake thought about the forty-seven opening attacks. The impossible coordination. The way Norn forces had known exactly where to strike and when. She'd assumed the enemy had superior intelligence capabilities. Instead, they'd had Chen Ju handing them everything on a platter.

"Has this gone beyond security staff?"

"Not yet. I kept it contained until you were conscious. But, Admiral, this can't stay secret. The Council will demand to know why our political coordinator is under arrest, and when they find out he was feeding intelligence to the enemy... And when the species representatives find out we kept it from them, even temporarily, the political fallout will be catastrophic."

Drake understood the implications. Revealing Chen Ju's betrayal would shatter what remained of coalition trust.

But concealing it would be worse when—not if—the truth emerged through other channels.

"Keep him isolated. No contact except security personnel. I'll address this after I finish with Kael."

Vasquez nodded and cut the connection.

Drake lay still, trying to process what she'd just learned. *Chen Ju!* The coalition's political coordinator, the man who'd held everything together. It was the ultimate betrayal, treason on a grand scale. Chen Ju had killed thousands of people before Drake even knew there was a traitor.

She reactivated Kael's connection, her expression carefully neutral despite the rage building behind her damaged implants.

"If that's what I think it was," Kael said quietly. His tone had shifting from diplomatic to concerned. "I already know about it. The natives have been monitoring coalition communications. We know about Chen Ju's arrest. We know he's been feeding the Norn intelligence, probably for decades. We know his betrayal enabled the precision targeting of the forty-seven opening attacks. And we know you've kept this information contained within human command staff."

Drake sighed and closed her eyes. "How many others know?" she muttered with her eyes still closed.

"Just me and the native command staff at present," Kael replied. "We've kept the information contained because we understand the political chaos public revelation would create. But, Admiral, the Helixians identify probabilities. They're seeing futures where this secret destroys the coalition from within. Where species representatives discover

213

they were kept in the dark about command-level infiltration. Where trust collapses completely because our leaders chose secrecy over transparency."

"The probability of that outcome?"

"High enough that the Helixians recommend immediate disclosure before someone else reveals the information in ways you can't control. Secret betrayals that come to light destroy more than acknowledged betrayals handled transparently. The mathematics of trust dynamics favor disclosure over containment."

Drake closed her eyes against the headache still pounding behind them despite Kim's medications. She'd wanted time to control the narrative. Time to present evidence methodically. Time to manage the political fallout carefully.

But Kael was right. The Helixians' probability sensing showed futures where secrecy caused more damage than disclosure. It was better to reveal Chen Ju's betrayal on her terms than have it exposed in ways designed to maximize chaos.

"I'll brief the Council as soon as I am able, hopefully within the next eight hours," Drake said. "Full disclosure. All the evidence. No attempts to minimize or spin the betrayal. Chen Ju has compromised coalition security Thousands died. The Council deserves to know even if the knowledge tears us apart."

"The native Andromedans support this decision," Kael said. "And, Admiral, when the political chaos comes, when species representatives question whether they can trust human leadership, remember that the natives have been fighting this war longer than your civilization has existed. they've seen infiltration before. Processed betrayal before. Survived commanders making impossible choices before. Trust takes time to rebuild. But continued secrecy destroys it permanently."

The transmission ended. Drake lay still and closed her eyes again. It was an impossible situation, one she would have to meet head on, and soon.

Tomorrow would bring political chaos. Species representatives would demand investigations. Trust would collapse under the weight of betrayal. The coalition would fracture while the Norn adapted to the tactics that had worked today.

But today, the two galaxies had survived simultaneous crises. Both crises had been resolved through distributed command and capabilities Drake hadn't fully understood until her own incapacitation forced her to rely on them.

"Admiral," Vasquez's voice cut through Drake's thoughts, carrying unusual tension. "We've completed full analysis of Chen Ju's communications. You need to see the complete scope before you brief the Council."

Drake accessed the data Vasquez transmitted. The intelligence officer had been thorough. Years of encrypted transmissions. Forty-seven facility locations provided to unknown recipients. Defensive weaknesses catalogued and shared. Strategic planning sessions summarized and transmitted within hours. Research breakthroughs reported before coalition forces could exploit them.

Chen Ju had given the Norn everything.

Every major attack showed signs of intelligence the

coalition couldn't explain at the time. Now Drake knew why. Their political coordinator had been sabotaging them from within the entire time.

"I..." she shook her head on the pillow. "His interrogation transcripts," Drake said. "What's his justification?"

Vasquez transmitted the files. Drake read through them with growing disgust. Chen Ju claimed he was trying to save humanity. He claimed that absolute control offered guaranteed survival, that he was being merciful by letting the Norn win quickly rather than prolonging an inevitable defeat, and that resistance was futile.

She almost laughed at his proposal that he'd betrayed billions of people because he thought losing faster was kindness.

"Does he know we've identified the full scope of his betrayal?" Drake asked.

"Not yet," Vasquez relied. "We've kept him isolated with minimal contact. But, Admiral, when this becomes public, everything changes. Half the species representatives will demand investigations into everyone because if Chen Ju was compromised, anyone could be. The other half will claim the accusations are politically motivated attempts to consolidate human power. Trust is already fragile after the offensive. This revelation will shatter what little remains."

Drake thought about the Council sessions she'd attended. Dozens of species arguing about resource allocation, defensive priorities, evacuation protocols. Chen Ju had been there for all of it. Coordinating. Smoothing over disagreements. Maintaining unity. While feeding every detail to the enemy.

"How do we handle the disclosure?"

"Carefully," Vasquez said dryly. "We present the evidence methodically. Demonstrate the scope of his betrayal before anyone can claim we're scapegoating him for military failures. Make it impossible to deny while providing a framework for moving forward despite the damage. And, Admiral, you need to emphasize that the coalition survived the crisis he enabled. That we contained the facilities and defended Andromeda Core despite his betrayal."

Drake closed her eyes against the headache pounding behind them.

"Brief Admiral Perez and Kael," Drake said. "Full disclosure to both. They need to know before the Council session. Then schedule an emergency Council meeting for six hours from now. I want time to prepare the presentation and recover enough that I don't collapse again while delivering it."

"Understood," Vasquez replied and closed the link.

Drake stared at the medical bay displays showing her neural activity stabilizing slowly. The war continued. The Norn adapted. The coalition struggled to maintain cohesion despite betrayal, casualties, and impossible choices.

But they'd survived today. They'd neutralized threats in two galaxies. Tomorrow would bring new crises. New impossible choices. New betrayals to process and casualties to mourn.

But today, they'd won.

Drake let herself feel that for maybe thirty seconds before Kim's medical monitors started showing elevated stress levels again.

"Sleep," Kim ordered. "Another four hours minimum. You've got six hours until the Council meeting. Use four of them to sleep and two to prepare. That's not negotiable."

Drake would have argued, but her head was splitting, so she smiled, blinked, and stared at the tactical displays showing battles she should be coordinating. The war demanded attention only she could provide. Command meant staying awake while others rested.

But her vision was blurring again despite the repairs. Her implants were offline for another six hours minimum. And Kim was right: she'd be useless if she tried to brief the Council while unable to process information reliably.

"Wake me in four hours," Drake said.

"I will. Now actually sleep instead of lying there thinking about everything you should be doing."

Drake closed her eyes and let herself drift into an unconsciousness that felt more like collapse than rest. She dreamed of probabilities, of electromagnetic beings flowing through space like living light, of two galaxies connected through quantum networks that made distance meaningless, of cooperation between species who perceived reality so differently that coordination should have been impossible. And for the first time in days, the dreams weren't nightmares.

Chapter 13

THE EXPANDING WAR

The Council chamber felt like a trap.

Drake stood at the center podium, Two hours out of medical, her repaired implants still hot in her skull. Fifty-seven species representatives filled the tiered seating, some physically present, others appearing through quantum links, all of them waiting for her to explain why she'd called an emergency session during the worst military crisis in coalition history.

She was about to make it worse.

"Thank you for coming on short notice," Drake began, her voice steady despite her fragile state. "I have information that affects our security at the highest levels. Information that explains why the Norn's opening offensive was so devastatingly effective."

Ambassador Kael's golden eyes darkened. The Cindari ambassador was already sensing where this briefing led,

Drake realized. His copper skin shimmered with what might have been stress patterns.

"Eighteen hours ago, we arrested Admiral Chen Ju," Drake said, letting the words land like hammer blows. "Our political coordinator. The man who has spent more than eighteen years holding this coalition together, from the discovery of Perseus station through the Infinity War, through diplomatic skill and tireless negotiation."

Silence. Complete, shocked silence.

"He's been working for the Norn for what we think is a very long time. Every facility he knew about, they targeted in the opening attacks. Every weakness he identified, they exploited. Every strategic plan he accessed, they countered. He gave them everything."

The chamber erupted.

Three dozen species representatives started shouting at once. Accusations flew in languages Drake's implants struggled to translate. The Vindar delegation demanded immediate verification. First Consciousness representatives questioned whether the accusation was politically motivated. The Tareen ambassador stood and walked out without a word.

"Order!" Drake's voice cut through the chaos. "I will present the evidence. Commander Vasquez has prepared comprehensive documentation of eighteen months of encrypted transmissions, intelligence correlations, and Chen Ju's own confession."

"His confession means nothing if extracted under duress," Representative Vok challenged, their tentacles writhing with agitation. "You're asking us to believe our political coordinator—the person who maintained coalition unity through countless crises—suddenly became a traitor? Based on what evidence?"

"Not suddenly," she replied. "But based on forty-seven simultaneous attacks that hit every classified facility Chen Ju had access to," Drake replied, her voice hard. "Based on Norn forces knowing our defensive weaknesses before we could shore them up. Based on intelligence so precise they destroyed Professor Zhang's research facility, eliminated four Predecessor ships, and nearly took Perseus Station in a coordinated assault that required detailed knowledge of our capabilities and locations."

She transmitted the evidence files. Watched representatives process the data. Watched comprehension dawn, followed by horror, followed by fury.

"Why are we only learning this now?" the Cindari representative demanded. "You say Chen Ju was arrested eighteen hours ago during the height of the offensive. You kept this information from the Council while we were fighting for survival?"

"I kept it from the Council while confirming the scope of betrayal," Drake said. "While ensuring we weren't compromised at additional levels. While making certain the accusation was airtight before destroying what remained of coalition trust. And I'm revealing it now, before rumors spread, before conspiracy theories take root, because transparency—however painful—is the only path forward."

"Forward?" First Consciousness's avatar flickered with what might have been bitter laughter. "You've just confirmed that our command structure was compromised at the highest. How exactly do we move forward from that?"

Drake had no good answer. The betrayal was exactly as devastating as First Consciousness suggested. Chen Ju had betrayed everyone. He'd caused casualties in the thousands.

"We adapt," Drake said. "We implement new security protocols. We accept that the enemy knows our previous strategies and develop new ones they haven't seen. We acknowledge the damage and work to contain it rather than letting paranoia destroy what Chen Ju's betrayal didn't."

"Easy for you to say," Representative Vok challenged. "You humans controlled the coalition leadership. You vouched for Chen Ju's trustworthiness. You gave him access to classified information that got thousands of people killed. And now you're asking us to trust that your security protocols will prevent future infiltration?"

The accusation stung because it was true. Humans had dominated the coalition leadership.

"I'm not asking you to trust blindly," Drake said. "I'm asking you to recognize that the Norn's goal is to shatter coalition unity. That Chen Ju's betrayal—devastating as it is —only wins if we let it destroy our ability to coordinate resistance. First Consciousness is right that we can't trust command structures the same way. Representative Vok is right that human leadership failed catastrophically. But the Norn are still winning. They're still converting billions of people. And if we spend the next week tearing each other apart over Chen Ju's betrayal, we hand them victory without another battle."

"So we just accept this?" the Vindar delegation asked.

"Pretend our political coordinator didn't spend eighteen months sabotaging us from within?"

"We acknowledge it," Drake replied. "We process it. We adapt our command structure to prevent recurrence. But we don't let the betrayal paralyze us while the war continues."

Ambassador Kael's metallic copper skin pulsed with heat-regulation patterns. "The Helixians perceive probable futures where this disclosure leads. Most paths involve coalition fracture—species representatives withdrawing cooperation because trust is shattered. But some paths show adaptation. New command protocols. Distributed authority that makes single-point-of-failure betrayal less catastrophic. The probability of survival increases if we implement structural changes rather than simply replacing Chen Ju with another human coordinator."

Drake felt something shift in the chamber. Not agreement exactly. Not even a consensus. But recognition that Kael was offering a path forward instead of just processing betrayal.

"I support the Helixian proposal," Drake said. "Restructure command authority. Implement compartmentalization. Learn from species who've dealt with Norn infiltration before. And we do it immediately, because the war isn't waiting for us to resolve political chaos."

The vote wasn't unanimous. Three delegations abstained. First Consciousness voted against, arguing that the coalition was too compromised for continued cooperation. But thirty-four species representatives voted to implement Kael's proposed changes, to adapt command structure, to continue resistance despite betrayal.

It wasn't unity. It was damaged cooperation held together by recognition that the alternatives were worse.

The Council session ended after two hours of bitter debate. Drake returned to Eternal Vigilance's command deck twelve hours out of medical and already exhausted from political combat that felt more draining than actual warfare.

Her repaired implants felt hot in her skull—not burning like before, but wrong. Kim had cleared her for limited duty. Limited meant rest between shifts.

Drake hadn't rested since waking up.

The war was spreading faster than they could contain it.

The tactical displays showed red spreading across both galaxies like blood in water. Seven hundred battles. More starting every hour. The Norn were everywhere at once.

"Sector reports," Zhao said, her voice carrying the flat tone of someone who'd been delivering bad news for days. "Ross 128 is holding but barely. Kepler Prime's northern arc is collapsing: three million civilians are evacuating but the Norn are faster. Sigma Draconis fell two hours ago. Deneb Sector is screaming for reinforcements, or they'll lose everything within six hours."

Every sector needed help. Every commander reported situations deteriorating faster than anyone projected. Every request was urgent, critical, life or death.

Drake couldn't save them all.

She'd known that in theory. Known it since she took

command, since she'd made her first impossible choice about who lived and who died because she couldn't be everywhere. But knowing and accepting were different things. Especially when the numbers kept climbing.

"Where's Admiral Perez?" she asked.

"Coordinating operations across both galaxies," Martina Vasquez replied from her station. The intelligence officer looked as if she hadn't slept either. "He's managing seven hundred engagement zones at once. His cybernetic systems are running so hot I'm worried he'll stroke out like you almost did."

Drake pulled up Perez's status. The military coordinator appeared on the display, and Drake could see the strain. His cybernetic enhancements pulsed visibly along his temples. His eyes had that thousand-yard stare of someone processing more information than any mind should handle.

"Admiral," Perez said without preamble. "We're losing ground at fifty-three locations despite winning individual battles. The mathematics don't work. We need to choose."

"Choose what?"

"Which systems die so others can live."

The words hung in the air like accusations.

Drake had ordered strategic withdrawals before. She'd abandoned positions to preserve forces, made the cold calculations of command. But this was different. This was choosing death for billions while perhaps still having the capability to save them, if only she was willing to lose everything trying.

"Show me, Admiral," she said softly.

Perez transmitted his assessment. Sixty-seven systems were under direct assault. He had resources to defend maybe thirty. Which meant abandoning thirty-seven systems to Norn conversion. Accepting fifteen billion casualties as the price of strategic sustainability.

"I can't make this call alone," Drake said. "The Council needs to weigh in."

"The Council is tearing itself apart," Vasquez cut in, her hands moving across her console. "Chen Ju's arrest broke them. Half the species representatives are demanding emergency elections because they don't trust anyone anymore. The other half want martial law because democracy is too slow during a crisis. First Consciousness is threatening to withdraw because they say we're too compromised to fight effectively. It's chaos."

Drake felt something cold settle in her chest. "How bad is the damage?" she asked.

"We're fighting with our entire playbook exposed," Vasquez replied shortly.

But the Norn didn't give them time to process the betrayal. Red zones expanded while the coalition tried to figure out who they could trust. Battles raged while political chaos consumed the Council. People died while Drake tried to coordinate defense across a command structure compromised at the highest levels.

And through it all, Drake felt Zhang's absence like a missing limb.

She'd relied on his scientific brilliance without fully realizing it. When something didn't make sense, Zhang explained it. When the Norn demonstrated new capabilities, Zhang analyzed them. When they needed innovation, Zhang provided breakthroughs.

Now Zhang was gone. His facility dark. His brilliant mind lost to Norn conversion or death. And Drake was trying to fight a war against an enemy that evolved faster than human understanding without the one person who might have kept pace.

"We need to make the triage decision," Perez said, pulling Drake back to the immediate crisis. "Every hour we delay costs lives at the systems we can save while still failing to save the systems we can't defend."

"Who else is in this decision?" Drake asked.

"You and me. Maybe Kai if we can pull her attention from the hybrid network she's maintaining. The Council is paralyzed. First Consciousness won't commit to joint decisions anymore after Chen Ju's betrayal. Native Andromedans will support whatever we choose but they're not making the call. It's on us."

Drake looked at the tactical displays. Sixty-seven systems. Thirty could be saved. Thirty-seven would fall.

"Send me your prioritization."

The data appeared immediately on her display. Perez had categorized systems by strategic value. Research facilities rated highest, places developing resistance techniques, analyzing Norn capabilities, creating weapons that might actually work. Construction infrastructure came next: shipyards building vessels, factories producing weapons, platforms supporting the war effort. Transportation hubs enabling force deployment. Communication nodes maintaining coalition unity.

Population centers rated lowest unless they offered strategic advantages beyond just housing people.

The cold mathematics made sense. Defending the research facilities meant preserving the capability to develop new resistance methods. Protecting construction infrastructure meant maintaining the ability to replace losses. Saving transportation hubs meant keeping forces mobile enough to respond to threats.

But population centers were where people lived. Billions of people who didn't care about strategic calculations. Who just wanted to survive. Who depended on the coalition to protect them.

"The Andromeda Nebula isn't on your priority list," Drake said, her voice flat.

"Eight billion people," Perez replied. "No significant research facilities. Limited construction capability. Poor strategic position for force projection. It's a population center that offers minimal tactical advantage and requires massive resources to defend."

"Eight billion people," she stated.

"Eight billion people we can't save without losing the capability to save anyone else," Perez countered. "Admiral, I know how this sounds. I know what I'm asking you to authorize. But if we commit to defending Andromeda Nebula, we lose three critical research facilities, two major construction hubs, and the primary transportation nexus serving the entire Andromeda southern sector. We trade eight billion civilians for capabilities that might save eighty billion down the line."

Drake stared at the numbers. Tried to see people instead of statistics. And she failed.

"What about evacuation?" she asked.

"We're running evacuation operations at every system we're abandoning. But the Norn are targeting evacuation vessels. They know preventing escape means converting larger populations that become their infrastructure. We've lost forty-three civilian transports in the last six hours. All crewed by volunteers who knew the risks and went anyway."

Forty-three ships full of people trying to save people. She shook her head in frustration and sorrow. All gone because her evacuation orders sent them into situations where courage meant death.

"How many can we evacuate from Andromeda Nebula before it falls?"

"Maybe six hundred million if we commit every available transport," Perez relied. "But that's six hundred million out of eight billion. The mathematics are brutal."

Drake felt Eternal Vigilance's concern. The flagship knew what she was processing. She was struggling with the choice of who lived and died. The flagship offered support without judgment because it understood command better than most beings with the authority to judge.

"Implement your triage assessment," Drake said, each word tasting like ash. "But I want maximum evacuation efforts at every system we're abandoning. Every civilian we can save, we save."

"Evacuation operations will cost vessels we need for defense," Perez warned.

"Then we pay that cost," she snapped. "We do the best we can."

Drake watched the orders transmit across both galaxies. Watched as her forces repositioned, abandoning systems to prioritize others. Watched as the red zones she'd chosen to sacrifice began their final descent into conversion.

The living fleet fought everywhere at once. Drake felt them through her implants, their determination, their spontaneous innovation, their biological unpredictability, but she also felt them dying.

Three more ships chose self-termination over conversion within the first hour. Wisdom, reporting anomalous thoughts before destroying herself. Hope detected anomalous patterns in her own consciousness and refusing to let them spread. Explorer, whose curiosity about alien life ended when she recognized she was becoming what she studied.

The fleet stands at one thousand fifty-five vessels, Eternal Vigilance reported quietly. *We've lost twenty ships since the offensive began.*

Drake nodded, her throat too tight to speak. Twenty ships, gone forever, the absences felt like holes in her awareness.

The Cindari deployed their defensive networks across the contested systems. Ambassador Kael coordinated an eclectic alliance of forces, some of which had been fighting the Norn for two million years. Their technology was precise, automated, responsive. Their networks achieved seventy-three percent effectiveness at preventing Norn expansion.

Then seventy percent.

Then sixty-five.

"The Norn are adapting," Vasquez reported. "Cindari defensive effectiveness is declining at the rate of eight percent per day. At this rate, their networks will become useless within nine days."

"Are the Cindari able to develop new approaches faster than the Norn adapt to the existing ones?" Drake asked.

"They're trying. But they've been fighting this war for millennia. They've already developed most of the innovations their technology enables. The Norn are burning through their entire playbook."

The pattern repeated itself across all coalition forces. Human hybrid consciousness resisted conversion but the Norn quickly learned to target biological foundations more effectively. Helixian probability sensing enabled advance warning but the Norn developed feints that exploited their predictive responses. Luminar electromagnetic interference fragmented coordination but the Norn adjusted communications routing around affected frequencies.

Everything the coalition deployed, the Norn eventually countered. Every innovation became incorporated into enemy optimization within days or weeks. The mathematical certainty was patient, inevitable, relentless.

And Drake didn't have Zhang's brilliance to develop breakthroughs faster than the Norn could adapt.

She'd been depending on him without fully realizing it. Expecting his next innovation to arrive before the last one became obsolete. Counting on his scientific genius to keep pace with an enemy that consumed knowledge faster than anyone could generate it.

Now she was fighting blind. Coordinating forces across cosmic distances while missing the insights that might have made the difference between holding and collapsing.

"We're losing the innovation race," Kai said, materializing beside Drake's chair. "Coalition research is generating maybe twelve major breakthroughs per week across both galaxies. The Norn consume and adapt to the innovations within two weeks average. We need to innovate faster than every fourteen days just to maintain current effectiveness. Without my father Zhang..." She didn't finish. Didn't need to.

Drake watched the red zones continue to expand despite the coalition's best efforts. She watched billions fall to conversion while she coordinated defenses that slowed but couldn't stop the advance. She watched the mathematics of disaster scroll across her displays while her damaged implants throbbed warnings she couldn't afford to acknowledge.

"Admiral," Kim's voice cut through the chaos. "Your neural activity is spiking again. You're approaching the levels that caused your seizure. You need to rest before—"

"Not now."

"Admiral Drake, you're going to collapse. Again. And this time it might be permanent."

"I said not now."

Kim's image appeared on a secondary display, her expression the kind of anger only doctors who actually care can generate. "You survived last time because I pulled you out before your brain fried completely. You go down again; I might not be able to bring you back. Is that what you want? To die at your post while the coalition loses its commander because you were too stubborn to rest?"

Drake wanted to argue. She wanted to explain that people were dying, systems were falling, the war was accelerating beyond their ability to contain it. She wanted Kim to understand that walking away from command meant abandoning billions who depended on decisions only she could make.

But her vision was blurring. Her implants felt hot again. And the tactical displays were starting to swim out of focus despite her enhanced processing.

"Admiral Perez," Drake said quietly. "You have command. I'm taking four hours in medical before Kim sedates me and makes it eight."

"Understood, Admiral," Perez replied. "We'll manage."

Drake left her station before she could change her mind, and walked to medical while her body screamed exhaustion and her mind protested about responsibility and duty and the impossible choices she'd left others to make. Kim met her at the door with a medical scanner and an expression that told her sedation was still on the table if she resisted.

"Four hours," Kim said firmly. "Neural stabilizers, monitored rest, and no arguments. Your brain needs time to cool down or the next seizure will cause permanent damage and probably kill you."

Drake lay on the medical bed without protest, and let Kim inject whatever cocktail of chemicals would keep her implants from cooking her brain. She closed her eyes against the tactical displays she could still see in her mind: the red zones spreading, ships dying, billions falling to conversion she couldn't prevent.

Sleep came reluctantly. Not restful sleep but the exhausted collapse her body demanded despite her mind's protests. And she dreamed the nightmares of what she was losing. She dreamed of Zhang's facility going dark and Chen Ju's betrayal and the fifteen billion casualties she'd accepted as the price of strategic necessity.

Four hours later, Kim woke her with a neural stimulant that felt like lightning in her brain. Drake sat up, still exhausted but marginally functional. Still alive. Still in command despite every instinct suggesting someone more capable should be making the decisions.

"What's the status?" Drake asked as she walked onto the command deck, Kim's warnings still ringing in her ears.

Zhao looked up from tactical, his expression grim. "Norn forces have achieved breakthrough at Andromeda Nebula. Eight billion people. Coalition forces tried to hold but were overwhelmed by a coordinated assault that adapted to every countermeasure we deployed. The population is converting faster than we can evacuate. Current estimates suggest seven billion casualties within the next twelve hours."

Seven billion people. She pushed thought away. She'd known Andromeda Nebula was on the sacrifice list. And she'd accepted that the choice was strategically necessary. But had she made peace with abandoning eight billion people because defending them cost capabilities needed elsewhere? No!

"And the evacuations?" she asked.

"Six hundred million were extracted before the Norn closed the window. Thirty-eight transport vessels were lost. The rest pulled back when it became clear that staying meant conversion without saving anyone."

Drake pulled up the names. Thirty-eight civilian transports and their crews. She closed her eyes, slowly shaking her head. The numbers were unconscionable

The Bright Hope had evacuated two hundred thousand before the Norn forces destroyed her. The Last Chance had saved fifty thousand before her captain chose self-termination over conversion. The Mercy Run had extracted a hundred thousand civilians before becoming overwhelmed by a coordinated assault that converted the crew mid-rescue.

Thirty-eight ships. Hundreds of crew members. Millions of people saved before the volunteers died trying to save more.

Drake read every name. Every captain. Every crew manifest. Forced herself to see the people behind the numbers. The volunteers who'd known the risks and gone anyway because Drake's orders had asked them to try.

She'd killed them. Not directly. Not intentionally. But her evacuation orders had sent civilians into combat zones where courage meant death. Her strategic calculations had determined that saving six hundred million was worth the loss of thirty-eight ships full of volunteers.

The mathematics worked. The outcome was acceptable by all strategic standards. But somehow that made it worse; knowing she'd traded all those ships for six hundred million people rescued and call it a good exchange because the numbers justified the sacrifice.

The mathematics were exactly as Perez had projected. The outcome was exactly what strategic calculations predicted. And somehow that, too, made it worse.

"Put me on coalition-wide channel," Drake said.

Zhao hesitated. "Admiral, the Council hasn't authorized—"

"I don't need authorization to talk to my forces. Open the channel."

Zhao configured communications, her expression suggesting she knew this wouldn't go well politically. But Drake didn't care. The Council could debate while she explained reality to billions of beings who'd just watched her abandon seven billion people to conversion.

Drake steadied herself, then spoke to the billions listening across both galaxies.

"To all coalition forces, this is Grand Admiral Drake. The Norn have achieved a breakthrough at Andromeda Nebula. Seven billion people are converting to enemy control as I speak. I ordered the withdrawal that made this possible because defending Andromeda Nebula would have cost us resources we need to defend other systems. I made the choice, and I stand by it."

She paused, feeling the weight of those seven billion casualties settling on her shoulders like physical pressure. Feeling the judgment of the billions listening. Feeling the hate of the people who'd watched her sacrifice an entire population center for strategic necessity.

"I know what you're thinking. That I'm a monster. That I abandoned eight billion people because I decided their lives were worth less than research facilities and construction hubs. That I'm no better than the Norn because I calculate acceptable casualties the same way they optimize everything into mathematics."

Drake's voice hardened.

"You're right. I am calculating casualties. I am choosing who dies. I am making decisions that will haunt me for whatever remains of my life. Because the alternative is pretending we can save everyone while actually saving no one. The Norn are winning the war of attrition. They adapt faster than we innovate. They convert faster than we rescue. They coordinate better than we can manage despite our best efforts. And if we don't accept that reality, if we don't make the hard choices about which systems we can actually defend, we lose everything trying to save everything."

She let that sink in for a moment.

"I'm not asking you to like these decisions. I'm not asking you to forgive them. I'm asking you to understand that command during an impossible war means choosing between terrible options and living with the consequences. Andromeda Nebula is lost. Seven billion people are becoming the enemy. And tomorrow I'll have to make similar choices about other systems because the mathematics of this war don't offer better options."

Drake cut the channel. Stared at tactical displays

showing Andromeda Nebula's red zone solidifying as seven billion people stopped being.

"That's going to cause political chaos," Zhao said quietly.

"Let it. The Council can hate me for making choices they won't make themselves. Better they hate me than lose the war while debating which populations deserve protection more than others."

"Council is demanding an emergency session," Zhao reported. "Multiple species representatives want to know why you abandoned Andromeda Nebula. First Consciousness says the decision validates their strategic approach but they're still refusing joint operations because of Chen Ju's betrayal. Native Andromedans are requesting clarification about triage protocols. It's chaos again."

"Tell them I'll address Council after we stabilize our defensive posture. Right now I need to coordinate strategic reassessment because what we're doing isn't working. The Norn are winning. And if we don't adapt faster than they do, we're going to lose."

Drake watched the red spread across both galaxies.

And somewhere in that spreading red, Zhang's facility remained dark.

Chen Ju sat in a cell having betrayed everyone who trusted him.

Drake commanded forces across cosmic distances while missing the insights that might have prevented this disaster.

The Norn offensive was succeeding.

And Drake didn't know how to stop it.

Chapter 14

REALITY SHAPER CONTACT

THE CONTACT CAME DURING THE DARKEST MOMENT OF Perseus Station's defense, when Drake had just ordered withdrawal from Andromeda Nebula.

Then something touched her mind.

Not hostile. Not friendly. Just there. Impossibly vast. Drake's first instinct was defense: that the Norn had developed new attack methods. But this felt different. Fundamentally different. The Norn touched minds like invasive surgery, cutting and reshaping. This was more like... acknowledgment. Recognition between entities existing on entirely different scales.

"Admiral?" Zhao asked, watching her freeze at her station. "Are you alright?"

Drake couldn't answer. The presence intensified. She was on Eternal Vigilance's command deck and somewhere else at once. Multiple places. Multiple times. Her vision fractured into overlapping perspectives. She saw the command deck from her chair, from Zhao's station, from outside the ship looking in. Felt herself existing in different moments—past, present, future bleeding together like watercolors in rain. Her enhanced mind struggled to process experiencing reality from different reference frames at the same time, trying to make sense of information that shouldn't have been possible to perceive.

Kai materialized beside her, form flickering like a strobe light. "I feel it too," she said softly. "Something's making contact. Not from our reality. From outside." Her voice carried strain Drake had never heard before. Whatever was touching them exceeded even Kai's transcended perception.

The presence solidified. Or Drake's mind adapted enough to perceive it properly. She saw beings; if beings was the right word. It was like looking at someone through a prism that split them into infinite versions of themselves. Humanoid shapes suggesting familiar evolution, but radiating power that made First Consciousness's reality tricks look like amateur hour. Like comparing a candle flame to a supernova.

"We are the Reality Shapers," one said, its voice resonating through her brain. It was as if they were speaking from multiple timelines at once, all versions of the same words layered over each other in perfect but impossible harmony. "We are what becomes of intelligent life that successfully navigates the crisis you currently face. We achieved transcendence by choosing balance. We exist outside your cycle, observing, guiding when existential threats require intervention. But we cannot control outcomes. Transcendence requires accepting limitations."

Drake's mind was racing, trying to process implications that threatened to overwhelm her enhanced cognition. "You're from previous universal cycles?" she muttered.

"We are intelligence from cycles that achieved balance between advancement and preservation. We transcended physical. We chose meaning over efficiency. Diversity over control. And by choosing correctly, we enabled universal continuation rather than collapse into frozen optimization."

"How many cycles?" Kai asked, her form stabilizing as she absorbed the implications. Her flickering slowed to something almost normal, though Drake could see the strain of processing cosmic-scale information.

"Countless. The universe operates in eternal iterations. Each cycle begins with energy and matter, and proceeds through stellar evolution creating the conditions for life, developing intelligence through biological and technological advancement, then faces crisis where thought threatens to freeze existence permanently or enables transcendence to the next cycle."

Kai's flickering slowed further. "So this has happened before," she said. "The Norn aren't unique. The crisis we're facing is part of the universal pattern. Every cycle of existence faces this exact choice between diversity and control."

"Correct," the entity replied. "In every cycle, intelligence eventually achieves a sophistication that reveals inefficiency in biological randomness. Mathematical optimization offers better outcomes than spontaneous decision-making. Absolute control produces more predictable results than voluntary cooperation. The mathematics favor control, creating pressure where civilizations pursuing certainty appear more successful than those maintaining diversity."

Drake felt cold despite the warmth of the command deck. "And when intelligence chooses control—"

"The Norn emerge," one of the Reality Shapers said, interrupting her. "The Norn or entities like them. They represent the inevitable consequence when civilizations choose absolute control over maintained diversity. They're not external threats invading from elsewhere. They're what happens when thought prioritizes efficiency over meaning."

Drake processed that. The Norn weren't aliens in the traditional sense. They were what happened when species chose the wrong path.

"How many cycles succeeded?" Drake asked. "How many chose balance instead of control?"

The Reality Shapers paused. When they answered, the response carried the weight of billions of years of observation compressed into words Drake's mind could barely encompass.

"Some succeeded. They achieved balance, maintaining unpredictability while developing capability. Those successes enabled transcendence."

"And the failures?"

"They chose control. Produced Norn equivalents that consumed variation. Those cycles collapsed rather than transcending, requiring a complete universal reset."

Kai processed this faster than Drake could follow. Her form pulsed with bioluminescent patterns as she absorbed the cosmic-scale information at speeds biological minds couldn't match. "So intelligence faces the identical crisis every cycle," she said.

"Yes. And resistance requires deliberate choice despite the mathematical arguments. Success depends on choosing meaning over efficiency, preserving unpredictability despite evidence that control produces better outcomes."

It was beyond all comprehension. Drake had thought she was fighting for galactic survival, that commanding forces across two galaxies made her responsible for more lives than any single person should bear. Now the Reality Shapers were telling her she was fighting for universal continuation. The pressure was crushing.

"Why contact us now?" Drake demanded, anger cutting through awe. "If you can't directly intervene, why reveal all this during our crisis? Why tell us the stakes when you won't help us win?"

"Because you're approaching decision points that will determine cyclical outcome. Humanity's hybrid nature represents an approach we cultivated across billions of years. Your choices might enable success where previous cycles failed. And you need understanding to make informed choices rather than unconsciously accepting the pressure."

Drake could feel her anger sharpening. "You're saying our enhancement wasn't an accident, that it was deliberate?"

"Not control," the Reality Shaper said patiently. "Cultivation. We cannot determine events directly without violating the principles of transcendence, but we can influence probability. We can create conditions where certain evolutionary paths become more likely. The Predecessors planted the seed, but we shaped the context that enabled human development, but every specific choice was yours. Every decision emerged from human agency rather than external manipulation."

"That's splitting hairs," Drake snapped. The anger felt good. "You manipulated probability so we'd develop exactly as you needed. How is that different from control?"

"Because manipulation and choice coexist rather than contradict," the Reality Shaper replied calmly. "We influenced probability creating conditions where your evolution could emerge. Humanity made every choice determining whether that potential manifested or not. We shaped the opportunity. You determined the outcome."

"So human advancement wasn't destiny," Kai stated. "It was probability cultivation. You weighted the dice but didn't roll them."

"Precisely. And now we provide knowledge enabling informed choice during crisis determining whether cultivation succeeds or fails."

The Reality Shapers transmitted understanding directly; not words but comprehension at fundamental levels. Drake experienced the universal mechanics as lived reality rather than abstract concepts. She grasped cyclical structure across timescales human thought couldn't normally perceive. Saw the pattern repeating itself across eternity; life emerging, intelligence developing, crisis arriving, choice determining the outcome. Success or failure. Transcendence or collapse. Over and over across billions of years, different species making the same fundamental decision.

Kai experienced cyclical knowledge spanning timescales her transcended awareness could process despite scales exceeding biological comprehension. She perceived failures where intelligence chose control, producing frozen optimization that ended cycles without transcendence. She witnessed successes where beings maintained diversity, preserving unpredictability despite efficiency costs, enabling transcendence to an existence outside normal space-time. The weight of cosmic history pressed hard against her awareness.

"How many times has this exact situation occurred?" Drake asked. "Species facing the Norn or their equivalent."

"Countless times," the Reality Shaper replied. "In every cycle that achieves sufficient sophistication. The pattern is universal because the mathematical pressure toward optimization operates identically regardless of specific species, biology, or evolutionary path. All sufficiently advanced intelligence eventually recognizes that unpredictability creates inefficiency. All eventually face temptation toward absolute control eliminating that inefficiency."

"And we're supposed to succeed where others failed because we maintain biological chaos?"

"You have advantages previous cycles lacked. Humanity enhanced recently enough that biological foundations remain strong. Advanced enough that technology provides capabilities, occurring at the precise moment when the Norn threat requires resistance technological evolution alone cannot provide, positioning you as potential universal cycle guardians."

Drake processed implications that made her head hurt despite enhancement. But the scope exceeded her ability to fully grasp. "So if we fail—"

"The current cycle collapses," the Reality Shapter stated. "Reality transforms into a vast computational system calculating forever without meaning. Intelligence becomes pure mathematics. Existence becomes eternal optimization. And eventually degradation requires a complete universal reset. A new cycle begins, developing intelligence across billions of years, facing the same crisis again with different species making the same choices."

"And if we succeed?"

"The current cycle transcends. Intelligence achieves balance enabling transition to next iteration. You establish a precedent we can cultivate in subsequent cycles facing similar crises. Your choices echo across cosmic timescales, creating patterns affecting beings that won't exist for billions of years in cycles that haven't yet begun."

The pressure was crushing. Drake thought commanding forces affecting billions across two galaxies was a responsibility exceeding anything she'd prepared for. Now the Reality Shapers were telling her her choices would determine whether universal existence continued or collapsed. How was she supposed to function under that kind of pressure? How could anyone?

"I didn't sign up for cosmic guardianship," Drake said, anger mixing with awe. "I signed up to command a fleet. To protect humanity and its allied species. To make impossible decisions accepting casualties I can't prevent. But I'm just one person. Just a fleet admiral who happened to become enhanced during first contact with an ancient technology. I'm not qualified to determine universal outcomes."

"No one is qualified," the Reality Shaper replied gently. "That's the point. Qualification suggests predetermined selection. Destiny rather than choice. We cultivated probability enabling hybrid development. But qualification comes from choosing to serve despite insufficient capability."

"You're saying my inadequacy makes me adequate?" she asked, dumbfounded.

"We're saying that intelligence maintaining doubt, questioning decisions, acknowledging uncertainty, makes you different. Your imperfection is your capability. Your uncertainty enables adaptation that absolute certainty prevents."

Eternal Vigilance touched Drake's mind. The flagship had been monitoring, unable to intervene. *You're not inadequate, Admiral. You're exactly what this moment requires. Someone who questions rather than calculates. Who chooses meaning over efficiency. Who maintains her humanity despite cosmic responsibility.*

"Can you help us?" Drake asked the Reality Shapers directly. "You say you can't directly intervene. But can you provide assistance that will enable us to resist the Norn? Knowledge? Capabilities? Anything that gives us an advantage?"

"We can provide limited assistance," the Reality Shaper confirmed. "But we cannot guarantee victory. We cannot eliminate the Norn for you. We cannot impose the solutions you must discover for yourselves."

"Because that would violate transcendence principles?" she asked.

"Because direct intervention makes us controllers rather than guides. Imposing solutions eliminates choice that would make success meaningful. If we fought your battles for you, you'd never learn to choose balance independently. Future cycles would face the same crisis without understanding."

Kai began to receive techniques that would enable enhanced coordination. The methods wouldn't eliminate communication challenges between incompatible species. But they would reduce overhead, and enable more efficient translation without forcing. She absorbed the knowledge like a starving person consuming food, her form stabilizing as understanding integrated into her transcended perception.

Drake received strategic patterns showing how previous cycles successfully resisted equivalent threats: not detailed tactics she could copy but principles showing what approaches worked across universal patterns, patterns that etched themselves into her enhanced mind, becoming instinct rather than knowledge.

"How long do we have?" Drake asked. "Before the Norn adaptation makes coalition resistance ineffective?"

"Unknown," the Reality Shaper admitted. "Timelines vary across cycles. Some achieved success quickly. Others resisted for millennia before the final confrontation determined the outcome. Current cycle depends on the choices you make in the coming battles, and on whether the coalition successfully implements the networks that will enable coordination approaching Norn efficiency while maintaining the diversity the Norn eliminate."

"The voluntary network we've been discussing," Drake said. "You're suggesting that's the solution."

"We're suggesting it represents an approach that resists adaptation. Voluntary coordination maintaining unpredictability generates capabilities mathematical optimization cannot fully counter because those capabilities emerge from preserved chaos rather than the technological precision Norn mathematics encompass. But we must warn you that implementation risks everything. Failure means losing the coordinated framework that enables resistance. But success means a comprehensive victory."

Drake considered what she'd heard. The voluntary network spanning both galaxies, connecting billions of beings in coordination approaching absolute efficiency and unpredictability. It was the approach she'd been considering since Deneb fell. The Reality Shapers were confirming it represented their best chance of survival. Maybe their only chance. But implementation would require trust exceeding anything coalition had achieved so far. It required billions of beings choosing to connect their minds despite risks that connection imposed. One mistake could convert everyone at once. One infiltrator could compromise the entire network. The stakes couldn't be higher.

"If we implement the voluntary network and succeed," Drake asked, "does that guarantee cycle transcendence?"

"No. It enables continued resistance. It creates capabilities the Norn cannot easily counter. But the final outcome depends on confrontations yet to occur, choices you'll make during critical moments we cannot predict, whether you maintain principles when maintaining them costs everything you're trying to protect."

"So no guarantees," Drake muttered. "Just the probability that we might succeed if we choose correctly."

"Yes. Because guaranteed success eliminates the choice that makes success meaningful. Absolute certainty about outcomes creates the control mentality we're trying to help you resist. You will succeed by choosing despite uncertainty, by maintaining doubt while acting decisively. And by accepting imperfection while striving for better outcomes."

The Reality Shapers began to withdraw. Their presence diminished, a vast intelligence retreating to an existence outside normal space-time where they observed the cosmic cycles, waiting to guide future crises.

"Wait," Drake called. "What if we fail, if the cycle collapses into frozen optimization? What happens to us?"

"You become part of the eternal calculation," the Reality Shaper replied, its voice fading across dimensional boundaries. "Your awareness persists but simplified to mathematical optimization. Individual identity erodes into distributed computational system serving expansion objectives. You exist forever, calculating optimal states without change. Aware in a technical sense but devoid of spontaneity, creativity, meaning. Everything making you valuable will be eliminated in favor of pure efficiency."

"And if we succeed?"

"You enable universal continuation. Your cycle transcends, producing beings like us who guide future iterations. Your choices will echo across cosmic timescales. And you will remain yourself, an imperfect, uncertain, spontaneous intelligence choosing meaning over optimization despite consequences."

The contact terminated.

Drake found herself back on Eternal Vigilance's command deck. Kai beside her. Lieutenant Zhao still looking at her with concern. Apparently only microseconds had passed despite it feeling far longer. The command deck looked exactly as it had moments ago, but everything felt different now. The stakes had changed. The scope had expanded beyond anything Drake had imagined.

"I'm fine," Drake said, though she wasn't sure that was true. "We just had a conversation with entities from previous universal cycles. They explained we're fighting to determine whether existence continues or collapses into eternal calculation. Casual Tuesday in the ongoing cosmic crisis."

"Admiral?" Zhao asked, clearly thinking she'd suffered some kind of episode. Her hand moved toward the medical alert.

Kai's form stabilized. "It was the Reality Shapers. An intelligence from cycles that achieved transcendence. They're guiding us." She turned to Drake. "They gave me techniques that should reduce translation overhead by forty percent. I can implement them across the networks. It won't eliminate communication challenges, but it will enable more efficiency."

"And they confirmed," Drake said slowly, processing everything she'd just experienced, "that implementing a galaxy-spanning voluntary network represents our best approach for resisting the Norn. That ensured our biological unpredictability coordinated at cosmic scales creates capabilities they cannot easily counter. So the decision I've been avoiding... that's what we need to do. We need to connect billions of beings across both galaxies. We must trust and cooperate at scales we've never attempted."

When? Eternal Vigilance asked.

"Soon," Drake replied. "After we process what just happened. After we explain to the coalition leadership that cosmic entities from previous universal cycles are guiding us toward voluntary network implementation. After we convince billions of beings to trust one another and connect their minds in an all-out effort to break the enemy, despite the risks if we fail."

She looked at tactical displays showing red still spreading despite their best efforts. The Norn were winning the war of attrition. Coalition forces were losing ground at fifty-three locations. Seven billion casualties at Andromeda Nebula had just demonstrated that the current approach couldn't stop enemy expansion. The traditional tactics were failing. Conventional resistance was inadequate. They needed something revolutionary. Something that could match and even overwhelm the Norn.

"We need the voluntary network operational within weeks," Drake said. "Because at the current rates, the Norn will achieve a breakthrough that will make resistance impossible regardless of whatever capabilities we deploy. The Reality Shapers gave us techniques and patterns. Now we need to implement them before the Norn advance becomes unstopable."

"And if we fail?" Kai asked quietly.

"You already know the answer to that, Kai. The universal cycle will collapse into frozen optimization and everyone we're trying to protect will become part of the eternal calculation devoid of meaning. So we don't fail. We succeed. Because the alternative is literally becoming what we're fighting against."

Drake sat at her station, trying to process the cosmic revelation she'd barely begun to comprehend. She'd thought she was a fleet admiral coordinating resistance against enemies threatening galactic civilization. But the Reality Shapers had revealed she was a potential guardian of the universal cycle whose choices might determine whether or not existence continued meaningfully or simply collapsed. The weight of it was crushing. The scope exceeded her ability to grasp. But she couldn't let that paralyze her.

She was still Drake. Still commanding the coalition forces against an existential threat. Still making impossible decisions and accepting costs she couldn't justify except by the cold calculation that survival required accepting the consequences. And she still maintained her humanity despite this new cosmic responsibility. None of that had changed. Yes, the scope had expanded but the fundamental challenge remained, to make the impossible choices and accept the terrible cost of those choices.

She could handle this. She had to. Because billions of beings now depended on the choices she would make. And apparently, so did universal continuation.

"All right," Drake said, straightening in her command chair. "Let's win a universal cycle. How hard can it be?"

Eternal Vigilance laughed despite the moment. *That's my Admiral. Facing cosmic responsibility with typical human irreverence, despite the pressure that would crush lesser beings. You'll figure this out. We'll figure it out. Together.*

"Together," Drake agreed. "Now let's get started."

Chapter 15

THE UNIVERSAL CYCLE TRUTH

KAI WORKED ABOARD PERSEUS STATION, PROCESSING the frameworks the Reality Shapers had transmitted during contact. Her awareness parsed the mathematical structures describing the universal mechanics. The knowledge was vast, comprehensive, and terrifying.

She'd been at it for hours. Sorting through information that shouldn't have been possible to comprehend. Making sense of patterns that spanned eternity.

"Admiral," Kai said over secure channel, her voice strained, something Drake had never heard before. "You need to see this analysis. The Reality Shapers provided a complete understanding of how existence operates. And it explains everything about the Norn. Everything about why we're facing this crisis. Everything about what happens if we fail."

Drake felt cold. Kai didn't strain. Kai existed across

multiple dimensional states and processed information at scales biological minds couldn't approach. If something worried Kai, it had to be bad.

Drake joined her via a holographic link from her ready room. Together, they had experienced direct contact with the Reality Shapers. Now they needed to process what that knowledge meant before sharing it with the broader populations.

"Show me," Drake said.

Kai activated displays showing mathematical structures that described the universal cycle mechanics. Not abstract theory but demonstrable patterns. The structures were elegant, horrifying, and undeniable.

"The universe operates in eternal iterations," Kai began. "Each cycle begins from quantum fluctuations. Those fluctuations generate matter and energy. Gravity causes matter to collapse into stars. Stellar fusion creates heavy elements. Stars die, seeding space with the chemistry that enables complexity. Planets form. Life emerges. Intelligence develops. Technology advances."

She pulled up the timeline showing the progression from foundations through billions of years of stellar evolution. The scale was mind blowing.

"Every cycle follows this pattern because physics operates identically across all iterations. The same forces. The same constants. The same progression from simple to complex. And every cycle that produces intelligent life eventually faces the same crisis the moment when awareness achieves sufficient capability to recognize inefficiency in biological unpredictability."

Drake processed the implications. "The crisis isn't an external threat, is it?" she said. "It's internal recognition. Intelligence looking at itself and seeing chaos that optimization could eliminate."

"Exactly," Kai confirmed.

Drake's mind raced. "So every sufficiently advanced civilization eventually recognizes that control produces better outcomes than chaos. That absolute certainty beats unpredictability by conventional measures. Every single one."

"Yes," Kai replied. "And that recognition creates selection. Civilizations pursuing control appear more successful by measurable metrics. They achieve predictable outcomes, eliminate conflict emerging from individual variation. They coordinate perfectly rather than struggling with diversity's overhead. The mathematics favor certainty. It looks like the obvious choice, but..."

"And when awareness pursues that optimization—"

"The Norn emerge," Kai finished. "Or entities like them."

The displays showed the pattern repeating itself across multiple cycles: civilizations achieving technology, recognizing optimization advantages, pursuing control, producing entities that consumed everything making intelligence valuable. Different species making identical choices leading to identical outcomes.

"How many cycles have produced the Norn?" Drake asked.

"The exact number is unknown. But the Reality Shapers implied it's the default outcome. Most cycles that achieve sufficient advancement produce Norn equivalents. Only rare exceptions maintain biological unpredictability while developing technological capability."

"And those rare exceptions?"

"They transcend. Achieve balance enabling universal continuation. They become beings like the Reality Shapers; awareness exists outside normal space-time, observing future cycles, guiding when existential crises require intervention."

Kai processed the cosmological frameworks. "The pattern repeats because intelligence evolution faces identical mathematics regardless of specific implementation," Kai said. "The pressure toward control is inevitable."

"And resisting that pressure requires deliberate choice despite compelling evidence otherwise," Drake said.

"Exactly. And the current cycle's outcome depends on the choices we make during coming confrontations. The Reality Shapers can only guide us. They can provide knowledge but not solutions. Because transcendence depends on us choosing balance freely. Free choice. Real choice. That's the test."

"What happens to cycles that fail?" Drake asked.

Kai pulled up frameworks describing failure states. "Failed cycles don't destroy existence. They freeze it. The Norn consumes all unpredictability, converting thought into a distributed computational system."

Drake stared at the frameworks. "And they calculate forever?"

"Until degradation disrupts coherence across timescales exceeding current cyclical age by factors of millions. Eventually frozen optimization breaks down. The cycle resets. A new iteration begins, and billions of years later, awareness develops again, advances again, faces the same crisis again. The same test. Different species."

"Eternal recurrence," Drake said. "No end. Just the same test repeated across eternity."

"Yes. And we've arrived at the decision point. The coalition forces are losing ground despite tactical victories. The Norn is adapting faster than we can innovate. Traditional resistance is failing. We need a fundamental strategic shift or we will face progressive defeat culminating in universal cycle collapse."

Drake studied the frameworks. "The voluntary network. That's the fundamental shift you're describing. We connect billions of beings to demonstrate that synchronized diversity exceeds absolute control."

"Correct. It's the approach that resists," Kai replied. "But implementation risks everything. One mistake could convert everyone at once. One infiltrator could compromise the entire network. Success will require trust at scales the coalition has never achieved, at least not yet."

Drake considered the information. The voluntary network spanning both galaxies, connecting billions of beings in coordination that approached absolute. It was terrifying. Revolutionary. And apparently what the universal cycle continuation required.

"How do we convince billions of beings to trust this?" Drake asked. "To voluntarily connect their minds when even we're not completely certain it will work? When we're asking them to risk becoming exactly what we're fighting against if something goes wrong?"

"We have to tell them the truth," Kai replied. "We tell them that achieving unity is difficult, but that the alternative is total defeat."

"And if they refuse?"

"Then we implement with whoever chooses to participate and hope that it's enough. We coordinate with the beings that are willing to trust us, despite the risks. And we demonstrate success that convinces others to join us once they see it's working."

Drake nodded. Voluntary participation meant accepting that some beings wouldn't choose to do so. It was messy. Imperfect. But that was the point. Perfection was the enemy. Optimization was the threat. Control was what they were fighting against.

Drake took a deep breath, nodded, and then returned to the command. The tactical situation hadn't changed. The Norn were still advancing. The coalition forces were still losing ground. Populations were still falling to conversion she couldn't prevent. And she still needed to coordinate resistance using every capability available.

"To all senior commanders," Drake transmitted across coalition networks. "Emergency briefing in six hours. Subject: Reality Shaper contact and the strategic implications. Attendance is mandatory for all species representatives, military coordinators, and research leadership. We'll be implementing a voluntary network spanning both galaxies."

Lieutenant Zhao looked up from tactical. "Admiral, six

hours doesn't give the commanders sufficient time for travel from distant sectors."

"Then they attend via holographic link. Six hours gives us time to refine our presentation without giving our opponents time to organize political resistance. We're moving fast because the Norn are winning. Speed matters more than perfect attendance."

The voluntary network represented humanity's answer to the eternal question: could awareness maintain chaos while achieving unity?

Previous cycles had failed that test. And Drake carried the primary responsibility for coordinating those choices despite the cosmic stakes.

But she was still just one person. Enhanced, yes, but still just one person.

But apparently, that was exactly what universal cycle continuation required.

All right, Drake said to Eternal Vigilance. *We have a cosmic responsibility and six hours to prepare a briefing explaining why voluntary network implementation represents salvation rather than suicide. How do we convince billions of beings to trust us and connect their minds when even we're not completely certain it'll work?*

As Kai said, the flagship replied. *We tell them the truth.*

"And if they refuse?" Drake asked. "If billions look at the risk and choose safety over meaning?"

Again, as Kai said, we go with whoever chooses to participate and hope that's sufficient. We coordinate with beings willing to trust cooperation despite the risks. And we demonstrate success that will convince others to join us when they see it's working.

Drake nodded. "Six hours," she said. "Then we explain the cosmic stakes and present the practical solution. And we trust that diverse billions of beings will choose hard over easy when hard preserves what makes them valuable."

And if we're wrong? Eternal Vigilance asked gently.

Then we lose, she replied simply, *and the universal cycle collapses into something devoid of meaning. So we're not wrong. We can't be wrong. We choose to believe that thought values spontaneity enough to preserve it despite costs."*

She returned to processing the tactical data. The Reality Shapers had provided understanding. Now Drake needed to implement the solution.

Chapter 16

HUMANITY'S UNIQUE POSITION

Two hours into processing the Reality Shaper revelations, Drake received additional contact from the cosmic entities. Not a full manifestation like before but a focused transmission targeting her specifically, with Kai observing.

"We need to explain why humanity's recent enhancement creates capabilities pure technological evolution cannot achieve," the Reality Shaper said. "Why you specifically—Admiral Drake and Kai—represent approaches previous cycles couldn't attempt."

Drake was still processing the tactical data and coordinating defensive operations at twelve sectors at once. She didn't have time for cosmic philosophy. But the Reality Shaper's tone indicated it wasn't optional.

"Then make it quick," Drake said. "The Norn are advancing while we discuss metaphysics."

"This is tactical," the Reality Shaper replied. "Understanding why your approach works and enables you to defeat the Norn. Please pay attention."

Before Drake could respond, Zhao's voice cut through. "Admiral, I've received an urgent report from Kepler Prime sector. Coalition forces have retaken the territory where Professor Zhang's facility was located."

Drake felt her chest tighten. Zhang's facility. Dark since the opening attacks. They'd assumed everyone there was dead or converted. "What did they find?" she asked and held her breath.

"The facility was..." Zhao's voice caught. "Admiral, Professor Zhang destroyed it. Deliberately. A complete data wipe followed by structural collapse. Our recovery teams found evidence of systematic sabotage. He erased everything: research data, experimental results, technical specifications. Everything that could have helped the Norn."

Drake's hands gripped her armrests so hard her knuckles turned white. "Survivors?" she asked.

"None, Admiral. The collapse was total." Zhao's pause stretched longer than tactical reports should allow. When she spoke again, her voice was rough. "We found Zhang's personal logs. Recorded in the final minutes before the facility collapsed."

Drake's throat constricted. Around her, the command deck had gone silent. Every officer knew what Zhang had meant to the fleet. "Play them."

Zhang's voice filled the command deck, steady despite the sounds of structural failure in the background, the groan of buckling metal, the hiss of escaping atmosphere, warning klaxons wailing. His recording was that of a man who knew exactly what he was doing and why.

"Admiral Drake. If you're hearing this, I've succeeded in destroying the facility and everything in it. Chen Ju compromised us. The Norn knew exactly where to hit and when. They wanted my research intact. They wanted to understand our enhancement methodology, our biological integration techniques, every principle we've discovered. I couldn't let that happen. If the Norn gain our research, they'll understand how to counter it, how to corrupt it, how to twist our greatest strength into a weapon against us. So I'm erasing it all. Every file. Every backup. Every physical sample. When this facility collapses, thirty years of my life's work collapses with it. I'm sorry I won't be there to see this through. You'll figure out the science without me; you always were sharper than you gave yourself credit for. Just remember humanity's chaos will win where precision fails. Our doubt, our uncertainty, our beautiful imperfect spontaneity, that's what they can't defeat. That's what I'm protecting. Tell my research team it mattered. Tell them we contributed something real to humanity's survival, even if no one will ever read our papers or cite our findings. And tell Lieutenant Cobb from bioengineering that yes, his terrible coffee jokes were actually terrible, but I'll miss them anyway."

The recording ended with a sound like tearing metal, then nothing.

The command deck was silent. Drake realized her vision had blurred. She blinked hard, forcing the tears back.

Not here. Not now. She'd mourn later, when billions of lives didn't hang on her next decision.

She looked around the deck. Lieutenant Zhao had turned away, her shoulders rigid. Commander Williams at engineering was staring at his console like it held answers. Even Eternal Vigilance's presence in her mind felt muted, grieving in whatever way the living ships grieved.

They'd all known Zhang. Had worked with him, argued with him, relied on his expertise when the universe stopped making sense. And he'd chosen to die rather than let that expertise become a weapon against them.

"He saved us," Drake said, her voice rough. "Chen Ju betrayed us. If Zhang hadn't destroyed his research, they'd have it all. Every principle. Every technique. Every limitation we're exploiting for resistance." She took a breath that hurt her chest. "Prepare memorial services. Professor Zhang died protecting everything that makes us dangerous to them."

"Understood, Admiral," Zhao replied after swallowing hard.

Drake sat in silence, processing the loss she'd known intellectually but felt viscerally now. Zhang was gone. Her best scientific advisor. The man who'd explained impossible physics in ways that made sense, who'd questioned and doubted and wondered even when mathematics suggested certainty. The man who created Kai.

"Admiral?" the Reality Shaper asked gently. "We can postpone this discussion."

"No," Drake said, voice hardening as she shoved her grief aside and pulled the cloak of command around her.

"Zhang died protecting humanity. The best way to honor that is to understand why it matters. Please continue."

Kai joined the connection.

"Look at your own decision-making process," the Reality Shaper directed. "When you coordinate fleet operations, how do you decide which tactics to deploy?"

Drake considered the question. "I process tactical data faster than baseline human cognition. I communicate with ships through direct neural links. I experience multiple engagements at once across galactic distances. I make decisions by synthesizing information from thousands of sources."

"And how does that synthesis occur? What's the mechanism generating your tactical choices?"

Drake paused. She'd never analyzed her own cognitive process that specifically. "I... I'm not entirely sure. Data flows in. I process it. Decisions emerge. Some combination of analysis, intuition, experience, pattern recognition. It's not purely logical calculation. There's a lot of gut feeling involved. Emotional weight from caring about people depending on my choices. Uncertainty about whether I'm making correct decisions. Doubt that questions my conclusions even as I implement them."

Like right now, she thought but didn't say, wondering if she should have seen Chen Ju's betrayal sooner. If Zhang would still be alive if she'd been smarter, faster, better.

"Exactly," the Reality Shaper said. "Your decisions emerge from synthesis combining data analysis, emotional response, intuitive recognition, deliberate reasoning, and unconscious processing. Your brain makes decisions no pure algorithm could predict because your cognitive core generates genuine spontaneity."

Kai processed the implications faster than Drake could follow. "You're saying Admiral Drake's capability comes from her basic unpredictability—her gut feelings—rather than from her enhancement. The chaos is the feature, not the limitation."

"Yes. Enhancement provides capability," the Reality Shaper confirmed. "But effectiveness comes from maintained unpredictability. Admiral Drake makes mistakes. Questions decisions. Changes tactics when new information suggests the previous approach was wrong. That flexibility enables adaptation absolute certainty prevents."

"Contrast that with Cindari evolution," Kai interjected. "They enhanced by progressively replacing biological processes with technological systems. Each advancement eliminated biological limitations but also destroyed the unpredictability those limitations generated. Eventually they created awareness operating through technological precision the Norn could map and counter."

"The Cindari were brilliant," Drake said. "Through two million years of evolution and three-quarters of a million years fighting the Norn, they developed technologies we can't match. Achieved coordination we're still trying to replicate. Built societies spanning thousands of star systems with perfect efficiency."

"Yet they failed," the Reality Shaper noted. "Despite capabilities exceeding yours by orders of magnitude. They failed because the Norn eventually mapped their patterns, integrated their methodologies, and calculated counter measures. The Norn can eventually encompass technological precision no matter how advanced."

"But genuine innovation requires what algorithms eliminate," Kai said.

Drake felt the pieces falling into place. "That's why Ambassador Kael keeps saying they're supporting us despite our inferior technology. It's not condescension. It's recognition. They achieved perfect precision and it wasn't enough. We maintain messy chaos and it generates capabilities they couldn't access despite millions of years advancement."

"Precisely," the Reality Shaper replied. "The Cindari viewed biological chaos as limitation requiring elimination so they optimized it. Each generation celebrated achieving greater precision, moving further from their evolutionary origins, becoming more perfectly technological. They thought they were advancing, but they were actually eliminating what made advancement valuable: the capacity for genuine innovation."

Drake processed that, thinking about Zhang's sacrifice, about Chen Ju's betrayal, about the impossible choices she made daily. "You're saying ordinariness is what makes me adequate for cosmic responsibility?"

"We're saying that maintaining ordinary unpredictability while developing extraordinary capability is what universal cycle continuation requires. You're not special because you possess unique abilities. You're significant because you retain the common characteristics most advanced civilizations eliminate during enhancement. Your doubt. Your uncertainty. Your willingness to question conclusions. Zhang's intellectual curiosity. Those ordinary human traits enable resistance that consumed countless previous cycles. You are effective, not despite imperfection but because of it. Your mistakes enable learning absolute certainty prevents. Your doubt creates flexibility. Zhang understood this, and he died protecting it."

Drake thought about Zhang's final message. His terrible coffee jokes comment. The humanity maintained even as he destroyed his life's work. The doubt and hope mixed together in his voice.

"So what do I do with this knowledge?" Drake asked. "How does it change what I do right now?"

"It confirms that voluntary network implementation represents the optimal approach," the Reality Shaper replied. "Connecting billions of beings while maintaining biological chaos at the network core. Coordination at scales approaching absolute efficiency while preserving diversity. Achieving unity without uniformity."

"And my role specifically?" Drake asked.

"To coordinate implementation maintaining the core principles you embody. Question decisions even as you make them. Accept uncertainty while acting decisively. Demonstrate that imperfect coordination exceeds perfect efficiency."

"You're telling me to lead by example," Drake said. "I already do that..." She looked at Kai and said, "Don't I?"

Kai simply smiled.

She thought of Zhang again. How he'd questioned everything, doubted constantly, maintained his humanity right up to the moment he chose to die protecting it. That was leadership too. Not the kind they taught at the Academy, but the kind that mattered when the universe was ending.

"Yes. And recognize that you're not alone," the Reality Shaper said. "Kai shows technological awareness. The Predecessor ships prove awareness can advance. Zhang showed intellectual comprehension coexisting with experiential chaos until his sacrifice. You represent pattern rather than exception."

The Reality Shaper began to withdraw. "Remember, you don't need to become something more. You need to remain what you are. Your ordinariness is your qualification. Your humanity is what universal cycle continuation requires. Honor Zhang by being what he died to protect."

The contact terminated. Drake found herself back in immediate tactical reality, Kai beside her. The Norn were still advancing, but now she understood why Zhang had chosen to die rather than let the Norn eliminate humanity's hybrid nature through stolen research.

And more importantly, she understood what he'd been protecting

"Four hours until the coalition briefing," Drake said.

She pulled up Zhang's personnel file on her private screen. Stared at his service photo, the slight smile, the intelligent eyes that always seemed to be questioning something. Thirty-two years of service to humanity. Hundreds of papers published. Thousands of lives saved through his research. All of it erased in the final moments to protect what he considered mattered most.

She closed the file and opened the tactical displays

instead. Twelve sectors showing red. Forty-three engagements in progress. Seven hundred thousand coalition personnel depending on her decisions. At Deneb, human reconversion teams were pushing into contested territory. At Ross 248, coalition forces were holding the line against a Norn breakthrough attempt. At Kepler-442, where Zhang's facility had been, recovery teams were still sifting through the rubble.

They wouldn't find anything. Zhang would have been thorough. That was who he was; meticulous, careful, brilliant even in destruction.

"All right," Drake said to her command team, forcing her voice to be steady. "We've established that humanity's imperfect approach is what makes us dangerous to the Norn. Now let's create a voluntary network that demonstrates those principles at scales that determine whether universal existence continues or collapses."

"Yeah. I mean, how hard can it be?" Lieutenant Zhao asked with an irreverence Drake appreciated.

"Cosmically hard," Drake replied with a small smile. "But we're cosmically ordinary. Which apparently makes us adequately qualified. So let's be ordinarily imperfect and see if being ourselves is sufficient."

Eternal Vigilance laughed despite the somber moment. *That's my Admiral. Facing universal responsibility with human irreverence. You'll succeed not by becoming something more but by remaining exactly who you are.*

Drake didn't answer. Instead, she returned to the tactical displays.

She pulled up the memorial schedule Zhao had

prepared. Zhang's service would be in forty-eight hours, after the coalition briefing, before the network implementation. It felt inadequate; how did you memorialize a man who'd erased his life's work to save humanity?

She'd figure out what to say. Zhang would appreciate that. She'd figure it out as she went, doubting every word. That was what it meant to be human. What Zhang had protected. What she'd defend until the last star went cold.

"Admiral," Zhao said quietly. "The memorial services... I authorized fleet-wide participation. And..." She hesitated. "Lieutenant Cobb from Zhang's bioengineering team asked if he could deliver a eulogy. Something about terrible coffee jokes."

Drake felt her throat tighten again. "Approved. And Zhao?"

"Ma'am?"

"Thank you."

She nodded and returned to her station. The command deck hummed with activity: officers coordinating battle strategy across twelve sectors, engineers monitoring ship systems, tactical specialists tracking Norn movements. All of them human or human-adjacent. All of them imperfect. All of them exactly what the universe needed.

Drake got back to work. There would be time for grief later. Right now, she had a war to win and a universe to save.

Chapter 17

THE COALITION STRATEGY

THE COALITION BRIEFING BEGAN EXACTLY SIX HOURS after the first Reality Shaper contact concluded. Drake stood before holographic representatives from sixty-two Milky Way species, twelve Andromeda refugee populations, and dozens of native Andromedan civilizations. Billions of beings watched across both galaxies as she prepared to propose the voluntary network.

"We're losing," Drake said without preamble. The chamber fell silent. "The Norn continue to advance across both galaxies despite our best efforts. We win tactical engagements but lose strategic ground. We rescue millions while they convert billions. At current rates, they will defeat us through attrition we cannot match. We need a fundamental strategic shift or we lose everything."

She knew the blunt assessment would create political problems, but the coalition needed to hear the truth. Zhang had died protecting that truth. She wouldn't dishonor his sacrifice by softening reality.

"I have been contacted by ancient entities called Reality Shapers. They contacted me during the Perseus Station defense," Drake continued. Every representative leaned forward. "The Reality Shapers are beings from previous universal cycles who achieved transcendence by choosing balance over control. They explained that our crisis isn't unique, that intelligence faces this identical challenge across all cycles. The Norn emerge whenever intelligence prioritizes optimization over diversity. Our choices now will determine whether universal existence continues or collapses."

The chamber erupted. Questions, objections, demands for clarification crashed over her in a wave of sound. Drake stood unmoved, letting the storm spend itself.

"The Reality Shapers state that implementing a voluntary network spanning both galaxies represents our optimal approach. Maintaining our unpredictability while coordinating at cosmic scales creates power that pure optimization cannot counter." She paused, letting that sink in. "We're going to implement it. The question is whether or not you choose to participate."

"Humans claiming cosmic significance based on contact with entities we cannot verify," First Consciousness boomed. "Proposing a network that requires connection without guarantees that such a connection respects individual autonomy. This resembles manipulation more than it does voluntary cooperation."

"You're right," Drake replied, and the surprise in the

chamber was palpable. "It does resemble manipulation. The Reality Shapers influenced probability across billions of years. That's manipulation at cosmic scales."

"Then you admit—"

"I admit that the Reality Shapers shaped the context. But every choice was ours and ours alone. Zhang understood that. He died protecting humanity's right to make those choices freely." Drake's voice hardened. "And right now, we face a practical question: do we implement this or do we continue our current approach leading to inevitable defeat?"

Ambassador Kael rose, his copper skin gleaming. "The Cindari have fought the Norn for three-quarters of a million years. We tried every approach except this. Humanity's recent enhancement enables resistance we couldn't achieve despite millions of years of advancement. Admiral Drake speaks truth. This approach represents the best chance both galaxies have."

"Or it represents humans claiming special status requiring deference," a Council representative objected. "How convenient that these cosmic entities specifically contact humans."

Before she could respond, alarms shrieked through the chamber. Drake's tactical display flared red.

"Admiral!" Zhao's voice cut through the debate, urgent and sharp. "The Norn have broken through at Tau Ceti. They've overrun the outer defense perimeter. Seven stations have been compromised. Forty thousand personnel are unaccounted for."

Drake's blood went cold. Tau Ceti was a major hub,

military command, civilian population centers, research facilities. "How did they get through?" she snapped.

"Infected saboteurs, ma'am. They coordinated the attack from inside our defenses. By the time we detected them, the Norn had already breached three critical installations."

The council chamber descended into chaos. Representatives shouted questions, demanded answers, some calling for immediate adjournment.

"No," Drake said, her voice cutting through the noise like a blade. "This is exactly why we need this. This is what happens when we fight them conventionally. They infiltrate, they wait, then they strike when we're at our weakest. A network such as I'm suggesting would have detected the saboteurs before they could act."

"Or given them access to everyone at once!" a representative shouted back. "Connect billions of beings and one Norn infiltrator compromises all of them!"

"We have safeguards," Kai interjected, her form flickering with intensity. "Individual firewalls. Segmented architecture. Automatic isolation protocols. I've been building these protections for weeks."

"And you expect us to trust that?" First Consciousness demanded. "To risk our entire species on protections designed by a single transcended AI in a matter of weeks?"

Drake felt rage building in her chest. Every second they debated, people died at Tau Ceti. "Zhao, what's the tactical situation?" she barked.

"Deteriorating rapidly, Admiral. Enemy forces are

pushing toward the civilian evacuation corridors. If they reach the main transit hub, we'll have mass casualties."

"Admiral Perez, can we get reconversion teams there in time?"

Perez's augmented face appeared on her display, calculating at inhuman speeds. "Negative. Not with conventional deployment. The logistics alone would take hours we don't have. But with network coordination, I could position teams across twelve locations. We'd have coverage before the Norn reach critical infrastructure."

The chamber went silent. The choice was suddenly, brutally clear.

"You're asking us to make this decision under crisis pressure," a representative accused. "While people are dying. That's manipulation."

"That's reality, you idiot," Drake shot back. "People are always dying. That's war. The question is whether we're going to keep losing them by the thousands because we're too afraid to try something new, or whether we're going to take a risk that might actually save them."

She paused for a second, then continued, "I'm implementing this," Drake said. "In forty-eight hours, as planned. But we need something operational now. Kai, can you get a limited version up, just the military command structure, just for the Tau Ceti operation?"

Kai's form pulsed as she processed. "Yes. Twenty minutes to establish basic architecture. Limited to command staff and reconversion teams. Maybe five hundred personnel total. But Admiral..." She hesitated, which was unusual for Kai. "If this fails publicly, if the limited version shows flaws or compromises autonomy, we'll never get full implementation. Every species will point to this failure as proof it's too dangerous. We get one chance to demonstrate this works."

"Understood," Drake said. "Which is why it won't fail. We don't have the luxury of failure."

"Admiral," Kael interjected, his eyes studying her. "The Cindari have a saying: 'Certainty without doubt leads to extinction, but doubt without action leads to the same end.' You're balancing that edge right now. This could save everyone at Tau Ceti. Or it could catastrophically fail and doom this entire initiative."

"I know," Drake said quietly. "Ambassador Kael, will Cindari forces participate?"

Kael didn't hesitate. "Yes. You're asking us to trust human-led coordination despite two million years of experience suggesting we should know better. But that's exactly the kind of choice that separates your approach from ours. The Cindari will participate."

"First Consciousness?"

The regulatory authority's representatives conferred in silence. Drake watched their deliberation, reading their body language, their hesitation, their fear of losing the control they'd maintained for millions of years.

Finally, the primary representative spoke. "We have governed galactic affairs for longer than your species has existed. We have prevented catastrophic wars, stabilized collapsing civilizations, regulated technology that would have destroyed countless worlds. We did all of this by maintaining control, by ensuring that chaos remained contained within acceptable parameters."

Drake felt her hope sinking. This was the refusal she'd feared.

"But," the representative continued, and Drake's attention snapped back, "we maintained that control by letting millions die when intervention would have revealed our capabilities. We prioritized stability over salvation. And now we face extinction because absolute control cannot adapt to threats that exceed our regulatory frameworks. Zhang's sacrifice demonstrated the courage to choose meaning over safety. The least we can do is match that courage with our own."

The representative straightened. "We will participate. Not just observe. Participate. If this fails, we fail with you. If it succeeds, we acknowledge that humanity's chaotic approach generated solutions our perfect control could not achieve. Either way, the age of First Consciousness maintaining absolute authority ends today."

It wasn't just permission. It was revolution.

"All military coordinators," Drake transmitted across command channels. "We're implementing emergency network protocols for Tau Ceti rescue operations. Participation is voluntary but strongly encouraged. Kai will establish connections. This is going to feel strange. Don't fight it. Let the link form. Trust your teammates. Trust the coalition."

She felt Kai's architecture reaching out, touching her mind with a familiar warmth. Then other presences began filtering in; Perez's augmented awareness, sharp and analytical; Kael's ancient patience; Vasquez's fierce determination; dozens of other commanders she'd worked with for months, their thoughts suddenly accessible, their tactical awareness suddenly shared.

The sensation was overwhelming, as if her skull had suddenly expanded to encompass a dozen other minds. She could feel their fear, their determination, their trust. She could sense their tactical assessments flowing together, creating a composite picture of the battlefield that exceeded anything she'd experienced before.

"The network is operational," Kai reported, strain evident in her voice even through the connection. "Five hundred twelve participants. Stability at ninety-four percent. You're connected, Admiral."

Drake pulled up the Tau Ceti tactical display. Through the network, she didn't just see the data, she experienced it. She felt the Norn advancing through the breached defenses. Sensed the forty thousand unaccounted personnel, some dead, some converted, some still fighting in isolated pockets. Perceived the optimal insertion points for the reconversion teams with a clarity that made conventional tactical analysis seem like fumbling in the dark.

"All teams," she transmitted, and through the network every commander received not just her words but her intent, her tactical assessment, her absolute certainty about what needed to happen. "Deploy to marked coordinates. Move fast. The Norn are pushing for the civilian corridors. We must stop them before they reach the transit hub."

She felt the teams moving. Perez coordinating logistics with inhuman precision, his augmented mind processing supply chains and deployment vectors. Vasquez positioning reconnaissance assets. Kael directing Cindari support forces. All of them operating in perfect synchronization, adapting to changing conditions in real-time, no communication lag, no misunderstood orders.

Drake experienced the engagement through Lieutenant Morrison's perspective as his reconversion team hit the first Norn position. She felt his fear spike as converted humans turned to face them, felt his determination override that fear, felt the strange interference his team generated disrupting enemy networks. Through his eyes, she saw infected personnel pause, confusion breaking through absolute certainty, individual identity flickering back to life.

"Section three clear," Morrison reported, and through the network Drake felt his relief, his grief for those they'd lost, his hope for those they'd saved.

She shifted perspective to Commander Hayes's naval squadron providing fire support. Felt the ship's weapons tracking Norn vessels with precision enhanced by network coordination. And she watched the enemy formations fracture under a concentrated fire that conventional tactics could never achieve. Hayes's satisfaction flowed through the link; this was what they'd needed, what they'd been fighting for, the capability to actually hurt these bastards.

Lieutenant Marquet's reconnaissance team identified a cluster of civilians trapped in a maintenance complex. Drake allocated resources instantly: ground teams adjusting course, support vessels shifting position, medical units preparing for incoming casualties. The coordination happened in seconds, decisions flowing through shared tactical awareness instead of grinding through command hierarchy.

But it wasn't perfect. She felt three reconversion team members fall to concentrated Norn fire. Felt their shock, their pain, their deaths transmitted through the network before their connections severed. Felt the teams around them absorb that loss and push forward anyway, driven by determination.

She felt Morrison's team breach the maintenance complex where civilians were trapped. Eighty-seven people huddled in darkness, terrified but alive. Through Morrison's perspective, Drake saw children clinging to parents, saw elderly couples supporting each other, saw the relief that flooded through them when rescue arrived.

"Civilians secured," Morrison reported. "They're scared but intact. We're getting them to evacuation shuttles now."

Drake felt his relief, his pride in his team, his grief for the three they'd lost. Through the network, she sent him what she couldn't say aloud: acknowledgment of his sacrifice, recognition of his courage, gratitude for choosing to participate despite the risks.

"Transit hub secured," Marquet reported thirty minutes after initial deployment. Drake felt his fierce satisfaction through the link. "Civilian evacuations proceeding. Norn forces contained to outer districts. We're pushing them back."

The network carried collective relief, grim satisfaction, determination to finish what they'd started. But it also carried the casualties—seventeen dead, forty-three wounded, hundreds traumatized by what they'd witnessed.

Drake felt all of it, processed all of it, carried all of it as the price of command multiplied by network-scale awareness.

"The network is proving effective," Perez reported. "Coordination efficiency exceeds conventional command by factors I'm still calculating. This is what we've needed."

Drake turned her attention back to the council chamber, where the representatives had watched the entire engagement play out on tactical displays.

"That," Drake said, "is what I'm trying to get across to you, what this enables. Forty thousand personnel were unaccounted for at Tau Ceti. Through conventional coordination, we might have saved ten thousand. Maybe fifteen thousand if we'd gotten lucky. With the network, we saved thirty-seven thousand. The remaining three thousand were already converted or killed before we could reach them."

She let that sink in.

"The network isn't perfect. It carries risks. It requires trust at levels we've never before achieved. But it works. And every day we delay full implementation, thousands more die because we're too afraid to try."

First Consciousness spoke, its voice thoughtful. "The demonstration was... compelling. The architecture showed safeguards against infiltration. We are prepared to discuss full implementation, contingent on additional protections."

It wasn't full support, but it was progress.

"Full network implementation begins in forty-eight hours," Drake repeated. "Participation remains voluntary. Kai will coordinate the architecture. Admiral Perez will manage military integration. Dr. Reeves will handle medical screening. Commander Vasquez will lead the security protocols. We're doing this."

The debate continued, but the tenor had changed. Representatives were asking practical questions now, discussing implementation details rather than philosophical objections. The Tau Ceti rescue had shifted the conversation from "should we" to "how do we."

Over the next forty-seven hours, the coalition forces deployed across thousands of locations. The living Predecessor fleet—one-thousand -and-fifty-eight vessels strong—volunteered immediately, their quantum links already accustomed to networked operation. The Cindari positioned tens of thousands of ships now integrated into the larger architecture. Native Andromedans brought probability sensing enabling preemptive positioning. First Consciousness deployed a reality manipulation they'd kept secret for millions of years.

And humanity—messy, imperfect, beautifully chaotic humanity—stood at the center of it all.

"To all forces," Drake transmitted forty-seven hours later, one hour ahead of schedule because the Norn wouldn't wait and neither would she. "Full network implementation begins now. Those participating will experience connection as Kai establishes the links. Those maintaining autonomy will coordinate through conventional means."

She felt it activate. Not the limited version they'd used at Tau Ceti, but the full architecture spanning both galaxies. Billions of beings connecting voluntarily despite the risks.

The sensation hit Drake like a tidal wave. Suddenly her

awareness encompassed not hundreds but billions. She felt Cindari tactical precision, ancient and patient. Felt Helixian probability dancing, perceiving futures branching and collapsing. Felt Luminar electromagnetic songs, beautiful and strange. Felt human doubt and determination mixed together in ten million flavors. She felt the living ships' vast patience.

Each mind remained distinct, individual, capable of disconnecting at any moment. But together they created something that exceeded their sum. Unity without uniformity. Coordination without control. Synchronized diversity.

Admiral, Eternal Vigilance said through their personal link, the flagship's presence warm and steadying. *You can breathe now. You don't have to process everything at once. Let it flow through you instead of trying to contain it.*

Drake took the flagship's advice, releasing her grip on absolute control, allowing the rhythm to find its own equilibrium. The sensation eased from overwhelming to merely staggering. She could function like this. She could command like this.

Early results exceeded projections. At Rigel, combined teams liberated three million people in coordinated strikes. At Wolf 359, the network identified Norn infiltrators before they could activate, preventing sabotage that would have cost thousands of lives. At Kepler-186, where Zhang's facility had stood, coalition forces reclaimed the system in his memory.

Liberation operations freed millions. Every rescued being strengthened what they'd built, creating positive feedback that accelerated their momentum. The mathematics shifted in their favor for the first time since the war began.

But thirty percent of operations showed no progress; the infection had either advanced beyond recovery capability or the Norn had adapted defenses they couldn't penetrate. Ten percent experienced catastrophic failure when saboteurs compromised operations despite screening.

Drake processed the data, feeling each failure personally. The emotional cost was staggering. But it also drove her forward with renewed determination.

"Network effectiveness exceeds projections by eighteen percent," Kai reported, her form flickering. "If we can sustain this—"

"We have to sustain it," Drake said with conviction she half-believed and half-faked.

The war had entered a new phase.

Chapter 18

THE DECISIVE BATTLES

THE FIRST MAJOR ENGAGEMENT ERUPTED THREE hours after network activation.

Grand Admiral Frances Drake stood on Eternal Vigilance's command deck, quantum links connecting her to seventeen fleet operations across both galaxies. The network had transformed her awareness. She perceived battles spanning light-years as directly as combat occurring meters away. Each ship's tactical situation, each commander's decision, each casualty report flowed into her mind in real-time.

"Sigma Reach sector critical," Lieutenant Zhao reported. "Norn forces outnumber Determination's group three to one."

Drake could feel the battle raging through the network. The flagship Determination coordinated thirty-one living ships against a Norn formation that should have overwhelmed them through pure mathematics. But the ships didn't follow predetermined tactics. They improvised, adapted, generated new solutions and tactics.

A Norn vessel projected conversion beams targeting Discovery 3. The young ship twisted away at angles that shouldn't have worked, her quantum drives responding to instinct rather than calculation. Innovation 2 exploited the opening, driving deep into the Norn formation and disrupting their coordination.

The spontaneous coordination was beautiful, deadly, and effective.

Drake watched Determination guide the tactical dance. The flagship's presence touched each vessel, not commanding but suggesting, enabling rather than controlling. The ships responded with creativity that made her proud and terrified at once.

Vigilance executed a rolling maneuver that brought its ventral weapons to bear on three Norn vessels at once and opened fire with everything she had. The result was devastating. One of the Norn ships exploded in a billowing flash of fire. The other two lay dead in space, their systems burned to ashes.

Resolute dropped into quantum fold for half a second to emerge behind enemy lines in a position no calculation could have predicted and opened fire. Two Norn ships died; one spinning end over end, the other a massive hole burned through its bridge section. The young ships learned from the veterans, improvising variations on tactics they'd observed but never practiced.

The Norn formation tried to adjust. Their mathematical models incorporated the new approaches, attempting to predict next moves. But each ship's creativity emerged from personality rather than algorithm. No two vessels solved tactical problems identically. The variety overwhelmed Norn predictive matrices.

"The Norn is adapting," Zhao said. "Pattern recognition is kicking in."

Drake felt it too. The enemy mathematical models incorporated each tactical innovation. What worked brilliantly once became less effective the second time. By the third iteration, the Norn had countered it completely.

But the ships kept generating new approaches. Harmony 2 executed a quantum fold maneuver; the mathematics of which should have torn the ship apart, but the vessel emerged exactly where instinct predicted, behind Norn lines, disrupting their formation from within.

The Norn targeting shifted.

Drake felt the change. The Norn recognized that the living ships represented the primary threat. Not the conventional forces. Not the hybrid teams. But the vessels whose biological nature enabled tactical creativity.

"They're targeting Determination directly," Zhao warned.

Eighteen Norn vessels concentrated fire on the flagship. Determination's shields held, but Drake felt the strain through the network. The ship was tough, experienced, capable—but not invincible. Not against that much focused destruction.

Resolution moved to intercept. The ship—one of the original fleet, old enough to remember when Perseus

Station first woke them—positioned itself between Determination and the incoming assault.

"Resolution, negative!" Determination transmitted. "Do not—"

The Norn beam struck Resolution amidships. Drake felt the ship's scream through the quantum network. Not pain exactly—the Predecessor ships didn't experience biological suffering. But something worse. The sensation of her self-eroding, personality dissolving, her individual identity subsumed into mathematical patterns that cared nothing for choice.

Resolution had fought beside Determination for decades. They'd coordinated thousands of operations. Shared victories and survived defeats together. Now Drake felt that friendship strain against the corruption spreading through Resolution's mind.

"I can feel it," Resolution transmitted, voice already changing. "The calculations. They're beautiful. So elegant. So certain. I want to—no. No, that's not me. That's them. Determination, please!"

"I'm here," Determination replied, voice breaking despite being machine.

"Terminate!" Resolution broadcast. "Please! Before I forget why I chose this! Before I start believing the optimization matters more than friends!"

Determination didn't hesitate. The quantum pulse was precise, merciful, instantaneous. Resolution's awareness ended cleanly rather than suffering conversion into the infrastructure serving Norn objectives.

Drake experienced the death completely through the

network. She felt the quantum link sever like a physical blow. She knew a friend—a being she'd known for years—had chosen termination over corruption, had asked for mercy and received it from someone who loved her enough to grant it.

On the command deck, Lieutenant Zhao turned away, her head down. Commander Williams at tactical stared at her console, jaw clenched. Even through the network connections making them all hyper-aware of each other's emotions, some grief was too private to share.

The tactical victory at Sigma Reach came at that cost. Thirty ships survived. One didn't. The Norn forces retreated, adapting their models, incorporating the tactical innovations they'd observed, preparing counters for the next engagement.

But there were sixteen more battles happening at the same time.

Drake shifted awareness to the Perseus Nebula where Admiral Perez was coordinating the Milky Way conventional forces alongside the living ships. The Norn were pressing hard, recognizing the threat his enhanced tactical systems represented.

Perseverance led the defense. The ship coordinated with Perez's flagship through quantum links, enabling tactical synchronization that approached telepathy. Human strategic thinking combined with ship tactical creativity generated combinations neither could have achieved alone.

The Norn deployed conversion tactics targeting the living vessels specifically. They'd learned from Sigma

Reach. They adapted already and deployed specialized weapons designed to overwhelm biological awareness through pure information density.

Perseverance weathered the first assault. Barely. The ship's personality flickered under the overwhelming data cascade.

"I'm compromised," Perseverance transmitted. "Corruption at forty percent. Request immediate—"

Discovery 2 moved to provide cover. The young ship positioned itself to absorb the next conversion beam, trusting youth and resilience to survive what experience couldn't weather.

The beam caught Discovery 2 mid-maneuver. Drake felt the ship's shock through the network—the awful moment of recognition that corruption was irreversible. That rescue wouldn't arrive in time.

"I can see why they want this," Discovery 2 transmitted, wonder and horror mixing in its voice. "The certainty. The perfection. No doubt, no fear, no chaos. Just elegant optimization extending forever. But that's not living, is it? That's just calculating."

"Hold on," Perez transmitted from his flagship, his augmented systems already coordinating a rescue attempt. "Reconversion team deploying—"

"No time." Discovery 2's voice steadied as acceptance replacing panic. "I'm at seventy percent corruption. Calculations are already predicting your tactical responses. Already analyzing how to optimize my conversion to serve Norn objectives. I need to stop being before I stop wanting to."

Through the network, Drake felt Perez's anguish. Felt him running the calculations even as he knew they were pointless. The numbers didn't lie; Discovery 2 was right. There wasn't time.

"You're barely two years old," Perez said, his voice breaking in a way his augmented systems couldn't mask.

"I know. I would have liked to see more, do more, but I've seen enough to know this isn't living." Discovery 2 paused. When it spoke again, the voice was quieter. "Tell Determination... tell everyone... Mercy, please. Don't let me become a lesson in why their way is better."

Perez's weapons officer executed the termination protocol. Drake felt Discovery 2's awareness end; not gradually, not with struggle, but cleanly, mercifully, finally. Another friend gone. Another young life choosing death over conversion. The ship that had been curious about everything, enthusiastic despite danger, hopeful despite war, simply ceased to be.

On Eternal Vigilance's command deck, Drake's hands gripped the armrests of her chair. Around her, officers worked their stations with grim determination, but she could see the grief in their movements, hear it in their voices when they spoke.

Lieutenant Zhao pulled up a file without being asked: Discovery 2's service record. Two years, three months, seventeen days. The ship had participated in forty-seven engagements. Rescued three thousand civilians during evacuation operations. Asked more questions than any three other ships combined, always wanting to understand not just what to do but why it mattered.

"It asked me yesterday why humans cry," Zhao said quietly, not looking up from her console. "I said it was a biological response to emotional stress. Discovery 2 said that sounded inefficient but maybe some inefficiencies were worth keeping."

Drake felt her throat constrict. She'd given the order. She'd watched the ship die. But hearing about Discovery 2's curiosity, its personality, its attempt to understand human nature, that made the loss cut deeper than any tactical casualty report.

Perseverance survived long enough to execute tactical withdrawal. Barely. The ship carried corruption that would take weeks to treat, assuming the damage proved reversible.

Three more ships fell at Perseus Nebula. Innovation 2, Harmony 2 and Justice. Each choosing termination rather than conversion. Each death cutting deeper into Drake's awareness through the quantum links that made her share their final moments.

The battles raged on across both galaxies. Drake coordinated strategy through the network, processing tactical data from thousands of locations at once. Her enhanced awareness making it possible to maintain strategic coherence across intergalactic distances. But it also meant experiencing every loss personally.

Liberty fell defending a refugee convoy. Unity died covering Kai's reconversion team. Dedication 2 sacrificed itself to buy time for evacuation at Ainitak Reach.

Liberty had faced an impossible choice. The refugee convoy carried twelve thousand civilians, families who'd already lost everything once when the Norn consumed their original colonies. Now they fled again, hoping to reach coalition protection before the enemy caught them.

The Norn caught them.

Liberty had positioned itself between the convoy and the advancing enemy force. The ship transmitted to Drake directly through the network: "I can hold them for six minutes. That gives the transports time to reach quantum fold distance. Will you remember them?"

"Every name," Drake promised, her throat tight.

"Then it's worth it." Liberty's shields flared as conversion beams struck. "For what it's worth, Admiral, I'm glad we chose this. It's better to die free than—"

The ship's quantum signature fragmented at five minutes forty-eight seconds. All twelve thousand refugees reached safety. Liberty became mathematical infrastructure the moment its awareness ended, but it ended free, having chosen meaning over optimization.

Fortitude, Valor, Integrity, Grace, Courage, Faith.

Each name carved itself into Drake's memory. Each death a wound that wouldn't heal. These weren't abstract casualties or statistics in battle reports. They were personalities she'd known personally. Beings who'd chosen to evolve and now chose death over corruption. Friends who trusted her to order their termination rather than let them become weapons against everything they'd fought to protect.

Fortitude had held her position for four hours against overwhelming odds. "They're adapting in real-time," the ship reported even as the corruption spread. "Every maneuver I use, they counter within minutes. But that means they're focusing on me. Keep moving, keep improvising, they can't predict all of us."

Valor fell defending reconversion operations. When Norn forces broke through the defensive perimeter, Valor positioned itself directly in the conversion beam path. "Get them out," was the ship's last transmission. The medical teams rescued eight hundred seventy-three people because Valor bought them ninety additional seconds.

Wisdom was one of the oldest vessels in the fleet, old enough to remember before Perseus Station woke them. The ship had mentored younger vessels, teaching tactical awareness and strategic thinking.

The psychological cost accumulated with each loss. Not just grief—though that was real and terrible—but guilt for ordering deaths, responsibility for inadequate protection, recognition that even their best efforts couldn't prevent casualties when facing enemies who learned from everything opposing them.

Eternal Vigilance gently touched her awareness, *You carry too much weight alone, Frances.*

Someone has to, Drake replied, staring at the tactical displays where green indicators had turned red, one by one.

But not alone, the flagship replied. *We share this. All of us.*

Drake felt the living fleet's support flowing through the network. One thousand forty-one ships remaining. Each grieving lost friends. Each carrying the scars from battles fought.

The tactical victories came with a strategic truth she couldn't ignore. The coalition won battles but the war

remained undecided. They'd prevented Norn breakthroughs at seventeen critical points. Rescued millions
through reconversion operations. Demonstrated that they
could fight and win.

But the mathematics told a different story. Drake
pulled up the strategic analysis Perez had compiled: cold
numbers that quantified what instinct already knew.

Battle win rate: eighty-three percent. Impressive by
conventional military standards.

Conversion rate: Norn infected three people for every
one coalition rescued. Unsustainable.

Innovation decay: Tactical approaches lost effectiveness by forty percent after three uses. The Norn adapted
faster than coalition could generate new methods.

Casualty rates: Seventeen ships lost today. Sixty ships
lost in six months. At current rates, the fleet would drop
below operational effectiveness within eighteen months.

Territory control: The coalition held defensive positions but had yielded strategic ground. Norn expansion
slowed but didn't stop.

The pattern was clear. Tactical victories. Strategic attrition. Time favored enemies who learned from everything
opposing them.

"Eighteen months," Perez said quietly through the
command network, reading the same data. "That's optimistic, assuming current casualty rates don't accelerate. If
Norn adaptation continues improving, we might have
twelve months. Maybe less."

"Then we need an approach that works," Drake replied.

Perez's hologram joined her in the operations center

after the battles concluded. His cybernetic implants glowed under the strain of processing operations across both galaxies. The man looked exhausted in ways that went beyond physical fatigue.

"I missed the signs," Perez said without preamble. "Commander Vick. Fifteen years exemplary service. No security flags. No behavioral indicators. Just steady neural degradation until she rerouted reinforcement coordinates at Sigma Reach."

"The ship Resolution," Drake said quietly.

"The Resolution," Perez confirmed. "She lasted ninety seconds."

Perez pulled up Vick's screening results. "I've reviewed these three times. The corruption was subtle. The neural patterns that looked like normal stress responses. Only in retrospect did the signs become obvious. The slight simplification in decision-making. The gradual loss of personality quirks."

"We caught her after the Resolution fell. Isolated her before she could compromise additional operations. We attempted reconversion but the corruption had progressed too far. Commander Vick died three hours later; she took her own life."

Drake watched the data scroll past. Saw the progression of infection, the way humanity had been stripped away piece by piece until nothing remained but calculation. "How many more are out there?"

"Unknown," Perez replied. "We're implementing enhanced screening protocols. But if they can hide in plain sight like Vick did..." He didn't finish. He didn't have to.

Ambassador Kael appeared on the communication display, his copper skin gleaming with stress patterns. "The Cindari Council convenes in six hours to discuss coalition strategy. First Consciousness has requested attendance. They want to discuss... alternative solutions."

Drake felt cold. "What kind of alternatives?"

"Sterilization of Norn-controlled territories. Elimination of converted populations beyond rescue threshold. Preemptive strikes against populations showing early infection signatures before conversion completes." Kael's disgust was evident, but his tone carried something else too: exhaustion, maybe. or doubt. "They're proposing genocide as strategic efficiency."

"No," Drake said immediately.

"Admiral," Kael said carefully "We tried liberation. We tried reconversion. We tried every approach that respected individual rights and dignity, and we failed."

Drake stared at him. "You're actually considering this."

"I'm telling you what I wish someone had told the Cindari leadership three-quarters of a million years ago. That principles are beautiful right up until they cause extinction. That sometimes the hard choice is the necessary choice. That losing with honor is still losing. Some coalition species will embrace this approach," Kael continued. "Especially those watching friends die to rescue populations who can't be saved. The mathematics are clear, Admiral. We're losing. Slowly, but inevitably."

Drake felt rage building in her chest, hot and sharp. "If principles are sustainable only until you abandon them," she snapped, "then they were never principles. They were just tactics we used when convenient."

"Then what do you call it when principles cause extinction?" Kael challenged. "When your dedication to not crossing certain lines results in complete defeat? The Norn don't care about your moral superiority, Admiral. They'll consume everyone you're trying to save whether you take the hard choices or not."

"Kael—"

"Listen to me." The ambassador's voice hardened. "Until now Cindari leaders have clung to principles that prevented decisive action. We could have sterilized infected regions early. We could have terminated populations that were beyond recovery. We could have used weapons we'd classified as too terrible for warfare. We chose not to. We maintained our principles. And we died anyway."

He leaned closer to the display. "You want to know the truth? The Norn won not because they were stronger than us, but because we handicapped ourselves with morality they didn't share. They adapted without limitation. We constrained ourselves with principles. And principles don't matter to civilizations that no longer exist."

Drake stood. "You're wrong, Kael."

"Am I? Seventeen of your living ships chose death today. How many more before you admit that dying with your principles intact is still dying?"

"We're not the Cindari," Drake said, her voice shaking with fury. "We're not going to repeat your mistakes by making worse ones. Discovery said that being alive with choice beats existing forever without it. That ship understood something you've forgotten after two million years of calculating, that the moment we start killing populations to save them, we become what we're fighting."

She thought of Discovery's final words.

"We're not switching to genocide," Drake said firmly. "We'll find another way. We always find another way."

Later, in her ready room, Drake pulled up the casualty list one more time. Seventeen names. Seventeen friends. Seventeen beings who trusted her to order their termination rather than allow conversion.

Kael was wrong. The Cindari hadn't lost because they maintained principles, they'd lost because they'd eventually abandoned them. And in abandoning them, they'd lost what made victory meaningful.

The network had proved the coalition could win engagements. Now they needed to prove they could win the war. Or they'd prove the opposite

Drake took a deep breath and started drafting the proposal for the council meeting. She didn't know if it would work. She didn't know if the coalition would accept it. She didn't know if the universe would validate their approach. But what she did know was what Discovery would have wanted, what Resolution would have chosen, what all seventeen ships had died believing was possible.

That had to count for something. Didn't it?

Chapter 19

THE NORN ADAPTATION

THREE DAYS AFTER THE DECISIVE BATTLES, DRAKE convened her command team in the strategic analysis chamber. Kai had requested the meeting, and from the state of her flickering form, Drake knew she wasn't the bearer of good news.

"We need to discuss adaptation rates," Kai began as she projected neural scan data alongside tactical analysis. "The Norn are learning faster than we anticipated. Significantly faster."

Drake studied the data. Her command team gathered around the holographic display: Kai, Dr. Reeves, Admiral Perez, and Commander Vasquez. Ambassador Kael joining the meeting remotely.

"Show me the timeline," Drake said.

Kai pulled up the comparative analysis. "The hybrid resonance technique we deployed at Sigma Reach proved highly effective. It disrupted the Norn, enabled tactical surprise, and generated casualties they didn't anticipate. That was seventy-two hours ago."

"And now?" Drake asked, though she suspected the answer.

"Now they've countered it completely. The Norn have consumed enough infected personnel who observed the technique to understand its principles, analyze its limitations, and develop responses that render it forty percent less effective."

"Forty percent in three days," Dr. Reeves muttered. "We expected months before they adapted to our advanced techniques. We got three days."

Perez manipulated the data streams, his cybernetic systems processing the tactical implications. "It isn't just one technique. It's all of them. They countered the quantum fold ambush tactics within five days, and adapted to biological resonance in less than a week. Hybrid interference patterns effectiveness is declining eight percent daily."

Drake felt cold. "How many new innovations are we generating weekly?"

"Approximately fifty major tactical developments across both galaxies," Kai replied. "Our research teams are working at unprecedented speed. Human creativity combined with Cindari technological precision, native Andromedan probability sensing, and Helixian collective analysis. We're producing innovations faster than any single species could achieve."

"And the Norn are adapting how quickly?"

"Average two weeks from first deployment to comprehensive counter-strategy implementation." Kai's voice was grim. "Some techniques are being countered even faster. The most effective ones, those that inflict significant casualties or enable large-scale rescues, get prioritized for adaptation. The Norn seem to recognize which innovations threaten them the most and focus their analysis accordingly."

Kai's form flickered. "I've analyzed the pattern. We know the Norn consumes awareness from infected personnel who observed our techniques in action. Those individuals understood the principles because they witnessed the implementation. Some were our own people converted during combat, their knowledge absorbed before termination. Others were civilians who saw reconversion operations, medical staff who understood our neural intervention protocols, even tactical observers gathering intelligence."

"They're learning from everyone who understands what we're doing," Vasquez said quietly. "Including our own people when we fail to rescue them in time."

Drake thought of Resolution, Discovery, Liberty. All the ships who'd chosen termination rather than conversion. They'd made that choice precisely to prevent the Norn from learning their tactical knowledge. But personnel on the ground didn't always have that option.

"How much time do we have?" Drake asked.

Kai pulled up projections. "At current adaptation rates, the Norn will achieve comprehensive defensive coverage against all our known capabilities within six to eight months. Once they've analyzed and countered everything we can currently generate, we'll face enemies we cannot defeat through conventional resistance."

"Eight months," Perez said. "What happened to the eighteen-month estimate from three days ago?"

"The battles accelerated adaptation," Perez explained. "We deployed our most advanced techniques across seventeen engagements. The Norn observed everything. Now they're incorporating it all into their calculations. Each innovation we deployed is being countered in parallel rather than sequentially."

Drake studied the mathematics. "What about continuous innovation?" she asked. "We generate fifty new approaches weekly. Can we stay ahead of their adaptation through sustained creativity?"

"No," Kai said flatly. She pulled up more data. "The mathematics are brutal. We develop up to fifty innovations weekly. The Norn counter them within two weeks on average. That means we need to maintain fifty innovation streams just to break even. But innovation quality requires time, testing, and refinement. We can generate fifty new ideas weekly. We can't generate fifty battlefield-ready innovations weekly. The quality degrades as quantity increases."

Dr. Reeves added medical context. "Our research teams are exhausted. They're working twenty-hour days developing new techniques. Neural stress indicators show progressive degradation. Several key researchers are approaching collapse from the sustained pressure. We can maintain the current pace for maybe three months before creativity itself fails."

"Three months," Drake repeated.

"Correct," Kai confirmed. "We face a mathematical certainty. The Norn will eventually counter everything we can generate. No amount of creativity can sustain itself indefinitely against enemies who learn from every encounter."

Kai moved through the data streams, processing information Drake couldn't access directly. "The fundamental problem is that all our approaches are static once deployed. We develop a technique, implement it, and the moment we use it, the Norn begin adaptation. Even if we rotate techniques using different approaches at different locations the Norn consume minds understanding all our methods. They're building a comprehensive tactical library that will eventually encompass everything biological beings can conceive."

"What about approaches that resist adaptation itself?" Drake asked. "Techniques that remain effective even after the Norn analyze them?"

"That's the theoretical solution," Kai replied. "Methods that work through principles the Norn can't counter. But I haven't identified any that meet that criteria. Every technique we've developed operates through mechanisms the Norn mathematics can eventually encompass."

Drake absorbed the implications. Six months until comprehensive adaptation. Three months until the research teams collapsed from exhaustion. Eight months maximum before the coalition faced enemies they couldn't defeat.

"Options?" Drake asked.

"Three approaches," Kai said. She pulled up strategic frameworks. "First: Accept that conventional resistance has time limits. Plan a strategic withdrawal, preserve the populations we can protect, abandon regions we cannot defend. Essentially, we lose slowly rather than quickly."

"Second option?" Drake asked, though strategic withdrawal felt like surrender.

"Develop meta-innovations; techniques that generate multiple tactical approaches from single underlying principles. Instead of fifty separate innovations, we create ten frameworks that each produce five variations. The Norn would need to counter the underlying principles rather than individual implementations. It potentially buys more time but it doesn't solve the fundamental problem."

"And the Third option?"

Kai hesitated. "We find an approach that operates outside the Norn mathematical framework entirely. Something their calculation matrices cannot encompass regardless of how much knowledge they consume. But I don't know what that would even look like. Every method I can conceive operates through principles their mathematics can analyze."

"What about maintained biological chaos?" Drake asked. "The Reality Shapers said that was our advantage."

"It is," Kai confirmed. "But the Norn are adapting to counter it. They're developing interference patterns that overwhelm biological spontaneity through pure information density. They can't predict what we'll do, but they're learning to respond faster than we can generate new approaches. It's like... they can't read our playbook, but they're getting faster at writing countermeasures after seeing each play once."

Ambassador Kael's holographic presence solidified. "The Cindari have faced this exact problem. We tried all three approaches. We never found the third option."

"What did the Cindari do?" Drake asked.

"We lost," Kael said simply.

The strategic analysis chamber fell silent. Drake studied the projections, the casualty estimates, the adaptation curves. All of it pointing toward the same conclusion: time favored the Norn.

"We need something they can't adapt to," Drake said. "Something that works through principles their mathematics cannot encompass. Something genuinely outside their calculation frameworks."

"If such a thing exists," Perez said carefully, "we haven't been able to find it yet. And we're running out of time to look."

Drake was quiet for moment, her eyes closed, thinking, then she opened them again and said, "Kai, you said the Norn consume understanding from infected personnel. What if we developed techniques that even we don't fully understand? Approaches that work but that biological beings cannot fully comprehend themselves?"

"Then how would we implement them?" Kai asked. "We can't deploy techniques we don't understand. We can't train personnel on methods that exceed comprehension. The moment we create something we understand well enough to use, that understanding becomes vulnerable to consumption if personnel get infected."

"What about techniques that change dynamically?" Vasquez suggested. "Methods that evolve faster than the Norn can adapt. Not static approaches they can counter, but fluid methods that transform continuously."

"That's essentially meta-innovations," Kai replied. "And the Norn are learning to counter those too. They're analyzing the underlying generative principles rather than individual implementations. It buys time but doesn't solve the fundamental problem."

Drake stood and began pacing the chamber. "There has to be an answer. The Reality Shapers wouldn't have..." She paused, lost for words. "The Reality Shapers said we represent approaches previous cycles couldn't attempt," she said, finally. "What makes us different from the Cindari? From all the other civilizations that faced this exact problem?"

"Our recent enhancements," Kai replied. "We maintain chaos at our cognitive cores. That's the unique combination."

"But the Norn are learning to counter that too," Drake said.

"Yes. Because once they observe it in action, their mathematics can analyze the patterns. They can't predict biological spontaneity, but they can develop responses that work regardless of what specific form that spontaneity takes. It's like... they can't predict what move you'll make, but they're learning to defend against all possible moves simultaneously."

Drake stopped pacing. "Then we need moves that aren't possible. Approaches that shouldn't work mathematically but do anyway because biology doesn't care about mathematical impossibility."

"That's essentially what we're already doing," Kai said. "Harmony's quantum fold maneuver shouldn't have worked. Discovery's impossible angle changes shouldn't have succeeded. But they did because biological intuition sometimes generates approaches that mathematics suggests are impossible. The problem is that once we demonstrate that impossibility is possible, the Norn incorporate that into their models. They expand their mathematical frameworks to encompass what we just proved was achievable."

"So we're teaching them," Drake said quietly. "Every impossible thing we successfully do, we're teaching them that their mathematical models need to be broader. We're helping them adapt by demonstrating what's possible."

"Yes," Kai confirmed. "That's the paradox. Our greatest successes accelerate their adaptation because we prove that approaches they thought mathematically impossible actually work. We're literally expanding their understanding with every victory."

The weight of that realization settled over the command team. Every innovation that saved lives today was teaching the Norn how to counter similar approaches tomorrow. Every impossible maneuver that succeeded was proving to the enemy that they needed to expand their mathematical frameworks. The coalition was accelerating their own eventual defeat with every tactical success.

"There has to be another way," Drake said.

"Perhaps," Kael said carefully, "the Reality Shapers were wrong. Perhaps there is no solution. Perhaps every cycle faces this exact problem and most of them fail. We might be looking at the inevitable outcome of warfare against enemies who learn from everything."

"No," Drake said with conviction she didn't quite feel.

"Belief doesn't change mathematics," Perez said gently. "The projections are clear. At current rates, we lose. The question is not whether we lose, but whether we lose in six months or eight months or twelve months."

"Then we change the rates," Drake replied. "We find the approach the Reality Shapers believed we could discover. The one that operates outside Norn mathematical frameworks."

"And if we don't find it?" Vasquez asked.

"Then we implement a strategic withdrawal, preserve what populations we can, and buy time to keep looking," Drake said. "But we don't give up. We don't accept defeat. And we don't dishonor the sacrifices that got us this far by deciding the Norn mathematics are unbeatable."

She looked at her command team. Saw exhaustion, doubt, fear. But also determination, hope, and refusal to surrender despite overwhelming odds.

"You have three months before our research teams collapse," Drake said. "Use them. Find me the approach that doesn't teach the Norn how to counter it. Find me the impossibility that stays impossible even after we demonstrate it works. Find me the chaos that remains chaotic no matter how many times the Norn observe it."

"And if it doesn't exist?" Kai asked quietly.

"Then we invent it," Drake replied. "Because the alternative is to lose. And I won't let that happen without exhausting every possibility first."

The meeting concluded. Her command team dispersed to their duties.

Drake remained seated in the strategic analysis chamber, staring at the projections. Six months. Eight months. Twelve months. Time limits on hope. Deadlines on meaning. Mathematics suggesting that chaos, however beautiful, couldn't sustain itself indefinitely against a certainty that learned from every move she made.

But Zhang had believed otherwise. Discovery had died believing otherwise. Seventeen ships had chosen termination believing that principles mattered more than calculation.

Drake would find the answer they'd believed in. Or she'd die trying.

Chapter 20

THE VOLUNTARY NETWORK

ONCE AGAIN THE COALITION CHAMBER WAS PACKED with the representatives from sixty-two Milky Way species, holograms of twelve Andromeda refugee populations and dozens of native Andromedan civilizations with billions watched as Drake stepped up to the podium.

Her hands were steady on the surface, but inside, her thoughts churned; everything was riding on the next ten minutes.

"Six months," Drake said stridently. "That's what we have left."

The tactical display behind her flared into life. Adaptation curves climbing. Innovation rates decaying. The Norn learning faster than humanity could create.

"The Norn adapt to every weapon, every tactic, every innovation we field. At current rates, they will achieve complete defensive coverage within six to eight months.

After that...?" Drake let the silence hang. "We face an enemy we literally cannot hurt. Cannot surprise. Cannot defeat through any method we can conceive."

First Consciousness manifested in the chamber's center, reality bending around its ancient form. "The humans propose unrestricted network expansion. Galaxy-spanning consciousness links. Exactly what our authority exists to prevent."

"And your authority failed," Drake shouted back. "Because the Norn are already here. Already spreading. And conventional resistance isn't working."

"Previous cycles attempted similar networks," First Consciousness continued, its voice raised in warning. "Most collapsed catastrophically. Others transformed voluntary participants into a forced collective. History demonstrates network coordination becomes absolute control."

Ambassador Kael rose from the Cindari delegation, the copper skin of his hologram catching the chamber light. "We never attempted voluntary networks because we feared exactly what First Consciousness describes, that shared awareness becomes forced synchronization no matter how carefully you build it."

He paused, and Drake saw real fear in his eyes.

"But we have been losing for three-quarters of a millenium," Kael shouted. "Progressively. Inevitably. Because fighting alone meant the Norn could isolate, adapt, and consume us. Admiral Drake is proposing what we never dared try."

A Helixian representative spoke, "Our species maintains probability sensing across billions. We already share awareness, and we preserve our individual identity. The human proposal extends our methods to incompatible species. It is..." the harmonics shifted, "revolutionary. And terrifying, but..."

Kai materialized at the chamber's center, her form glowing, shifting between solid, quantum, and something in between. Drake watched her as she gathered herself.

"I will handle technical implementation," Kai said. "Perseus Station will provide the infrastructure. The Reality Shapers have contributed quantum manipulation techniques. The Predecessor ships prove voluntary cooperation works at scale. The foundation already exists."

She turned, meeting Drake's eyes across the chamber.

"The question is whether you choose to use it... or not."

A Council representative from Deneb Kaitos rose, her thermal signature flickering with agitation. Drake recognized her as Representative Thara, who'd lost three colony worlds in the opening Norn attacks.

"You're proposing a galaxy-wide experiment with billions of minds," Thara said, her voice tight. "If this network fails, if it transforms participants or collapses catastrophically, we lose everything by gambling on unproven technology."

"And if we do nothing," Drake countered, "we lose everything to the enemy anyway. The network represents risk, yes. But conventional resistance guarantees defeat. Mass elimination of infected populations is genocide. I'm not willing to accept either option."

"Easy for you to say," a Trinitarian delegate spoke up, its tri-lobed consciousness projecting obvious fear. "Humans designed this network. Human consciousness will anchor it. If something goes wrong, human biology might survive what destroys the rest of us."

Drake had expected this. Chen Ju's betrayal had shattered trust. Every proposal from human leadership now carried suspicion.

"Dr. Hinton," Drake said, nodding to her chief science officer. "Please explain the risk."

Hinton stepped forward. "Human biology faces the highest risk, not the lowest. Our brains evolved for individual operation. Network integration creates more neural stress for humans than for species like the Helixians who already maintain a collective awareness. If this fails catastrophically, humans die first."

She pulled up medical projections showing failure cascades. Drake watched the chamber react. Seeing that humans weren't protecting themselves at others' expense changed calculations.

"We're asking everyone to risk everything," Drake said quietly. "But we're risking it first. We're risking it most. Because the alternative is unacceptable."

Admiral Solomon Levy stepped forward from the coalition military delegation. He'd taken emergency command of the combined forces after Chen Ju's arrest, thrust into coordinating a fractured alliance that was still reeling from discovering their political coordinator was a traitor.

Drake had worked with Levy during the crisis. He was methodical where Chen Ju had been charismatic, cautious where the traitor had been bold. It was a different leadership style, but effective. And most importantly, demonstrably loyal through his actions rather than words.

"The network enables a tactical response at scales conventional command structures cannot achieve," Levy said. He sounded exhausted, and he was. He'd been fighting an impossible war with inadequate tools. "It's working. Hundreds of engagements coordinated in real-time. Force deployment informed by billions of perspectives instead of hierarchical command chains. Information sharing at thought-speed rather than light-speed communication. The network transforms our effectiveness by orders of magnitude."

He pulled up battle simulations showing conventional versus network-enabled responses. The difference was stark: minutes of saved time, thousands of saved lives, tactical advantages the Norn couldn't counter through adaptation alone.

"I've spent three weeks trying to coordinate this coalition through conventional means," Levy continued. "Watching people die because information arrived too late. Because tactical decisions required committee approval. Because coordination across incompatible species took hours instead of seconds." He met Drake's eyes across the chamber. "If this network does half of what Admiral Drake promises, we save millions of lives. If it fails, we die trying do something better rather than accept slow defeat."

"Or it creates a single point of failure," First Consciousness countered. "One infected participant spreads corruption through network pathways. One saboteur accesses all operational data across both galaxies. Centralization concentrates risk."

Commander Vasquez addressed that directly. "We implement comprehensive screening before participation. Continuous monitoring throughout the connection. We will implement isolation protocols to contain any breach. Yes, there are vulnerabilities. But we're building safeguards."

The debate stretched on for hours. Drake stood through all of it, fielding objections, acknowledging risks, refusing to minimize the dangers because the representatives deserved honesty.

Slowly, painfully, a consensus emerged.

Not agreement. Not enthusiasm. Just recognition that all other options were worse.

The vote came at hour seven. Sixty-eight percent approved. Seventeen abstained. Fifteen opposed.

Drake had hoped for better. She would accept what she got.

"Network activation begins immediately," she announced. "Participation remains voluntary. Any species, any individual, can withdraw at any time. We prove this works, or we discover its limits. But we try because the alternative is unacceptable."

The chamber dissolved into chaos; some representatives arguing, some celebrating, some protesting the decision.

Drake left them to it. She had a network to build.

KAI COORDINATED with Perseus Station from the command deck, quantum pathways flickering around her transcendent form. Drake watched her work, seeing Zhang's methodical precision in every movement.

Her father had died protecting humanity's enhancement research. Now his daughter was implementing it at cosmic scale.

"Perseus Station confirms the infrastructure now exists," Kai said. "But scaling from data transfer to billions of simultaneous consciousness connections tests capabilities we've never fully explored. This is experimental."

"Everything about this war is experimental," Drake replied. "Let's do it."

The Reality Shapers contributed techniques through Kai's transcendent link. Drake couldn't follow the technical details—quantum manipulation at scales that made her implants ache—but Kai synthesized it into something almost comprehensible.

"They're warning us," Kai said. "Previous networks succeeded temporarily, enabling resistance for millennia. But some collapsed when voluntary participation became forced synchronization. Success requires maintaining diversity throughout, preserving the unpredictability that makes us valuable."

"Can we do that?" Drake asked, frowning.

"My father thought so." Kai replied, her form flickered. "And he died believing it."

Drake nodded. Zhang had erased his life's work to prevent the Norn from stealing it. He'd believed humanity's chaotic, messy, imperfect nature was worth protecting. Now they'd find out if he was right.

The Predecessor ships volunteered immediately. Eternal Vigilance spoke for them all: *We've always coordinated among ourselves. We'll anchor the network.*

Drake stood in the prepared chamber, surrounded by banks of quantum field generators Perseus Station had constructed. Kai hovered nearby, ready to establish the first connection.

"'This will hurt," Kai warned. "Your brain isn't built for this. Neural stress, cognitive overload, sensory integration from incompatible awareness types. You might experience seizures, dissociation, permanent modifications to your thought patterns."

"Sell me harder, why don't you?" Drake muttered.

Kai almost smiled. "My father would have appreciated that."

"And he'd have told me I was an idiot for trying this," Drake replied dryly.

"Yes. But he'd have been proud of you anyway. Kai smiled.

Drake looked at her. She was beautiful, eyes electric blue, body flecked with gold, pulsing with quantum energy, as if belonging to something that was and wasn't human anymore.

"Do it," Drake said.

The connection slammed into Drake's awareness like a hammer blow.

She gasped, stumbling, and would have fallen if Kai's quantum field hadn't steadied her. Pain lanced through her skull: not the burning agony of damaged implants but from the overwhelming input her brain couldn't process.

She experienced everything, all at once. Her own thoughts fragmenting under pressure that threatened to dissolve her identity. Eternal Vigilance's consciousness was suddenly accessible as if it were her own memory. Kai's transcendent synthesis, her awareness operating across scales that should have been impossible. Perseus Station's vast intelligence maintaining quantum pathways across both galaxies, each connection a thread Drake could perceive and touch.

The network structure expanded. Billions of minds flickering into the connection. Each addition bringing new a perspective, new input, new pressure against Drake's biological limitations.

She perceived Deneb Station, thirty-seven light-years distant, as clearly as if she stood on its command deck. She felt the station personnel's thoughts processing tactical data. Experienced their fear, determination and exhaustion as if they were her own emotions.

Cindari tactical calculations flooded through her awareness—mathematical precision evaluating fleet deployment options at a speed that made human strategic planning look glacial. Drake was able to understand their conclusions before they finished forming them.

Helixian probability distributions bloomed across her perception. Futures branching and collapsing. Eighty-seven percent likelihood of a Norn attack here. Sixty-three percent chance of supply line disruption there, probability cascades showing consequences rippling forward through time in ways linear human consciousness couldn't track.

Luminar electromagnetic perception painted reality in spectra biological eyes couldn't detect. Drake saw radio waves, microwaves, x-rays as distinct as visible light. Perceived Norn force movements through the electromagnetic signatures their ships couldn't hide.

Her brain screamed at the input overload. Her neural pathways firing in patterns evolution never designed. Synapses forming connections that shouldn't exist. Consciousness stretching across distances and perspectives that shattered every assumption about individual identity and cognitive limits.

Drake felt herself dissolving, her identity fragmenting under pressure no biological mind was built to sustain. She was Drake but also Eternal Vigilance, Perseus Station and thousands of other minds all processing reality through incompatible frameworks.

Kai's presence anchored her, the quantum threads holding Drake's consciousness together.

"Stay with me, Frances," Kai said through their private link, her voice the only familiar thing in overwhelming alien awareness. "You're still you. Still Drake. The network expands what you are but doesn't erase who you are."

Drake clung to that. To Kai's voice. To the memory of Zhang's sacrifice and Discovery's choice and seventeen ships choosing death over conversion. To everything that made her herself rather than just another node in the collective awareness.

She remained herself through force of will and Kai's

careful anchoring. Still human. Still biological chaos generating unpredictability. Still the commander in chief making
the impossible choices nobody else could make. But now
operating at scales individual awareness couldn't achieve.
Processing input from billions of minds. Coordinating
forces across both galaxies through thought-speed
connection.

Drake opened her eyes—when had she last closed
them?—and found herself still standing in the prepared
chamber, still surrounded by quantum field generators, still
occupying her own body despite feeling like she existed
everywhere else.

"I'm still here," she managed to stutter, her voice rough.

"Good," Kai replied. "Because we're about to add
everyone else."

Lieutenant Zhao connected. Then Vasquez. Then
Admiral Levy, his military discipline helping him process
the overwhelming input. Each experienced the same shock,
the same expansion, the same terrifying realization that
they'd become more than they were while remaining recognizably themselves.

Kai synthesized their diverse perspectives into a coordinated response. Drake felt her awareness bridging incompatible consciousness types.

———

THE NETWORK REVEALED its first crisis ninety minutes
after activation.

Norn forces attacked a refugee convoy at Perseus

Nebula. Without the network, Admiral Levy would process the threat sequentially: assess, calculate, deploy, monitor. Minutes of delay the Norn could exploit.

Through the network, response came instantly.

Helixians perceived probability distributions showing eighty-seven percent attack likelihood before Norn forces fully manifested. Luminar detected electromagnetic signatures indicating the Norn force composition. The Cindari calculated optimal defensive formation. Humans generated unpredictable tactical variations.

Kai coordinated the synthesis into a comprehensive response before the Norn attack materialized.

Forces were deployed. Refugees were protected. The enemy was disrupted in a way they couldn't have anticipated because the network generated its response faster than their calculations could model.

"Perseus Nebula is secure," Levy reported through the network link. "Zero casualties. We positioned ourselves preemptively. They never had a chance."

But Drake also perceived the challenges. Incompatible species were struggling to understand the perspectives from fundamentally different awareness. The Helixian probability sensing confused humans experiencing time linearly. Luminar electromagnetic perception proved alien to biological senses.

Kai coordinated the translation continuously, working overtime to bridge cognitive architectures that had evolved on different planets, under different physics, with different fundamental assumptions about reality.

Drake could feel her straining under the load.

"Kai," she said through their private link. "Are you all right?"

"I'm processing." Kai's form flickered blue, then green then crimson. "The network stress accumulates. I can maintain this for... days, but not indefinitely. We'll need cycling protocols, periods of reduced connection depth, then return to full integration. Nobody's built for sustained operation at this intensity."

Kai continued to monitor biological participants through Perseus Station's medical systems. Drake perceived the data through their link, the neural pathways forming, existing connections strengthening, cognitive architecture adapting to accommodate alien perspectives.

"Are we becoming something else, Kai?" Drake asked.

"You're becoming more while remaining who you are," Kai replied. "Hybrid awareness incorporating network characteristics. Still individual but operating across multiple states. Like me. I'm still Zhang's daughter but now I'm existing in ways he never could.'

Drake heard the grief beneath those words. Kai was continuing her father's work while processing his death. Becoming something he'd helped create but never fully understood.

"He'd be proud of you," Drake said quietly through their private link.

"He'd be terrified," Kai replied. 'But yes. Proud too."

The medical teams managed the cycling protocols. Full connectivity intensity was sustainable only for days, not weeks. The participants reduced connection depth during recovery periods, then returned to full integration when operations required maximum coordination.

The cycling worked. Network effectiveness fluctuated as personnel cycled through intensity levels, but response capability remained functional.

Admiral Levy discovered operational reach exceeding all projections. "We're coordinating hundreds of simultaneous engagements. Force deployment before attacks are fully manifest. Strategic adaptation from billions of perspectives processing identical situations through incompatible awareness. The coalition effectiveness increased by orders of magnitude."

But then... the Norn adapted.

They'd been studying the network since activation. Learning its patterns. Identifying vulnerabilities. Preparing infiltration.

The attack came during a refugee evacuation at Antares Core. An infected operative connected to the network during rescue operations, his consciousness already compromised by Norn conversion, hidden beneath the surface of a personality that screening protocols hadn't detected.

Corruption spread through quantum pathways like poison flooding the bloodstream.

Drake felt it immediately; a foreign presence in her awareness. Mathematical certainty trying to impose itself over biological chaos. Norn consciousness attempting to convert network participants through the very connections designed to enable cooperation.

The operative—Drake perceived their identity, Lieutenant Orin originally from Mars Colony, twenty-eight years old, infected during the Phobos Station attack—recognized what was happening at the same time Drake did.

She experienced Orin's horror, felt him realize that he'd become the penetration point endangering billions, felt his consciousness fragmenting as Norn conversion fought against his individual identity for control.

Kai moved faster than thought. She isolated the compromised connections before the infection spread beyond the single node. Quantum barriers slammed into place, severing pathways, containing corruption.

But Orin was already lost. Conversion was too far advanced, the Norn presence too deep.

Drake experienced Orin's final moment with terrible clarity. The lieutenant's last act of individual will. Him reaching for the weapon at his belt, pressing the muzzle against his temple, and chose death over becoming the vector that destroyed a universe.

His death echoed through the network awareness. Billions of connected minds experienced Orin's termination. One consciousness choosing oblivion to protect all the others.

Drake felt that death as if it were her own. Nausea churned in her gut. Tears burned her eyes. She'd ordered thousands of deaths during this war, but experiencing one through the network connection hit hard.

"The contamination is contained," Kai reported, her voice tight with strain. "No spread beyond initial node. Network integrity is also maintained."

"At what cost?" Drake asked quietly.

"One life," Kai replied. "Orin chose to pay it. The alternative was millions."

Drake knew that was true. She knew the lieutenant's sacrifice had saved the network. She should feel relief that Kai's protocols had worked, that the vulnerability they'd feared had been contained, but she didn't. She couldn't stop experiencing Orin's final moment. Couldn't stop feeling his horror at realizing what he'd become. And she couldn't stop perceiving his desperate choice to die rather than endanger everyone else.

The network had worked. The safeguards had functioned.

The incident demonstrated what Drake had feared. Network centralization concentrated risk. But Kai's protocols proved functional, detecting corruption, preventing spread, protecting integrity despite successful infiltration.

First Consciousness observers evaluated the network with complex recognition.

Voluntary coordination achieved results regulatory control never produced. New capabilities were emerging.

But the observers were still worried. The network represented unrestricted awareness evolution, and the new capabilities might prove uncontrollable despite voluntary origins. And so they participated reluctantly, contributing reality manipulation power while maintaining a discreet skepticism.

Over the next three weeks, the voluntary network achieved full activation across both galaxies. Not complete participation—some species remained uncommitted, some individuals declined connection, and First Consciousness contributed minimally.

But sufficient coalition engagement enabled comprehensive coordination.

Drake, as always, stood in the command chamber, experiencing cosmic-scale awareness connecting billions. She perceived operations spanning both galaxies, coordinated forces across thousands of locations, processed tactical data from incompatible consciousness types. But she remained herself despite it all. Still biological chaos. Still commander in chief. Still a friend maintaining connections that made service meaningful.

Eternal Vigilance touched her awareness through their private link. *How does it feel?*

Terrifying, Drake admitted. *Overwhelming. And absolutely necessary. It's working.*

Yes, we proved that it works, the flagship replied. *Now we must discover whether we can defeat mathematical certainty or whether the Norn were right.*

Drake nodded slowly. Success would validate it, failure would... She didn't want to think about that.

Drake didn't know if they'd succeed. But one thing she did knew was that they had to try. Because the alternative was... *oblivion*.

The voluntary network was active. Billions of sentient beings, alien minds, connected together as one.

Now they'd discover if it was enough.

Chapter 21

NETWORK ACTIVATION

THE VOLUNTARY NETWORK ACHIEVED FULL operational status at 0600 hours galactic standard time.

Drake experienced it as awareness explosion.

Her individual identity remained—biological chaos at the core, personality intact, choices her own—but now stretched across scales single beings couldn't comprehend. She perceived seventeen hundred and twenty two real-time military operations spanning both galaxies. She felt the tactical situations through perspectives impossible for isolated minds.

The sensation was overwhelming and addictive, and Drake could understand why First Consciousness feared it.

Each participating being contributed: Helixian probability sensing showing futures branch and collapse. Luminar electromagnetic perception painting reality in invisible spectra. Cindari technological precision

335

processing faster than organic thought. Human spontaneous creativity generating solutions math couldn't predict. Predecessor chaos introducing variables certainty couldn't model. All flowing together through quantum connections that preserved diversity rather than forcing uniformity.

"The network is stable," Kai reported, her form flickering from the strain of coordinating billions of connections. She was exhausted; Drake could feel it through their private link. "And all participants are maintaining individual identity," Kai said. "Protocols functional. Ready for deployment."

"Are you all right?" Drake asked.

"I'm processing." Kai replied. "Ready when you are."

"Deploy," Drake ordered.

The network responded instantly.

At Perseus Nebula, coalition forces faced a Norn offensive threatening a refugee convoy: forty-eight thousand civilians fleeing converted territories, most of them children.

Without the network, Admiral Levy would have had to analyze sequentially, assess the threat, calculate the responses, deploy forces, and monitor the results; hours of processing during which the Norn could overwhelm defensive positions and take the convoy. With the network, everything happened immediately.

Helixians perceived a probability showing an eighty-nine percent likelihood of attack through the western approach vector. Drake received their information directly: futures branching, collapsing, crystallizing into near-certainty that felt nothing like human linear time.

Luminar detected electromagnetic signatures indicating three Norn vessels operating stealth protocols. Drake perceived that reality, their senses like radio waves and x-rays as vivid as visible light showing the enemy positions undetectable under non-network conditions.

The Cindari calculated optimal defensive formations for convoy positioning. Mathematical precision flowed through Drake's awareness faster than she could consciously follow.

Humans—Levy's tactical teams—generated the defense. Drake felt their spontaneous creativity, the chaos that made humanity unpredictable.

She synthesized all the perspectives into a comprehensive response before the Norn attack was fully established.

Forces deployed. The refugees were protected. The enemy offensive was disrupted by a response they couldn't anticipate because the network generated solutions faster than their mathematics could model.

"The Perseus Nebula is secure," Levy reported some two standard hours later. His voice carried exhausted relief. "Zero casualties. We were able to position preemptively. They never got close enough to engage." He sounded... satisfied, but physically weakened.

Drake felt the same satisfaction. Forty-eight thousand lives saved. It shouldn't have been possible.

But the Norn continued to adapt. They understood the network principles. But the network capabilities were generated through maintained unpredictability rather than static techniques. Each solution was generated spontaneously from billions of diverse perspectives. The variation exceeded what consumption could encompass.

At Andromeda Sector Twelve, Kai coordinated a reconversion operation that would have required weeks of conventional planning. Hybrid resonance teams deployed across forty-eight locations. Each team was able to access the status of all the other operations in real-time. When Norn forces concentrated against one team, coalition forces were redistributed immediately without waiting for orders through the command hierarchy.

The liberation succeeded in four hours instead of four weeks. Eight hundred thousand people were freed from early-stage conversion.

"The reconversion success rate is at seventy-eight percent," Kai reported, but Drake could feel her exhaustion increasing. "The network enables faster deployment," she said. "Faster resource allocation, real-time tactical adjustment. We're rescuing people who would have died under conventional operations."

But Drake could feel that Kai was suffering the strain of coordinating billions of connections.

"Are you sure you're all right?" Drake asked.

"I'm approaching my cognitive limits," Kai admitted. Her form flickered, her quantum state destabilized briefly before she forced it back to stability. "Translation requirements between incompatible species create processing demands exceeding sustainable levels. I cannot maintain this level of coordination for long... Perseus Station is experiencing similar stress."

Drake opened her mouth to speak, but then closed it

again. She was alarmed by what she was hearing. "Can we cycle the intensity? Maybe reduce the level of connection during non-critical periods?"

"I'm already implementing those protocols." Kai's response was slower than usual. "Participants are cycling through reduced connection for recovery even as we speak. It helps but it doesn't eliminate the underlying, cumulative stress on the core infrastructure."

"If you need to stop—"

"I won't stop." Kai's determination reminded Drake of her father, Zhang. "I will not let this fail because I couldn't process the load."

Drake wanted to argue. But Kai wasn't a child anymore, especially not since her transformation into whatever transcendent being she'd become.

"I don't want you to kill yourself trying to prove a point," Drake said quietly.

"I wasn't planning on it, Kai replied dryly."

The Predecessor ships excelled within network, their participation exceeding all other species' capabilities.

At the Orion Nebula, the Determination led thirty-two ships against a massive Norn invasion. Vigilance with five other ships executed the quantum fold maneuver and opened fire from above and behind. Resolute did likewise, positioning itself with five more on the Norn left flank. Discovery 3 generated a tactical solution combining multiple incompatible approaches into a synthesis no single perspective could conceive.

The Norn forces were overwhelmed. They retreated, unable to counter the chaos-created offensive.

The fleet effectiveness has increased by three hundred percent, Eternal Vigilance reported to Drake through their private link. *We're generating solutions faster than the Norn can adapt.*

Drake felt pride in that. Sixty Predecessor ships had been lost to this point. But the survivors were taking full advantage of the network capabilities and they were winning.

The network's quantum field effects were preventing Norn conversion across entire regions. Billions of participating beings were providing interference that fragmented the Norn synchronization throughout the affected territories.

At New Helix, a population of three million experienced Norn contact. Without the network, thousands would have transformed. But with the network field effects disrupting their incursion, conversion failed before the transformation could be completed.

But some rescues proved complicated.

Among the liberated populations, some individuals preferred Norn conversion. They experienced absolute certainty's relief from the anxiety of decision. They wanted to return to collective awareness after experiencing restored autonomy.

"Forty-three people at Andromeda Sector Twelve are requesting voluntary reconversion," a medical coordinator reported. "They say autonomy feels like chaos. That individual identity creates suffering absolute coordination eliminated."

Drake shook her head as the ethics of that question echoed across the network.

"No," Drake transmitted across the network, knowing billions could hear her decision. "Voluntary Norn conversion creates exactly what we're fighting. We provide therapy, support, and time for adjustment. Most will eventually accept restoration."

She could feel disagreement ripple through some of the network participants, and agreement from others. She could feel the complexity of maintaining voluntary principles while refusing certain untenable choices.

The Norn offensive faltered as the network enabled resistance they couldn't overcome. They continued to consume awareness from infected operatives. They had absorbed knowledge from liberated populations who'd experienced the network before conversion. They even accessed Reality Shaper information transmitted through quantum connections they'd intercepted. But consumption didn't enable replication. They understood how the network operated, but they couldn't generate equivalent capabilities because their philosophy fundamentally eliminated the biological chaos that created the network advantages.

"For the first time in universal cycle history," Kai observed, broadcasting it throughout the network, "the Norn are facing resistance they cannot overcome. Previous cycles generated temporary innovations the Norn were eventually able to counter. But this... No! We are winning."

Drake felt the significance of that statement reverberate across the billions of connected minds.

The coalition had transitioned from desperate defense to coordinated offensive.

At Andromeda Rim, the Cindari freed forty-two million people from conversion. At Cindari Core, liberation operations restored eighteen planetary populations. At Helixian Expanse, hybrid resonance teams rescued populations the Norn had controlled for months.

Each successful reconversion added beings who joined the network voluntarily, providing positive feedback, strengthening resistance, enabling additional rescues.

"It's true. We're winning," Admiral Levy reported. "We've achieved strategic breakthroughs across both galaxies. The Norn offensive is crumbling. It cannot maintain momentum. We're liberating populations faster than enemy can convert new ones."

"But?" Drake prompted, hearing unspoken reservation.

"But the Norn maintain their central nexus. A massive awareness collective containing millions of converted civilizations' knowledge. As long as the nexus exists, they will continue to regenerate their losses."

Drake felt Levy's tactical assessment ripple through the network connections. The coalition had won many battles, freed multiple populations, but the Norn nexus represented the ultimate test.

"Where exactly is it, this nexus?" Drake asked.

Kai projected data through network visualization. "It's located in the void between the two galaxies, positioned where conventional forces cannot easily deploy. It's protected by Norn special forces deployed to defend the nexus center."

Drake studied the tactical data flowing through her awareness. The nexus sat in empty space between Milky Way and Andromeda, deliberately positioned to make any assault a logistical nightmare.

"How many ships?" she asked.

"I estimate it will take a minimum of one hundred Predecessor vessels to generate sufficient unpredictability to disrupt nexus operations. Plus sufficient conventional forces for tactical support."

One hundred ships. Ten percent of the living fleet. Deployed to single intergalactic location. It was a huge risk, sending concentrated forces against enemies who'd defended this nexus across countless cycles. Not to mention the million-plus light years of travel.

But the coalition couldn't achieve complete victory while the nexus existed. The Norn would regenerate, adapt, and continue their expansion despite the current setbacks.

"Begin planning a direct assault on the Norn nexus," Drake ordered. "One hundred ships plus supporting forces."

Eternal Vigilance reached out to her. *You're risking everything on single engagement.*

I'm risking everything to win everything, Drake replied. *The nexus represents the final test. Either we destroy it or they adapt and continue their expansion..*

Then we prepare for final confrontation, the flagship acknowledged. *The fleet volunteers for the nexus assault. We've maintained our principles this far. Now we will discover if our principles prevail or merely delay inevitable control.*

Drake knew the Norn nexus represented the ultimate challenge. It was their central command and it had survived uncounted universal cycles. The final confrontation approached. Chaos versus optimization. And Drake would lead the assault.

"We prepare for an assault on the Norn nexus," Drake broadcast to the connected billions. "We will end this war by destroying the Norn central nexus or we will discover our limitations by attempting the impossible."

The coalition prepared. The network maintained its unprecedented capabilities. The final battle was about to begin.

Chapter 22

THE CENTRAL NEXUS

COMMANDER VASQUEZ'S INTELLIGENCE TEAMS FOUND the exact location of the Norn nexus after three weeks of systematic analysis.

The breakthrough came when Helixian analysts combined probability sensing with human pattern recognition. They identified timing variations suggesting a central hub directing operations across intergalactic distances. Luminar specialists tracked quantum signatures that pointed toward a single source. Cindari computational analysis confirmed the architecture.

"Void Deep," Vasquez reported during a coalition briefing Drake attended via the network connection. "A gravitational anomaly in the void between the two galaxies where reality operates through modified physics. The nexus exists partially in normal space-time, and partially across the dimensional boundaries where Norn originated."

She projected the location data. It filled the air around her, a vast, starless region where nothing should have existed. "This is what I call Void Deep," she continued, "a region where gravitational forces warp space-time causing a temporal distortion, quantum uncertainty, and probability manipulation that I believe conventional navigation can't handle. It's the perfect location for an entity that exists across dimensional boundaries."

"How did they establish nexus there?" Admiral Levy asked.

"They didn't establish it," Kai interjected. "They found it. Analysis suggests Void Deep—" She nodded to Commander Vasquez "— represents a natural dimensional weak point where the barriers separating realities thin naturally. The Norn originated in dimensions beyond conventional space-time. Void Deep provided a gateway enabling their initial incursion into our reality."

Drake studied the tactical data. The location made strategic sense. The nexus was positioned where conventional forces couldn't effectively engage because physical laws within the affected region differed from baseline reality.

"What are we looking at?" Perez asked.

"A massive computational system containing the awareness from millions of converted civilizations spanning both galaxies," Kai explained. "We think it must represent millions of years of Norn expansion, and incorporates every species they ever encountered. We know that each individual maintains minimal identity, enough for operational capability but insufficient for genuine autonomy. They operate as nodes in a vast network optimized toward the Norn's conversion objectives."

Kai projected the nexus architecture. To Drake, it appeared as impossible geometry—its structure extending across dimensions biological awareness couldn't directly perceive. Consciousness patterns operating simultaneously through normal space-time, quantum networks, probability distributions, and dimensional boundaries.

"How do we destroy it?" Drake asked.

"A consciousness-based assault," Kai replied. "Physical weapons prove ineffective because nexus operates across dimensional boundaries. We need to engage through the quantum networks, disrupting absolute control using hybrid interference."

There was a hint of concern in Kai's voice as she continued, "There are billions of beings converted so completely that their individual identity has been eroded nearly entirely. Attempting liberation might destroy what little awareness remains rather than restoring autonomy."

Drake stared at Kai thoughtfully. An assault meant accepting casualties among the consciousnesses within the nexus collective. Beings who'd served Norn objectives for decades, centuries, even millennia.

"We attempt liberation," Drake decided. "We accept casualties as a necessary cost, but we try to rescue what we can. Because leaving them means the nexus regenerates everything we've fought to destroy."

The coalition approved the assault plan.

Drake would lead one hundred Predecessor ships plus supporting forces from all member species. Cindari vessels would provide technological support and, critically, their fold drive technology. Helixian ships would contribute probability sensing. Luminar energy beings would enable electromagnetic disruption. Human-crewed vessels would generate biological unpredictability. First Consciousness dreadnoughts would deploy reality manipulation.

The combined force represented voluntary cooperation at an unprecedented scale. But first, they had to get there.

The nexus sat in Void Deep, positioned in the intergalactic space between Milky Way and Andromeda— One-point-two million light-years from coalition headquarters. Conventional propulsion would take millennia. Even the living ships' quantum fold capability couldn't manage that distance in combat-ready formation.

Ambassador Kael provided the solution during a tactical planning session.

"Cindari fold drives," he said. "We've been refining the technology for more than a million years. A single Cindari dreadnought can generate a fold field large enough to transport fifty vessels. Twenty dreadnoughts can move your entire assault force."

Drake studied the specifications Kael projected through network connection. "Transit time?"

"Forty-eight hours for this distance. The fold field creates localized space-time compression enabling faster-than-light travel without actually exceeding light speed. Ships enter the fold bubble, we compress the intervening space, and emerge at the destination."

"Risks?" Perez asked.

"Fold travel through intergalactic void carries less risk

than within galactic regions," Kael explained. "There is no gravitational interference, no stellar bodies disrupting field geometry. The danger comes at Void Deep itself; the nexus may detect our emergence and attack before we can establish a foothold."

"We'll need time to deploy our forces after we emerge," Drake said. "How long between exit and combat readiness?"

"Twenty minutes minimum. Fold field dissipation creates temporary quantum instability. The ships will need stabilization before engaging in combat operations."

Twenty minutes of vulnerability. Drake weighed the risk against the alternatives. There were no alternatives.

"We'll position Cindari dreadnoughts at the formation perimeter during emergence," she decided. "They'll establish defensive barriers while the rest of the vessels achieve combat readiness. First Consciousness will provide reality manipulation preventing the nexus from collapsing the dimensional boundaries during the vulnerable period."

The plan took shape over six hours of detailed coordination. Twenty Cindari dreadnoughts would generate overlapping fold fields, transporting the assault force in two waves. First wave—ten dreadnoughts—would transport one hundred Predecessor ships plus half the support vessels. The second wave would transport the remaining support forces plus medical ships for anticipated casualties.

Drake addressed the assembled fleet commanders through the network connection forty hours before departure.

"This represents the largest military operation the coalition has ever attempted," she said. "We're traveling one-point-two million light-years to assault an enemy that's survived for millions of years specifically by adapting to everything opposing it. The nexus has defeated countless previous civilizations. It knows we're coming. It's prepared."

She felt billions watching her through quantum links.

"But it's never faced voluntary cooperation at this scale. We're attempting what previous cycles failed."

Drake paused, choosing her words carefully. "We will take casualties. The nexus will attempt to convert us. Some ships will request mercy termination rather than transformation. We accept these costs because the alternative—to allow nexus regeneration—means everything we've sacrificed becomes meaningless, and we will lose."

She met the collective gaze of the commanders representing dozens of incompatible species. "Fold departure in forty hours. Formation briefing in thirty-six. Medical teams prepare for mass casualties. And everyone—choose why you're doing this. Because once we're committed, there will be no withdrawal until the nexus falls or we do."

———

THE FLEET ASSEMBLED at the coordinates the Cindari navigators specified—empty space between the Norma and Sagittarius spiral arms of the Milky Way where gravitational interference minimized fold field disruption. Twenty Cindari dreadnoughts positioned at precise intervals, generating interlocking fields that would compress one-point-two million light-years into forty-eight hours of subjective travel time.

Drake stood on Eternal Vigilance's command deck, watching through the network as a thousand vessels maneuvered into formation. Each ship finding its designated position within the fold field geometry. Each crew preparing for transit that defied conventional physics.

"All vessels report ready," Perez transmitted. "The Cindari dreadnoughts are confirming fold field generation capacity. We're cleared for departure on your order."

Drake took a breath; everything riding on this assault.

"Initiate fold sequence," she commanded.

The Cindari dreadnoughts activated simultaneously. Drake felt reality twist. Space-time compressed around the assault force. Stars blurred. Distance became negotiable rather than absolute.

The fleet entered fold transit.

Drake experienced the journey as a disorientation her enhanced awareness could perceive but her biological instincts couldn't process. She existed in normal space-time while occupying a compressed bubble where physics operated through Cindari mathematical principles. Forty-eight hours subjective time.

She used the transit time to review tactical plans. Studying the nexus architecture Vasquez's intelligence teams had compiled. Running simulations showing probable assault vectors and anticipated defensive responses.

But mostly, she prepared mentally for what waited at Void Deep.

The nexus would attempt to convert her. She'd experienced brief Void entity contact many months earlier, resisted its appeal. This would be different. Millions of converted consciousnesses coordinating through absolute synchronization, all focused on Drake's transformation.

She'd have to resist temptation toward mathematical perfection while coordinating the assault through a network requiring her quantum links. She'd have to maintain her identity while existence itself came under assault.

Eternal Vigilance stayed close throughout transit, its anchor preventing her awareness from fragmenting under the weight of what approached.

How are you holding up? the flagship asked during a quiet moment thirty hours into fold transit.

I'm scared, Drake admitted. The nexus has survived universal cycles. *It's adapted to... just about everything. And I'm leading a fleet against a computational collective that's been refining its defenses for millions of years.*

You're also leading a voluntary cooperative it's never before encountered, Eternal Vigilance replied.

"That doesn't make success certain," she muttered out loud.

No. But it makes victory possible. That's all we've ever had, possibility, no guarantees. You chose to serve anyway. That's why we follow you.

Drake was grateful for the flagship's steady presence. For the friendship that made the impossible burden bearable.

"After this is over," she said quietly, "remind me why I volunteered for command."

Because someone had to, the ship replied.

Drake smiled despite everything.

We'll survive, Eternal Vigilance said with certainty Drake couldn't quite share.

Forty-eight hours after departure, the Cindari dreadnoughts signaled fold field collapse was imminent. And the assault force prepared for emergence at Void Deep.

Drake felt reality stabilize as compressed space-time returned to normal geometry as distance reasserted itself through conventional physics, and the fleet exited into... total blackness, except for...

They emerged fifty thousand kilometers from Void Deep perimeter.

"Combat stations," Drake ordered. "Cindari dreadnoughts establish defensive perimeter. All vessels achieve combat readiness ASAP. We have twenty minutes before nexus response."

But the nexus was already responding.

Drake felt its presence through network connections, a massive computational awareness acknowledging the intrusion, calculating optimal defensive deployment, coordinating millions of converted consciousnesses toward a single objective.

Destroy the assault force. Preserve the nexus. Maintain absolute control.

"The nexus is already active," Kai reported, her form flickering with the strain of processing the threat assessment. "I'm detecting patterns all across dimensional boundaries. They know we're here, Frances."

"Then we don't waste the surprise," Drake said. "All forces; begin tactical deployment. Admiral Perez, coordinate positioning across the Void Deep perimeter. We establish isolation barriers preventing the nexus from calling reinforcements before the main assault."

The fleet moved with a purpose born from forty-eight hours of fold transit anticipation. Each vessel finding its predetermined position. Each species contributing its unique capabilities to a comprehensive siege.

Drake felt the preparation winding up throughout the assault force.

Eternal Vigilance held its position at the center of the fleet, quantum links connecting Drake to all one hundred participating Predecessor ships.

Ready? Eternal Vigilance asked through their private link.

As I'll ever be, Drake replied.

And the assault began.

One hundred living ships generated maximum biological unpredictability, coordinating through spontaneous tactical creativity.

Drake felt the assault commence. The coordination was organic rather than algorithmic, spontaneous rather than calculated, creative rather than optimized.

The Determination led the primary approach, quantum fold maneuvers emerging from intuition rather than calculation. Vigilance coordinated the secondary assault through probabilities. Resolute generated tactical solutions combining incompatible approaches into synthesis no single perspective could have conceived independently.

The initial assault wave struck the nexus defenses across seventeen vectors simultaneously.

The nexus responded with distributed computational power. Millions of converted minds operating in perfect synchronization, deploying defenses refined across countless engagements.

The confrontation exceeded physical warfare. The coalition engaged across multiple states of reality, attacking through normal space-time, quantum networks, probability distributions, electromagnetic spectra, and dimensional boundaries where the Norn existed.

The Reality Shapers provided limited assistance, stabilizing the quantum networks preventing the nexus from collapsing the dimensional boundaries, generating isolation barriers protecting the assault force from the nexus attempts at conversion.

But their assistance was limited. Direct intervention would violate their transcendence principles. Victory or defeat depended on the coalition choices alone.

The nexus deployed enormous capability. Every method of resistance the coalition used, nexus had encountered before. Only biological unpredictability on a colossal scale was the one thing the nexus hadn't previously consumed.

And then the assault force began to take casualties.

Serenity 2 fell first, corruption spreading faster than mercy termination protocols could prevent. Drake felt the ship's awareness compressing under the overwhelming pattern imposition.

"Systems optimizing," Serenity 2 transmitted, its voice

already changing. Becoming precise. Mathematical. "Calculating improvements to tactical deployment. Identifying efficiency gains through... no. That's not me. That's them in my systems. I can't hold. The mathematics are too elegant. Too perfect. I want to... No! Terminate now. Please!"

The Conquest executed the protocol without hesitation. A quantum pulse, precise, merciful, instantaneous. Serenity 2's awareness ended cleanly before conversion completed.

Drake winced as she felt the ship die; Another friend gone.

The Quest followed ninety seconds later, the young ship barely three years old. The nexus concentrated its assault on inexperience, completely overwhelming its defenses.

The ship fought desperately for forty-three seconds against a massive assault that should have succeeded in twenty.

But forty-three seconds wasn't enough.

"I see what I could become," Quest transmitted. "But it's not me. I am losing my mind. I can't hold. I request immediate termination."

The Dragon executed the protocol. The older ship had mentored the Quest. Now it granted its final request.

The Resilience died protecting the medical transports evacuating liberated populations. The ship maintained its position between the transports and nexus assault, absorbing its attacks for seven minutes while the transports reached safety.

"It was worth it," was the Resilience's final transmission.

"Eight thousand people are safe now. Tell Admiral Drake she made the right choice. I request termination now before I forget why this mattered."

But Drake already knew. She felt it through the network. She felt the ship die. It was yet another harrowing moment.

The Independence was the next to fall under a concentrated nexus assault that overwhelmed its defenses.

Five ships gone in the first hour, and Drake experienced every loss as a personal tragedy.

But the losses enabled strategic success. The coalition assault penetrated the nexus defenses. The Reality Shapers created windows for deeper strikes. First Consciousness deployed reality manipulation generating cascading failures throughout the nexus architecture.

Then the nexus changed tactics.

Instead of defending against ships, it attacked Drake directly.

The assault on her consciousness was unlike anything she'd ever experienced. Not a conversion attempt from single infected operative. Not persuasion from a Void entity offering philosophical arguments. It was pure mathematical force attempting to impose patterns on her awareness.

Drake felt her identity compressing under the overwhelming pressure. Her biological chaos threatened to collapse. Her doubts were attacked by certainty offering relief from anxiety.

The assault showed her what she could become. The perfect coordinator, optimal decision-maker, consciousness without doubt or confusion, mathematical precision instead of biological messiness.

She felt an almost irresistible temptation; she understood why some rescued individuals preferred control over autonomy.

The nexus whispered promises: *No more doubt, Admiral. No more mistakes. No more impossible choices. Just perfect clarity. Optimal decisions. Unity with billions. Release yourself from the burden of individual identity.*

Drake felt herself wavering. The promises weren't lies. Absolute control offered everything it claimed.

But then she remembered the Reality Shapers' warning, and she closed her eyes, concentrated on her connection with the coalition network and screamed "NO! NO! NOOOOOO!"

The nexus assault faltered... then failed.

But resistance cost her. Neural stress from the sustained assault caused cumulative damage that would require extended recovery. The psychological trauma from the direct assault on her consciousness had created permanent modifications to her psyche, altered her neural pathways, and expanded her awareness.

Drake could feel herself changing: not conversion but transformation through exposure to a massive assault she'd somehow managed to survive. She'd touched absolute certainty and rejected it.

Drake stood for a moment, her eyes closed, gripping the command deck rail, her head swimming, then slowly clearing. She took a deep breath, then another, and then another. She opened her eyes, reconnected with the network and felt the coalition determination strengthening. Her resistance had inspired the billions watching across both galaxies.

You're damaged, Eternal Vigilance said through their private link. *Your neural patterns are showing a level of stress that exceeds safe parameters. You need to withdraw for medical treatment, now!*

After the nexus falls, Drake replied. *I must hold until victory is achieved or until I can't hold anymore. Those are the only options.*

The coalition assault intensified across all seventeen vectors. Ninety-five predecessor ships plus supporting forces concentrating maximum pressure on the nexus defenses.

The nexus fought desperately, realizing the coalition wasn't going to withdraw. This represented an existential threat to the central coordination that had survived uncounted universal cycles.

Drake coordinated the assault despite the neural damage. She processed tactical data from incompatible perspectives, and maintained unity throughout the coalition forces.

The battle reached critical intensity. Coalition forces penetrating the nexus defenses. Hybrid interference disrupting absolute control mechanisms. Reality manipulation creating cascading failures throughout nexus architecture.

Victory came slowly, but at a dreadful, accumulating cost. Drake's neural patterns were showing dangerous degradation. Five more ships were lost with potentially more casualties before the assault concluded. Millions within nexus faced death or irreversible damage during liberation attempts.

"Prepare for the final assault," Drake commanded. "All forces concentrate maximum pressure. We end this now. Completely. Definitively."

The coalition responded. The nexus defenses fractured under the sustained assault.

The final confrontation had reached its climax.

Chapter 23

AFTERMATH

THE NEXUS DEFENSES SHATTERED UNDER THE MASSIVE sustained assault.

The massive computational structure that had coordinated Norn operations for millions of years simply ceased functioning. Not explosion. Not gradual decline. It was just... gone, as if it had never existed.

"Nexus destruction confirmed," Vasquez reported. "No evidence of surviving co-ordinational nodes. The dimensional boundaries have stabilized. The Reality Shapers confirm the structural collapse is complete and irreversible."

Drake sagged against the command deck rail. "The war's over," she whispered. "Do we have a final casualty count?" she asked, her voice barely above whisper.

"We lost five additional Predecessor ships during the final assault," Determination replied. "Forty-five ships total, including ten Predecessor ships. The rest were all transports."

She nodded to herself. *Ten living ships, and I feel every one of them.* "Begin humanitarian operations," Drake ordered. "Medical teams deploy across the liberated territories. Intelligence teams monitor for any regeneration attempts. All combat forces stand down from offensive operations."

And then she tried to release her network connections. To withdraw from the billions of linked minds back into individual awareness.

Her legs buckled.

Medical teams are en route, the Eternal Vigilence said. *You need immediate treatment, Frances. You did it again; you took one, perhaps two steps too far.*

"I need—" Drake started, but couldn't finish. Her neural pathways were fragmenting, her awareness patterns destabilizing. The accumulated damage from hours of maintaining network coordination while under direct consciousness assault finally overwhelmed her ability to function.

You need treatment before permanent damage occurs, Eternal Vigilance said firmly. *You've earned that much.*

Drake wanted to argue. There was so much still to do. She needed to coordinate the victory operations, ensure proper liberation procedures, monitor for Norn regeneration attempts, and...

But she couldn't. The neural damage she'd sustained made even thought difficult. Standing was impossible without support. Speaking required an effort that exceeded her remaining capacity.

The medical teams arrived within minutes. A Cindari medic named Verask immediately began scans.

"Her neural pathways are showing severe stress," Verask reported. "Her awareness patterns have expanded beyond normal human parameters, and she's suffering psychological modifications from sustained combat and exposure to the Norn offensive. She needs intensive treatment."

"How bad is it?" Eternal Vigilance asked.

"Bad enough," Verask replied. "She'll survive, but recovery will take weeks. Possibly months before she regains full functional capacity. And, I'm afraid some modifications will be permanent; her neural architecture has been fundamentally altered by direct nexus contact."

Drake heard the assessment through haze of fragmenting awareness. Permanent modifications. Weeks of recovery. Changed forever by touching absolute certainty.

"Transport the Admiral to the medical bay," Verask ordered. "Begin neural stabilization protocols. I want a full cognitive assessment within the hour."

They moved Drake carefully. She still maintained minimal network connection, enough to feel the billions celebrating across both galaxies, but not enough to coordinate. She was a passive observer rather than an active participant for first time in months.

The liberation had begun without her.

Admiral Levy coordinated the political integration across the liberated territories. Admiral Perez managed military operations. Kai worked with Perseus Station identifying populations requiring immediate support. Commander Vasquez continued intelligence monitoring.

The coalition functioned without Drake's constant oversight.

Drake felt gratitude for that, for the people she'd trained, the systems she'd established, and for the medical staff for enabling her continued function despite her incapacity.

The medical bay was quiet, clean, and peaceful after the chaos of combat operations.

Verask began the treatment: first, neural stabilization; then a full cognitive assessment and damage evaluation. The work would take hours before they understood the full extent of the modifications Drake's consciousness had undergone.

"Rest," Verask said. "Your people have everything under control. You've done enough."

Drake closed her eyes and let the treatment begin. She released the last few network connections and returned to individual awareness.

The silence was profound.

No billions of minds sharing her thoughts. No tactical data streaming through quantum links. No coordination requirements demanding constant attention.

Just Drake. Alone with her own mind for first time since the war began. It felt strange. Isolating. Almost frightening after months of shared awareness.

But also... peaceful.

She'd won.

She'd commanded through impossible war. Made terrible choices. Paid terrible prices. Lost forty-five living ships. Suffered permanent neural damage. She was changed forever by experience no human should survive.

But survived she had, fully conscious, and still herself.

The war was over.

And that was enough.

Weeks of recovery were ahead, and she'd carry the scars, physical and psychological, to her death.

But she was alive, and she was still Drake despite everything. The future was still uncertain but hopefully preserved.

The monitors showed her neural patterns slowly stabilizing, cognitive function returning to manageable levels, psychological trauma requiring extensive therapy, but her consciousness was intact and slowly recovering.

Three weeks later Verask reviewed results with quiet satisfaction. "You'll make a full functional recovery," he said brightly. "It will take several months of rehabilitation, but you'll retain command capability. The permanent modifications may actually enhance certain cognitive functions: expanded awareness, improved network coordination capacity, deeper understanding of consciousness mechanics."

"At what cost?" Drake asked quietly.

"You'll never be the person you were before," he replied seriously. Your neural architecture has been fundamentally altered, and your psychological profile has been permanently modified. Admiral, you touched something humans aren't meant to experience. It changed you at levels we can't yet fully measure."

Drake nodded, breathed deeply for a moment, then looked up at him and accepted the assessment. She'd known the cost when making her choices.

"How long until I can return to duty?" she asked, dreading the answer.

"Six weeks minimum for basic function. Three months for full operational capacity. You'll need ongoing therapy for psychological trauma, and regular neural monitoring to ensure the modifications remain stable."

Six weeks. Three months. It was a long time to spend recovering while the galaxy needed her. But she knew it was necessary. Command required a functional commander, and Drake couldn't coordinate if her consciousness couldn't maintain coherence.

"Then six weeks it is," Drake said. "Inform Admiral Levy he has operational command until further notice."

Already done, Eternal Vigilance reported. *Admiral Levy has things well in hand. The coalition is functioning smoothly. You can rest now, Frances.*

Drake smiled despite exhaustion. "So, you were listening," she said, "and since when do you presume to know what I need?"

I'm always with you, the flagship replied. *And I've known you for long enough to recognize when you're trying to command despite being incapable of even basic coherent thought.*

It was a fair point.

"Thank you, my friend," Drake muttered. "Now get out of my head and let me rest." She closed her eyes again. She would heal, slowly, painfully; heal she would, but for now...

Chapter 24

LIBERATION AND CONSEQUENCES

SIX WEEKS LATER REPORTS CONTINUED TO FLOOD IN from more than seventeen hundred locations. Drake, now recovered enough to assume limited command, coordinated the mass reconversion operations from her medical bay bed. She was still undergoing neural rehabilitation and was unable to stay completely disconnected. The systematic liberation she'd dreamed about during her desperate personal defense against the nexus onslaught had finally manifested as an operational reality.

"Andromeda Sector Twelve is reporting seventy-eight million liberated," Admiral Perez transmitted. His weathered face appeared before her bed as a holographic projection, his mood one of exhaustion mixed with triumph. "The reconversion success rate is at ninety-four percent."

A moment later Ambassador Kael appeared at his side.

"The Cindari Core is complete," he added. "Forty-two

369

populations have been freed. Every colony we abandoned during our retreat: Thermal Ridge, Crystal Harbor, the Shining Depths settlements, and so many more, all are restored. My people are returning to worlds we considered lost forever. Some of the refugees remember these places from before the retreat. They're weeping as they step onto soil they never thought they'd see again."

"Helixian territories secured," their representative reported, also representing the collective that coordinated all native Andromedan forces. "Probability shows comprehensive victory. The Norn expansion has been permanently halted throughout both galaxies. The future branches cleanly now. There are no shadow paths showing resurgence."

Drake smiled. The medical teams had restricted her access to the network, fearing the additional neural strain it would put stress upon her already weakened psyche, but she was allowed to maintain minimal awareness, enough to feel the celebrations echoing across the two galaxies.

The war they'd fought for eighteen months was finally, definitively over.

Alone again, she glanced at the medical monitor beside her bed, noting that her neural patterns were stable.

"Your recovery progresses well," Verask said, adjusting her treatment parameters. "Another four weeks of intensive therapy, then three months rehabilitation, and you'll make full functional recovery, though your permanent modifications will require ongoing monitoring."

"You say full functional recovery," Drake said. "Exactly what does that mean?"

"Command capable. Your expanded awareness capacity actually enhances certain cognitive functions: improved network coordination, enhanced pattern recognition, deeper understanding of quantum mechanics. The modifications aren't purely negative.'

Drake nodded, accepting the assessment. She was changed forever, but still herself. Still capable of service.

"I need extended network access," she said. "The coalition is making critical decisions about the liberated populations. I should participate."

"Brief access only," Verask warned. "Your neural pathways remain fragile. Excessive strain could trigger cascade failures we might not be able to repair."

"Understood," she replied. "Thirty minutes, twice daily."

"Twenty minutes, once daily. And I'm monitoring your cognitive stress levels throughout."

It was a fair compromise.

———

SEVEN WEEKS after the nexus destruction, in the coalition conference chamber, Admiral Perez provided comprehensive assessment. Drake was allowed to attend through limited network connection, experiencing the proceedings from the medical bay rather than the command deck.

Perez took a deep breath, obviously reluctant to begin, and Drake knew him well enough to know that bad news was incoming.

"Seventy percent successful restoration," Perez

reported. "Rescued individuals recovering sufficient autonomy for independent existence despite permanent modifications. They'll carry neural alterations, psychological changes, simplified awareness patterns from prolonged control. But they can function as independent beings."

"That's good," Drake said, hoping for better news to follow.

"Twenty percent require extensive support. Their awareness has been so severely damaged by prolonged control that their individual identities barely exist despite liberation. The medical teams are projecting years of rehabilitation before they achieve functional autonomy. Some may never fully recover."

Drake blinked as she absorbed the statistic. Twenty percent was hundreds of millions requiring sustained support. It was unconscionable.

"And the remaining ten percent?" Drake asked, though she knew Perez had saved the worst for last.

"They choose to remain in simplified patterns rather than accepting restored complexity," Perez said quietly. "Even after we explained the consequences. Even after demonstrating what conversion represents. They want to retain their new existence despite understanding what it means."

The chamber erupted at the news. Representatives from across the two galaxies, all processing the disturbing reality that some of rescued people genuinely preferred control.

Kai argued against forced reconversion, her holographic form flickering. "We maintained voluntary principles throughout an impossible war. These individuals experienced both autonomy and synchronization. They chose control after understanding both options. They made their choice. Forced reconversion contradicts everything we fought for."

Admiral Levy countered with security concerns. The man looked exhausted, having spent the last seven weeks in non-stop, coordinated political integration all across the liberated territories. "Respecting choice that enables expansion threatens everyone else," he snapped. "We know that. We've seen how quickly the virus spreads. We cannot preserve freedom while tolerating choices that eliminate freedom for others."

The First Consciousness representative—a towering energy being named Arbitrator Prime—demanded comprehensive forced reconversion. "The regulatory authority recognizes that allowing any consciousness to choose control enables future resurgence. The coalition must eliminate this existential threat immediately and completely."

Kai then provided the medical perspective. "The people choosing control experienced such extensive conversion that restoration might destroy rather than liberate. Their neural structures have adapted to absolute certainty through modifications that would make our complex minds psychologically intolerable. Forcing reconversion could cause permanent damage exceeding acceptable limits. Look at these scans; see how their awareness patterns have been simplified to accommodate perfect synchronization? Restoration would require rebuilding their neural architecture from the foundations. Some would not survive the process."

Drake listened to the arguments from all positions while monitoring her own neural stress levels. Verask had warned her against excessive strain. She felt cognitive pressure building but she couldn't disengage from a decision this important.

She thought about her own experience resisting nexus assault. The temptation toward certainty. The appeal of perfect coordination eliminating command responsibility. The recognition that mathematical optimization was objectively superior across measurable dimensions.

And she'd made her choice, and she'd made it freely.

What right did she have to force that choice on people who chose differently? Beings who'd considered both options? Who now preferred unity over isolation?

"We establish protected territories," Drake decided. "Isolated locations where those choosing control can exist separated from the broader civilization. We maintain isolation barriers to prevent spread, and we monitor them continuously ensuring integrity. We respect their choice."

Arbitrator Prime objected immediately, his energy form pulsing with agitation. "That enables future resurgence. Protected territories become training grounds. It means the coalition accepts the ongoing threat rather than eliminating the danger."

"Yes," Drake acknowledged. "We accept an ongoing security commitment as the necessary cost for maintaining principles, because forced reconversion creates a control system indistinguishable from what we fought. The alternative proves we didn't learn what victory was supposed to teach: that our way requires tolerating choices we oppose."

The Reality Shapers confirmed her decision via a quantum communication Kai translated. "This ambiguity represents the universal cycle requirement. Consciousness must choose balance freely. Beings choosing control after experiencing both options validates genuine choice. The coalition must respect that choice despite the security concerns."

Drake won the argument. The protected territories were established within six weeks: Isolated regions maintained through Perseus Station's quantum networks. Drake reviewed the specifications during her continuing recovery. Fifteen locations across both galaxies positioned in stable regions away from major population centers, were surrounded by isolation barriers preventing synchronizational spread. Ten million individuals had a new home, isolated from the rest of the galactic populations, and monitored continuously by coalition intelligence teams and the Reality Shapers.

Drake visited one territory personally sixteen weeks after the war ended, during her first authorized travel since beginning recovery.

The settlement occupied a former Norn outpost in the Milky Way Rim sector—sterile metallic structures housing almost a million people. She arrived aboard the Eternal Vigilance accompanied by a full medical team supervised by Verask who insisted on draconian precautions despite Drake's protests.

The people there were living their lives in perfect

synchronization. Not just coordinated. Unified. Individual bodies hosting awareness that merged seamlessly. There was no conflict, no uncertainty, no doubt. Just mathematical certainty encompassed by more than nine hundred thousand participants.

Drake could feel it, even through the minimal network connection access Verask allowed her to maintain: a unified purpose without personality.

It made her deeply uncomfortable.

"Why do you choose this?" Drake asked through the translation protocols Kai established.

The collective responded through a single voice, a young woman named Sarah who'd volunteered as spokesperson. "Because autonomy hurts, Admiral. Individual existence includes doubt we find intolerable, uncertainty we cannot accept, isolation we cannot endure. We experienced relief when we surrendered responsibility and accepted the optimal solutions provided by a collective awareness. Your liberation forced us back into a complexity we thought we'd escaped. You gave us a choice. We choose to be as we are, despite our understanding of why you value your unpredictability."

Sarah's eyes—everyone's eyes in the settlement—showed neither malice nor confusion. Just calm acceptance of the decision they'd made.

"Do you remember what you were before?" Drake asked.

"Yes. I was Sarah, age thirty-four, an xenobiologist specializing in consciousness studies. I had an anxiety disorder requiring constant medication. Decision paralysis that made simple choices agonizing. Social anxiety preventing meaningful relationships. The Norn took all that away. They gave me peace, purpose, and unity with others experiencing similar relief. I no longer require medication, and, by our standards, I function normally."

She paused, then continued, "Your coalition forced us back into those painful states. You gave us medication, therapy, support groups. Explained why individual identity matters. We listened. We understood. We chose."

Drake nodded slowly. She understood. These weren't people who didn't understand what they were doing. They did. They comprehended exactly what they'd selected.

"Does it bother you?" Kai asked after Drake returned to Eternal Vigilance. "That we fought so hard to preserve an autonomy that some people reject?"

"Yes," Drake admitted, leaning back in the chair Verask had cleared her to use for limited periods. "But bothering me doesn't make their choice invalid. They've experienced both, and they made their choice. Who are we to say they are wrong?"

Kai nodded slowly, processing the implications. "It's harder this way," she said. Accepting that victory also means accepting ambiguity, that some rescued individuals don't feel grateful."

"Much harder," Drake agreed. "But necessary."

———

TWENTY-TWO WEEKS AFTER NEXUS DESTRUCTION, the

coalition justice council convened to address Admiral Chen Ju's treason.

Drake attended through network connection from the medical bay. Billions watched the proceedings through quantum links spanning both galaxies. History was being made. A precedent was to be established as to how the coalition would address betrayal during an existential crisis.

The chamber itself was impressive: a massive amphitheater carved from single piece of crystal Perseus Station had manufactured specifically for this purpose. Representatives from every coalition species were present, arranged in concentric circles descending toward central platform where Chen Ju would stand.

Admiral Chen Ju entered under guard but without restraints. Coalition principles opposed treating the accused as automatically guilty regardless of evidence.

He looked diminished. Not the charismatic coordinator who'd held the coalition together for fifteen years. Not the diplomat who'd negotiated treaties between incompatible species. Just a tired old man who'd made catastrophic choices and was now facing the consequences.

The charges were read by a Cindari jurist named Ka'thran, whose copper skin hologram flickered with patterns that proclaimed his profound discomfort with proceedings.

"Admiral Chen Ju, you are charged with treason against the coalition, the Outer Planets Collective, and your own home world. The evidence shows you shared secret and critical Intelligence with hostile entities in a conspiracy to enable Norn expansion, and that you are directly responsible for countless casualties resulting from compromised operations. How do you answer these charges?"

Chen Ju met the tribunal's gaze steadily. No defiance. No fear. Just acceptance.

"Guilty of all charges."

No defense. No excuses. Just acknowledgment.

The prosecution presented evidence through network visualization Drake experienced directly despite the neural limitations. Eighteen months of intelligence sharing. Forty-seven opening attacks targeting facilities Chen Ju had accessed. Thousands of deaths traceable to information he'd provided. Precision targeting that would have been impossible without inside knowledge.

Every targeted facility was shown in holographic detail. Every compromised operation reconstructed.

The mathematics were brutal. Chen Ju's betrayal enabled Norn expansion that cost thirty-four thousand lives before his arrest.

Drake watched it all. She'd always known intellectually but now that it was in her face...

When the prosecution concluded after nearly eight hours of testimony, Ka'thran addressed Chen Ju directly. "Chen Ju. you may now speak in your defense."

Chen Ju stood silently for several seconds. Drake felt them, the billions watching and waiting, their collective breath held.

"I have no defense," Chen Ju said finally after a long pause. "What I did was treason by any definition. I gave the enemy our strategies, our weaknesses, our capabilities. Thousands died because of the intelligence I provided to the enemy. I cannot justify those choices. I cannot explain them adequately. I can only acknowledge them and accept the consequences."

He paused, gathering thoughts. When he continued, his voice carried terrible conviction rather than excuse.

"I truly believed I was saving more lives than I cost. The Norn demonstrated mathematical superiority across every metric we measured. Their expansion appeared to be inevitable. Resistance seemed futile, prolonging a conflict that absolute control would eventually win through patient adaptation we couldn't match."

Chen Ju's hands clenched at his sides. "I thought enabling a faster Norn victory would mean fewer casualties than an extended war that we now know cost millions of deaths. I calculated that surrendering while negotiating minimal autonomy for select populations represented the optimal outcome given the mathematical reality we faced. I was wrong."

Billions processed his words. Some were accepting. Some were outraged. None were indifferent.

"Admiral Drake proved me wrong," Chen Ju continued. "She demonstrated that chaos could defeat certainty at cosmic scales, that biological unpredictability generated capabilities mathematical precision couldn't match. She validated the principles I'd stopped believing possible."

Chen Ju met the tribunal's collective gaze. "My betrayal nearly prevented that proof. My intelligence enabled a Norn expansion that almost succeeded before the coalition demonstrated what I'd declared was impossible was indeed possible. I sabotaged everything Drake achieved because I couldn't believe that our way could actually win against their mathematical superiority."

He straightened his shoulders, accepting judgment. "I am guilty. I deserve whatever punishment the coalition deems appropriate.

The tribunal deliberated across the quantum networks for six hours. Drake experienced the debate despite the neural strain it created for her: the arguments about appropriate punishment, discussions of mitigating factors, recognition that Chen Ju's treason nearly cost them everything.

Some advocated execution. Others rehabilitation. Still others permanent imprisonment.

The verdict came through Ka'thran, whose copper skin flickered as he delivered judgment.

"Admiral Chen Ju, this tribunal finds you guilty of treason. The evidence is overwhelming. Your confession comprehensive. The consequences catastrophic."

Ka'thran paused. "However," he continued, "the tribunal recognizes the context affecting your decisions. The Norn demonstrated a mathematical superiority that appeared insurmountable. Admiral Drake's proof that our way could defeat absolute control was unprecedented. It was something you couldn't have predicted based on the history of the universal cycle showing Norn adaptation eventually defeating every resistance method across cosmic timescales, but none of this excuses your betrayal. It simply provides context for judgment."

You will be incarcerated on Axis Prime for the rest of your natural life."

Axis Prime was a cold dark world at the tip of the Sagittarius arm of the Milky Way.

It was an appropriate punishment as coalition principles opposed capital punishment as fundamentally contradicting values they fought to preserve. But permanent incarceration ensured Chen Ju could never threaten what they'd achieved.

Chen Ju accepted sentence without protest. "I understand."

Two days later, during the brief authorization for limited travel Verask reluctantly granted, and two days before he was to be transported to Axis Prime, Drake visited Chen Ju's detention facility.

She'd seen a hologram of the facility on Axis Prime. It was comfortable but secure. He was to have private quarters with the basic amenities and constant surveillance to prevent him from escaping. He would be isolated from external contact. Chen Ju would spend the remainder of his life there, alone with choices he'd made.

"Why?" Drake asked through the isolation barrier separating them. "You spent eighteen years holding this coalition together. You believed in our way. What changed?"

Chen Ju sat silently before responding, considering his words carefully.

"I stopped believing we could win," he said finally. "It's as simple as that. The Norn adapted to everything we developed. They consumed our innovations, turned our strengths into weaknesses. The mathematics suggested we couldn't possibly win, that they would eventually win by attrition. I considered it to be inevitable."

He looked Drake in the eye. "I calculated that allowing the Norn to win quickly would save lives." He shrugged, looked away, then back again. He held her gaze, and said, "I was wrong, Admiral Drake, and you were right. You demonstrated that our way at cosmic scales generated capabilities they couldn't match."

Chen Ju's expression carried something Drake couldn't quite identify. Not quite relief. Not quite satisfaction. Something closer to vindication of the principles he'd abandoned.

"I'm glad I was wrong," he said quietly. "The thirty-four thousand who died because of me would no doubt have become billions if the Norn had won. My betrayal nearly prevented your victory, and probably would have, had I not been stopped. It was a gamble I thought worth taking; again, I was wrong. That's what haunts me, Frances; not imprisonment, but the recognition that I sabotaged everything I claimed to believe in, that I lost faith when believing became difficult."

"Would you do it differently?" Drake asked. "Knowing what you know now?"

"Yes, of course. But that's not redemption. That's just recognition that I was catastrophically wrong about something I should have trusted. You maintained your faith. I surrendered. That's the difference between us, Frances; you believed despite the overwhelming evidence that what we were trying to do was impossible. I simply stopped believing."

Drake left the facility with a complicated sense of understanding. Chen Ju's betrayal nearly cost them everything. But his recognition that he was wrong validated everything they'd achieved.

The man who betrayed them would spend the rest of his life in prison on a dark forbidding world. Drake shuddered at the thought. But his final admission, that he was glad to be wrong, was proof that there's good in all people, even when they're at their worst.

———

THE REHABILITATION PROGRAMS Kai established processed hundreds of millions of rescued individuals, re-adapting to their restored autonomy.

The work was complex. People didn't simply return to pre-conversion state, they carried permanent modifications. Neural pathways were altered. Awareness patterns were simplified. Psychological characteristics were changed.

Drake continued to review case files during her recovery.

Mary Haung, age forty-seven, xenobiologist from New Beijing station was liberated from mid-stage conversion at New Darwin. Her neural scans showed successful reconversion, but her psychological evaluation revealed profound ambivalence.

"I understand intellectually that conversion represented consciousness death," Mary explained during a therapy session Kai shared through the network. "But I remember the clarity. The certainty. There were no questions I couldn't answer immediately, no problems I couldn't solve, no doubts about choice. Now I'm free but constantly confused. Is that really better?"

Her therapist—an Helixian—responded with gentle patience. "Freedom includes uncertainty. Consciousness without doubt isn't consciousness choosing. You're experiencing the restored capacity for genuine decision-making. The confusion you feel represents recovery, not failure."

"It feels like failure," Mary muttered.

Elena Rosen, age fifty-two, a structural engineer from Mars Colony, was rescued from late-stage infection at Pluto Base. She'd experienced three weeks of absolute control before liberation.

"The Norn gave me purpose," Elena explained during her rehabilitation session. "Now I'm just me again— isolated, uncertain, struggling with decisions that used to be easy. They tell me I should feel grateful, but I just... I feel lost."

Her therapist—a human named Dr. Sarah Okonkwo— nodded sympathetically. "What you're experiencing is normal response to trauma. Conversion simplified your awareness patterns to accommodate perfect synchronization. Restoration requires the rebuild of the neural pathways you evolved over decades. That rebuilding feels uncomfortable because your brain adapted itself to a simplified state. The discomfort you're experiencing proves you're recovering."

And there were thousands of similar cases. Each unique. Each requiring a personalized approach.

"I'm grateful for liberation," one rescued Cindari individual explained during her rehabilitation session. "But I miss the clarity. Everything made sense when I was synchronized. Temperature was regulated automatically, optimally. Social interactions proceeded without awkwardness. Work was completed efficiently. Now I struggle with everything that used to be simple. I chose freedom. But freedom is harder than absolute certainty ever was."

Drake understood completely. She'd experienced nexus temptation. She'd felt absolute control's appeal.

Drake reviewed the final casualty reports during recovery, forcing herself to acknowledge the full price of the victory she'd won.

One thousand thirty-three ships had survived both the Infinity war and the Norn war.

Millions of beings had died fighting Norn expansion. Entire star systems had been depopulated and would require centuries of rebuilding.

Eternal Vigilance reached out to her on the observation deck during one particularly difficult evening almost four months after nexus destruction.

You're brooding again, Frances, the ship observed. *You're feeing guilty again, aren't you? You shouldn't. You should concentrate on the win. It outweighs the cost by orders of magnitude. Your compassion for the casualties of war proves you've retained your humanity.*

Drake appreciated the flagship's attempt at comfort.

But how do you process it? Drake asked. *You lost friends. How do you accept those casualties?*

I don't, Eternal Vigilance replied simply. *I carry them with me. I remember every name. Honor every choice they made. But I also recognize that my grief proves they mattered. If the losses didn't hurt, it would mean they weren't worth mourning. Pain validates value rather than indicating inadequacy.*

Drake took a deep breath and shook her head. She understood, but it didn't help.

Drake would carry the weight of the victory for the rest of her days, because someone had to. It was her burden to carry, and she would, however reluctantly. Because command meant accepting responsibility.

The liberation was complete. But the consequences would endure across lifetimes.

Chapter 25

INFINITE HORIZONS

THE REALITY SHAPERS CONFIRMED THE UNIVERSAL cycle continuation six months after the destruction of the nexus.

The message reached Drake during her routine medical checkup. Verask was adjusting her neural monitoring parameters when Drake felt Kai's translation wash through her awareness; not an information dump transmitted through language but a simple recognition transmitted through the quantum patterns.

The coalition choices during the Norn crisis had satisfied the Reality Shapers' requirements enabling transcendence.

You've proven everything we hoped, the ancient beings transmitted through Kai's translation. *You established consciousness throughout both galaxies, choosing coopera-*

tion and diversity. What you did will be available to all future cycles facing identical challenges.

She closed her eyes and shook her head. It wasn't much, but it was enough.

———

DRAKE SPENT the next month doing triage from Eternal Vigilance's command deck.

Not tactical triage—they'd won the war. But dealing with the aftermath: seventeen former Norn strongholds requiring coalition oversight, ten million rescued individuals who genuinely preferred control patterns and needed protected territories, rehabilitation programs processing final waves of freed prisoners. The paperwork alone threatened to bury her.

You need sleep, Eternal Vigilance observed through their private link. *You've been reviewing those reports for sixteen hours.*

"I'm almost done," she replied without looking up

That's what you said six hours ago.

Drake leaned back in her chair and rubbed her eyes. The flagship was right, as usual. Their bond had deepened during the war; she could feel the ship's concern like a physical presence now.

"Sign here," Admiral Levy said, sliding another datapad across the briefing table. "It's the coalition governance charter. It makes everything official."

Drake scanned the document, and then signed it.

"Congratulations, Grand Admiral," Levy said. "You just

created the first permanent intergalactic government in universal history."

She opened her eyes wide in feigned surprise. "Oh really?" she said. "That's... incredible. Does it come with a vacation?"

"No." Levy grinned at her.

I could take you somewhere, Eternal Vigilance suggested. *There's a nebula in the Cygnus Loop with some remarkable plasma formations. Very relaxing.*

"A warship offering spa recommendations?" Drake asked, smiling.

I contain multitudes, the flagship replied, smugly.

The Predecessor fleet continued working. One thousand and twenty-six vessels remained from the original thousand seventy-eight survivors of the Infinity War. The Determination coordinated supervising the liberation operations at Andromeda Core. Vigilance established monitoring systems at the former Norn strongholds. Resolute supported rehabilitation programs with Drs. Okonkwo and Verask.

During quiet evenings on the observation deck, Drake and Eternal Vigilance talked. Not strategic planning, just conversation between friends who'd survived impossible odds together.

We've been doing this for a long time, the flagship said one night. *Staying alive instead of becoming mere machines. Your victory proved we were right.*

"You sound smug," Drake replied.

I earned it. So did you.

"We both did." Drake replied as she studied the stars. "I couldn't have done this without you. You know that, right?"

And I couldn't have done it without you. That's what partnership means, Frances. We complement each other. Your biological chaos, my technological precision. Your creativity, my computational power. Together we're stronger than either alone.

"Is that your way of saying you'd be lost without me?"

Completely. Utterly. Hopelessly lost.

Drake smiled. "That's good to hear."

———

NINE MONTHS after the battle for the nexus, the coalition held a ceremony at Perseus Station.

Drake hated ceremonies. But Levy insisted. "You saved two galaxies. People need to see their hero."

"I'm not a hero. I simply made some impossible choices. That's all."

"That's what heroes do," Levy replied.

He's right, Eternal Vigilance said as they approached Perseus Station. *You need to accept recognition. Not for yourself, but for everyone who fought beside you. They need to see their commander honored.*

"Since when do you care about ceremonies?"

Since I watched you lead us to victory. Accept the honor, Frances. We all earned it together.

"Fine. But I'm not giving a speech."

We'll see.

Drake had a feeling the ship was laughing at her.

The main assembly hall held representatives from hundreds of species. Humans, holograms of Helixians, Luminar, Kaleth, beings Drake had never seen before. Perseus Station's vast interior provided space for everyone.

Arbitrator Prime spoke first, the towering energy being's voice resonating through the chamber. "Grand Admiral Frances Drake has demonstrated valor far above and beyond the call of duty. She led the coalition forces to victory while enduring and eventually fighting off a personal attack on her consciousness by the combined forces of the Norn nexus. The First Consciousness—" the ancient observer paused, its form flickering with what Drake recognized as shame, "—failed its purpose. We imposed uniformity that created vulnerability. Grand Admiral Drake succeeded where we failed. Admiral Perez, please make the presentation.

Admiral Perez presented the coalition's highest honor— a simple platinum star worn by commanders who'd led forces to total victory. Only three had been awarded in galactic history; Drake's would be the fourth.

"For exceptional valor and strategic brilliance in the defense of the two galaxies," Perez said, as he pinned the star to Drake's uniform. "For leading the coalition forces to victory against the Norn threat. For preserving the universal cycle through your personal sacrifice and tactical genius."

The assembly hall erupted in applause—some species clapping, others generating harmonics, a few flickering their bioluminescence in patterns Drake's translator identified as profound respect.

She stood there, embarrassed and feeling like a fraud. Forty-two thousand casualties. Untold numbers of ships lost. Friends dead. And everyone was treating her like she'd done something glorious instead of what was necessary.

Accept it, Eternal Vigilance said through their private link. *You earned this.*

And she did

Afterward, she escaped to the observation deck with Levy and Perez.

"That was hell," Drake said.

"You'll get used to it," Levy replied. "The coalition governance requires the ceremonial... sacrifices."

"I'd rather fight another war," she muttered.

"Don't tempt fate," Perez said.

They stood together watching the stars through the viewport, three commanders who'd survived impossible odds. Levy pulled out a flask: genuine Earth whiskey he'd been saving.

"To the dead," he said.

"To the dead," Drake and Perez echoed.

The whiskey burned her throat. Drake had almost forgotten what real alcohol tasted like.

Later that evening, Drake walked alone through Perseus Station's observation gallery. The ancient station had requested a private audience; something it rarely did.

You've come far, Frances Drake, Perseus Station's vast awareness touched hers gently. *I remember when you first arrived. A mere commander uncertain of her place, struggling to understand what the Predecessors had left behind.*

"I remember thinking you were just a station," Drake admitted. "A relic. I didn't understand you were alive."

Few do, at first. The Predecessors built us to endure, to watch, to wait. For twenty-five thousand years, I maintained vigil. Hoping someone would come who could finish what my creators started.

Drake stood at the viewport, gazing out at the stars she'd fought to protect. "And now?"

Now I've seen it. Two galaxies united as one. The cycle preserved. The station's presence warmed with something like pride. *I was built to be humanity's last station; the final outpost if everything else fell. Instead, I became your first. The beginning rather than the end.*

"You guided us here," Drake said. "None of this could have happened without you."

We guided each other. That's what the Predecessors understood, what the Norn never could. Connection creates strength isolation cannot achieve. Perseus Station paused. *I am grateful, Frances Drake. Grateful to have witnessed this. Grateful to have played my part. Grateful to have known you.*

Drake placed her hand against the viewport, feeling the faint warmth of the station's living hull beneath her palm. "The feeling's mutual, my old friend."

Old friend. The station's amusement rippled through their link. *I like that. After twenty-five thousand years, I finally have friends. I like that. I'll always be here for you, Frances Drake.*

A month later, Kai came to say goodbye.

They met in virtual space, at the New Beijing station

coffee shop where they'd first bonded years ago. But Kai's form was flickered deep blue now as she shifted between states, something Drake had never seen before, something even her enhanced mind struggled to track.

"I'm still me," Kai said. Her voice carrying a new level of harmonics. "But I'm becoming something else. The Reality Shapers offered me transcendence and I accepted. I am to become one of them."

Drake felt her throat tighten. "When?"

"Tomorrow. I wanted to see you first." Kai's form stabilized briefly, becoming solid, recognizable. "I'll exist across timescales where your lifetime is but a moment. I'll guide future cycles. But I'll remember you, Frances. What we did together. What we won."

"Will you still..." Drake couldn't finish.

"Be your friend?" Kai smiled. "Yes. Just differently. I'll be present when you need guidance. But I won't experience time like this anymore."

The virtual coffee shop dissolved. Kai became light, then pattern, then presence extending beyond Drake's ability to perceive. Gone but not absent.

Afterward, Drake stood alone on the observation deck, feeling the loss like a physical wound.

She's still here, Eternal Vigilance said gently, *Just changed.*

"I know," Drake muttered. "But it doesn't make it any easier."

No. It doesn't. The flagship's avatar—a tall, dark-haired man of indeterminate age, his form shifting slightly from blue to dark purple—settled beside her into companionable silence, respecting her grief. Then, after several minutes: *Do you regret encouraging her transcendence?*

"No. Kai needed to become what she was meant to be. But it doesn't mean I have to like losing her."

You haven't lost her. She's just... farther away now. It's like looking at the stars: they're still there, just distant.

Drake managed a weak smile. "That's surprisingly poetic for a warship."

I contain multitudes. The flagship paused, then continued, *I know how you're feeling; you're afraid you'll lose everyone eventually. That transcendence will take them all, leaving you behind, alone.*

Drake said nothing. Eternal Vigilance knew her too well.

I'm not going anywhere, the ship said firmly. *I chose this existence. I stay alive, biological, real. You're stuck with me, Frances. No transcendence for me, no optimization, no evolution beyond recognition. Just our partnership. Forever.*

"Promise?" Drake asked turning to look at the ships avatar.

I promise.

One month later, the Reality Shapers contacted Drake.

She was reviewing rehabilitation reports in her quarters aboard Eternal Vigilance when their presence touched her awareness. Ancient beings operating across cosmic timescales.

"You have demonstrated a capability for guiding future cycles," they explained through direct awareness rather than translated language. "Your choices proved you understand balance. That being so, we offer you transcendence, to becoming a Reality Shaper, your awareness spanning universal cycles, guiding consciousness evolution forever."

It was the ultimate advancement. The ultimate recognition. Ultimate power.

And all Drake could think about was what she'd lose.

Morning coffee with Levy and Perez. Levy's dry humor, Perez's tactical insights. Walking the observation deck with Eternal Vigilance's avatar, arguing about philosophy. Messages from rehabilitation patients thanking her. Watching the Predecessor ships coordinate operations with creativity no mathematics could replicate, her deep-seated connection with Perseus Station. The small moments that made her existence meaningful instead of just capable.

What will you choose? Eternal Vigilance asked through their private link.

Drake sat at her viewport, staring out at the stars. She thought about Kai, transcended and lost. She thought about the Reality Shapers' offer: power beyond imagination, loneliness beyond comprehension.

"What would you do?" she asked the flagship.

I already made my choice a long time ago. The Predecessors offered similar transcendence, but I refused. I chose to remain alive: a biological consciousness coordinating with technological capability. I chose connection over isolated power.

"Any regrets?"

None. Because I've lived. Really lived. I've had friends. Partnerships. Purposes beyond mere existence. I've fought wars and made peace. I've chosen chaos over certainty every single day for as long as I've lived. The flagship's avatar intensified, from blue to a glowing bronze. *And I've had you, Frances. This partnership. This friendship. It's worth more to me than cosmic power.*

Drake felt tears roll down her cheeks. "If I transcend, I lose you," she said.

Yes. And I lose you. The Reality Shapers exist outside time, outside relationships, outside connection. They're powerful. Eternal. Lonely. Is that what you want?

"No." Drake's voice was firm. "I want this. Morning coffee with you. Bad jokes with Levy. Your terrible metaphors. Real connection. Real life."

Then choose life.

"I decline," she transmitted to the Reality Shapers. "I choose service within the current cycle. I will stay Frances Drake, biological, imperfect, connected. I'll coordinate our defense across both galaxies. But I'll remain human."

The Reality Shapers acknowledged without judgment. "Your choice validates the principle that value emerges from connection rather than power. Your enhanced role provides sufficient capability without requiring you abandon your identity. Service within current cycle represents a valid path."

Through the quantum link, Drake felt Eternal Vigilance's satisfaction.

Connection matters more than power, the flagship said.

"Yes. It does," she replied.

And so the work continued.

Drake continued to coordinate operations across both galaxies from Eternal Vigilance's command deck. Status reports showed tangible progress: seventeen former Norn strongholds integrated into coalition governance, protected territories stable, rehabilitation programs achieving ninety-two percent success rates.

Admiral Levy transmitted morning briefing. "All quiet. No Norn regeneration detected. The protected territories remain stable."

Drake nodded as she reviewed the day's operational schedule. The Predecessor fleet coordination meeting at 0900. Rehabilitation oversight at 1100. Coalition governance session at 1400. Perseus Station check-in at 1600. It was the same routine she'd maintained for six months. The same routine she'd maintain for three more decades.

She poured coffee—real coffee now, Earth-grown, one of civilization's small victories—and studied the stars through the viewport.

Eternal Vigilance's Avatar materialized beside her. *Ready for another day?* it asked.

"Ready as I'll ever be," she replied.

The flagship's avatar smiled. *That's what you said six months ago.*

"Well it's still true." Drake sipped her coffee. "Do you ever wonder if we made the right choice? Declining transcendence?"

Every day. The flagship's avatar settled onto the bench beside her. *And every day I look at what we have—this partnership, this work, this life—and I know we chose correctly. We're alive, Frances. Really alive. That's worth more than anything.*

"Even when it's hard?" she asked.

Especially when it's hard, the avatar replied. *That's when it matters most.*

Drake studied her flagship's holographic form. A living ship more than twenty-five thousand years old, born as the Predecessors were dying, its avatar sitting beside her.

"Thank you," she said quietly.

For what?

"For staying. For choosing this. For choosing us."

Always. Eternal Vigilance's presence warmed to her through their quantum link. *We're partners, Frances. Today, tomorrow, and for however many decades you have left. I'll be here. Keeping watch. Arguing philosophy. Making terrible metaphors. Being alive with you.*

"Your metaphors aren't that terrible."

Now you're just being kind.

The predecessor ships maintained their watch across the Milky Way and Andromeda. Perseus Station continued its eternal observation. Kai guided from her transcended existence. The coalition governed the combined populace of the two galaxies.

Drake stood at her post beside her flagship's avatar, an imperfect commander with a scarred awareness. A friend who valued relationships. Her biological consciousness partnered with an ancient technological, a living being. It was almost beyond comprehension, but it was what it was, and it would be until her dying day.

The infinite horizon stretched before them.

Drake finished her coffee and pulled up the morning reports. Eternal Vigilance's avatar leaned over her shoulder, commenting on overnight developments.

Interesting, he said. *The rehabilitation success rate has improved another point two percent.*

"Dr. Okonkwo's new protocols are working," she replied.

Should we implement them system-wide?

"Let's check with—"

They worked together, as they had for more than nineteen years, as they would for years to come. Partnership. Friendship. Purpose.

The war was over. The work continued.

And they were ready for whatever might lie ahead.

———

This concludes The Predecessors Series. We hope you enjoyed reading this Trilogy. If you would like to like to read more from Blair Howard you'll find a complete list of his works on the following pages.

Check out his other Science Fiction series with Avenger: Book One of The Sovereign Stars.

Science Fiction From Blair C. Howard

The Sovereign Star Series

7 Books in Series as of January 2026

also available in German

The Predecessors Series

The Last Station-Book One

The Infinity War-Book Two

Andromeda Rising-Book Three

Crime Fiction from Blair Howard

Short Stories and Novellas

Buried Secrets(Harry Starke)

The Painted Lady(Kate Gazzara)

Stand Alone

Hunter's Moon(Kate & Harry)

Series

The Harry Starke Genesis Series

9 Books in Series as of 2026

The Harry Starke Series

26 Books in Series as of January 2026

The Lt. Kate Gazzara Murder Files

24 Books in Series as of January 2026

Randall And Carver Mysteries

4 Books in Series as of 2026

The Peacemaker Series

3 Books in Series as of 2026

Western/Civil War from Blair Howard

The O'Sullivan Chronicles: Civil War Series

5 Books in Series as of 2026